RIDER'S REVENGE

THE LAST RIDERS, #10

JAMIE BEGLEY

Young Ink Press Publication
YoungInkPress.com

Edited by C&D Editing,
Diamond in the Rough Editing & Hot Tree Editing
Cover Art by Cover Couture
Map by C&D Editing

Connect with Jamie,
JamieBegley@ymail.com
www.facebook.com/AuthorJamieBegley
www.JamieBegley.net

MAP OF TREEPOINT, KENTUCKY

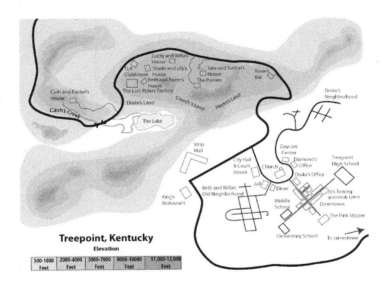

Heroes can be found in everyday life, but legends ... those are rare. Those you have to search for...

PROLOGUE

J o swam through the cool water of the small lake hidden in the woods behind Rachel and Cash's house. Rachel had offered to let her swim there any time she wanted. Usually it was early evening when she came out here. If she didn't see any cars or motorcycles outside Rachel's house, then she would take a quick dip. Tonight, though, it was so dark she couldn't see her hand in front of her face, and the lights from Cash's cabin that could normally be seen through the inky darkness were off.

She dunked her sweaty hair under the water. The night was muggy, and she had serviced a three-car pile-up on the outskirts of town.

Jo swam until she was nearly exhausted, banishing the sight of the dead body being wheeled to the coroner's van. Thankfully, the victim had already been covered in a body bag before she had arrived.

The sheriff had told her that the victim had been from out of town and had ignored the warning for the sharp curve. The BMW had taken the curve too fast, not seeing another car had stopped, waiting for a car in the incoming lane to pass so they could go down the side road that led to a home.

All three cars had been involved in the accident, four people had headed to the ER, and one to the morgue.

"I need to find another job," Jo said out loud to herself as she floated aimlessly on her back.

Staring up into the tree branches that fanned over the water, she had drifted out farther than she had thought. She didn't bother lifting her head, knowing exactly where she was in the small body of water.

The faint sound of a motor from the road didn't have her lifting her head. The main road wasn't close, but sounds carried in the woods surrounding the lake. With Rachel and Cash being out of town to visit Cash's relatives, she didn't expect any of Cash's friends or Rachel's brothers to stop by for a visit. Even if they did, they wouldn't stay long, seeing that they weren't home.

As the sound of the motor grew closer, Jo lowered her legs, treading water to stay in the shadows of the trees on the side of the lake.

"Dammit," Jo muttered softly, seeing a motorcycle's headlight coming to a stop at the bank, the lone light hitting the water.

She moved farther into the shadows, her chin dipping into the water in case the light hit her. She castigated herself for not taking the time to put on her swimsuit.

She had ridden her bicycle from the scrapyard. At least whoever the lone rider was who was enjoying his cigarette wouldn't be able to see it from where it was leaning against a tree several feet away.

Jo remained still, making small movements to stay afloat as he smoked. When the smoke drifted toward her, she realized whoever it was, they weren't smoking a cigarette.

When he lifted the joint toward his mouth again, Jo recognized Rider.

She cursed to herself. She detested that particular Last Rider. Shade, she had talked a few times before and after her father had been murdered. He had even loaned her enough money to keep her business going when she had been overwhelmed with the debts her father's death had left behind. If Shade hadn't loaned her the money, the new tow truck her father had talked her into buying would have been repossessed.

The few times that she had been unfortunate to talk to Rider, he had grated on her nerves. The first time she had met the handsome biker, he had expected her to fall for him as if he were God's gift to women. The second time, he had thought she was interested in women.

Every bone in her body had screamed at her to take the Casanova down a peg or two. The only reason she didn't was because Jo knew he was friends with Rachel and because his ego was so overblown that dynamite wouldn't make a dent in his pearly whites.

A stray breeze had her shivering in the water.

Dammit, how long does it takes to smoke a joint? she thought wrathfully as she waited for Rider to leave.

When she saw him flick what was left in a glowing arc, then turned off his bike, she knew she was in trouble. His headlight disappeared, giving only the dim shadow of him undressing.

Her head spun at trying to figure out what to do as she warily watched his movements.

Rider headed toward the opposite side of the lake from where she was swimming. When she heard the scape of a rock, she knew he was climbing the rock overhang.

Was he going to stand there or ...?

Her unfinished thought was answered as soon as she heard the splash.

She started swimming for the bank where she had left her clothes and bike. Her heart was pounding in exertion as she swam.

The tips of her toes had just grazed the bottom when she felt a muscular arm curl around her waist.

"Let me go!" Jo screeched, trying to jerk out of Rider's restraining hold.

"Who do I have here? A mermaid coming to keep me company?" his amused voice came from behind her as she struggled against him, kicking her bare feet at his shins and thighs.

"Let go!"

"What's the hurry?"

Jo sputtered out the water that was threatening to drown her as he turned her around to face him in the dark. The sleek feel of his skin under her palms heightened her anxiety of being alone with him in this isolated spot.

"I want to leave." Jo was angry at herself for the slightly hysterical tone she could hear in her own voice. When men saw a weakness, they were quick to take advantage.

"I can't convince you to stay?" His husky voice had a seductive, assertive tone that had him increasing her efforts to get away from him.

It might be pitch dark, but she could see the sexual promise that had the cool water feeling as if she was trying to escape being dragged down into quicksand.

With her nails, she scratched his hands, determined never to be a victim to a man's desires again. "No!"

He released her, and she frantically started swimming toward the bank.

"Come on, Rach; the least you can do is keep me company until Cash gets here."

She stopped swimming to turn back toward him, dumb-founded. "You think I'm Rachel?"

"Who else would be skinny dipping in Cash's swimming hole?"

Was he pretending not to know who she was? Jo could have sworn he had known. Then she admitted to herself that if she hadn't seen who he was when he had been smoking, she wouldn't have known.

"No, I'm not Rachel." Jo had lowered her voice, hoping he wouldn't recognize her voice from the few times she had been around him.

"Want to tell me who you are, then?" The seductive intent turned flirtatious.

"It doesn't matter. I have no interest in keeping you company." She flipped onto her stomach and started swimming again. "Just stay where you are until I can get dressed and leave."

"You must not know who I am if you think I'm a gentleman."

Jo swam harder at hearing the sound of splashing behind her.

"Don't you dare get out of the water before I leave."

As soon as she was able, she took off in a run, going toward the vicinity she had left her clothes and nearly tripping over them.

Tugging on her shorts as fast as she could, then her T-shirt, her heart was pounding out of her chest, leaving her unable to hear where he was in the water. Twisting as she tried to tug her stubborn damp T-shirt down, she heard the sound of a twig breaking.

"Don't!" She bent down, trying to find her panties and bra. Finding her bra, she shoved it into her back pocket, giving up on trying to find her panties. She then slipped into her tennis shoes, water still running down her legs. "Where are you?" She raised her head, trying to peer through the pitch darkness.

"I'm still in the water."

"You're lying." She carefully maneuvered herself toward her bicycle.

"Now, why would I lie?"

She was making a fool of herself. "Are you laughing at me?" Feeling relief as she finally grasped her handlebars, she turned it toward the road.

"A little."

Her head practically did a exorcist spin as she tried to determine where he was.

"You don't have to worry about me. You're going to break your neck running around in the dark."

"It's not my neck I'm worried about," she muttered, getting on her bike and starting to peddle as fast as she could without seeing where she was going.

As soon as she didn't think she was being followed, she turned on the faint headlamp. A minute later, her wheels were on the pavement, heading back toward town.

It was dangerous riding this curving road in the dark. A car could mow her down before they even knew she was there. If Rider hadn't shown up, she would have gone up a couple of feet and took a small dirt trail that would have led her back to town.

Most of the town had forgotten that trail was there. It was overgrown and wasn't big enough to get a car through, but it was nice to walk it after she would ride her bicycle up the main road. She only knew of its existence because she been raised on going on road calls by her father's side.

Jo slowed down, coasting down the hill toward town, seeing The Last Riders' clubhouse lights blazing as she passed.

Looking up the hill where the house sat, she saw a couple

of the members watching as she rode past. She lowered her head, pretending she hadn't seen them, relieved when she turned the corner and was out of sight.

———

TWO MINUTES LATER, a motorcycle pulled into the parking lot. Rider parked, already knowing the gloating that would be waiting for him as he climbed the steps to the porch.

"You're looking all wet." Moon snickered.

"I told you that you were wasting your time," Razer taunted.

"It was worth a shot." Rider laughed. "You don't know if you don't try."

"How bad did she shoot you down?" Razer asked.

"She pretended she didn't know it was me."

"That must have hurt." Moon laughed.

Rider gave a mocking grin back. "I pretended I didn't know it was her, either."

The men just shook their heads.

Moon looked at him curiously. "You mind if I take a shot at her next?"

"Go for it. It won't work." Rider shrugged at the other biker. "Not for you anymore than did for me."

"So, if you can't get in her panties, no one can?" Razer rolled his eyes at Rider's cocky attitude.

"I didn't say I didn't get in her panties." Reaching into his pocket, he twirled out a lacy pair of panties on his fingertip.

"I'd ask, but I don't want to know. Brother, one day, a woman is going to bring you back down to earth, just like Beth did to me."

"Won't ever happen. Why settle for one woman when I can do them all?" There wasn't a woman who existed now or in the future who was worth getting shackled to.

Unlike Razer and the other brothers who had fallen in love, none of them were like him. Even Shade, who Rider would have sworn didn't have a heart, had fallen under a woman's spell.

Not him. Never him. No woman, and certainly not Jo, would ever be able to give him everything he wanted. It wasn't possible. There would always be another woman's pussy to explore and make his for a time before moving on to the next one. Half of the fun was the chase. Once that was over, half the fun was gone.

"I wish the women could hear you."

Rider tossed Jo's underwear to Moon. It was bizarre to him that Razer or any man would settle for one woman. Hell, women never gave up anything. They expected the ring, the picket fence, and kids. What did the men get? The pleasure of having them in their bed and, if they were lucky, one night of fucking per week. He could have a woman sucking his dick for him with a snap of his fingers. Would a wife do that? Hell no.

"You're just jealous they love me." Rider pulled his damp T-shirt away from his broad chest. "I need to get a shower and change. Later."

Rider didn't miss the amused glances his friends threw in his direction, so he gave a parting shot to Razer.

"Beth promised me she would heat me up a plate of food that was left over from your dinner. I've got to hurry. I don't want it to get cold." Satisfied that he had found his mark, he went inside, while Moon blocked Razer from lunging toward him.

"Cool it."

"That fucker better find his own woman quick." Razer jerked his arm away from Moon's grip. "Or I'm going to kill him."

Moon held his laughter back, afraid that the other man

would throw him off the porch. "He only does it to piss you and the other married men off. I don't know why you all let him get to you."

"Because nothing gets to him ... ever. He managed to fool our wives into believing he's a dumb schmuck. And he's managing to get a piece of our pie. Hell, he's not even content with that. He's trying to steal the *whole* fucking pie."

Moon shook his head. "Brother, you all fucked up, and now you're trying to close the gate. Rider is one Last Rider that I plan on keeping any woman I'm interested in away from. If I were you, I'd handle him differently."

"Oh, yeah, old wise one? What in the fuck would you do differently?"

"Find Rider a woman to keep him occupied so he won't have enough energy to chase after your women."

"How are we supposed to do that? A whole clubhouse of women and the ones in town haven't slowed him down."

"Because they aren't the right woman."

"Like who?"

"Ask Shade. He and Rider used to party hard together before he married Lily. He'll know which woman would attract his interest."

Razer stared at the panties that Moon was twirling on his finger. "I might have a few ideas of my own."

Moon grinned. "Jo's hot, sexy, and she virgin territory to the men in the club."

Razer's jealously disappeared. Grinning back, he asked, "She shot you down, too, didn't she?"

"Like a shooting star." Moon moved away from the door, seeing Razer had calmed down.

"You sure you want us to try to hook Jo up with Rider? He doesn't share his bikes. Nor does he share the candy he cons Willa into making for him."

"He'll share Jo. Rider will never fall in love with a woman the way you and Shade have done."

"You never know. Never underestimate the power of a woman to steal their way into your heart."

"We still talking about Rider?" Moon laughed.

Razer laughed, too. "I guess you're right. Crazy thought, right?"

They were still laughing when a shooting star flashed across the sky, gaining their attention that had already been affixed on the night sky.

"Did you see that?" Razer asked, turning toward Moon to see if he had also seen it.

"Maybe it's a good luck sign that you'll be able to get Rider off your back."

"It could also be an omen that Jo is going to shoot Rider down like she did you."

"She's going to shoot him down; that's a sure thing. The question is: what are you and the brothers going to do when she does?"

Through the open door, he saw Rider coming down the steps with his hair neatly brushed and with an anticipatory smile on his face. Razer knew he would go home to find the man sitting at his table, eating the leftovers that he had planned to eat for lunch the next day. And he knew the married brothers where just as fed up with him as he was.

"I'm going to do what The Last Riders always do."

"What's that?"

"I'm going to make it happen."

One by one, booted feet stepped into the clearing a quarter mile away from The Last Riders' clubhouse. As Rider took his place next to Train, his eyes went around the circle, stopping on each of the brothers.

Cash's inscrutable expression gave no clue what he was thinking as he stood next to Viper. Meanwhile, the president of The Last Riders made no pretense of the burning hatred for the men they had been waiting for, wanting to serve their own brand of justice. The men thought they were too smart to be caught, that their victims wouldn't live to point a finger at them. Regrettably for them, their victims had survived, and now their fates were sealed. They would be taken out of society before any more damage could be perpetrated by them.

Rider couldn't blame Viper. He had no sympathy for anyone who fucked with The Last Riders. Each of those they would be serving justice on today knew what The Last Riders were capable of and had taken their own lives in their hands when they had hurt someone the club protected.

The Last Riders might hate the prisoners, but their

vengeance was never taken lightly. Only those who deserved their wrath found themselves unable to escape the club's justice. It wasn't like they didn't respect the legal system; The Last Riders just didn't believe those who had committed certain grievances against them deserved to escape into the forgiving arms of the law. They wouldn't be given a chance to plea to a sympathetic jury or parole board. The Last Riders were their jury, and no mercy would be given to them.

Knox stood on the other side of Viper, his sheriff's uniform at home as he stood straight in his jeans and T-shirt, proudly wearing his vest with the patches he had earned through the long years of being a Last Rider. Razer's expression was just as fierce, waiting for Shade and Moon to arrive so they could get started. There was an empty spot next to Razer where Shade would stand when he arrived.

Rider couldn't help looking toward Lucky, his own fury building at the jagged scar that could be seen over the collar of his T-shirt. Behind Lucky, Stud and Calder stood. Viper had invited them to keep them from snatching justice out of The Last Riders' hands.

Turning his head to the side, Train caught his eyes. The brother knew he had misgivings about them being there. Rider silently assured him of their silence.

Looking forward again at the sounds of a shuffle, he saw Shade and Moon throw a struggling man into the center of the circle. None of the brothers made a sound as Shade took his spot, leaving the man heaving and standing alone as Moon stepped outside the circle, leaving the clearing to retrieve their next victim.

Rider's eyes went to Viper's as his deadly calm voice filled the quiet air that had been filled with respectful silence for the solemn act they were about to carry out.

"Bear, you know why you're here?"

The muscle-bound man straightened, turning to face Viper and spitting a glob of bloody spit onto the dirt. Rider wondered if it was Shade or Moon who had managed to get a punch in before delivering him to Viper.

"I'm not a fucking idiot. You're going to kill me because I tried to kill Lucky. Fucking cowards. You're too afraid to take me on man to man. I could beat any man here, and you know it!"

"Lucky," Viper unemotionally called out the brother's name.

Lucky stepped out into the circle, coming face-to-face with the large man who nearly took his life. "There're not many men who can brag that they got one over me. I got sloppy. That's on me. As a Christian and pastor, I should be able to stand here, turn the other cheek, and offer you forgiveness. It's taken me a lot of soul searching to realize you're not worth me being unable to look at my God, wife, son, and congregation with your death staining it."

Bear's relief was palatable in the clearing, believing he was going to get away scot-free, unaware that the mountain he was standing on was going to be his final resting place.

"I'm not sorry to say the other brothers don't feel the same," Lucky cut short Bear's relief. "A strike against me is a strike against them. They don't have the same connection to God as I do. They also don't have a problem looking their wives or children in the eyes, knowing they took out a piece of shit like you." Lucky reached into his leather vest, taking out seven cards. Rider knew how many there were because there were seven original members who were waiting to complete what Lucky felt honor-bound to relinquish.

Holding the cards, he fanned them out. "We're going to give you a fair chance to live, which is more than you gave me. Each of these cards represents one of the brothers. You'll each be given your choice of weapon. None of us will interfere, but only one man is going to be walking out of this circle."

Bear didn't make a move to choose a card. "I'll take all you fuckers on if you're going to be fair."

"We're not the one who came up behind someone and bashed them in the back of the head with a crowbar, then slit his throat when he was unconscious. Choose before I change my mind and show you what I'm capable of when my back isn't turned."

Bear reached out, taking a card, then contemptuously flicking it at Lucky. The card spun in the air, hit his chest, and then fell in slow motion to the ground.

"It's a five," Lucky called out to the brothers, then went back to his spot in the circle, putting the remaining cards back in his vest.

None of the members needed to ask who the five-card represented.

Rider stepped into the circle, grinning good-naturedly at Bear. The biker thought he had the upper hand. Rider could tell from his straightened posture, already planning to take him down in his mind.

"I'll let you pick your weapon of choice first. Pick whatever you want. I think we can come up with whatever you want," Rider offered, not caring which one he picked, just hoping the asshole would at least make their fight interesting.

"I want a gun. I wouldn't mind putting a bullet in your head. It's what I should have done to Lucky."

"I think we can accommodate you with the first half of what you want. Viper?"

Rider watched as Viper moved forward, taking a gun from the back of his waistband and handing it to Bear.

"There's only one bullet in the chamber—use it wisely,"

Viper advised before turning his back to Bear and returning to the rim of the circle.

Bear appeared stunned that Viper had actually given him the gun.

"You sure you don't want to make it easy on yourself by putting that bullet to good use and blowing out your own brain?" Rider drew his attention back to him.

Bear laughed in his face. "If The Last Riders keep their word, I'll be back at the Destructors' club, drinking a beer before they get done burying you."

As Bear bragged, Rider didn't take his eyes away from the gun, watching him steady it in his hand and raising the barrel toward him as his thumb went to the trigger. Bear had intended to finish his sentence with a bang, but before he could pull the trigger, Rider struck his foot out, knocking it out of his hand.

Bear tried to take a running dive for the gun where it had landed by Razer's foot. No sooner had Bear's chest hit the ground than Rider stepped on his spine, hearing the *whoosh* of air escape his lungs as Bear tried to reach for the gun with his fingertips.

Keeping his booted foot on Bear's back, pinning him to the ground, Rider reached down for the gun. His good-natured expression then vanished as he bent, pressing the barrel of the gun to Bear's forehead.

"You stupid fucker. You should have taken me out before bragging about it." Pulling the gun away, Rider straightened, handing the gun to Razer, who neatly tucked it into his waistband as Rider removed his foot from Bear's back. Standing still, he waited for Bear to get to his feet.

When the large bear of a man came at him, Rider dug his heels into the dirt, steadying himself to keep from being thrown down. Bear was used to taking his opponents down with his size.

Rider began pummeling Bear's ribs, forcefully driving the oxygen out of his lungs. Bear tried to jerk away and regain his breath, but Rider didn't let him, following him in the confines of the circle, using all his strength to hold him in place. When Bear stumbled backward into Cash, Cash shoved him back toward Rider.

Rider caught the first glimpse of worry from Bear, realizing he may not succeed in taking Rider down as the man took his eyes off him for a second, looking for a gap between the brothers that he could get through to run for his life.

There wasn't one.

When Bear turned back to him, Rider was waiting, smashing a fist into his nose and sending a spray of blood over his T-shirt. Regretting he had worn his favorite shirt, he hoped that Jewell or Stori would be able to get the blood out. He didn't want any reminders of Bear. The son of a bitch deserved to be forgotten.

Bear frantically swung his fists wildly, trying to drive him away, or hoping to get lucky and connect with some part of his body. However, Rider fluidly dodged his fists, methodically wearing Bear down by hitting him in his vulnerable spots.

It wasn't the first battle to the death that Rider had taken part in. Bear might have gotten into numerous fights, but unless he had fought with his life on the line, he wouldn't be able to beat Rider's experience.

Bear hunched over, trying to protect his ribs, so Rider viciously punched him in the jaw. When Bear tried to jerk his head from being struck again, Rider hit him in the chin, then the mouth, satisfied when he heard Bear's jaw bones shatter. Damn, how he loved the sound of bones breaking.

Like a predator, he circled Bear. Raising his arm, Rider brought his elbow down on the back of Bear's neck, driving him to his knees. Then Rider reached out, taking a swatch of

Bear's hair and exposing his throat as he reached down to take a long knife out of his boot. He pressed it to the flesh he had exposed.

"How does it feel to know I could slit your fucking throat and you can't do a damn thing about it?" he goaded the biker who was gasping in pain from his injuries.

"Fuck you."

Laughing down at him, Rider carved a thin line across his throat. "You're not my type, but your sister is. She's going to need a shoulder to cry on when you go missing."

"My sister wouldn't let you smell where she pisses."

Rider released Bear's hair to circle him. As Bear's head fell forward, Rider then snapped his foot out, kicking Bear in the jaw and sending the man to the dirt, whimpering.

"She'd fuck me and beg for more. Your sister is a slut," Rider continued to goad, disappointed the man wasn't putting up a better fight. "I bet it won't take me an hour to get in her pussy."

"I'll take that bet." Viper's mocking voice drove Bear into a mindless fury that had him getting off the ground and barreling toward him.

As Bear charged toward Viper, Rider blocked his path by plunging his knife into Bear's stomach. He jerked it out then plunged it in again, this time in Bear's side between his ribs.

Bear dropped to his knees, dazedly staring up at Rider before falling to his side.

Rider used the tip of his boot to toss him onto his back. Then, crouching down next to him, he surveyed Bear's injuries. None so far had dealt a killing blow. He had no intention of making his death easy. He wanted to send Bear to hell screaming in agony.

Taking his knife, he split Bear's T-shirt in half, exposing his chest. Meticulously, Rider then carved Lucky's name on the flesh of his chest.

"That's so you won't forget why you're going to hell." After making a sprawling Y, he stabbed him again in the stomach, using his weight to let the knife sink deeply. "I expected you to be more fun to kill, Bear. Instead, you're boring me, and I hate being bored."

Rider used his hand to close Bear's mouth, shutting off his oxygen. Bear's eyes started bulging out as he struggled to breathe. Terror had his legs sawing in the dirt as he struggled to get out from under him.

The man Rider was slowly killing was going pale and shaking as shock began to set in. When his eyes closed, Rider jolted him conscious with a hard slap on his cheek.

Rider couldn't understand the unintelligible words coming out of Bear, pressing his mouth closed with the palm of his hand and sawing his tongue in half with his teeth.

"Your prayers are too late."

He used what was left of Bear's T-shirt to wipe his bloody hand before standing and heaving Bear over his shoulder, easily carrying the heavy weight as the brothers parted to let him through the circle. He walked over the rough ground to the deep hole that all the members had taken turns digging. Hurling the heavy weight, he was happy to see that Bear had landed face up.

Reaching behind his back, he took out his revolver then emptied the barrel into Bear's legs, making sure each kneecap and hand had bullets in them before he gave Bear the final words he would hear addressed to him.

"Did Lucky look at you the same way you're looking at me when you threw him down that ditch?" Rider sadistically mocked the man staring up at him. "Don't worry; I'm not going to bury you alive. You have company coming on your way to hell."

Leaving Bear staring up at the bright blue sky, Rider walked back to the circle, passing Stud and Calder as he returned to his spot. The two men had known The Last Riders would exact justice for Lucky. They had wanted a piece of Bear, too, but unfortunately, you couldn't kill a man twice. Both Stud and Viper had argued back and forth about who had the right to deal with Bear. The Last Riders had won when Stud had given in for a favor in return.

The freshly turned soil next to Bear's plot held the body of a woman whom the Destructors had exacted their own form of revenge on. He hadn't asked for an explanation from Shade when he had been woken last night and been told to meet him in the clearing. Nor had he asked for any about the dead woman and why Crazy Bitch was there. The three of them had buried the woman, then drove to the diner in town to eat breakfast.

When his stomach growled, Train gave him a disgusted look. He had eaten two plates at lunch and was already hungry. He shrugged it off. He was a man of big appetites.

His attention was diverted from thoughts of food and sex when Crash willingly entered the circle after being escorted by Moon. The brother had asked to stay, but Viper had refused. No one was allowed to witness punishments administered by the original members. However, Viper had made the exception for Stud and Calder for Bear, who were now leaving with Moon.

Crash and the brothers waited expectantly for the man who had to lean down to dodge a low branch. Viper and Cash stepped to the side, making room for the late arrival.

The Gavin who strode into the middle of the circle to face off against Crash wasn't the same Gavin who Rider had partied with during their leave in the Navy, nor when they had started the club in Ohio when the original members had been a force of nine.

Rider could still remember their ride to Ohio when they had left the service, fucking and drinking their way through state by state until they had found themselves staying a weekend in Ohio. The weekend had turned into a week, then another. When they hadn't found the enthusiasm to move on, they had decided to make Ohio their home, content to build the club until Gavin had come up with the idea to branch out and start another charter in Kentucky, where Gavin had found a house and property large enough to build the factory and house the men. It was a fateful decision, one that each of the members were still struggling with equal parts of regret and happiness. Many of The Last Riders had found their wives in Kentucky, while Gavin had lost the woman he loved and the life he had led.

Gavin was dressed all in black, from his boots to his jeans. His black leather jacket was unzipped, the black T-shirt underneath showing his massive chest. He had regained the weight he had lost during his captivity with the Road Demons, and he was no longer the pasty white wraith he had been in the rehab center. Now, his skin glowed with health and vitality ... until you looked into his eyes that were as dark and mysterious as a still, murky lake, not showing what lay beneath the surface.

Crash paled at the forbidding stranger that Gavin had become. Hell, Rider was thankful he wasn't the one who would have to fight him, and he was always ready for a good fight. Gavin scared the Jesus out of him, and he didn't scare easily.

"Gavin ..." Crash started, but broke off at the intense hatred on Gavin's face that spoke volumes of how much Gavin loathed him. "Broth—"

Gavin struck his hand out, backhanding Crash's cheek. "No brother could do to me what you did. I wouldn't do to my worst enemy what you did to me. I don't have to tell you what they did—they sent you the videos. I would have died before I had let someone I called brother suffer through what I did."

Crash started crying. "I didn't know what to do—"

When Gavin flashed his hand out again, Crash didn't even try to avoid the fist that knocked him back a step.

"I know what I would have done. I know what every brother in this circle would have done. I fucking know what Stud and Calder would have done, and they aren't Last Riders!" Gavin moved closer to Crash, bearing down on him like a vengeful dark angel determined to wreak havoc and pain to the person who had betrayed him.

"You ate and slept in your nice, clean bed, while I slept in filth and had to piss in a bucket! You ate food on a plate, while I ate leftover slop. You fucked women who you *wanted* to fuck, while I fucked men and women who wanted to get their sick kicks out of me."

"I'm sorry!" Crash cried harder at Gavin's condemnation.

"If I could kill you a thousand times, it would never pay me back for what I went through."

"I know—"

Gavin struck out again, hitting Crash and doubling him over. "Shut the fuck up."

Rider was surprised Crash was still able to stand.

Thinking about all the times he had spent partying with Crash made him sick; he had known all along where Gavin was and hadn't tried to tell anyone. It reinforced what he had already learned at his own father's betrayal—treachery knew no boundaries when their own wants and needs were at stake. Crash had been weak, and so had Rider's father.

Unlike Gavin, Rider had walked away, not taking his revenge on his father. He had sworn it would be the last time he would. If anyone ever fucked him over again, he would settle the score, just like Gavin was about to do.

Some revenge was sweet like Bear's. Others, like Crash's, were bittersweet.

Regardless, The Last Riders would dispense their justice. Gavin would be sleeping in Viper's old bedroom, while Crash would be in a cold grave.

Crash's spine stiffened until he stood straight again. "I did what I could. That's why they kept you alive so long."

"Thanks for looking out for me." Filled with scorn, Gavin moved to Crash and wrapped an arm around his neck before Crash could react. "I'm going to do what I wished someone had done for me the first month Memphis and you left me to rot in the Road Demons' basement." Gavin twisted Crash's neck unnaturally until Rider heard the snap of his neck before Gavin tossed him away.

"You were supposed to save some for the rest of us." Viper bent down to take Crash's pulse.

Rider could have told him it was a waste of time. When the Reaper killed, he only shared with the devil.

2

The parking lot of the diner was nearly empty when Jo neatly slid the tow truck into a parking spot at the side of the building. The lone, small, red compact parked by the dumpster was easily identified as Carly's. There weren't many vehicles in Treepoint that she couldn't recognize. She had been born and raised in the small town, other than the years she had moved away with her mother, Jo reminded herself.

Jo also knew who the expensive motorcycle sitting in front of the building belonged to. If she didn't want to fill her thermos with her morning coffee, she would have done a U-turn in the parking lot and left. Unfortunately, the only other place to get coffee so early in the morning was at the Quik Stop, and Freddy didn't open for another hour.

"If that asswipe says one thing to me, I'll bash him with my thermos," she mumbled under her breath as she grabbed the stainless-steel thermos from the console. It was the same one her father had used every day before his death.

Tucking it in the crook of her arm, she opened the door, then slid out of the truck onto the pavement. Her boots splashed the water puddle onto her ugly green Dickie's coveralls. Uncaring that the bottom of her jumpsuit was now bearing a dark stain, she shut the door and continued toward the diner, ignoring the sprinkling rain.

She was at home in the elements. It was only the male species that gave her pause. And the biker who rode the huge monster sitting right outside the door was definitely a male.

Determined not to run like a scared rabbit this time, she flung the door open with more force than necessary, sending the glass quivering and the bell over the door pealing madly. Anti-climatically, Jo looked around the empty restaurant as she took a seat at one of the swing chairs at the counter, setting her thermos down in front of her.

Looking around again, she frowned, having expected Rider to be sitting at one of the tables or booths, with Carly talking to him as she waited on him. There was no sign of either of them.

She had watched enough scary movies to become worried and was about to call out for Carly when the waitress came out of the women's restroom, smoothing her tumbled hair down.

"Morning, Jo." The middle-aged woman had a blush staining her cheeks as she made her way behind the counter.

"Good morning, Carly. I was getting worried about you." Jo returned her greeting, wondering if Rider had left his bike to go across the street to visit Knox at the sheriff's office.

Carly's blush deepened. "Sorry. I asked Rider to look at the toilet for me. It won't stop running."

Jo didn't blink at the lie as the bathroom door opened again and Rider came out. The biker, unlike Carly, wasn't embarrassed at being caught in the women's restroom with a woman.

Tearing her eyes away from his sardonic smile as he took

a seat in one of the small booths for two, she swung her head back to Carly.

"What can I get you this morning?" The waitress unashamedly winked at Rider as she asked for Jo's order.

"I just need my thermos filled and an egg sandwich to go." She ate most of her meals in the truck so she would be ready when a call came through the radio.

"You want a cup of coffee while you wait for me to make your sandwich?" At Jo's nod, Carly went for the coffee cups, pouring two. After Carly set one in front of her, Jo watched as she then carried the other coffee to Rider.

Swinging her chair forward, Jo felt uncomfortable watching the casual flirtations between them. She impatiently stared down at her watch. She hated not being in her tow truck before seven. It was ten to now.

The town was too small for the morning rush of traffic most larger cities experienced, but as small as Treepoint was, mornings were inevitably her busiest time. The calls would range from cars not starting to flat tires. Days like today would be filled with wrecks caused by the rain-slickened roads or by dodging a deer fleeing a hunter's arrow.

Dumping a large dollop of creamer into her coffee, irritated that Carly hadn't given her a spoon, she leaned over the counter and reached for one in the silverware container underneath the counter. Successful, she stirred her coffee, able to see in the reflection of the stainless-steel coffee machine that Rider and Carly were still talking.

She spared another quick look at her watch. It was now five to.

She took her spoon out of her coffee cup and deliberately let it drop to the counter. In the reflection, she saw Carly and Rider's heads turn toward her before Carly murmured something and took off toward the kitchen.

Satisfied that her objective had been achieved, Jo took a

sip of her coffee, unconsciously strumming her fingertips on the counter.

"What's your hurry?"

The sound of Rider's voice from the booth had her swinging around on her chair. "Some people have work to do."

"Who you are referring to? Carly or yourself?"

"Both."

His narrow-eyed stare raked over her. His arm was hooked over the back of the booth, long legs sprawled out to the side, owning the space with his masculinity oozing out of every pore in his body.

To have a man like Rider focus on you took all the sarcasm out of a woman. It was everything she could do to force the single word out of her mouth.

Swinging her chair forward, she concentrated on her coffee and not the dark brown-haired man who made her self-conscious of the stains on the hem of her coveralls and his bird's eye view of her ass straining the coarse material.

Hearing footsteps coming from behind her, she gripped her coffee tighter. She hated it when men came up from behind her.

She sensed when he sat down next to her at the counter without turning her head.

"You mind?" A powerful shoulder blocked her view as he reached across the counter, retrieving a spoon for himself.

"Help yourself. I did." She cattily spared a brief glance as Rider settled back in the chair.

Rider's lips curled into a sensuous smile as he dropped his eyes to the zipper she had closed up to the base of her throat. "Sorry I took so long to order. I couldn't make up my mind on what to have for breakfast."

"Really? I assumed a man your age would know exactly what he wanted."

"You'd think so, but I couldn't make my mind up if I wanted sweet or salty." His smile grew wider.

She hadn't been born yesterday. There was no mistaking his comparison.

"Go for sweet." Giving him the snippet of advice, she then cringed when his loud laughter filled the diner.

"You're cute when you're irritated."

She condescendingly snapped her head toward him. "I'm not irritated."

"Yes, you are. You're pissed because you're embarrassed you caught me and Carly making out before you came in."

"Why would I be embarrassed?" She looked down her nose at him.

His smug, good-looking face struck a chord of another man she detested. Handsome men like Rider always believed every woman was for the taking. Long lashes she would give her eye teeth for surrounded what should be plain brown eyes but were the color of fall leaves, mysterious and ever-changing, depending on his mood, and right now, he was laughing at her.

"You're both consenting adults. What I'm becoming mad about is that it's taking Carly seven minutes to fry an egg, and you thinking I want to talk to you."

His smile slipped, his eyes changing into the swirls of colors matching his mixed emotions that she wasn't giving the flirtatious comeback he was used to from other women. She didn't do flirting. That ability was beyond her now.

His good humor might have slipped, but Rider's massive ego wasn't gone for long.

"Wow, someone got out of the wrong side of the bed. If I'm bugging you, I'll return to my table." He made the offer, not expecting what was coming next.

"Please do."

Her coffee cup poised in the air, about to take a sip, she

paused at his surprise. For a brief second, she thought she saw something terrifying in his expression before he swung out of his chair, leaving his coffee behind. She expected him to return to his table, gaping after him as he made a beeline for the door.

Jo was still staring at the door when Carly came out of the kitchen, carrying the plastic container with her sandwich. "I put in some bacon and a muffin to tide you over until lunch since I kept you waiting. The grill takes a while to heat."

"Thanks. I appreciate it." Taking out her wallet, she carried her food to the register as Carly filled her thermos.

"Where'd Rider go?"

Feeling like a bitch, Jo guilty added another couple dollars to Carly's tip. "He left."

"Oh." The red lipstick turned into an unbecoming pout as Carly gave her the thermos.

The loud motorcycle engine sounded, making them stare out the plate glass window as Rider reversed and drove out of the parking lot.

"I thought he wanted breakfast."

"He must have changed his mind. Thanks." Jo hurried away before Carly could ask more questions about Rider's departure. She ate at the diner a lot and didn't want to worry what Carly was doing to her food out back every time she placed an order.

Cursing under her breath, she went back to her truck, where she choked her sandwich down, hating herself.

She despised being a bitch. She really did. That part always came out around men, despite her efforts that each time would be different.

"I'm going to be a lonely old woman who no one will remember, not even my name when I die."

She was so lonely she ached. Rachel was her only female friend in town. Married to Cash Adams, she was kept busy with a small child and worked for The Last Riders, who her husband also worked for.

Rachel would invite her over for dinner regularly, so much so that she had quit accepting her invitations, sensing Rachel was inviting her because she knew how lonely she was.

"Would it have killed you to be nice?" she asked herself out loud.

The best part of her job was that she was her own boss. The worst part of her job was she spent the majority of her time alone.

Static filled the cab of the truck just as she snapped the plastic lid closed.

"You there, Jo?"

"I'm here," she answered, pressing the button on her radio to answer the familiar voice of the sheriff.

"I need a car towed. I'll text you the address." Her cell phone pinged just as he stopped speaking.

Looking at the address, she pressed the button again. "Give me ten minutes. I'm leaving the diner now."

Frowning, she backed out, turning the massive wheel to aim the truck at the road. She tried to think of who lived in that part of town. It was nearly at the county line. She usually never got calls from that direction unless they were involved in a car wreck.

Pressing down on the gas, she held on to the steering wheel with both hands. There weren't many townspeople who lived that far out of town, mainly older people who had been born in the hollars and still lived there. Many of them lived in multi-generation homes, not wanting to give up their privacy by living around others. Why live in a house with a small yard when you can live with your parents and have the forest at your doorstep?

Slowing, she put on the blinker before turning down a

paved, two-lane side road. The road was so narrow she had to honk her horn when she went around a curve, warning oncoming vehicles approaching in the other lane. They were dangerously sharp curves. Two medium-sized cars would have trouble navigating the hairpin curve. Her truck was so large it almost took up the entire road.

The flashing lights of the sheriff's car ahead showed she was on the right backroad.

Maneuvering the large tow truck to the side of the road, she then grabbed her clipboard hanging from the dashboard and mentally prepared herself as she opened the door. Jumping down from the truck, she walked over to where Knox and his two deputies were standing, staring out into the creek bed where a car was sitting. The front of the small car had nearly been flattened, with the windshield broken and smashed inward.

She had been driving her late father's tow truck long enough to know she was dealing with a fatality.

Taking out her ink pen, Jo wrote down the description of the vehicle and that Knox had requested it be moved before she handed the clipboard and the pen to Knox.

"What happened?" she asked him, seeing the deputy take more pictures before wading into the water to snap more.

"It seems like Ben accidentally hit the accelerator instead of the brake, and it shot forward, taking them over the hill."

Jo's heart twisted in grief. The Warrens were an older couple and had been married since high school. She guesstimated they had both been in their seventies. She had met them in town and the few times they had needed to get their car towed.

"Are you done? If you are, I'll hook the car up."

"Go ahead. The state police just left. Lloyd is just taking pictures for my files," he answered, scrawling his signature on her form.

Taking it from him, she climbed back into her truck.

Pulling out in a wide arch, she backed the truck up to the small creek. Stepping back outside, she grabbed the steel chain that would ease the totaled car forward onto the back of her truck.

The drizzling rain cast a gloomy shadow on the dismal sight of the mangled car. As she worked, she tried not to look inside what was left of the interior, not wanting to remember the evidence of what had happened within.

Jo hated jobs like this, when she knew the victims. Ben had been a large bear of man despite his age, and Mary had been so small a hard breeze would have blown her away.

Blinking back useless tears, she went back to her truck to push the button that would pull the mangled vehicle on the bed of her truck.

"It never gets easier, does it?" Knox said, coming to her side to watch grimly.

"No, it doesn't. Thanks for not calling until they had been taken away."

"It's my job, and I didn't want to be here. No sense you having more nightmares."

Jo looked at him. "I don't have nightmares." Expressionlessly, she went to the other side of her tow truck, making sure the car was locked in place before returning to where she had left Knox. "I'll be by your office for my money tomorrow." With that, she brusquely opened her cab door and climbed inside before he could say anything, ignoring the quizzical way he looked at her.

She expertly nudged her truck to miss Knox's squad car as she mentally called herself an idiot for taking offense at the mention of nightmares.

She wished she could have nightmares. At least that would have been normal. Even as a child, though, her life had been as far from normal as you could get.

Her earliest memories were of her mother and father fighting over his drinking or her complaining about why he never came home. Many nights they had eaten alone, and then she had been woken in the middle of the night by their loud arguments. She had learned to pull the blankets and pillow over her to drown out them out.

Despite the fights, her mother had stayed, while constantly threatening to leave and take Jo with her. Then her mother's duty to her finally outweighed keeping her marriage intact.

Jo's fingers tightened on the steering wheel. What had triggered her mother's decision was a night that she still blamed herself for, regardless of what her mother and her therapist had tried to convince her of.

She wasn't placing the sole blame on herself. There was plenty to share with the four boys who still remained untouched for the crime they had committed.

She had been a naïve fifteen-year-old when the seventeen- and eighteen-year-old high school jocks who had Treepoint at their beck and call decided she was going to be their trophy for winning their championship game.

Jo swallowed down the bile rising in her throat. It had been years, yet she could still remember every detail of that night.

Blowing her horn as she went around the curve, relieved the main road was just ahead, she relived that night. The alcohol-fueled breath breathed down on her breasts, rough hands parted her thighs, while she felt other hands using their bruising strength to pin her arms down. Pressing her foot down on the accelerator, the tow truck barreled toward town just as the sun rose high in the sky.

When Jo flipped on her windshield wipers, she realized the mist blocking her vision wasn't from the rain outside.

God, how she wished she could wipe away that night with a flip of a switch.

Slowing down when she hit the city limits, she drove past the church, then the police station. Ironic that they were on the same street. Retribution or forgiveness. She hadn't been able to achieve either since she had come back to town.

The Dawkins were too powerful, not only with wealth but family and friends that made *him* untouchable. She had been untouched before Curt and his friends had lain their disgusting hands on her.

No matter how many Sundays she had spent in church, she hadn't been able to find forgiveness in her soul for them, nor had she been able to find justice from the law. Her reaction to Rider showed that she hadn't put the past behind her.

The Warrens had died unexpectedly. When they had gone outside to their car, they hadn't known that it would be the last time they would walk out their door. The same damn thing could happen to her. Accidents happened all the time. One had taken her own father's life. Any unfortunate accident could take her life, and everything she had been waiting to do would be unfinished.

Excitement and fear coursed through her veins. To achieve her plan, she needed a patsy.

A grin tugged at her lips. Pretty boy would be perfect. No one would suspect him. He would also be protected by the sheriff who wouldn't let anything happen to him.

It was perfect. Freaking perfect.

3

Rider took the steps two at a time, going upstairs of the clubhouse and heading to his bedroom. He passed Jewell's open door and halted in the hallway, watching as she tugged her top over her pert breasts.

"You want to be late with me?" Giving her a smoldering look that would light a fire in her pussy, he strolled into her room.

"I already have to pull from the punishment bag this week because of you." Jewell gave him an irritated look as she sat down on the edge of her bed to put on her shoes. "If I keep being late, Shade will take over the factory again."

Undeterred, he sank down onto the bed next to her, sliding his hand underneath her tight top, traveling up her bare spine to pull the material tighter so he could see the outline of her nipples poking out. "Shade won't take over again, not when Lily is expecting at any minute." Rubbing his jaw along her chinbone, he felt her shiver in his arms. "Loosen up. I want to spend the morning in bed with you." With his free hand, he moved to the cleft of her thighs, rubbing her pussy in firm strokes.

"Damn, Rider." Jewell started falling backward at his urging, lifting her hips greedily at his movements. "I shouldn't have let you talk me into having a day off."

With his chest, he crushed her breasts flat as he unsnapped her jeans. "Call in sick."

"Shade would have to fill in for me. He would be up here before I can hang up to see if I'm lying."

With a final swish against her clit, he removed his hand from her wet pussy. "Wake me up during your lunch hour."

He started to get up from the bed, but she pulled him back down.

"I didn't say I wouldn't do it. Just what would happen when I do."

He laughed, settling back down alongside her. "Want me to call in for you?"

Licking her bottom lip, Jewell unsnapped his jeans, parting the material to reach down and pull out his hardening cock. "Yes, I'm kind of busy." She parted her hungry mouth, slipping over the head of his cock.

As a hiss of air escaped through his clenched teeth, he shifted slightly, reaching for his cell phone in his back pocket and hitting Shade's number before putting the phone to his ear.

"What do you want?" Shade's sleepy voice had Rider smiling up at the ceiling as he lay back to give Jewell more of his cock.

"Jewell isn't feeling well. I talked her into taking the day off."

"Then you can go work for her." Shade definitely wasn't happy to be woken up with the bad news that the factory's manager needed the day off.

"Can't. I'm busy." He pushed Jewell's head farther down. The woman could suck cock with her hands tied behind her back. He would know.

"Get un-busy. I'm not filling in for Jewell because she wants to spend the day with you."

"Come on, Shade. When Lily has the baby, it'll be three months before Jewell will be able to take off." Another hiss of air escaped him when Jewell closed her mouth tighter on him.

"I'll work until one. Lily has a doctor's appointment at one thirty. Either you or Jewell better have your ass in the office at one."

Rider grinned down at Jewell after Shade had disconnected. Tossing his cell phone on the bed, he kicked his boots off, then settled back on the rumpled bed to enjoy his blowjob.

"Aren't you going to be late?" A female voice from the doorway had him raising his head.

"Jewell's sick."

Ember came farther into the bedroom. "It must be catching. I'm feeling hot myself." The sultry woman lay on the bed next to him, enviously watching Jewell suck his cock before dipping her mouth to kiss his.

Thrusting his tongue inside her mouth, he returned the kiss, sharing with her the lust that he and Jewell had been building.

"Shade will be pissed if you don't show," he warned, smoothing her T-shirt out of his way. Ember's tits were heavier than Jewell's, the scrap of black lace was more of a decoration than holding them confined in their cups. Rider raised himself, laving the skin between her breast and nuzzling the lace aside to suck one rosy nipple into his mouth.

"You going to make it worth the punishment?" Ember's eyes glittered salaciously back at him.

"Don't I always?" he mumbled against her tit, giving her

nipple a playful nip before he released her breast. "Sit on my face."

Not needing further encouragement, Ember jerked off the bed, removing her clothes in a rush.

When she positioned herself over him, his tongue was waiting to taste her. Surrounding her clit with his lips, he then pushed his tongue into the slit of her pussy, driving inside the wet channel.

Ember moaned, placing her hands on either side on his head as Jewel sucked harder on his cock, wanting her share of his attention. He had no qualms that he wouldn't be able to satisfy both women.

Rider grabbed Ember's hips, pulling her farther down on his mouth. He loved having his mouth on a woman's pussy, almost as much as he enjoyed having his cock in a woman's throat. The power of keeping them in his control as they sought to please him was a heady feeling of euphoria that most men could find in a bottle of liquor or drugs. Women, however, were his choice of drugs. He was addicted to their taste and smell, almost as much as the sounds of their moans when they begged to come.

Moving his hand from Ember's hip, he used it to take his cock away from Jewel, hearing his cock pop out as he rolled over, reversing positions with Ember. With his hand still on his cock, the other went to the back of Ember's neck, raising her to meet his cock. Opening her mouth, she sucked him as he slid to the back of her throat. His cock twitched, spilling his semen into her experienced throat.

"Strip for me," Rider croaked out to Jewell, jutting his hips out to ride out his orgasm.

Jewell crawled off the end of the bed. Her hand at her top, pressing it to her flat waistline, she tortuously inched it upward, moving her hips and feet to imaginary music.

By the time her top was off, he had pulled his cock out of

Ember's mouth and had started finger-fucking her to the movements of her hips.

"Play with yourself," he ordered Jewell as he fucked Ember faster.

Jewell went to the opening of her jeans before sliding them downward.

"Without the jeans." He spoke louder to be heard over Ember's moans. "When I get done with her, I'm going to fuck you. You want it, you're going to have to work for it." He jutted his still half-hard dick in her direction.

"Maybe I don't want it," Jewell teased, taking her hand out of her jeans, then sexily peeling her jeans over her hips.

"You want it." He grabbed his cock with his free hand, stroking it into another erection.

Jewell wantonly kicked off her jeans, then raised one foot to the edge of the bed, giving him an eyeful of her glistening cunt. Wetting one long delicious finger, she sank it into her pussy.

His erection, never far away when a pussy was near, nudged Ember's squirming waist.

"You think you deserve it more than Ember?" he taunted Jewell, taking his finger out of Ember's clenching pussy and putting it in his mouth, licking her juices off before he reached for a condom on the nightstand. "She's in bad shape."

"So am I," Jewell whimpered.

"Two waiting pussies, one cock. What's a man supposed to do?" Rolling the condom on in the same movement he got off the bed, he moved to stand behind Jewell.

As he shoved her headfirst onto the bed, her hands splaying out to catch herself, Rider pounded his cock into her tight pussy, feeling her clench him like a fucking glove.

"Rider! What about me?" Ember mewled like a cat in heat.

"Come here." He motioned her closer to Jewell. When she

had scooted her ass close enough, he positioned her until she was lying on top of Jewell.

Rider gritted his teeth. The sight of two greedy pussies had him thrusting harder inside of Jewell.

As Jewell and Ember began kissing each other, his fingers went to Ember's pussy as he continued fucking Jewell. He dug into Ember's ass cheeks, taking his cock out of Jewell then sliding it into Ember. He gave her several hard strokes before he pulled out then plunged back into Jewell. He alternated fucking each woman until his skin shone in sweat.

He gripped Ember's other ass cheek over the faint purple bruise he had left there last night before he had gone out to meet Carly at her apartment. There was something immensely satisfying to see his mark on her. It wasn't as sweet as the one he had left on Carly's shoulder, or the one he had put on Jewell's tit, or the one he had wanted to give Jo.

Thinking about the way the woman had blown him off had him pounding even harder into Ember. There weren't many women who he couldn't get his dick into, yet Jo was the one who grated on his pride.

Ember caught his attention by breaking off from kissing Jewell to suck on Jewell's neck. Rider snaked his hand out, taking a handful of her hair and pulling her mouth away from the woman's neck.

Clicking his tongue at her for being bad, he said, "You know I don't like anyone to mark any of the women but me."

"S-sorry," Ember sobbed when his hand landed heavily on her bare ass.

"It okay ... this time." He soothed his hand over the red mark.

"Thank you. I won't do it again." Ember had to hold on to Jewell's shoulders to keep herself from being knocked over from his penetrating thrusts.

"You're such a good girl," Rider crooned as he switched to

Jewell's pussy. He fucked her so hard that both women and the bed rocked. He was about to switch again when he felt Jewell's pussy tightening. Knowing she was about to come, he rewarded her by angling upward to hit the spot that would drive her over the edge. When she pulled Ember into a voracious kiss, he knew he had succeeded. Then, when her legs stopped shaking, he pulled his dick out, giving Ember his whole attention.

Leaning forward as he fucked her, he placed his mouth on her shoulder. Biting down, he gave her another mark.

Ember's whimpers of pleasure had his own lust overwhelming him. He sunk down onto both women in a sexual frenzy that nearly blew his fucking mind into a desire-ridden haze that lasted all morning.

HOURS LATER, Rider lifted one eye to look at the clock sitting on Jewell's nightstand. Yawning, he carefully moved off a sleeping Jewell's back without waking Ember, who was sleeping on the other side of him. Shifting out from underneath her, he sidled across the bed, getting to his feet. Walking naked from the room, he showered in the bathroom before going to his bedroom to dress.

His bed was still unmade from the night before, pillows and sheets hanging off the side. Taking the pillowcases off the pillows and bunching the sheets into his arms, he carried the dirty laundry downstairs to the basement. Seeing the washing machine was empty, he started the load before going out the side door to the path that led down to the factory.

The green metal building sat below the clubhouse, sitting on the back portion of the parking lot. The lot was filled with the employees' vehicles from town, and a large box

truck at the back was ready to be fill
would go out at the end of the day.

He had a minute to spare when he w

Shade eyed him critically before st̪
have the seat behind the desk.

"Jewell's not coming?"

"I thought I'd give her a break. She's exhausted." Sitting down, he rolled the computer chair closer to the desk.

"I told Viper that Jewell and Ember didn't come in today."

Shade didn't communicate his actions often. When he did, it was usually for a reason. He was letting him know he was angry at being asked to work that morning.

"Viper will dock their pay." Rider angrily stared across the desk at The Last Riders' enforcer.

"Why should they be paid to stay in bed and fuck you?" Shade unrepentantly locked eyes with his. "I had shit to do this morning. I promised to spend the morning with Lily at the church. She had promised to be there to help Rachel and Willa get ready for the auction."

Rider's anger dissipated. Shade wouldn't have let Lily out of his sight to go to the church without him. Not only had his morning fuck session inconvenienced Shade and Lily, but Rachel and Willa.

"Lucky and Cash pissed, too?"

"What do you think?" Shade didn't make the effort to lessen his guilt.

"I'm sorry. If you had told me you had shit to do, I would have worked, or sent Jewell to work."

"Would it have made a difference?"

"Probably not at the time," he admitted. His cock always took precedence over what everyone else wanted. It was a fault of his character, and he saw no reason to change it. That's why he was single and available to any woman at any time.

s why I waited to tell you. Brother, you know me; about you doing what makes you happy, but when it erferes with work, we have a problem, because then I have o step in or Viper does, and then you're interfering with shit that makes *us* happy."

"You happy? You've never been happy a day in your life," Rider scoffed at the use of happy and Shade in the same sentence.

Shade's lips thinned into a firm line. "Then let's put it another way. The next time one of the women wants to call in sick on a day you're off, they better have a doctor's excuse or start looking for another job."

Fuck. Jewell and Ember were going to be furious at that decree. He wasn't happy with it himself.

"Point taken. If they call in sick, it won't be because of something I've done."

"Good." Once he had said his piece, Shade moved on, reaching for a check that was lying on the desk and giving it to him. "Give this to Jo. She should be here in thirty minutes. She's bringing Killyama's car. Have her park it in the bay. Train wants it to be a surprise."

"That piece of crap? We should be paying Jo to keep and scrap it."

"The Destructor women have a sentimental attachment to it, which Train understands."

"To each their own." He wouldn't give a nickel for that scrap of heap. He didn't care how much money Train had paid to have it restored.

When Shade turned his head toward the window that showed The Last Riders clubhouse and the path that led to Shade's house, Rider turned to see what he was looking at.

Rider swallowed hard, envious of the man the woman belonged to. She was walking elegantly toward the factory despite her protruding belly. The raven-haired beauty was strikingly beautiful when she wasn't pregnant. Pregnancy magnified her beauty, as if she glowed from an inner warmth surrounding her protectively.

"Looks like Lily is ready for her appointment. If you don't go, she'll be late." He put the check underneath the calendar in plain sight to remind himself to take it outside when Jo arrived.

"If something comes up, call Viper. My phone will be off until we come out of the doctor's office."

Rider nodded, pretending to focus on the e-mails that needed to be answered and evading Shade's searching, keen gaze.

"Rider ..."

"Don't keep her waiting."

When he looked again, Shade was gone.

He went to the window, standing to the side, watching Lily's face when she caught sight of Shade. She practically ran into his arms despite being away from her husband for only a few hours and her being heavily pregnant.

He gripped the cord of the blinds, jerking it taut and lowering them, removing the couple from sight as Shade reached her.

The happy couple were expecting their second child. Lily had come a long way from the teenage girl he had first seen at the lake. She had been afraid of her own shadow back then. Maturing as a wife and mother under Shade's protection and love, Lily had become a stunningly sweet woman. Any man would envy Shade's marriage.

Physically exhausted, he leaned wearily against the windowsill. He hadn't slept for over thirty-six hours, other than the brief ten-minute nap he had taken after fucking Jewell and Ember. He had to be physically and mentally exhausted before he would be able to sleep the four or five hours he would manage to attain every other day. The thoughts drumming through his skull kept him from finding the relief of slumber. No alcohol, nor the number of women he fucked could assuage the need that gave him the motivation he needed to see a new day start. That and The Last Riders.

The brothers might not have a blood bond, but they had shared hell together and had survived, forging a friendship that was stronger than blood.

Women like Lily were princesses and were meant for men of power. Just as Winter was Viper's, the president of The Last Riders.

Rider was just a soldier. He was meant to live and die for the club. If he failed in his duty, then one of the brothers could be hurt. He had failed in that duty once before. Never again.

He wasn't The Last Riders' backup when things went to shit. He was their fail safe.

4

"Late night?" The snickering from the doorway had Rider straightening.

"You need something, Curt?"

"Just wanted to see if you wanted to get a beer after work?"

Rider would rather rip his toenails off than spend an evening pretending to be friendly with the disgusting man. However, he gave him a jaunty thumbs-up as he returned to the desk to deal with the e-mails.

"Ask Moon if he wants to go. The last time we hung out, he wanted to know why you didn't invite him," he smoothly lied. It was going to ruin what was left of Moon's workday to find out he would have to spend the evening with Curt and his buddies at Mick's bar. If he had to suffer, there was no reason Moon didn't have to, too.

Curt's chest swelled with pride that The Last Riders were fighting over his friendship. "Sure thing. I wouldn't want to cause problems between you guys." Hesitating, he turned to look over his shoulder before turning back toward Rider. "Should I invite Gavin?"

Rider wanted to laugh at Curt's wariness. All the factory workers were leery of Gavin. Hell, most of the brothers were also.

"I'd give that a pass if I were you. Gavin prefers to spend his evenings working out."

That was the truth. His friend spent hours working out after work in the basement of the club. Viper had converted part of it into a gym after Winter had been attacked to help her recover. It had also become useful after Cash's motorcycle wreck. All the brothers made use of the top-of-the-line equipment.

"I know he's a friend of yours, but he gives me the creeps." Curt looked over his shoulder again to make sure no one had come up behind him.

Rider concentrated on the e-mails to keep from giving Curt the cutting remark he deserved. The only person who had a creep factor was Curt. Every time he had to hang out with him, he felt like taking a hot shower to cleanse the feeling of stepping in dog shit from his soul.

Viper had ordered him to make friends with the repulsive, sorry excuse of a man. That was after Jo had confronted Curt at Mick's bar when she had returned to town. Train, Knox, Cash, and Rider had witnessed it. When they had gone back to the clubhouse, they had asked for permission to make Curt disappear. Unfortunately, Viper had denied the request after Shade had informed them of the repercussions. Curt was a member of a large family who would make waves if he disappeared. Instead, Viper had Shade and Cash come up with a plan.

The only way The Last Riders hadn't been caught seeking their own brand of justice was they played it smart and bided their time until they were able to strike. It was taking longer than they had believed it would take. The son of a bitch was cagey, never admitting to anything he had done.

They had hoped to find evidence that he had touched an underage student from the high school, but again, he had outmaneuvered them by marrying the girl when she had become pregnant. Now the girl was over eighteen and refused to admit that Curt had touched her when she was still underage.

Willa had tried to make friends with Megan during the brief time she had worked with her, to no avail. Lucky's wife had been heartbroken when Curt had forced Megan to quit. Then she was even more upset when she had quit the job she had taken in King's restaurant. Leaving her alone and without support when she had miscarried Curt's baby, Megan had gone over the deep end and tried to kidnap Viper and Winter's baby. The Last Riders had chipped in to get the girl counseling. However, once again, Curt had stymied them by locking her away in a mental health facility. Even if they could convince her to testify against Curt, her mental state would be used against her. The Last Riders wanted to see Curt behind bars, but not at the cost of causing more pain for Megan.

Sooner or later, Curt would fuck up, and The Last Riders would be waiting.

Rider reminded himself to take a couple aspirins before going out with him tonight to combat the headache that Curt always gave him.

"I need to get busy if I'm not going to keep you waiting after work," Rider said when Curt lingered in the doorway.

"Wouldn't want to hold you up. Mick's will be full with it being Friday."

Rider glared at Curt's back as he left, hating that he would have to spend the better part of the night at Mick's instead of at the party The Last Riders had every Friday night at the clubhouse. Several of the brothers were riding in tonight from Ohio, and he had been looking forward to spending the night with them and the women who were anxious to become full members.

His day had gone to shit ever since he had seen Jo at the diner.

Left alone, he was able to finish the e-mails. Then he needed to check the progress on the orders that were waiting to be filled.

Stepping out of the office, he checked the work board in the middle of the factory to see which orders were being worked on and those still waiting to be packaged.

"Fuck." He was surprised Shade hadn't ripped him a new asshole. The workers were backed up with him, Jewell, and Ember not working this morning. Train being off for the next three days hadn't helped either.

Taking off his jacket, he took the packing list for the largest order and got busy, losing track of time. It was only when he was lifting a heavy box and the front door opened, spilling the bright light inside, that had him looking toward the front door and remembering that Jo had been scheduled to deliver Killyama's car.

Carrying the box to the popcorn machine, he set it down to finish after he checked out the car.

Before he could stop her, Jo had gone to the office. Rider met her when she was about to come out of the empty room.

"Shade or Train around?" Her frosty voice was like a Brillo Pad on his ego. He could understand her not reciprocating his flirtatious behavior, but damn, she didn't have to act like he was a slimy slug.

"Nope. Will I do?" He gave her a phony smile that all the brothers would recognize, deliberately maneuvering his body so Jo would have to brush past him or remain in the office.

She stared down her nose at him, remaining where she

was. "I have Killyama's car. Can you sign for it, or should I text Train?"

Her blue-gray eyes made no effort to hide the contempt she felt for him. From their first meeting, she had taken one look at him and formed an opinion of him that he hadn't tried to change, but damn, it was getting harder and harder to resist bringing the woman down a peg or two. Several reasons stopped him. He had been in the bar when Jo had drawn a steak knife on Curt, exposing him and Jared as her rapists when they had been in high school together.

Rider would have taken that into consideration of her behavior toward him because of him being a male, but Jo hadn't treated Moon or any of the other brothers to the same contempt she had him. Moon had treated her to the same flirtatious attitude as he had, but she had given him a tolerant smile as if he were a kid trying to get his first date.

The second reason was she was friends with Rachel, and if he pissed off Rachel, then he would have to deal with Cash. All in all, it was too much work for him just to score a piece of ass that he could get by pressing one of the many women's numbers that were available for him to choose from.

He folded his arms against his chest. "I can."

Her eyes turned bluer than blue when he didn't move out of her way.

"You first." She motioned for him to go ahead of her so she wouldn't have to brush past him.

Giving her a cocky smile that he was sure would lower him even more in her estimation of him, he moved partially to the side, giving her a scant inch more space. "Ladies first." He expectantly waited for what she would do next.

She disappointed him when she reached for her cell phone. "Perhaps it would be easier for me to deal with Shade."

"Don't bother. He's with Lily at her doctor's appointment,

and Train is in Lexington with Killyama—they've gone to a race. I don't understand. What's the problem?"

"You know what you're doing. From the way the women in town talk about you, I'm surprised you're trying to do something as mundane as copping a feel, giving me little room to go past you."

"I've never been called mundane before. What does it mean?" Rider treated her to a fake frown of puzzlement.

"I know you're not stupid. Rachel said you're an engineer. If you don't know what mundane means, then you didn't get your money's worth out of your college education." Jo gave him a once-over as if he were a spoiled piece of beef at the store that no one wanted.

Damn, he should have expected Rachel would tell Jo.

"If you're done having fun at my expense, I haven't had lunch yet, and King is waiting for a tow."

"I wasn't making fun of you." His frown became sincere.

"Really? It seems that way to me."

"I was trying to flirt with you—"

"Again, you surprise me. I've made it pretty obvious I'm not interested in you."

"It doesn't hurt to try, does it?" He was enjoying their comebacks. Like a teeter-totter, their volleys had their ups and downs.

"It does when you're bugging the piss out of me."

For the first time in his life since turning thirteen, a woman stared at him coldly without a spark of sexual interest.

Turning, he walked to the front door, going outside and holding the door for Jo. "Shade said to put it in the bay. I'll open the door for you." Not waiting for her reply or even if she was going to make one, he went to the side of the factory toward the back. At the swipe of his palm, the metal door rose.

The back of the factory had two bays. One where the box trucks could load the packages to be shipped or where they received their supplies. The other bay, which he was giving Jo access to, was only used by The Last Riders. It housed his private collection of bikes, and the other brothers' bikes and vehicles they owned. It also housed the security system for the factory and the clubhouse.

Jo backed up the trailer, stopping short of the metal door. Rider watched as she then lowered the car using the wrench, setting the car neatly inside the bay. It was covered with a tarp that she removed with a flourish.

He walked around the car slowly. It didn't look like the same car. The four-door had undergone a dramatic change inside and out. The puke-green color was gone, and the candy-apple red was striking.

Opening the driver door, Rider poked his head inside, amazed at the transformation. The black leather upholstery shone and smelled brand-new. The whole car did. It had been restored with an eye to detail from the gauges that been cracked and broken to the side panels.

Rider gave an appreciate whistle, rising to admire the work of art that had been accomplished. "Damn, whoever Train found to restore it did a hell of a job," he complimented, running his hand over the roof.

"I need a signature." Her voice pulled him out of his absorption with the car.

Taking the clipboard, he scrawled his signature, thinking about how much crow he was going to have to eat when Train came back on Monday.

"I'll have to ask Train who did it. I have a car in Ohio I've been hesitating to get restored."

"He's a friend of mine." Reaching into the pocket on the front of her coveralls, she took out a business card, then handed it to him.

Staring down at the card, he saw the business was in Virginia.

"If you're interested, send him a picture of your car, and he can give you an estimate."

"I'll do that ... after I check him out. I want to see his reviews."

"I met Carl when he restored a car for one of my customers. I think he's done a couple. He said he's retired and just take jobs he's interested in. I don't think he has any reviews," Jo explained as she bunched the tarp up and tied it down on the trailer.

Staring at Killyama's car, he decided to text the number on the card anyway.

"Give me a sec before you leave. Shade gave me a check to give to you from Train." He remembered as Jo was about to get into her truck.

At her nod, he went to the door that led to the inside of the factory from the bay. Not wanting to keep her waiting, he hurried, telling Nickel he would be right back when he tried to ask a question. Grabbing the check from the office, he then turned, retracing his steps.

Opening the door into the bay, he heard Jo talking to someone, so he skirted a row of bikes, coming up behind the back of the tow truck.

"You're getting ugly in your old age."

Curt was the one being ugly, using a disparaging tone, trying to belittle the woman out of sight and sound of anyone.

"Go fuck yourself, Curt. Wait ..." Scornfully, her words lashed out like a whip. "I fucked you. It wasn't great. Why not give the girls under eighteen in town a break and take a flying leap off Black Mountain?"

Rider strode out, making his presence known when Curt took a step toward Jo. "You looking for me, Curt?"

"I was taking a cigarette break," Curt answered defensively.

"Did you clock out?" Rider questioned with a raised brow, not missing the retaliatory glare he gave Jo before he went to the back door. The metal door slammed shut with a loud bang at the force Curt used.

Rider turned to look back at Jo. "If he gives you any trouble, call Shade. He'll deal with him."

"I don't need Shade's help to deal with Curt. He's a scared little mouse unless he has his friends or cousins with him."

"Scared little men like Curt are the most dangerous," he warned.

"Curt wasn't wrong. I am getting older and uglier. I'm not fifteen anymore. He messes with me, he'll get more than he's bargained for." She met his gaze with a steely determination that had him becoming afraid for her.

Curt might seem like a lazy bastard, but when assholes like him became angry, they didn't care who they hurt.

He had to quell the worry beginning to burn a hole in his stomach. He should have just kept his fucking mouth closed. Jo was an independent woman who didn't need or want advice from him.

"Here's Train's check." Handing it to her, he then swept his hand over the pad, closing the bay door. "You have the keys?"

Jo gave him a searching look before taking them from her front pocket and giving them to him. "That's it? No flirting? No 'you want to go out'? You offer to have Shade deal with Curt when you could have said something a minute ago. When you get shot down for good, your true colors come out. It's good to know I didn't waste my time with you."

He closed his hand around the keys in his palm, biting his tongue to keep himself from saying what he wanted to say. Instead, he lowered his lashes, gave her the sensual smile he gave to women, and said, "I didn't say anything to Curt because I didn't think you would appreciate me making you look weak in front of him."

Jo's jaw dropped, and she took a step back when he took a step forward, making sure she caught a whiff of the expensive cologne he paid to be made just for him.

Giving her a wry look for backing away, he bent down to pick up the buffing rag that had fallen out of her pocket. "I stopped flirting with you because you told me to. If you're having trouble making up your mind, we could have dinner tonight at King's."

"I'd rather eat glass if I was starving to death than have dinner with you. You were fucking Carly in the bathroom this morning, and you have the nerve to ask me out for dinner tonight? Invite Carly; it would make her night after you left without saying goodbye."

If Jo thought she would make a dent in his pride at her refusal, she was mistaken. You had to care about a woman to worry about what they thought of you. He didn't believe women were helpless and couldn't take of themselves. He had learned to his own detriment that they had a survival instinct that was more cunning than a man's.

"That's too bad. King's chef is the best in Kentucky." Going to the side of her tow truck, he opened the door for her. "I'd better be getting back to work."

"Tha ..." she began to say as she started to step up onto the footrest when Rider reached out before she could react, plucking her off her feet and plopping her down gently on the driver's seat.

Jo stared down at him in surprise. He quickly shut the door before she could hit him.

"You take care." Giving her a jaunty wink, he went to the back door of the factory, already putting her out of his mind.

Some women could make men cry in their beers because

men wanted them so badly. Jo wasn't one of those women. She was a ball buster. It would take a strong man to survive the shitstorm of trying to win her. It wasn't a challenge Rider was interested in winning.

The married brothers had fought a battle of falling in love and lost. As much as Jo intrigued him—the hard rise in his jeans testified to that fact—it wasn't enough to have him beating down her door or chasing her tow truck.

Laughing sardonically to himself, he went to find Nickel. Helping him unjam the popcorn machine wasn't as much fun as provoking Jo, but it was a hell of a lot safer.

5

"So, are you coming to dinner or not?"

Jo rubbed her temples. She had been refusing Rachel's dinner invitation for the last fifteen minutes and was beginning to get a headache at Rachel's determination that she come.

"I've already told you no ten times. I'm eating at home and, God willing, I can get a few hours' sleep before getting called out. What's the big deal if I come tonight?"

She was going to stop by the grocery and buy herself a TV dinner, then watch one episode of *The Walking Dead* before going to bed. Her red-headed friend's temperament was showing through, though, refusing to accept her refusal.

"I didn't know Cash has to work late tonight, and I made a big pot of chicken and dumplings. Mag, Ema, and I can't eat it all. All that food is going to go to waste if you don't come. Please, I'll make you some deviled eggs."

Her stomach growled at the tempting bribe.

"What time will everything be ready?" She gave in to the inevitable two pounds that she would be walking away with from Rachel's home cooking.

"Six. Don't be late!" Rachel gave her a grin before going to talk to Beth and Lily about the church store charity auction at the counter.

There was no denying Rachel when she made up her mind. Jo had had no intention of joining the committee until her friend had badgered her into agreeing.

Looking over the rack of clothes, she saw Shade sitting outside in the parking lot, waiting for Lily to finish.

Carrying two plain shirts and a thick sweater, she carried the items to the counter to pay for them and finish the meeting that had been interrupted when Beth had to wait on a customer.

"I think it's a brilliant idea!" Beth was saying to her sister when she reached the counter. Willa, the pastor's wife, seemed just as pleased.

"I think so, too!" Rachel's beaming smile showed how happy she was with whatever idea Beth and Lily had come up with while she and Rachel had been talking.

"What idea?" Jo asked, reaching for her wallet.

Lily started ringing up the clothes Jo had set down. "I read about a charity auction for bachelors to raise money. I told Beth about it, and we think that would be an inexpensive way to raise money for the church. The auction we had last year only raised five hundred dollars, and we wouldn't have raised that if King hadn't given that steak dinner for four."

"Who do you think you'll be auctioning off? There aren't many bachelors in the congregation." Jo didn't want to dull their enthusiasm, but she couldn't think of any of the bachelors in church who she would pay fifty cents to go on a date with.

Lily's face fell, as did Rachel's. Meanwhile, Willa and Beth stared at each other. Jo could practically see the wheels turning. Then Beth's face brightened.

"There's no reason the men have to be from the congregation. I'm sure I could talk Rider and Moon into volunteering."

"They'll probably be auctioned off quickly with all the women in attendance." Lily laughed.

Jo was the only one not laughing as the other women agreed.

"Why does it have to be the men in town we auction off? Why can't some of the women?" Rachel waved at two customers coming into the store.

Jo didn't like the way the conversation was turning, nor the four pairs of eyes trained on her.

"No. And before you start pestering me, there aren't enough deviled eggs in the world to make me volunteer." Jo dumped the change Lily had given her from her purchase into the donation jar that sat next to the cash register.

"Jo, don't be like that! It's for a good cause. It's for the toy drive for some of the children on the list. It's the only present they'll get for Christmas," Lily pleaded. Her violet eyes had Jo looking away.

"No." It wasn't as strong as her first refusal, but she held on to her determination not to make a fool of herself when none of the men in town bought a date with her.

"We don't want to force you into doing something you don't want to do."

Lily was making her feel terrible. Even the other three were looking at her like she had just squashed a butterfly.

"No one would bid on me." With the defense, she revealed her fear.

"Yes, they would," Lily assured her. "And if none of the men bid on you, I will, and you can go out to dinner with me and Shade."

Jo rolled her eyes. "I'm sure he would enjoy that."

Sweet woman she was, Lily missed the sarcasm in her voice.

Jo gritted her teeth when Beth, Willa, and Rachel offered to bid on her, too.

Feeling like she was about to give in, she clutched at straws, trying to make the women see reason. "How about I pinch in volunteering to set up the dinner? I could buy a couple of presents, too."

"It won't be as much as I can talk Shade into letting me bid."

Lily's downcast expression had words slipping out of her mouth Jo had no intention of uttering.

"I'll do it."

Lily clapped her hands, squealing in glee. She came from around the counter and pulled Jo into a tight hug. "Thank you! I promise you won't regret it. I'll make you a special dinner when I win you," Lily promised light-heartedly.

"Quit jumping around. That can't be good for the baby."

Lily's smile widened as she pulled back to pat her belly.

"Now that we have that settled, let's figure out who we're going to ask if we can auction them off." Rachel reached underneath the counter, taking out a yellow pad, and then taking a pen out of the cup beside the register.

"Rider and Moon for sure. If we're lucky, we'll make enough money to buy all the presents for the children on the list and have enough left over to put together a box of groceries for a Christmas dinner to give to each family." Willa stared down at the long list of families who had applied for aid from the church.

"You really think you'll make that much money?" Jo asked skeptically, looking down at the names, sick at the thought they might not raise enough.

"If I were single, I would buy Rider for five hundred,"

Willa blurted out, then blushed, ignoring Jo's skeptical question as she took the pad away from Rachel.

Jo looked at the woman in surprise. She personally didn't think he was worth over a buck-fifty, but to each her own. At least she would have a front row seat to see the women in town making fools of themselves. *At least I won't be alone*, she consoled herself, already regretting auctioning herself off. The only reason she didn't back out were the names on the list. Every child deserved to have their wishes come true on Christmas morning.

"I can ask Mick," Jo suggested. "A couple of the older women have been chasing him since I was a little girl."

Willa wrote Mick's name down on the pad. "Anyone else?"

"I can ask Dustin." Rachel offered up her youngest brother.

"I can ask Bliss to ask Jessie Hayes if we can auction her or one of her brothers," Beth said.

"Just ask Jessie. I don't want Dustin getting in a fight during the auction." Willa just wrote down Jessie's name.

"You sure? Men would buy more tickets to the auction if they thought they could get a front seat for a fight," Rachel disagreed, not worried her brother would be on the losing end of any fight.

Willa gave Rachel a quelling glance. "Anyone else?"

"I can't think of any." Jo picked up her bag to leave before she was suckered into volunteering to sell another book of tickets to the auction.

"If we get everyone on the list, that'll be enough." Willa picked up both lists. "If any of you think of anyone else, let me know. I better get back upstairs. I left Lucky watching the baby."

"I'll see you tonight, Rach. Bye, Willa." Giving Lily and Beth a steely-eyed glance, she reminded them of their promise. "And you two better not leave me hanging."

Lily raised her hand. "I swear."

"Me, too." Beth sighed. "But I think you're worrying about nothing. One man is going to snap you up when I get done with you."

Jo stopped dead in her tracks. "What does that mean?"

"It means I'm going to help you get dressed that night. I don't trust you not to show up in those coveralls, or one of those shirts you just bought." Beth's eyes narrowed on her oil-stained coveralls.

Jo frowned. She hadn't planned to wear her coveralls, but she had planned on wearing the red shirt she had just purchased. "What's wrong with the red top I just bought? I thought it would be perfect to wear during Christmas."

"Other than it used to be pink? I donated that top last week when Razer washed it with one of his red T-shirts."

"It's red now," Jo argued.

"If you can call that color red, you're color blind."

"What color would you call it?" Jo opened the bag, taking another look at the top that Beth was making fun of.

"Ugly."

Jo closed the bag. "You could have told me that before I bought it."

Beth moved behind Lily, using her as a shield. "I thought you were just buying it to be charitable."

"I'll remember that the next time you get your car stuck in the snow," Jo threatened her. "I'm wearing it."

"Lily, you better bring Shade's checkbook to the auction, then." Beth sidled farther behind Lily.

Her antics had Jo laughing and not paying attention to what she was doing as she went out the door and barreled into a hard body.

When she rocked back on her heels, hard hands steadied

her. Instead of releasing her, though, the arms pulled her closer.

"Baby, if you wanted me, all you had to do was ask. You didn't have to throw yourself at me."

The plastic bag in her hand connected with the smug face inches from hers.

Rider's jaw dropped at the hit. Jo saw the women in the shop were just as shocked at her unexpected reaction.

Jo felt every finger on the hands that gripped her arms to steady her. For a split second, she saw a flicker behind his eyes that swelled her heart with fear, but then she shook the fear off when his face relaxed in a disarming grin.

Releasing her, he placed a hand over his heart. "Shot down again! I'm going to need two cupcakes to get over my disappointment, Willa."

As Rider moved around her, Jo jerked her head around to see that Willa had returned from upstairs, carrying one of her bakery boxes.

"What's so important that you promised me one of your cupcakes to get me here? You trying to get me in trouble with Lucky? He says I'm not allowed to come here asking for freebies."

Jo dumbly stood as Rider opened the bright pink box and took out a cupcake that had a mound of frosting that was so high she knew Willa had put extra on it to convince Rider to be auctioned off.

She had wasted a perfectly good cupcake on him. Hell, Rider would have paid to be in the auction. A group of women fighting over him would make that egocentric asshole's year.

When Willa rubbed some of the frosting off his cheek after he took a bite, Jo let the door shut.

What did women see in him? She wasn't blind. Rider was handsome and had a body most women would lust after, but he was seriously spoiled by the feminine interest showered on him. He treated women like they were a smorgasbord, and he wanted to taste everything being offered.

"The meeting over?" Shade rolled down his window when Jo walked past his car to get to her truck.

"Yes, Lily should be out in a minute," she said, stopping to talk to him. Pride had her hating to ask for the favor she was going to have to ask for. "I haven't received a check from the city for the tows they owe me. Can I pay you next week?"

"I've told you to make payments when you can." His expression didn't betray what he was thinking, but she always felt like a loser when she had to ask for a favor from him.

"I don't like owing money to my creditors, especially when I work for my money and it should have been here. The city used to pay me monthly. Now they've managed to hold the paperwork until I'm lucky if I get it in three." The unnecessary explanation wouldn't matter to Shade, yet it made her feel better. She didn't want him thinking she couldn't manage her money better.

"I'm not a creditor; I'm a friend. I'll get my money when I get it. I'm not going to worry about it, and you shouldn't either."

"Thanks, Shade. I appreciate your help. How did Train like the car?"

"He's debating giving it to Killyama. Rider offered to buy it from him."

"Train's not going to sell the car he bought for his wife as a gift."

"No, but he's enjoying letting Rider think he will."

A joking Shade wasn't one she was used to dealing with. He never talked about the other men in his club, and never about how they interacted with each other.

"I'll tell Carl that Train likes it. I'll see you next week."

Excusing herself, she was glad to escape his presence. There was something about Shade that made her feel as if he could look inside her soul and know what she was thinking. It made her nervous and on edge. She was amazed Lily was married to him. The meek and mild woman didn't have a mean bone in her body. Shade, on the other hand, seemed like he would have no problem crushing her spirit.

Lily had clearly felt comfortable enough to spend whatever amount needed to keep Jo from being embarrassed. Even Beth had joked about Shade's checkbook. Maybe she had misjudged him. Maybe he wasn't the hardass she had assumed he was.

Doubting herself, she wondered if she could have misjudged Rider, too. Her misgivings rose as she climbed into her truck, tossing the bag onto the passenger seat before starting the engine.

Since she had returned to Treepoint, she had been planning on taking her revenge for the night that had irrevocably changed her and her family's life forever. That it would take even longer if she changed her plans had her wanting to ignore the conscience that was screaming to be heard.

She was about to hit the gas when Rider came out of the church store. His confident swagger had her teeth clenching as he waved at Shade before taking off for the diner. Her eyes followed him as he jogged across the street. Instead of going into the diner, though, as she had expected, he tapped on the side window. Was Carly waiting for him?

A minute later, her question was answered when Curt and Justin came outside. She couldn't hear what they were saying from where she was sitting, but she could understand the bro pat on Rider's back as they went to the side of the diner, all three men piling into the truck. That they were good friends was obvious.

Jo couldn't bear to watch any longer, turning her head forward again, not wanting them to see her watching.

She might have misjudged Shade, but she had hit a bull's-eye with Rider. She didn't know why she was feeling guilty anyway. All his lawyer would have to do was make sure there was one woman on the jury, and he would get off.

As she turned the wheel to refuel her truck, she caught a faint scent wafting from the heavy material of her coveralls. It took a second to realize it must have been pressed to Rider's body. His cologne was spicy and musky, making her think of dark nights and sex.

Dammit! She hit the steering wheel, accidentally hitting her horn. She mouthed "Sorry" at the car that was passing in the oncoming lane.

She hadn't felt desire since she was fifteen, and the thought of Rider being the one to send tingles to her nipples was unbearable. It was like betraying everything she believed about herself. She wasn't the same naïve girl she had been. She was a grown woman. She had grown past childish dreams of happily ever after and wanting a Disney movie named after her.

Composing herself, she pulled into the gas station and refueled her truck. Back inside, she drove home to take a shower and change her coveralls.

After loading the washer with the coveralls that smelled like Rider, she pushed the start button, wishing she could wash away the feeling of desire he had risen as easily.

"I promised that you would get the justice you deserve," she said out loud, reaffirming the pledge she had made to the lonely fifteen-year-old girl she had been. "You've waited long enough."

Law found in a courthouse wasn't the only way to right a wrong. She had tried to find justice there and hadn't. It was time to give mountain justice a turn.

6

"You trying to catch trespassers?" Jo asked as she walked across Rachel's front porch.

The old woman sat in her wheelchair, staring off into the woods that led to the lake.

"I wish," Mag scoffed. "It would give me someone to talk to."

Jo bent down to kiss her wrinkled cheek, placing a comforting hand on her back. "I'm here. Go ahead and talk my ear off."

Cash's grandmother was one of the oldest residents in Treepoint. She had raised her children by bootlegging and made no excuses for how she had made ends meet. Despite her tough attitude toward life, they had grown closer when Jo had returned to town.

When she was younger and her father would take her with him to go buy alcohol from Mag, she had been terrified of the woman. Then, when Rachel asked after church one day if she would stay with Mag for the weekend for her and Cash's anniversary, she had hesitated but agreed. The older woman had become one of her closest friends, and it broke her heart every time she talked about dying.

"And you get plenty of company. They just don't want to hear you telling God you're ready for Him."

She snorted. "Like it's doing me any good—I'm still sitting here."

"Rachel, Cash, and I wouldn't know what to do without you."

Another snort had her grinning and hugging her, despite her trying to shrug her off. Jo then sat down on the rocking chair next to her wheelchair.

"What has you so down today? It's been a beautiful day, and the food Rachel's cooking smells delicious. I've been looking forward to the deviled eggs all afternoon."

"She puts too much mustard in them, and her dumplings don't have enough salt."

Rachel rocked the chair, listening to her complaints. "The last time you told her she used too much mayonnaise."

"I'd rather have more mayonnaise than mustard." Mag's dentures snapped in irritation as she complained.

"I'll eat the ones you don't want."

"I didn't say I wouldn't eat them, just that they aren't as good as the ones I make."

"Ahh … so you're upset because you didn't make them?"

"They never let me do anything fun anymore."

Jo turned her head, seeing Mag's unhappiness that she could no longer do the things she enjoyed. Rachel said the last time she had tried to let Mag cook, she had set a dish towel on fire, and was salting food, even the desserts, until they were inedible, or was using enough fat to give herself another heart attack.

"I can't blame them for the cooking. When I let you make hamburgers, you set the stove on fire."

"I had it under control."

"I can't help you get them to let you cook again. Cash had to buy a new stove. What else do you miss? Maybe I can help with that."

"I miss going to Rosie's. Mick doesn't come and see me anymore."

"Rachel caught him giving you a pint of whiskey."

"I want to sit at the bar and have a cold beer and eat a hamburger. You could sneak me out."

Jo lowered her voice so Rachel couldn't hear. "I'll see what I can do. Rachel asked me to stay with you this next weekend. If she and Cash say it's okay, we can hit the bar, but you have to promise me you'll behave."

"Then I don't want to go. If I didn't want to have fun, I would get Cash to take me. He's become a stick in the mud. He watches everything I eat as much as Rachel does."

"They don't want to lose you. I can't blame them," Jo said softly.

"I'm in my nineties; a loud fart would take me out."

Laughing, Jo stood, pushing the wheelchair inside when Rachel called out that dinner was done.

Rachel gave her a flustered look when they came through the door.

Jo gave her a questioning glance as she pushed Mag's wheelchair to the head of the table. Ema was buckled into her chair, eating a deviled egg.

"Something wrong?" Jo took a seat at one of the table settings.

Rachel gave her a worried frown. "Cash called and said that he's on his way home with Rider. Cash told him what he was having for dinner, and he invited himself."

"Why should she give a damn that boy is coming to dinner? She eats a lot, but that's a big pot you have on the stove."

"Mag, I've told you not to use that word in front of Ema."

Rachel brought her hands to her hips as she reprimanded the old woman.

"When Cash stops playing that music he listens to, I'll stop." Mag huffily turned toward Jo. "Why don't you like that boy? He's not as good-looking as my grandson, but he ain't married either. If I were five years younger, that boy wouldn't know what hit him."

Rachel laughed, giving Mag a glass of iced tea before pouring one for Jo.

"Jo hit him with a bag this morning."

"What that boy do to get you to hit him?"

Jo concentrated on plucking an egg off a platter and shoving it into her mouth, deciding not to answer.

"Rider joked that Jo had thrown herself at him when she accidentally bumped into him," Rachel helpfully answered when Jo didn't.

"It's what I would have done."

Mag probably would have done more than that in her younger years, Jo thought, finishing her mouthful.

"I wouldn't deliberately throw myself at Rider if he were the last man on earth."

"You're a lesbian?" Mag gave Jo a pitying pat on her shoulder. "You don't know what you're missing. I thought about it once in my twenties. There's no comparison between dick and—"

"Mag, please behave," Rachel said, looking out the window. "They're here. Save your past stories until we're alone."

"Why? Nothing happened. She didn't look as pretty when I sobered up."

Jo couldn't help it. The woman was a cross between Joan Rivers' caustic tongue and Roseanne Barr's tactlessness. She was wiping her tears of laughter away when Cash and Rider came inside.

Cash gave Rachel a kiss before giving his daughter hers. The toddler pursed her lips, giving her father a kiss before squealing for Rider when he moved closer to the table, wanting a kiss from him, too.

"That child is smarter than you. You need to take a lesson from her," Mag advised Jo, moving the deviled eggs closer to her to take three, uncaring that she was making her the center of attention.

"Are you going to hit me again if I sit down here?" Rider mockingly hesitated before taking the chair next to her.

Jo gave him a withering glance. "I'll try to restrain myself," she said mockingly back.

At her comment, Cash's mouth opened as he sat down next to Rachel.

"I'll tell you later." Rachel forestalled the obvious question about why she had hit Rider. "Let's eat. The food is getting cold." Rachel filled a plate with dumplings, giving it to Cash before handing the serving spoon to Jo.

Jo only put a spoonful on her plate before passing the spoon to Mag. She also only took a small serving of the mashed potatoes and the green beans.

"You didn't take much?" Rachel frowned at the small portions that Rider more than made up for, mounding his plate high when it was his turn.

"According to Mag, I eat too much," Jo said, picking up her fork.

"She was only jok—"

"No, I wasn't. She's already eaten four eggs since she's gotten here." Mag cut off Rachel.

Jo laughed, not insulted by the woman. Besides, she *had* eaten four.

Mag's bluntness was refreshing. She made no pretenses about what she was thinking or observing.

Jo ate, remaining silent as Rider, Cash, and Rachel talked.

Listening, she came to realize that Rider was close to the small family.

During the meal, he had gotten up to make himself coffee, preferring to drink that during his meal. His easy familiarity as he opened cabinets for the coffee and mugs, and a drawer for the spoons had her surprised. She hadn't known Rider was a frequent visitor. Jo spent a couple of evenings with the couple and had never seen Rider there.

Jo blasted herself for making her opinions known. She had been vocal in her disdain of Rider. Thinking back, she realized Rachel would change the subject or divert her attention.

She had been aware of Cash's friendship with the club, but hadn't known it extended to their family circle.

"Would you like a cup?" Rider asked, carrying his own cup to the table.

"No, thank you." She ate self-consciously, just wanting to eat and make her excuses to leave.

Jo gave Mag a wondering brow when Rider refilled his plate with even larger portions than his previous one.

"He's a growing boy." Mag beamed from across the table at the man who had stopped growing long before tonight.

Jo turned her head to the side. "How old are you?"

"Thirty-four," he answered instantly.

Jo reached for the dumplings, daring Mag to make a snide comment with a sidelong glance.

The old woman shrugged. "It's your ass."

"Mag ..." Rachel dropped her fork to her plate.

"It's okay." Jo reassured Rachel she wasn't offended by stealing the last egg from the platter that Mag had been hoarding close to her plate.

"I like a woman with a big appetite." Rider nudged the potatoes closer to her.

Jo nearly grinned back at the amusement in his eyes.

Smothering the smile down, however, she continued to eat, ignoring the potatoes, even though she wanted them. Rachel's were silky smooth, and she wasn't stingy with the butter when she made them.

She hadn't made a dent in her second plate when Rider leaned back in his chair, patting his stomach. "What's for dessert?"

"I didn't make any." Rachel's eyes lowered, but Jo caught the slight quiver of her lips. Her friend couldn't lie worth a damn.

"No self-respecting woman from the mountains would cook a dinner as fine as this one and not make a dessert to go with it." Rider sniffed the air, as if he was a hunting dog on the trail of a meal.

Rachel gave him a harassed look before going to the kitchen, where Jo heard her open the oven door then shut it. She returned, carrying a covered dish. After setting it down on a heat pad, she removed the top.

Jo forgot the food on her plate when she saw the cobbler. No one in the county could make cobbler as good as Rachel's. She had won numerous contests no matter which flavor she made, and unless she was mistaken from the dark blue juice seeping out from underneath the crust, she had made her specialty—blackberry.

Rider was already reaching for the spoon when Rachel brought ice cream and bowls for everyone.

"You're lucky you never invited me to dinner before you married Rachel, or I would have stolen her from you." Rider groaned after taking a bite.

"Like you could have caught her." Mag snorted. "Cash only caught her with my help."

Cash placed his arm around the back of Rachel's chair. "You're not how I caught her. Rachel fell in love with the greenhouse I built her. She loves being able to grow blackberries in the winter while everyone else has to use frozen ones."

Rachel brushed her fingers over Cash's lips, removing the sugar from his bottom lip. "That isn't why I fell in love with you. I fell in love with you when you told my brothers I was pregnant, and I wouldn't marry you."

Jo swallowed the lump in her throat when Rachel's expression went from unashamedly loving to one of extreme sadness. Bending her head over her bowl, she gave Rachel and Cash their privacy as the memory of the child they had lost was revived.

The child would have been their second. It was only during the last couple months that Rachel had resumed her natural vivaciousness. Even her vibrant hair color had been toned down, the curls lacking their healthy sheen.

Jo had been relieved when Rachel had slowly come out of the shell she had withdrawn into. She was sure Cash had been that reason. The happily married couple had worked through their loss, and their marriage had grown stronger through the tragedy they had shared.

Forcing herself not to take another serving, Jo placed her spoon in the empty bowl. Standing, she carried her dishes to the kitchen, then came back to remove the rest of the dishes as Cash and Rider talked about an order they needed to work on tomorrow.

"You don't have—"

Jo laid a hand on Rachel's shoulder before she could get up. "Don't you dare. You cooked dinner; I can do the dishes." Taking Cash's and Rachel's plates, she went back and forth, leaving Rider's plate since he was still eating.

She was loading the dishwasher when Rider carried his to the sink.

"You can stack them after I rinse them off." Rider didn't give her time to protest, taking over the job.

She didn't want to be in the small kitchen with him, but other than coming off as a bitch, she had no alternative. She had no idea how to make small talk with him, so she remained silent, moving around him to get the dirty pots and pans for him to clean.

It was only when Rider cleared his throat that she realized he might be having trouble talking to her, too.

"I contacted the number on the card you gave me. He's coming to the factory to take a look at my car and give me an estimate."

"That's good," she said stiltedly. "What kind of car is it?"

"1970 Dodge Charger."

Surprised, she looked up from the dishwasher. "I expected you to say a Corvette or a Mustang."

Rider stopped scrubbing the heavy pot that Rachel had used for the dumplings. "You think I'm a Stang man?"

Jo's lips quirked. "A bright red one."

Rider laughed, shaking his head. "With the right engine, a Charger can beat a Stang."

"I'm not going to disagree with that." She shrugged. "I figured you just wanted to drive it, not race it."

"I plan to do both."

"You plan to race around town?"

"Hell yes. When I get it restored, I can shove it up Greer's ass when he pulls up next to me in his truck."

"Being friends with the sheriff will come in handy. Lesser mortals like me have to worry about tickets."

"Knox wouldn't write me a ticket if he caught me racing. He would kick my ass."

She expected him to deny her ascertainment that he wouldn't face the same repercussions as others. It eased her guilty conscience. She seriously doubted Knox would give him a beating for breaking a traffic violation.

"It would be worth it. Greer's a nut where that truck of his is concerned. The one he bought Holly is almost as big."

Rider gave her a look of unholy amusement. "How bad do you want to ram his truck with yours when he revs his motor at the stop light in town?"

"It's everything I can do not to flatten it," she admitted.

"Your truck could do the job." His encouragement had her seriously thinking about it. Greer always managed to get behind her at the stop light. He would rev his motor, making his truck jerk forward incrementally until it would be nearly kissing her bumper.

"Knox would haul me off to jail if I tried."

"I could get you out. Go for it."

"Nope. I'm not stupid enough to mess with the Porters. They treat their vehicles like family. They can be vindictive."

"Are you talking about Greer or the Porters as a whole?" Rachel asked, coming into the kitchen carrying Mag's empty plate.

"Mainly Greer, but you have to admit you, Tate, and Dustin stick together like glue when you get mad at someone." Jo took the plate away from Rachel, sticking it in the dishwasher.

"Most families from the mountains usually do. Sometimes it's hard, especially when Greer gets pissed off for no reason. The rest of us have to pick and choose who we're going to feud with." Rachel didn't try to deny the close relationship she shared with her family.

"Make it simple; narrow it down to three," Jo joked, nudging Rachel with her shoulder, so she could open the lower cabinet door to get the pack of dishwashing detergent.

Straightening back up, she caught Rider's eyes on the swell of her breasts she had inadvertently exposed. Her lips tightened, and she gave him a dirty look as she started the dishwasher.

"Thanks for dinner, Rachel. I'll see you at church." She didn't say goodbye to Rider, moving around him so she wouldn't have to touch him as she went into the dining room.

Kissing Ema on her cheek, she then said goodbye to Cash, frowning when she realized Mag must have gone to her room. She regretted not being able to say goodbye to her. However, like a scalded cat, she wanted out of Rider's vicinity before she ruined the evening by saying something sarcastic to him.

Going out the front door, she was relieved to see Mag was sitting out on the front porch. She hadn't even bothered to turn the porch light on, sitting in the darkness.

Jo placed a hand on her shoulder, feeling how frail the woman was becoming. "Don't leave, Mag." Jo bent down, brushing her cheek with a kiss before rubbing her cheek against hers.

Mag covered Jo's hand, patting it. "Ain't going nowhere tonight, but soon. The leaves are almost gone."

"I hate that old saying." Jo sat down next to her knees, laying her head on Mag's arm.

When she was younger, her mother had often repeated the saying when one of her older relatives had passed away, explaining in a matter-of-fact voice that leaves fall off so that new ones can take their place. As she grew older, one by one of her relatives had passed during the fall and winter months. She wasn't as superstitious, but now that all her relatives were gone, it gave her a feeling of foreboding that Mag had seen her last spring.

"You're a sweet girl to worry about an old woman. I still remember your pa driving up with you sitting on that cushion so you could see over the hood of his truck."

"I used to be scared of you." Jo used to be as afraid of her as much as she loved her now.

"You were afraid of your own shadow. You still are."

She raised her head. "No, I'm not—"

"Then why don't you give that boy a chance?"

"Who? Rider?"

"Don't play stupid with me. You know who I'm talking about. You're not getting any younger. You should be chasing after the boy as if he were on fire."

"Not everyone wants to get married and have children."

"You forgetting you always came carrying that pretend diaper bag and the baby doll your pa bought you in that plastic carrier? You treated that doll like it was the real thing. You played with that doll long after most girls in the county were already going on dates. You want to lie about not being interested in men, go ahead. But you'll never make me believe you don't want a bunch of youngins."

"I grew up."

Mag squeezed her hand tightly. "Yes, you did. I would have handled it differently if I had been your ma. I'm not faulting her, but your pa should have killed those bastards instead of leaving it to God. God helps those who help themselves."

"Yes, He does." Jo stood, removing her hand from Mag's grasp. "Don't stay out here too long; you'll take a cold."

"I'm too mean to take a cold. Think about what I told you."

"I will, I swear. Night, Mag."

Jo left the old woman. Mag thought she had promised to think about chasing after Rider, but her mind was on what she had said about God.

Sadness clouded her vision as she walked to her truck. Mag had a better chance of seeing another spring than she did.

A drizzling, freezing rain slid down the nape of her neck, increasing the sense of foreboding she had felt on the porch.

She wouldn't get much sleep tonight. The roads would become treacherous as the temperature dropped during the middle of the night.

Jo gave a last look at the shadowed exterior of the cabin in her headlights. She was about to pull out when her lights hit Rider's motorcycle. If he left now, he would make it home safely.

Braking, she reached for her phone. She typed out a text message, then pushed Send. Finished, she pocketed her phone, driving away.

The dismal darkness swallowed the large truck into its misty depths as she left the cabin's lights behind.

"Your ma never teach you it's impolite to eavesdrop, big ears?" Mag snapped.

Rider unapologetically walked out onto the porch. "If you knew I was listening, why didn't you say something to Jo?" Rider moved to the front of Mag's wheelchair to stare down at the cunning woman.

The sound Mag made was a cross between a snort and grunt as she shifted herself into a more comfortable position in her wheelchair. "You couldn't have been listening too closely if you missed how I was trying to set you up with her."

"I didn't miss it. I just wanted to see if you would admit it."

"The only advantage to getting old is being able to say whatever the hell I want."

"Something tells me you never had that problem."

"Life's too short to give a fuck about what anyone says."

"Mag ..." Rachel hissed, coming out from inside the house.

Rider couldn't help grinning when Mag's shoulders

drooped at getting caught once again for her choice of words.

"Girl, I came out here for peace and quiet."

Rachel lovingly wrapped a thick blanket around Mag's shoulders. "It's too cold to stay out here."

"If you came out here to bug me, you can take your ass back inside."

"Actually, I came out to tell Rider that Jo texted me, saying the roads are getting bad and you should head home or stay the night."

Rider leaned against the porch post, hiding his surprise at Jo's concern. She hadn't liked that he had caught a glimpse of her breasts, and she had become even madder that he hadn't hidden his appreciation of the sight.

"I was just leaving." Rider zipped up his jacket and turned the collar up. He grimaced at the cold wind as he burrowed his hands into his jacket pockets. He had left his gloves in his saddlebags.

He wondered if Jo had a jacket and gloves in her truck. The top she had been wearing was too thin to offer much protection.

"Five more minutes, Mag, or I'll push you inside myself," Rachel said, giving Rider a wave as she went back inside.

"You sure you don't want me to push you inside?" he asked, straightening from the post and already walking to the edge of the porch, knowing she wouldn't.

"I know you don't want any advice, but I'm going to give it anyway." Mag grabbed the wheel of her wheelchair, turning it toward him.

Hesitating, he turned back. "I've been known to take advice, if it's good."

Her narrowed gaze sharpened. "You remind me of my husband. Cash ever tell you he was a carny worker?"

"No." Rider kept the amused indulgence pasted on his features, sensing she was staring through him.

"Well, you do. He had the same good ol' boy charm that had most of the town wasting their money to win a fifty-cent Teddy bear. Don't try to fool me, little boy. I see exactly who you are." Mag wheeled her chair closer. "You're out for yourself, and you don't give a damn about anyone else."

He grimly let his amicable pose drop as he moved closer to her, letting his intimidating shadow fall over her. "That's not a nice thing to say about a person." He had dropped his voice to the menacing level he had used with seasoned soldiers he had served with when they had underestimated him.

"You think you can scare me?" Mag gave a cackle of harsh laughter. "I've taken on men who would scare you shitless."

"I don't get scared."

"You're scared of Jo."

This time, it was him laughing. "I'm not afraid of Jo."

"She's not a dumb whore. You can't pull the wool over her eyes. Jo will never give you the time of day until you show her the real you. She can take the ugly you're hiding. That girl loved her pa like he hung the moon, despite him being a drunk. Her mother dragged her away from Treepoint because she'd had enough when those boys raped Jo. Her good-for-nothing pa wouldn't even let her report what they had done to her." Mag ferociously condemned Jo's father for being such a coward. "The only reason he lasted as long as he did was because of her. She's hocked everything she has to hold on to that scrap of land he left her. There aren't many women who could love like that, but Jo is one of them. For what it's worth, you need to get your ass in gear and not let her get away before some other man steals her."

His gaze flickered, moving away. "You can't steal what doesn't belong to you."

"You a Last Rider?"

"Yes."

"The Last Riders have been taking what they want since they moved here."

"If they want it." He shrugged. "I don't want Jo."

"I've said my piece. It's cold out here, and I'm done talking to a man who will run all over town for a good meal, but isn't smart enough to latch on to one who will cook for him every night."

Rider knew she wasn't really talking about food.

"Jo doesn't cook." Unwisely giving the flip comment, he moved to open the door for her so she could swing her wheel around to go inside.

"She can learn how to cook. She just needs someone to light her fire. I guess that little matchstick you're carrying around isn't up to the task. Ignore my advice; I take it back. You haven't got the good sense God gave you to lick a postage stamp."

Rider gaped at the woman as she wheeled off. Was she using another metaphor to insult his skills as a lover, comparing a postage stamp to a pussy?

Cash's feisty grandmother, whose bones were gnarled with age and arthritis, rolled away, unconcerned that Rider could snap her neck and make it look she had fallen off the porch.

Taking a step back into the house, he saw Cash sitting at the table, eating another bowl of dessert.

"Don't even think about it," Cash cautioned. "What'd she do?" He nodded toward where Mag had disappeared.

"She insinuated I didn't have enough brains to lick a postage stamp."

"She must be down in the dumps. Mag doesn't insinuate shit. She's not afraid to speak her mind."

"That old bitch isn't down in the dumps. She's mean as fuck."

"Careful. Rachel will hear you."

Rider decided to do what he should have done before talking to Mag—leave. It wasn't often someone could spark his temper, but the woman had needled him with her barbs that had slipped under his thick skin.

Shutting the door on Cash's smirking face, he strode across the porch, his fury distracting him from the sleet. When his boot heel hit the step off the porch, his foot slid from under him, leaving his upper body half on and half off the porch and his legs tangled on the ground.

"Dammit!" Rider swore, trying to get up. It took three times before he managed to stand. The ground was a frozen sheet of ice.

Aggravated, he carefully limped back up the steps, going back to Cash's door and knocking.

A second later, Cash opened the door.

"It's too slick to ride home."

Cash opened the door to let him inside. "You should have left when Rachel warned you instead of shooting the shit with Mag."

Rider clenched his fists, still mad at Mag, and now irritated at falling. Plus, his hand had been cut by one of the porch boards. The last thing he needed was having Cash laughing at his predicament.

He shouldn't have left the clubhouse. If he had stayed, he would be cuddled up in bed with one of the women from Ohio who wanted to become a member. At the time, it had been a brilliant move. With so many brothers visiting, it meant a long line at dinner. He hadn't expected to be gone so long. Now he was stuck at Cash's for the night on his fucking couch alone.

Taking his jacket off, he hung it on the wall, then went to

the couch to take his boots off as Cash went to find him a blanket.

He turned on the television and lowered the volume so as not to wake Rachel and Ema. He didn't give a fuck if he disturbed Mag.

"Here you go." Cash handed him a blanket and a pillow. "You need anything else?"

"No." He grumpily tossed the pillow to the end of the couch. "Go to bed. At least one of us can work off that meal. Make damn sure I don't hear any sounds coming from your room, or I'll be dragging your ass out of bed to drive me home."

"It won't kill you to go without sex."

That was easy for Cash to say. He was going to bed with a hot redhead.

"I can go a night without sex, but why would I want to? I'm living every man's dream—a different woman every day, a job I love, and a great place to rest my head at night, especially if I have a couple of women keeping me company."

Cash moved around the couch to take one of the chairs, propping his legs on the coffee table. "It isn't my dream, nor do I think it's any of the brothers'."

Rider opened his mouth to disagree with him, but Cash's serious expression stopped him.

"I'm on the opposite side of the fence than you are. I think most men hope to find the woman who will help them change their ways and make them a better person, to make coming home worth it, despite an argument from the night before. A woman who makes you feel as special as you think are." Cash's lips curled into a confident grin.

"I don't need a woman to make me feel like that. I already know I am."

Cash shook his head. "I don't think you do." He pinned his gaze on him, unwavering as Rider flipped through the channels on the television. "Rider … how long are you going to hang on to the past? Delara and Quinn are ancient history."

"Go to bed, Cash. If I wanted someone to preach to me, I'd call Lucky."

Rising, Cash frowned down at him in irritation. "I'm no preacher, but I am a friend who can see you're on a one-way track going nowhere."

"Maybe so, but it's my track to ride, and you had no problem riding on it before you married Rachel."

"No, I didn't. I'm going to bed. I can see I'm wasting my breath. Try not to eat the rest of the cobbler. I want some for breakfast." Cash left him alone in the living room.

As soon as he heard Cash's bedroom door close, he went into the kitchen and made himself a bowl of cobbler before sinking down on the couch to enjoy an old movie he had found. When Cash woke in the morning, he wasn't going to be happy that Rider had unashamedly finished off his cobbler. He would wait until he got to work before telling him that he had seen Rachel had made two and the other was hidden in the back of the fridge.

He finished the movie and was halfway through the second one before he was able to fall into a light doze. The habit had become ingrained when he was in the service, when it had been a matter of life or death to be aware of his surroundings.

At the camps where he had been stationed, night was when many attacks had occurred. The enemy used the opportunities to sneak past their guard under cover of darkness. Sleep deprivation became a way of life for many, especially the few who had been sent out on special missions like Shade, Gavin, and he had been assigned.

Shade had been a sniper, eliminating enemies with a single bullet. Gavin had been the primary diver navigator;

the water had been his battlefield, setting explosives or dismantling those that had been set. He could lead a team through dangerous waters, rising from the depths to take out a target, then slip back before the enemies even knew he had been there.

Rider stared blankly at the television. It was the information he had fed to his superiors that had given both men their targets to eliminate. He was a SEAL-in-training when he had been called into the commander's office.

Standing stiffly in front of his commander's desk, Rider had watched as he had flipped the file he had been reading toward him.

"I've been reading over your background. Many of your superiors think you're going to wash out of SEAL training. Why is that?"

Rider didn't need to pick up his file to read the comments of those who had devoted their lives to the service. They believed he didn't have the ambition to succeed where others who were smarter and had trained years to become a SEAL had failed.

"Is that why you wanted to see me, sir?" Dread at hearing that he had failed to make it through the class burned through his gut.

"All your superiors might not think you can make it through, but one thing they all had in common was that they all liked you. I talked to each of them. They said they don't know if you had the commitment to be a SEAL, but each of them said they would share a beer with you when you got back.

"Your superiors all like you, and so do the men. You talked several of them out of DOR."

"It's good to know I'm so well liked, sir." Rider didn't take it as a compliment, and he didn't think Commander Nellis did either. At that, he was wrong.

"You were ranked in the top five in the physical portion of your exams, and the top three in intelligence. I've seen your physical performance since you have arrived at BUD/S, but when I've seen you with the men, I haven't seen the intelligence you are capable of. Why is that?"

"Sir, if you had to go down a blind alley in the middle of the night, would you rather have Wizard or Maze beside you?" Rider asked. Wizard was the smartest one in their class. Maze was the strongest.

His commander astutely stared across the desk at him. "I would pick you. That way, I have the best of both." Nellis closed the file, placing it in his top drawer. "Which is why I sent for you. I'm going to recommend you to be the sensitive site exploitation explorer. Your natural friendliness could be honed into a skill that my team could use."

An assignment with Nellis's team was everyone's goal. That it was offered to him was unexpected. The commander only picked elite SEALs to fill his team's ranks.

"I would be honored to be a part of your team, sir."

"You don't have to blow smoke up my ass. I just need you to do the jobs I assign you. I think you'll be a natural at finding out intel for the sites we're going to be striking and facilitating the other members' safety."

"I won't let you down, sir."

"I don't think you will, or I wouldn't have chosen you. Dismissed."

Rider had left the meeting on top of the world. The military had been the only family he had left. Every step he had made since leaving home had become fueled with the desire to become a SEAL. To become a member of a team that most of his friends had aimed for gave him a sense of accomplishment that he had never had or had been able to achieve working for his family's business.

Looking back now, Rider grimaced. Now, he could see

what his younger self hadn't been able to see. In layman's terms, he had been a stool pigeon, seeking out and making friends who would make his team's attacks successful. At the time, he hadn't been aware the cost he would have to pay. Now he knew.

If he had to do it over, he would have told Nellis no. But he hadn't, and now he had to live with the consequences of it every fucking day.

Unable to sleep, he prowled around the living room, feeling caged. He couldn't escape the memories, so he turned off the television and let himself out of the cabin. He would crash and burn before he stayed cooped up any longer.

Being more careful going down the steps this time, he was able to make it to his bike without ending up on his ass. Then he slowly rode home, expecting to feel his wheels skid on every curve. He gave a sigh of relief when he made it back to the clubhouse.

He walked up the back walkway instead of taking the steps, even though he was sure one of the brothers would have salted them, just as they had the walkway.

No one was in the kitchen, but the living room was filled. The Ohio members had spread out to sleep on the floor. Others were still sitting around, talking or playing pool.

"Rider, you're back!" A feminine squeal from one of the couches had him changing his mind about getting a beer.

"Mercury, I see Moon is keeping you busy." Rider watched the sensual woman's mouth play over Moon's cock before swallowing more than half of his length into her mouth. That she had accomplished the feat had his dick burning behind the zipper of his jeans.

She was naked from the waist down. Rider assumed that Moon or one of the other brothers had fucked her upstairs, then brought her downstairs to share.

"Where's Jewell?" he asked Moon, who managed to gather his scattered wits to answer.

"Upstairs with F.A.M.E."

He hadn't had a threesome with the new brother yet, but it didn't change his plans.

Going to the bar, he left Moon to finish as he grabbed a beer and talked to Diablo and Trip. He had served with Diablo and had convinced him to join The Last Riders when he had gotten out of the service. Trip had served with Diablo after Rider had left, so he had met him in Ohio when Trip had tagged along. Diablo had decided to stay and become a member, but Trip had left for a couple of years before deciding to come back and make Ohio his home. He had just become a full-fledged member last year. Rider still winced at the memory of being selected to battle the brother for the right to belong.

"How are the roads?" Diablo asked.

"Bad enough none of you will be able to go back in the morning." Rider opened his beer, wishing Moon would finish. Any other time, he would have joined him on the couch, then taken Mercury upstairs, but he had seen F.A.M.E fuck before. It was going to take a lot of stamina to out-fuck that brother, and he had no intention of coming in at second best.

Trip shrugged, unconcerned. "I don't mind riding on bad roads. It's the fuckers who are with you that scare me."

Rider was finishing the last of his beer when Moon finally moved away from Mercury to play pool with Gavin and Viper.

Rider would have joined them at the pool table if he was sure Gavin wouldn't make an excuse to leave and go upstairs. Gavin tried to avoid any interaction with him, no matter how Rider tried to resume their friendship.

Mercury's tits swayed in his vision as she walked toward him, reaching for him.

"I was going to ask if you needed a break, but I can see you don't." He groaned when she cupped the hard-on he was planning on drilling into her cunt.

"I don't get tired. You're the one who didn't get much sleep last night."

Rider gripped her ass cheek, pulling her closer and rubbing his dick into her belly. Delving two fingers between her cheeks, he found the small rosebud he was searching for and twisted the anal plug he had put there before leaving to eat dinner with Cash.

Placing his beer on the bar, he turned her until she faced the stairs. "Ladies first." Removing his fingers, he swatted her ass with a firm hand. Then he watched as Mercury's ass jiggled as she walked.

"Later." Excusing himself, he followed her up the steps, enjoying the tantalizing glimpses of the plug buried there on each step to the upper floor.

When the door next to his opened, he motioned toward the doorway, and Mercury went in the direction he wanted.

Rider took off his shirt as soon as he came through the doorway, sparing a quick glance at Jewell who was riding F.A.M.E's cock in the middle of the bed.

Jewell's lids lowered when Rider lifted Mercury to position her on the bed, her ass pointed toward the hallway.

He was just placing a knee on the mattress when Nickel came in.

"Damn, I walked in the right room."

Rider rubbed his aching eyes, then kneaded his neck muscles to ease the bunched-up muscles that screamed in protest every time he moved his head. He was getting too damn old for the nighttime Olympics he had been participating in over the last week.

The Ohio members had used the weather as an excuse to delay their departure, and he had made it his personal mission to try to out-fuck every one of them. He had succeeded with everyone but Diablo, whose dick had to be made out of steel, or he was popping Viagra by the handfuls.

"Someone is asking for you out back," Shade said, coming up from behind him.

Rider taped the order he was working on, then put it in the mail cart to be mailed. "Thanks. It must be Jo's friend. He texted me that he'd be in town today."

"Rough night?" Shade didn't return to his office, walking beside him as he made his way out the back of the factory.

"Rough week," Rider corrected him. "I miss the brothers when they're gone, but damn, I'm so sore a ten-year-old could take me down."

"I'm sure you'll recuperate by nightfall." Wryly, Shade opened the door.

Rider didn't know what he had expected Carl Norris to look like, but the grizzled old man smoking a cigarette and dressed in tattered jeans and a T-shirt without a jacket to cover his tattooed arms wasn't the image he had pictured in his mind.

"Carl?" Rider asked as he approached him, reaching out to shake his hand.

The old man threw his cigarette to the ground before taking his hand. "Rider?"

Rider nodded. "It's nice to finally meet you. I've wanted to get my car restored for the last three years. Anyone who can restore Killyama's car, I knew would be able to handle my baby."

Carl dropped his hand. "Let's see it before I make promises I can't keep."

Rider introduced Shade as he pressed the button for the garage. When it raised enough for them to get under the door, Rider pointed at the car he wanted restored.

It took several moments for Carl to tear his eyes away from the bounty in the garage. When he finally looked at the vehicle in question, the admiring gleam he had used to view the other cars and motorcycles diminished. His hands went to his back pockets as he walked around it, bending down to look inside before continuing his inspection.

"Does it even start?"

"No." Becoming disenchanted with Carl's behavior, Rider was ready to pull the plug on giving him the job. It was only the loving detail he had shown to Killyama's car that kept him from going back inside the factory.

"Pop the hood."

Rider walked around the hood of the car to open the door and pop the hood open. Getting out, he walked back to the front to see Carl staring down at its empty shell that should have housed the motor.

Carl reached up, then slammed the hood back down. "Do you just want it running, or do you want it restored to pristine condition?"

"I want it to look like it was just rolled out of the showroom."

"Going to take a few bucks." Carl walked back outside as he pulled his cigarettes out of his back pocket.

Rider shared a quick glance with Shade as they followed him. "I'm not worried about the money. I just want it done right."

"That I can do. It might take a few months for me to find the parts, but I can restore it. I'll send Jo over to haul it to my place." His lanky body was walking away before Rider realized he was done talking and was leaving.

"That's it?" Rider asked, hurrying after him before he could get inside his bright cherry '60s Chevrolet truck.

Carl stopped. "What else is there to talk about?"

"You don't need a deposit?"

"Oh." Carl took a long draw of his cigarette. "I forgot. How does five hundred sound?"

"That's all?"

"A thousand sounds better, but I'll take five if it's in cash."

If he hadn't seen Killyama's car, he would have kicked the man off the parking lot. However, Train had trusted him with his wife's car, and Rider knew that Killyama would have killed Train if anything bad had happened to the car he had depended on Carl to restore.

Rider took out his wallet, counting out a thousand dollars, then handing it to him.

Carl took the money, shoving it into his back pocket. "I'll send the receipt with Jo."

"That was ... different," Shade remarked as they watched

the man who didn't seem to have enough strength to boost himself into his truck, much less restore a car drive away. "The good news is that he can't make your car any worse than it already is."

"Let's hope not. I'd hate to fuck up an old man." He was seriously debating the wisdom of getting it restored by someone who seemed more interested in a cigarette than making money.

"I wonder if he's any relation to Greer," Shade joked, slapping him on the back.

Rider turned to snap at Shade as they started to go back to the factory when he saw a flash of movement out of the corner of his eye. Coming to an abrupt stop, he gaped at the empty road.

"Did you see that?" he asked Shade as he was about to open the factory door.

"See what?"

"That black car that just drove by."

"I didn't see anything." Shade let the door close, moving back to his side.

"He had to be clocking sixty." No one from town would be stupid enough to drive on the curvy road at that speed. The hairpin curves had most drivers going twenty-five, maybe thirty-five if they were feeling lucky.

Shade cocked his head to the side, listening. "You had to have imagined it, or we would have heard their ass crash."

"I didn't imagine it. It had to be doing sixty. It was black with tinted windows."

Shade's eyes narrowed on the empty road. "No one in town has a car like that that I know of."

"Me either." Rider mentally pictured the townspeople with the cars that he had seen, not coming up with any who drove a car resembling the one that had flashed past him.

"What does it matter anyway? It's no skin off our noses if

someone wants to end up in the morgue. We've got work to do."

"I'm coming."

Rider followed Shade inside, unable to resist a lingering look back at the road, looking for the car that had glided over the pavement like a phantom seeking a victim.

"REMIND me why I'm sitting here instead of being at home in bed?" Rider shoved his empty plate away. Exhausted, he only wanted his bed and to gain a few hours of sleep to recharge.

"We're here because all the women are at King's restaurant, decorating for the auction tomorrow night," Shade reminded him.

"It's past ten. They should be home by now. I'm surprised you let Lily go alone."

"King's there. He and Evie are going to drive her home. He's going to text me when they leave the restaurant. I couldn't resist letting my father-in-law deal with two pregnant women."

The door of Mick's bar swung open as a lone woman entered. The two men seated at a corner table stared, recognizing the woman who confidently strode in to take a seat at the bar.

"They must be almost finished. Jo was on the list of helpers Lily organized." Shade took out his phone, checking to make sure he hadn't missed a text.

"Getting worried?" Rider gave it ten minutes before the brother would be calling to check on his wife.

They could hear Jo ordering a burger, joking with Mick that she was too tired to go home and make one for herself.

The hand on his beer bottle tightened. Rider was tempted to carry it over to the bar and try his luck with her one more time. However, she had shot him down too many times to know it would be a wasted effort. She never gave him the time of day, unless he needed a vehicle towed or forced himself to dinner like he had at Cash's the week before.

He critically surveyed the woman dressed in loose-fitting coveralls with her brown hair pulled back into a ponytail. She didn't scream femininity, nor was she particularly attractive, making no effort to wear makeup or wipe away the oil smear that rested on one of her cheekbones. She hadn't even changed out of her work clothes to decorate the restaurant, even knowing she would be surrounded by other women who hadn't a hair out of place when they had left the clubhouse.

Her most appealing characteristic to him was her stand-offish attitude, not her looks. He always liked a challenge, but not enough to get his tired ass out of his chair and take another shot at her. She was a challenge he was saving for another day when he was bored and wide awake. He had to be on the top of his game to deal with the cutting remarks she dealt.

"Why don't you take a picture? It would be easier than you sitting here, staring holes at her."

Rider's lips quirked in a smile. "Just trying to make up my mind if I want to order another one of Mick's burgers."

"What you're wanting isn't on the menu," Shade replied wryly.

Rider shrugged. "What makes you think I want Jo?"

"She's breathing, isn't she?"

Rider gave a low laugh. "It takes more for a woman to get my attention than breathing, despite what you and the other brothers think."

"Like what?" Rider didn't like the way Shade was staring at him.

The brothers all thought he wasn't aware they wanted

him settled down. He had to admit he had egged it on by becoming close to most of The Last Riders' wives. The only one he hadn't been able to hoodwink was Killyama. That bitch was too smart for her own good. Rider didn't hold it against her, though.

Train's wife was a bounty hunter. That alone made her more suspicious-natured. Her two partners were former Army Rangers who he had occasionally worked with, which gave her another advantage.

"That's for me to know."

"So, you've heard all the brothers want you tied down with a woman?"

"Moon couldn't keep a secret if he had to," Rider acknowledged. "I knew Razer and Viper were becoming pissed. What surprised me was Moon saying you were on board, too."

"Moon has been talking." Shade's face didn't change expression.

They didn't mind Rider watching when they wanted to add some spice to their Friday parties, but they were steadily growing worried that the women would fall under his spell and the unthinkable would happen—that he would fuck them without their husband's permission or presence. In other words, they didn't trust him.

There was a small doubt in the back of each of their minds. Him being in a committed relationship would remove their doubts.

He might come across as a laidback fool, but he was anything but. He was loyal to the brothers and would never take what belonged to another, despite the temptation.

"Don't blame Moon. A little birdie also told me."

"Jewell needs to keep her mouth closed. She only told you because she enjoys sleeping in your bed."

"Maybe it was Jewell, or maybe it was Stori." He shrugged.

"I take turns who spends the night with me. I don't have any favorites."

"Keep telling yourself that. Jewell thinks she is." Shade gave him a warning glance.

"No, she doesn't. Jewell knows exactly where she stands with me, and that's right under me."

"I won't tell you that you're begging to be brought down a peg or two, but you are."

"I'm not scared. You and the other brothers can try to your hearts' content to get me married off. If that means I have someone new to fuck, I won't complain. Just don't expect me to put a ring on her finger."

Shade shook his head at him. "It's like talking to a brick wall. I was trying to get you to slow it down with the wives and give the brothers a break for a while, but I can see it's a waste of time."

Rider grinned. "Is that why you invited me out for dinner and a drink? I thought it was because you know that Jo comes out every night for dinner and you wanted me to see her."

"If that was what I had planned, I would have chosen a better time and place when she's not looking so exhausted after working all day, then volunteering to decorate a charity event. But that's just me. Never thought a woman who worked her ass off to pay bills she's not responsible for was sexy, but with you, I never know," he said sarcastically.

At Shade's words, Rider took a longer look at Jo. Damn Shade.

Jo did look tired, and she was only able to eat half her burger before they heard the radio she kept by her side blaring out in static, asking for a tow.

Taking out a bill from the front pocket of her overalls, she laid it down on the counter, then slid off the stool.

"Thanks, Mick," she called out, hurriedly leaving the bar with Mick staring after her worriedly.

"Why doesn't she sell her father's business and start fresh?" He had assumed she would after her father died. When she hadn't, but instead had come to the factory every month to pay back the money that Shade had lent her, he had seen a determination and a level of trustfulness in business that many people would blow off in this day and time. Jo had old-fashioned values that were so rare they were nearly extinct.

"Maybe she has something most people don't have any more—integrity."

Rider cocked an eyebrow in Shade's direction. "That's high praise coming from you."

He wasn't about to tell him that his thoughts were mirroring his. He didn't want anyone to know he was giving Jo a second thought. Give the brothers a chance, and they would run with the idea and have him married to Jo before he knew what hit him.

"Lyle left her nothing but debts. She has maxed out most of the credit she had built up before moving back to Treepoint. He talked her into that new tow truck and building another garage to make repairs to the state vehicles. She wasn't able to get the contract from the state, so it was for nothing. She doesn't make enough towing to pay the bills, much less the lawsuits that were filed by the city for the damages when he wrecked in town."

"She's paying for that, too?"

"Yes. I tried to talk her into declaring bankruptcy, but she won't."

"I need another beer." Rider left the table to go to the bar. He didn't want to know Jo's problems. He had managed to stay single by not getting involved in women's personal lives.

What he didn't know couldn't bother him. It kept him detached and from drawing closer to any of his fuck buddies.

"Give me another beer, Mick. Might as well give me one for Shade, too. He must be thirsty from all the talking he's doing."

Rider reached for his wallet to pay for them as Mick stopped stocking glasses to reach down for the beer, setting them on the counter.

"What's he talking about?" Mick asked. Everyone in town knew Shade wasn't much of a talker.

"Jo." Rider raised his voice so Shade could hear. "The brothers—"

"She's a sweet girl. Life's handed her a raw deal."

Mick's worried frown had Rider's shoulders slumping. He should have kept his mouth shut.

As the bar owner cleared away the remains of Jo's meal, he continued, "She pretends she's too tired to cook every night, but I brought her over some of my lasagna so she could have a home-cooked meal, and her fucking stove didn't work. Then, when I went to put it in the refrigerator, it didn't work either. If Lyle were still alive, I'd beat the hell out of him for not seeing that girl was better taken care of."

"I'm sure she got them fixed by now." Taking the beers, he tried to make his escape, only to be thwarted by Mick.

"Not likely. That was two weeks ago, and she's still eating dinner here every night. I offered to buy her new ones, but she won't let me. Said she prefers eating here or at the diner. Won't take any help from me, and I've known that little girl since she was barely tall enough to climb on one of my barstools."

"I'm sure it will work itself out for her." Backing away from the bar, he returned to the table, where Shade was waiting. "Remind me only to come here on the weekends. He'll talk your ear off when he's not busy." Settling back down, he took another drink of his beer, ignoring Shade and wishing Lily or King would text him so they could leave.

"You live in your own world."

Unconcerned, Shade's sharp jibe did not insult Rider. It was true.

"If it doesn't need fixing, why fuck with it?"

"I used to think that way, too."

"You still do." His eyes narrowed on Shade. "The only person you're capable of caring about is Lily."

"Do you really believe that?"

Rider wasn't afraid of the harsh features of the man sitting next to him.

"We may be friends, Shade, but I have no doubt in my mind, if you felt Lily was threatened, you would take out anyone who hurt her, no matter who it is."

"That's true, but that's true about any of the brothers and their wives."

Rider agreed. "That's why I plan to stay single. Besides, if I get married, who would be the brothers' backup?" His eyes gleamed in the dim light. "I have to keep myself available if anything happens, so I can give the women a shoulder to cry on."

"Brother, you're not my backup. If I get my ass killed, I'm going to make sure you bite the dust before I do."

"I'm too pretty to die," Rider boasted, knowing he was pissing Shade off. He would rather take a punch from him than keep talking about Jo.

Shade ominously stared at him. "I was trying to give you a heads-up about what the brothers were going to try to do. I can see you don't need my help."

"Nope. I've already got it covered." Downing his beer, he stood. "You ready to head back to the club?"

Shade shook his head. "What's your hurry?"

"I'm fucking tired. I'm not interested in talking about or

doing Jo. If the brothers are worried about me coming between them and their wives, they should be talking to them, not making plans to take me out of the equation. I might joke around to irritate them, but they should know—and that includes you—that I wouldn't steal another man's woman."

"I can't speak for the others, but I'm not worried about you stealing Lily from me."

Shade was simply stating a fact. Rider had watched the interaction between the couple and knew Shade believed it. However, Rider didn't have the same faith that any woman would be completely faithful, despite how much in love they claimed to be.

Lily was a sweet woman and had fallen in love with the club's enforcer. He was happy for Shade, but did he think it would last forever? No, he didn't.

He had known Shade since he had joined the Navy. He had only known one other man who could kill with such deadly accuracy and remain untouched by the carnage he had left behind. He had taken both of their backs during the years he had given to the military. The only time he had failed was when he had been taken in by a woman's lies. Twice he had been lied to by women whom he had believed loved him, and it had nearly cost numerous lives. He had no intention of falling for lies from a woman again.

Quinn and Delara had promised him forever. Neither had kept their words. Forever to a woman meant until something better came along.

"Take it from me; no woman is infallible."

One second, Shade was sitting, and the next, he was standing, menace pouring out of him like a volcano getting ready to explode.

"Don't class Lily with other women. You've had your ass handed to you on a platter by bitches who had their own agendas, so I'm making allowances, letting your mouth spout shit you don't know anything about. But if you ever —and I mean *ever*—compare Lily to the relationships you've been in, then you better make a dentist appointment first."

He had foolhardily stepped into a quagmire by taking his irritation at the brothers trying to hook him up with Jo out on Shade. Despite his protests that he didn't want a woman in his life, if he ever did change his mind, it wouldn't be Lily. Even if by some miracle she did divorce Shade, she deserved a man to give her his whole heart, not a man like him who only had bits and pieces left.

Rider watched his friend angrily walk off. Shade was sensitive to any slight he felt toward his wife.

Going outside after paying their tab, he saw Shade already getting on his bike.

"Sorry, brother. I may be the best-looking brother, but I'm damn sure not the smartest."

"The holidays are coming up. Maybe you should visit your family and deal with the shit that's been festering for a while."

His jaw clenched. "Nothing's festering."

"Then you're more of a man than me. I would have a shit-load to get off my chest if I were you."

Rider looked away from Shade's perceptive gaze. "I'm not you."

"No, you're not. If you were, you would've dealt with it a long time ago."

"Nothing to deal with. It is what it is."

Rider stared out at the deserted road, avoiding Shade's eyes, when the car he had seen earlier in the day flew by. His clenched jaw dropped as the dark car drove past without a sound, gliding over the pavement, the windows so tinted he had no hope of seeing the driver inside.

"Look!" The car was rounding the curve before he could get the word out.

Shade turned only to see the empty road. "At what?"

"The car I was telling you about."

"I didn't hear or see anything. What has given you a hard-on for this car anyway?"

"It's an old Camaro. Either a '67 or '69. I just wonder whose it is. I've never seen one around town." Motorcycles had his heart, but old cars were a close second.

"Ask Jo; she knows every car in town. What does it matter anyway?"

"It doesn't. I'm just curious. Jo will be at the auction tomorrow night; I'll ask her."

"The only way you're going to get Jo to give you the time of day is to win the date with her. Moon's been saving his paychecks to score that prize."

"He has?" Rider took his eyes off the road, trying to discern if Shade was manipulating him into bidding. The cold bastard didn't give anything away.

"Unlike you, Moon enjoys a challenge."

Rider slung a leg over the seat of his motorcycle, then started the engine. "The brother always likes to bite off more than he can chew. Jo will chew him up and spit him out when he makes a pass at her."

"When's the last time you heard of a woman turning Moon down?"

"There's a first time for everyone."

"Yes, there is."

Rider jerked his head to the side at the sound of laughter in Shade's voice, but the brother was already riding away. Shade never laughed unless Lily was near. Was he laughing at the thought of Moon being shot down or the disgruntlement he hadn't been able to hide over Moon going to bid on Jo?

Moon didn't have a chance in hell of scoring a touchdown with Jo. Even if he did win the auction, Jo would never drop her guard with Moon. The woman was too smart to be taken in by the smooth charm that had most women dropping their panties for Moon. That's what he told himself all the way home. By the time he parked his bike at the clubhouse, he was ready to punch himself in the face at why he gave a fuck anyway.

The only thing he would be bidding on tomorrow night was the peanut butter candy that Willa had made before she went to the church to decorate. She hadn't even asked him to taste test it before she had sealed it and took it with her.

He would have to stop by the bank in the morning to make sure he had enough cash on him to win that candy. Moon could win Jo.

He knew exactly who was going to win the prize of the night.

Jo was walking down Main Street toward the church store when she saw the flyer taped on the light pole. Blanching, she tore it down, crumbled it into a ball, and then shoved it into her pocket with the other two she had torn down.

If she saw one more of those flyers with her name listed to be auctioned off, she was going to kill Lily, who was the one who had come up with the idea to plaster the advertisements around town. She would wait until after the baby was born before getting her payback. She didn't forget about Willa, Winter, and Rachel, who had agreed, despite her objections.

Though the four women had bulldozed her into agreeing, the sight of her name on the list had her seriously debating pulling out of the auction.

She had planned to go to the thrift store to find a dress to wear for that night, but she had been unable to face whichever woman was volunteering that day. Instead, she had turned toward the department store.

As she viciously swung the door open, her bravado lasted

about five seconds when she was confronted with numerous racks of women's clothes, having no idea where to start.

"May I help you?"

Jo dragged her eyes away from the price tag of a mustard and cream sweater to a petite brunette who had her wishing she was back in her tow truck.

"No, thank you. I'm just browsing." She dropped the cardboard price tag as if her fingers had been burned. Taking a step to the side, she was about to slink out the door when the saleswoman gave her a reassuring smile.

"Then I'll leave you alone. I've been marking down several items, in case you're interested." The saleswoman pointed at a section on the wall toward the back.

Taking a hesitant step, Jo moved toward the section the woman had indicated, relieved when she didn't follow.

She had no hope of finding something affordable in the store, yet she looked through the expensive clothes, planning to leave as soon as the clerk was out of sight.

Sliding the hangers around, she wasn't really paying attention to the clothes until one caught her attention. The cocktail dress was two-toned and was midlength. The ice-pink strapless top held her captivated with its little jacket and the black bottom. It was elegant and refined and would probably cost more than she would make in a year.

Biting her lip, she reached for the price tag, then frowned when she couldn't find it. Pulling the dress down from the wall, she reached inside to search.

"That's my favorite, too. If it came in my size, that would be going home with me," the clerk joked, sleekly taking the dress from her. "I'll put it in the fitting room for you."

Before Jo could protest, she found herself meekly following her into the fitting room.

"I'm Aly. Just call out if you need any help."

"I'm Jo."

The clerk smiled. "I know who you are. I realized you didn't recognize me when you didn't say anything. We went to high school together. I was sorry to hear about your father. He used to fuss at me to buy a new car when I had to keep calling him for tows."

Jo looked closer at the woman, trying to place her.

Aly's smile widened. "Picture me with a mouth full of braces and add about eighty pounds."

Jo's jaw dropped. "Allison Warren?"

Allison was one of the few girls in school who had tried to make friends with her. Unlike her, Allison had been popular. Jo had never tried to return the friendly overtures, too embarrassed that she lived in a junkyard and her father was the town drunk. Plus, she hadn't been able to return the invitations that Allison had extended to her.

"I'm sorry about your parents. They were fine people."

Aly's eyes watered. "I still don't believe it."

"I went to the funeral home to pay my respects. I didn't see you."

"I was in Colorado, snowed in. I saw your name on the register. You sent flowers also. I was going to send a thank-you card, but I haven't been able to actually make myself write them yet."

"I understand." She impulsively reached out to hug the woman, finding herself enfolded in a warm hug of shared grief.

Jo hadn't been able to bring herself to send out cards after her father's death for a couple of months after he had died. The cards had brought the grief to the forefront as the final step of something she could do on her father's behalf.

"Are you going to stay in Treepoint?"

"No, I'll be leaving after I settle my parents' estate and sell their house. I graduated from vet school and have a mobile practice in Colorado. I haven't decided where to go next, but

I won't stay in Treepoint for the same reason I didn't come home after I graduated. Treepoint can't support two vets, and Sy's been in business for years. I'm working here through the holidays. Then I'm thinking of Alaska. Lily promised to lend me some of her books to help me make up my mind." She smiled widely again, shaking off her grief. "Enough about me. Go try on your dress, and let me see when you're ready."

Going inside the dressing room, Jo numbly stared at the dress. It would be a waste of time to try on a dress she couldn't afford, much less probably couldn't fit into.

"I'm waiting," Aly reminded her from outside the dressing room.

Seeing no way out of the uncomfortable situation, Jo unzipped her coveralls. Undressing, she then slid the dress over her head, feeling the material glide over her lovingly. She waited until she had put on the small, waist-length jacket before turning to see herself in the mirror.

The dress looked as if it had been made for her, emphasizing her breasts and hips while skimming over the small pouch of her stomach that she was self-conscious about.

"Jo?" Allison called out as Jo stared in amazement at her reflection.

"I'm coming." Opening the door, she stepped out.

Aly eyed her approvingly. "I wished I had your height. You look stunning, Jo. It will be perfect for tonight."

"You know about the auction?" Jo rubbed the luxurious material of the dress.

"Lily talked me into buying tickets and gave me a flyer to hang up in the employees' lounge when she and Rachel came in to buy their dresses."

"I'm going to kill her," Jo muttered. "After the baby is born," she qualified.

"You couldn't hurt a fly, much less Lily."

"Wanna bet?" Jo turned in the dress, wanting to see the back. Damn, it looked just as pretty from the back.

"Yes." Aly turned her around to face forward again. "You have to buy this dress. You'll be the prettiest woman at the auction."

"I already have a dress to wear tonight," Jo lied, wishing she could buy it, but knowing she couldn't afford to. "I better get changed. I'm sorry I've wasted your time."

"You're not going to get it?" Aly asked in dismay. "Whatever dress you have can't compare to the way you look in this one."

Jo's hand lingered over the collar of the jacket instead of removing it, as she had been about to do. "I can't afford it." She dropped the pretense that she had another dress, telling the truth to the woman she hadn't seen in years.

Aly gave her the same smile she had given her every time she had asked if she could sit next to Jo in the school cafeteria. "The dress is 70 percent off, and I'll give you my discount." Aly pushed her toward the dressing room. "Get changed."

Jo changed, coming out with the dress draped over her arm.

"What size shoes do you wear? There's a pair of black heels I just marked down on clearance that will match the dress perfectly."

Beginning to feel like she was sinking into the tidal wave of Aly's exuberance, Jo told Aly her shoe size, then waited by the counter for her to retrieve them.

Jo had no idea how she was going to pay for the dress, much less the shoes that Aly was intent on selling her. She was about to make a break for it when Aly returned, proudly showing her the shoes.

"Those are Gucci." Jo might not know much about dresses, but she knew shoes. The high heels were black, but they had a pink heel that matched the color of the ice pink of the dress. "Aly, there's no way I can afford—"

"Yes, you can; trust me. These are last season's and have been discounted three times. It's a final markdown. I'm giving you my discount for them, too." Aly scanned the shoe box, then removed the jacket from the dress, pulling out the price tag from the sleeve. "That'll be twenty-eight dollars." Aly reached for a garment bag and began maneuvering the dress inside.

The total was so low it took several seconds to believe she was hearing Aly correctly. There was no way the items totaled to that low of a sum.

"Aly … I can't let you. You'll get fired." Jo looked up at the closed-circuit camera over the register.

"Jo, I won't get fired for letting you use my discount."

"Even with your discount, there is no way these cost twenty-eight dollars."

"Well, they are … It's not like there is a big call for cocktail dresses in Treepoint. You're actually saving the store money on shipping it back to the warehouse. Will that be cash or charge?" Aly asked determinedly.

Reaching into her coveralls pocket, intending to pull out her money, she instead grabbed the three flyers. Blushing, she threw them into the trash can sitting beside the counter, mortified that Aly had recognized them from her hastily concealed expression.

"You want me to take down the one I put in the lounge?"

"Please." Jo managed to find her money, giving it to her. "And if you see any others that Lily put up, I would appreciate it."

"I go for a walk during my lunch hour. If I come across any of them, I'll take them down."

Jo gave her a grateful glance when Aly handed her the purchases. "Are you coming tonight?"

"Are you kidding? Lily wouldn't leave until I promised to go. For someone so sweet, she can be very determined when she sets her mind on something."

"Tell me about it," Jo concurred in exasperation. "Rachel, Winter, and Willa are just as bad."

"Maybe we should marry a handsome biker and join the club," Aly teased, walking with her to the front door.

"I prefer men who drive cars," Jo said primly, not about to admit to Aly or herself that she found any of The Last Riders attractive.

"I usually agree, but I've seen a few of the bikers in town since I moved back. I wouldn't mind getting acquainted with a couple of them. I had several friends in Colorado who rode motorcycles. You should broaden your horizon."

"No thanks. My horizon is broad enough without adding a Last Rider to the mix. I'll see you tonight." Jo had never been able to joke and tease like most women, even before she had made the mistake of trusting Curt. Looking back, she could see that her naïveté had painted a target on her back to unscrupulous boys who took it as willing.

She had been withdrawn as a child, too affected by her parents' constant fights to make friends easily. Then, as she had grown older and heard the hurtful remarks made by her classmates, she had drawn further away. Her first foray into drawing someone into her solitary existence had ended in disaster, not only for her, but her parents hadn't been able to survive the fallout.

She made a quick stop at her house before going on a call of a stalled car that was blocking traffic on Main Street.

Her gloom drew darker as she approached the car, her gut clenching when she recognized it.

The emergency lights of the car were blinking, and Knox was in his uniform, directing traffic to go around it.

Driving past the car when Knox motioned her forward, she rolled her window down. "Find another to tow him."

Knox walked to her window. "He's blocking traffic."

"Then help him push it to the side, or call Greg. Curt won't get a tow from me." She resolutely stared back at the aggravated sheriff as the cars behind her started honking.

Expecting him to blast her with curses, she was surprised when he nodded, then pushed a button on his radio attached to his jacket. "Greer, call Fuller Towing in Jamestown; tell him I need a tow. Then come here and help me move this car." Once he released the button, he returned to directing traffic.

As she drove past Curt's car, she looked down and saw the malicious way he watched her. Raising her hand high enough for him to see, she flipped him off, uncaring of the Christian values that Lucky tried to instill in his parishioners every Sunday.

She would starve and lose everything she owned before she would ever give Curt a tow.

Listening to the weather report, she decided to fill up her gas tank. The entire state of Kentucky was under a snow advisory. If she was lucky, the snow would hit before it was her turn to be auctioned off.

After refueling, she checked her tires and the extra snow chains she kept as spares. Some of the roads at higher elevations were treacherous and could be snow covered, leaving unwary drivers stranded. She had learned to be prepared.

Many of the mountain inhabitants didn't have the money for a tow, and she would lend them the chains until they could return them when the weather was better. It was bad for business, as were the free tows she would give to any hard luck story that too many of her customers had told her. Her father had told her numerous times not to listen to them, but it was hard to do when she had volunteered in the church store and knew how desperate many of them were.

When she was finally satisfied that her truck was as equipped for the snowstorm as she could make it, Jo got back inside her truck and turned the heat up higher. Seeing the digital clock, she muttered to herself. If she didn't hurry, Lily or Rachel would be calling, wanting to know where she was.

Curt's car was gone, and traffic was back to normal when she drove back down Main Street. It only took five minutes to get home.

As soon as she made the turn onto her property, she felt a sense of unease. Feeling ridiculous, she drove past rows of dilapidated cars that had been crushed and stacked on top of each other, making it impossible to see her house until she rounded a small curve. Jo's foot hit the brake when she did.

The front of her house had been egged. One of Curt's friends, or a family member, had beat her home.

Edging her truck closer, she parked in front of the ramshackle home. She knew the fucking cowards were gone and weren't waiting for her inside. The security alarm she had installed herself would have gone off if any of her windows or doors had been opened.

Looking at the rapidly darkening sky and the yard that offered many hiding places for anyone who could be waiting for her, she flipped her glove department open, taking out the small snub-nosed pistol that had belonged to her father. She slid it into her pocket before getting out.

When she climbed her front steps, eggshells cracked under her boots. It was going to be a mess to clean. The goo was already freezing to the porch and the siding of the house.

Keying in her security code, Jo opened the front door, then shut it behind her, determinedly putting thoughts of the waiting mess behind her. She didn't have the time to deal with it now and be at King's on time.

After resetting her alarm, Jo took a quick shower, wishing she had spent the extra money to install a camera on the outside. She should have anticipated Curt's reaction and have come back home immediately. It was the only spot where she was vulnerable, and he had taken advantage when her back had been turned.

Drying off, she went into her bedroom, searching through her drawers for a strapless bra and seamless panties she could wear under her dress. She found what she needed in the back of her lingerie drawer. She had purchased them when her college roommate had gotten married, and she had been a bridesmaid. Luckily, they still fit.

Padding barefoot across the cold, wooden floorboards, she shut her bedroom door, then turned the old radiator on high, shivering in the cold air. Once she was dressed, the room was warm enough that she could concentrate on her makeup and hair.

When she was finished, she stared into the cracked mirror she'd owned since she was a young girl. Jo reached out, touching her reflection in the mirror, then her cheek. It was slightly unreal that the image in the mirror was actually her.

Going to her closet, she went to the tips of her toes in her new heels, reaching for an old shoe box. Grasping it, she tugged it down until it was within her reach. Opening the box, she took out the small black velvet clutch purse she had bought at the thrift store. When she had seen it on the wall, Jo had thought the vintage purse was beautiful and had bought it on an impulse. Lily hadn't known who had donated it, but whoever it was had taken care of it, wrapping it in tissue paper and a cloth bag.

Jo wasn't used to carrying a purse, usually shoving the items she needed in her pockets. Sliding the small amount of cash she had on hand, her license, and the pistol, she had to force the snap to close.

Grabbing a clean pair of coveralls, a change of clothes, and her boots before turning off the heater, she then gingerly made her way outside to her truck.

She nearly fell into the seat after clambering up her truck in her heels. Smoothing out her dress, she shut the door with a sigh of relief. She would be lucky if she didn't fall on her face when she got out.

It had grown colder in just the short time she had gone inside her house. Relieving her fears that Curt or one of his minions would be waiting for her to leave, she told herself that the bastards would be safely tucked away somewhere warm.

Evil always preferred warmer temperatures. The place she was determined to send Curt was going to make him feel right at home.

IT WAS ALMOST CLOSING time when Shade walked into the department store.

Aly excused herself from a browsing shopper to meet him at her cash register. Opening the drawer, she took out the receipt she had hidden under the drawer.

"Eight hundred, forty-three dollars, and sixty-two cents."

Shade handed her his credit card without balking at the amount.

Motioning for him to sign the electronic receipt, she pushed a button on her register to spit out his paper receipt when he was done. Giving to him, she watched as he folded it neatly and placed both the receipt and the card back in his wallet.

"Thanks, Aly. Don't forget, this is just between us." His

threat wasn't obvious, but the chill he gave out had her hastily reassuring him of her silence.

"I won't forget. I won't mention it to anyone in town or any of the others in the club."

"I appreciate it. I wouldn't be happy if Moon or any of the other brothers asked me why I bought Jo a dress."

She hadn't asked any questions when he had come into the store that morning as Lily was putting up the flyers outside, and she didn't ask for any now. She enjoyed the few times she had been allowed entry into the Friday night parties at The Last Riders' clubhouse to ever jeopardize being able to go back.

"Mum's the word."

"Exactly."

As Aly watched Shade stride away, she nervously licked her lips. Damn, Lily was a lucky woman. Maybe she would get lucky herself, and Jo would make good on her threats. She would have no problem giving Shade a shoulder to cry on if something happened to Lily.

Aly rolled her eyes at herself. Nothing was going to happen to Lily. God was probably just as afraid of Shade as everyone in town was. Still, she had no intention of pulling those posters down. A slim chance was better than none at all.

"What kind of pie is that?" Moon tried to move closer to the table, but Rider refused to budge, crossing his arms over his chest to keep him from getting too close. He didn't want Moon's fingerprints in the snowy perfection of Willa's candy.

Rider stood guard over the table where the baked goods were going to be auctioned off. He hadn't moved since he had arrived. Besides, King's bar and restaurant was filled to overflowing, and the only space available was near where he was standing. That was because he had glowered every time someone moved closer to inspect the variety of treats that the church hoped would provide the funds needed to help those in need.

Moon wasn't about to be scared off as others had been. Dodging him to go to the other side of the table, he lifted up a place card and read it out loud.

"Buttermilk pie. Why doesn't it say who made it?"

"Because everyone in town knows who made it. Tate Porter's wife, Sutton, made it. You should bid on it. It's delicious."

Moon looked at it skeptically. "It doesn't look that great."

"It is; trust me. You won't regret it. It's like silk on your tongue."

"Is it as good as Willa's candy?"

"Better," Rider unashamedly lied.

"You going to bid for it?" Moon gave the pie another skeptical glance.

"No, I'm not going to bid against Tate. You see that shotgun in the gun rack in the back of his truck?"

"No way to miss it. It's really that good?"

"Better."

Moon bent over, trying to get a whiff of the covered pie. "I'm going to bid. I'm not afraid of the Porters." Straightening, he oozed confidence.

Rider nearly snickered at him. He wouldn't touch that buttermilk pie with a ten-foot pole. Willa's candy would go last, and that meant Moon's pocket would be lighter after he paid for Sutton's pie.

Rider was turned toward Moon with the bar and restaurant at his back when several people jostled him, making it difficult to turn and see what was going on. The cold air hitting him told him that someone had come in.

As an elusive scent wafted by him, his nostrils flared at the delicate perfume that filled his senses, bringing his dick to attention like a needle on a compass. He rudely used his elbows so he could turn around, wanting to see who was wearing the perfume.

Cash and Rachel were taking their coats off, and Shade was helping Lily with hers. Sliding closer to Rachel, he leaned forward to smell her perfume. Rachel gave him a withering look.

Rider stepped away. It wasn't Rachel. Her scent had been spicy, not delicate.

Moving toward Lily, he picked up the glove she had

nervously dropped when he had gotten too close. Lifting the glove to his nose, he then immediately gave it to Shade when his face turned red with fury.

"What the fuck?" Shade snatched Lily's glove from him.

Rider hastily stepped back. Lily's perfume wasn't the one he was searching for either. Lily's was too sweet. The one he was after was more floral, but not overpowering with nuances of jasmine and clover. It made a man think of sex on a rainy day or fucking in front of a fireplace. It reminded him of home.

He tried to look around the room, but most of the men were his height or taller, concealing most of the women. Fuck, he couldn't go around the restaurant sniffing all the women.

"Sorry," he apologized to Shade and Lily, going back to the auction table, where Moon had taken residence.

"Did you see who was behind me when I was talking to you?"

Moon shook his head. "No. Why?"

"Never mind."

Rider's attention was no longer focused on the auction. One by one, he scoped out the crowd. The Porters were grouped together, so were the Colemans and the Hayes. The three families had been feuding longer than he had been in Treepoint. He believed even they didn't know what had started the bad blood between them.

His eyes moved on to the old biddies who belonged to Lucky's church. Most of them haughtily stared at those around them who were holding drinks from the bar. Lucky and Willa were standing by the arch of the door that led toward the restaurant, greeting those who had just arrived.

Evie, who looked like she could give birth at any time during the auction, and King were trolling around the room, making sure that everyone had drinks, both alcoholic and none. Bliss and Drake were talking to the city council. Viper and Winter were settling at a large table where The Last Riders had congregated. His eyes were moving away from the table when Lily waved at someone who was coming from the bar.

Rider's eyes went to the area Lily was waving at, and then he started walking toward her, confused as to who she was greeting, when he noticed a woman sidled between Knox and Diamond, their height previously obscuring her from his view. His mouth dropped open when he recognized the woman.

"Excuse me. Lily wants me."

Rider heard the soft sound of her voice, not recognizing the sultry tone, used to the tart one she normally used when addressing him.

"Holy hell. Who is that?"

"Jo," Rider answered Moon's question, despite wanting to keep the fact to himself, but he knew Moon wouldn't stop until he found out.

"That can't be Jo."

Rider felt the same disbelief as Moon as he took in the dress that clung to curves he hadn't known the woman had. He had caught a glimpse of her breasts when she had been at Cash's, but the generous expanse of cleavage she was showing tonight was enough to make him swallow his tongue to keep from drooling.

"It's her. She has her radio in her hand." Rider couldn't believe the sophisticated woman who had gone to Lily's side was Jo. He hadn't believed she owned anything other than jeans or coveralls. He for fucking sure had never seen her hair curled and wound into a bun on top of her head with tiny ringlets escaping.

He watched as she talked to Lily then Beth as she entered the group. Her hands moved as if she were emphasizing a

121

point she had made. When she opened her clutch and took out a wad of paper, Rider knew what it was.

"Seems she doesn't appreciate the flyers Lily put up as much as we did."

Rider felt Moon move from the other side of the table to better see Jo.

"She looks fine in that dress. Is there an ATM in here?"

"No." Rider knew Moon was worried he didn't have enough money in his pocket to win the auction for her.

He didn't.

"There's one in the diner," he offered, knowing it was out of order.

"I'll be right back."

"Take your time." Rider waited until Moon went out the door before he made his move.

He stealthily walked through the crowd until he was standing behind Jo. Razer was standing slightly back behind Beth, faking an interest he didn't feel. Rider asked him who was babysitting their kids while deliberately listening to the conversation the women were having.

"How many of those flyers did you put up?"

"A few." Lily wasn't upset at Jo's question. "I told you about them. I even showed you the mock-up before I sent them to the printers."

"The mock-up you showed me didn't have my name on the list, and it damn sure wasn't the very first one. I would have remembered that."

"I didn't think you would mind."

"Well, I do. Lily, it's embarrassing."

"I'm sorry. I didn't mean to embarrass you. It is for a good cause."

"You don't sound very sorry."

Rider's lips curled in amusement at Jo calling out Lily for not being sorry. Even Shade was having trouble keeping a straight face. All the club members knew that Lily, as sweet as she was, could be ruthless when it concerned her charity.

"What are you going to be bidding on tonight?"

"This and that," Rider answered when he realized Razer had answered his question and asked one of his own.

"I bet one of them will be the peanut butter candy. Good luck. King told me he would be bidding. He plans to sell it by the piece to his customers."

Rider only half-listened, trying to get closer to Jo to smell her perfume. When he did, the scent had his balls tightening.

A tug on his sleeve had him returning to awareness as Razer moved him away from Jo just as she turned, startled at seeing him so close to her.

"Can I help you?"

Trying to come up with an excuse, too afraid he would stutter if he did, he shrugged like a lame-ass idiot, then turned toward Razer for help.

His friend raised a mocking brow before stepping in to rescue him. "Rider was trying to get Lily's attention to start the auction. I think there's something he wants to buy."

"We should have started ten minutes ago!" Lily grabbed Jo by the arm, rushing by him. "Come on, Rider. I have everyone listed on the flyer in the order they're to be auctioned off. You're third."

"I'm first!" Jo's screech was drowned out as King saw Lily's wave and jumped onto the small stage that The Last Riders had built, despite King's protests.

"Of course. I didn't want you called out before it was your turn."

For a pregnant woman, she had no problem rushing Jo through the crowd. Rider had trouble keeping up with the crowd converging on them.

Dustin Porter shoved him back when he tried to help Jo

onto the stage. Rider wanted to tear her hands off his shoulders when he easily lifted her, setting her on it.

Gritting his teeth, he stood next to the stage, ignoring Dustin's triumphant smirk.

Tate and Greer were going to be raising the younger brother's son if the cocky man didn't back off.

Rider tried to glower at him like he had been when he had been standing guard at the table, but Dustin was either unwilling or too stupid to understand what he was trying to silently warn.

Rider searched the room, glad Moon hadn't made it back yet.

"Thank you all for coming tonight." Lily took the microphone King gave her, standing in front of the stage. "The funds will go into making many children's Christmas this year, provide groceries to their families, and the backpack meals for the students that are out of school for the holidays. Thank you." Lily handed the microphone back to King and started organizing the others who were to be auctioned off into a line. He was behind Dustin, and Moon was behind him.

"We're going to start the auction off with someone the whole town knows. Jolene Turner runs the towing company, so not only are you getting a dinner date with her, but she's throwing in a coupon for a year's free emergency towing. Now, who wants to start the bidding off?"

Jo looked like she was about to jump down from the stage and take off at a run. Her luminous eyes looked like a deer caught in the headlights of an oncoming semi.

"I will." Dustin waved his hand. "A hundred dollars."

"The tow will cost you more than that. Who can do better?" King rattled off like a master auctioneer.

"Here!" Rider gave a low groan when he heard Moon's yell from the doorway. "I bid two hundred."

Another male voice, one he couldn't see who it belonged to, bid five hundred. It sounded suspiciously like Shade.

Rider didn't lift his hand, hearing the bids go back and forth between Dustin and Moon until it reached twelve hundred dollars. Moon had gradually found enough space to make it to the stage. At his final bid, Dustin's face showed he wouldn't be able to raise it any higher.

Moon's victorious expression vanished when Lily called out a bid for thirteen hundred.

"Is that fair?" Moon asked King, crestfallen, as Lily gave him a sheepish look at his glare.

"I don't know. How about it, Lucky?"

The crowd looked toward Lucky, who nodded, while Rider saw Willa elbow her husband.

"It's not in the rules that the organizers can't bid. It's all for charity. Let's please keep that in mind, and keep it friendly and fun," Lucky tried to soothe Moon and the crowd.

Moon huffily turned back to the stage. "Fifteen hundred dollars!"

"Sixteen." Lily's voice wasn't as loud Moon's, but it effectively had Moon bidding until his last bid was two thousand.

Lily started wringing her hands and was trying to look over the crowd for her husband. Again, Moon was about to claim victory. Meanwhile, Jo had been growing paler each time Moon had outbid Lily.

"Two thousand dollars!" King shouted out. "Going, going …"

"Twenty-five hundred dollars." Rider kept his gaze pinned on Jo as he shouted out his bid.

Murmurs and gasps could be heard throughout the crowd. He didn't even look when Moon and Dustin both turned toward him.

"Moon?" King's piercing gaze went to the other man.

"Twenty-eight hundred."

"Rider, you going to raise that bid?" King shouted out as the crowd hushed to listen.

Jo cast a pleading glance toward Lily, who was motioning toward Willa. Lucky's wife's hands went up helplessly, showing she didn't have enough to give her to meet the bid.

Rider grinned up at Jo wickedly. "I believe I am."

11

Jo had never prayed for her radio to go off, but she did now as the crowd confronted her to see who would win the date with her. Surreptitiously, she used the folds of her dress to shake the radio to make sure it was still working. Any other freaking time, the radio would be blaring at her. Now, when she needed the distraction the most, it remained silent, not providing her with the excuse she needed to flee the embarrassment of being the center of attention.

Lily wasn't helping either. She had moved away from the stage in what she hoped was an effort to find someone to lend her enough money to win the auction for her as she had promised.

"Three thousand."

Rider's bid had the crowd talking excitedly among themselves as Moon countered his bid.

"Thirty-one hundred."

The torture of listening to the bids had her wanting to put her hands up and stop the auction herself. Only the thought of making a bigger embarrassment of herself than she was doing now stopped her.

"Thirty-five hundred." Rider's bid had Jo taking her eyes off Lily and going to his.

Her palms grew clammy with her nerves. The man she was familiar with was gone; it was as if a stranger was staring back her. Her instinct to flee went into overdrive at the unwavering intensity in his gaze. The casual and lanky pose that characterized his familiar, charming appeal was missing, replaced by a predator who was staking his claim for a tasty meal it was about to devour.

She shook her head as if silently denying the thought, and then looked back at him, only to see his gaze become resolute.

Her thoughts frantically raced for a way to escape the ordeal.

"Thirty-six hundred."

She wanted to look toward Moon at the sound of his uncertainty, knowing from the sound that he was reaching the end of the money he had available. Rider must have realized it, too, moving in for the kill.

"Four thousand."

Her shoulders slumped when there was no counter from Moon.

"Four thousand dollars," King repeated Rider's bid. "Going, going …"

Every second that tried to delay the end of the auction had Jo holding her breath, praying for divine intervention.

"Gone. Congratulations, Rider. Dustin, you're next. Hop on up." King waved for Dustin to take the stage.

Jo was so anxious to get off the stage that she moved to the edge without thinking how to get down. Any other time, she would jump down, but fear of falling onto her knees in front of the audience had her hesitating.

Moon's helping hand appeared in her sight, and she was about to take it when she was lifted off her feet. Her eyes widened on Rider as he lifted her down to the floor, his hands lingering on her waist.

"Thank you." The ingrained habit taught to her by her mother had her thanking Rider, but it didn't stop her from pulling away from his lingering touch.

Scanning the crowd for the person she was searching for, she was about to awkwardly make an excuse to disappear from sight when Rider's words stopped her.

"I'll pick you up at six tomorrow night for our date."

Feeling uneasy, she wanted to refuse and tell him hell would freeze over first before she went out on a date with him, but she stopped herself when Willa and Winter's ecstatic faces came into view as they managed to squish between Knox and Cash.

"Jo, Rider's bid was more than we expected for the whole auction!" Winter grabbed her hand, pulling her into a tight hug.

Jo remained mute when she found herself turned to Willa, who was so happy she had tears brimming in her eyes.

"I was so worried—we worried—we wouldn't have enough money to buy the toys, much less make food baskets. Thank you both so much. I can relax for the rest of the auction and enjoy myself."

Jo felt like a Grinch on Christmas morning at Willa's heartfelt gratitude.

"I'll be ready at six, Rider. Willa, have you seen Lily?"

Willa frowned, looking over her shoulder. "She was just here a moment ago. I'm sure she'll show up in a minute. It's so crowded that it's hard to spot her."

"If you see her, tell her I'm looking for her." Jo had a few choice words for her when she found her.

Her dark thoughts were interrupted by the clapping of the audience.

"Congratulations, Carly," King called out as Dustin jumped down from the stage.

Jo lowered her lashes to observe Rider's reaction to Carly having the winning bid, then wished she hadn't when she realized his gaze was still fixed on her.

Her nipples tautened under the shimmering ice-pink bodice of her dress.

Pulling her small jacket closed, she took a step back from the heat that was emanating from his body. Fanning her face, she searched fruitlessly through the crowd again.

"It's getting stuffy, isn't it? I'm going to go stand by the door and try to catch a breeze."

Willa and Winter's brows rose at her hasty departure.

Rider didn't move as she tried to move around him, hemmed on each side by Winter, Willa, Rider, Cash, and Knox, she found herself closer to Rider. When the arrogant man bent down, she could have sworn he was sniffing her throat.

Shock held her still. Then she found her hands on his finely textured gray shirt that had been tucked into his black slacks.

"Excuse me."

"What perfume are you wearing?"

"Rider, it's your turn. Let's not keep the ladies waiting."

King's announcement over the microphone didn't deter Rider as his nostrils flared as if he could smell the agitation that was seeping from her body at the unwanted attraction that was assailing her feminine parts.

She could have sworn on a stack of Bibles that she would never, ever be able to respond to any male, much less the boy toy who was an inch away from her. She would rather be tied down on a rack than admit the truth to herself, despite the proof that her panties had grown damp, and the dress she was wearing had begun to feel like an uncomfortable weight that held her in place.

Though Jo knew her judgment of men had been warped since her attack, there was no way she was going to allow herself to become another of Rider's women.

Using the memory of the night she had been raped to restore her equilibrium, she moved away from the group.

She must have become oxygen deprived. Jo excused herself as she found a lone spot near the doorway to watch the auction. Each time someone entered or exited, the cold air lifted the fog that had surrounded her, reassuring her that she was back on an even knell.

The cold air wasn't the only thing that brought her to her senses. Watching the bidding war over Rider helped.

The mass of women who had moved closer to the stage had the men forced to the back. Jo didn't look at the stage, where he was standing, focusing on the women instead. Even the older married women in the congregation were bidding as their husbands grew angry.

"We have an extra seat at our table. Come and join us."

Jo hadn't felt Shade's approach, too intent on the auction. The biker gave her the heebie-jeebies with the purposeful way he was looking at her.

"No, thanks. It will make it easier if I get a call."

"No one will be calling. Everyone in town is here." Shade lightly took her elbow. "Lily wants to talk to you, and I would rather you talk to her with me present. She's looked forward to this auction, and I would hate to see it get ruined because you're upset with her."

Jo found herself escorted through the crowd as Shade walked beside her. She had no intention of denying that she was angry with Lily, pregnant or not.

"She convinced me to be in the auction. The only reason I agreed was because she promised to buy me."

"Your bid exceeded the money Lily had tucked into her purse. If you're angry, be angry at me. She had asked me to go to the diner to get more cash from the ATM, but it's out of order. When I got back, your auction was over."

She found herself maneuvered into sitting next to Lily, and her anger died away at her sheepish expression.

"I'm so sorry ..."

Jo didn't miss Shade's hardening expression as his wife began her apology.

"It's fine, Lily. We shouldn't have made the plan. Besides, how bad could a date with Rider be?" She tried to ease Lily's guilt. "Let's look at the bright side; there are going to be a lot of happy children Christmas morning."

Lily gave her a bright smile that had her forgetting why she was even angry in the first place. It was impossible to be angry with the woman who didn't have a mean bone in her body. She could understand how Shade had fallen in love with her. Everyone did, and she was no exception.

Lily held a special spot in most of the townspeople's hearts from the first time Pastor Saul had introduced her to the congregation as a child whom he and his wife had adopted. Since then, she had grown entrenched in their hearts. Jo could count on her fingers the number of people she could consider a truly good person, and Lily was one of them.

On the other hand, Shade wasn't. She didn't need to know particulars to form her opinion on that. It was in the vibes he put off. Despite her father's assurances that he was a fine person, and the loan he had given her for the truck, her instincts screamed to be wary of him.

She had ignored her instincts the night she had been raped. It had been a hard lesson to learn, but she had learned it. She knew Shade had no interest in her as a woman, but her instincts shouted at her that he did have an ulterior motive for extending the credit. The sooner she could pay the loan back, the happier she would be, and would finally stop expecting for the other shoe drop at what his motive was.

"Not many women would complain about having to go on a date with Rider."

Jo winced that Viper had overheard her choice of words to Lily. As the president of The Last Riders, she expected him to be angry. That he wasn't showed in the lopsided grin he gave her.

"I'm not like most women." Jo refused to be embarrassed or pretend she hadn't meant her words.

"Don't worry; he'll probably spend most of the time eating. He has a bottomless pit for a stomach." Winter had everyone sitting at the table agreeing.

"Order the meat lovers platter and a trio of desserts on King's menu, and Rider will fall asleep before you can drive him home," Willa laughingly suggested.

"Or order the special at the Pink Slipper and swing by the Donut Hut. They always put him in a sugar coma."

Jo didn't know the name of the woman who had offered the last suggestion. She had seen her in town occasionally, either in the diner or riding on the back of one of The Last Riders' motorcycles. Either the dark-haired woman had never been in an accident, or her car had never needed a tow, or her only form of transportation was with one of the bikers.

Carly, who was walking past their table on the way to the restroom, paused, standing over the seated woman. "Jewell, I expected you to be front and center to win Rider's date."

The diner's waitress's snide attitude had the others at the table stiffening, except the woman whose identity Jo was wondering about.

"Why pay for something I can have for free?" Jewell

leaned sideways, draping a graceful arm over the back of her chair, lifting her chin to stare straight back at Carly.

Carly looked like she was about to rip every strand of hair out of Jewell's head. Her lips tightened so much Jo could practically hear her teeth grinding.

"Going, going ... gone!" King's voice over the loudspeaker broke the tense moment. "Congratulations, Aly. Moon, you're next."

"Looks like we lost out." Carly shrugged, moving away toward the restrooms.

The brewing catfight between the two women never materialized.

Jewell turned forward in her seat and began speaking to Diamond as if the brief exchange had never happened.

The encounter between Jewell and Carly only reinforced Jo's opinion of Rider, as well as the throng of women who trailed after him to the table she was sitting at.

When he went to take an empty chair from another table to move to the one his friends were sitting at, Jo stood.

"Take mine. I want to congratulate Aly."

Jo disappeared into the crowd before anyone could stop her.

Aly was flushed with her success. The elegant woman dressed in a sophisticated dress of black velvet looked as excited as if she had won the Heisman trophy.

"Congratulations." Jo tried to keep from being squished between the Porters and the Hayes as King began the auction for Jessie Hayes.

"For a while there, I thought I was going to have to take a bank loan to win," Aly gushed.

Lily and Willa had been fanning themselves with the flyers when they had heard the amount of the winning bid. Aly's four-thousand five hundred-dollar bid had exceeded hers. For that, Jo was grateful. If the bids of the night remained high, then no one in town would be discussing the high bid Rider had made for her.

"I wanted to thank you for this afternoon. I appreciate you letting me use your discount."

"No problem. Anytime. Seems like we're both going out with the same man."

"Yes, it does."

"We'll have to see which one of us can convince him into another date."

Jo's lips quirked. "That's going to be a no-brainer. I'm hoping he can convince you to stay in town so you won't be so anxious to leave after the holidays," she said sincerely.

A curious expression crossed Aly's face. It seemed like she was about to say something until Shade came up to them to tell Aly that Lily wanted to talk to her.

A crimson flush heightened the color on Aly's cheeks.

"I'll talk to you later, Jo." The woman went toward the table she had just left as if the hounds of hell were after her.

Jo gave Shade a curious look, sure he had something to do with the terrified expression Aly had veiled when her gaze had swung from Shade's to Jo's. Why would Aly be frightened of Shade?

That fortified her resolve to remain detached from anything to do with The Last Riders. She needed to remember that any friendship between her and Rachel and Lily would have set limits she wouldn't broach. The two women would remain loyal to their husbands, despite any friendship they had with her.

"Your message has been received. You can relax now." It took all her courage not to back down when Shade's brows lowered.

"I don't know what you mean."

"I'm not an idiot, Shade. Why didn't you want me talking to Aly?"

"I merely repeated Lily's message. Don't read more into it than there was."

"Lily is pregnant, not helpless. Does everyone jump when you ask them to?"

"Usually. Don't assume an ulterior motive when there isn't one. I didn't assume anything when you left the table when Rider arrived."

Shade had more than his fair share of arrogance. All The Last Riders did.

Jo dropped the subject. As long as he didn't expect her to jump through hoops to keep him happy for the loan he had given her, she would leave Aly's reaction alone. She didn't want Shade delving into her reaction to Rider's appearance.

"I need to get back to Lily. Enjoy your date with Rider tomorrow." His parting shot had her fighting back a nasty reply.

Finding a quiet spot in the back corner of the bar where she could watch the rest of the auction without having to talk to anyone, she mentally distanced herself until she could leave.

Ordering a cup of coffee from the bartender, she sipped it as the auction moved toward the desserts.

She couldn't help laughing when she saw Moon triumphantly lift Willa's candy container over his head as the crowd gathered, jokingly asking for a piece.

Rubbing the back of her neck at the sensation of being watched, she looked around. The auction over, music began to play over the loudspeaker, and couples began to fill the lounge area to dance.

Jo told herself now that the auction was over, she would wait a couple minutes before calling it a night.

Still looking around at all the activity, she was able to see clearly into the next room when Knox swung Diamond around. Rider was standing at the entrance of the bar, blocking any chance of her leaving without speaking to him.

She swallowed compulsively at the tight ball of fear lodged in her throat. His posture and determined gaze had her looking over her shoulder, sure another woman had been the cause of his close scrutiny. When she found no one behind her, Jo paid for her coffee, slipped from the stool, and used the dancing couples as camouflage to navigate across the dance floor.

Trying to look over Viper's broad shoulders and Winter's head, she saw Rider was no longer standing in the doorway. Instead of being relieved, she became even more high-strung about his whereabouts.

She stayed at the fringe of the dance floor, hoping the couples would obscure her position. She clutched her purse and radio tighter, feeling ridiculous for playing cat and mouse with a man who was putting off the signal she had misinterpreted as him having found a juicy mouse he had every intention of devouring it if it came close enough.

"That's not going to happen," Jo muttered under her breath, searching the bar area for another exit. How could there not be another exit?

Her instincts were screaming for her to run.

Turning in a half circle, she spotted him on the other side of the dance floor, talking to Cash and Rachel, his arms held loosely by his sides.

Jo wasn't fooled. His taut body could easily outrun her to the doorway, which his posture promised he would do if she tried to escape.

Licking her dry lips, she took a step back and bumped into a couple about to enter the dance floor. Her lips parted to mumble an apology, but it went unspoken at Curt's sudden, hostile appearance. He was with Carly.

She was already ill at ease with the large crowd, Rider's

strange behavior, and now faced with the man she detested with a hatred that had festered for years. Her breath grew ragged.

She shakily brought her hand up to her throat, trying to draw a deep breath.

"Are you okay, Jo?" Carly reached out, touching her arm.

Jo pulled away from her touch, needing to get away from Curt's close proximity. Her breaths grew shallower as her lungs fought for oxygen, and she blinked back black dots as her knees started to buckle.

A firm hand surrounded her waist, tugging her into a hard body. Her fingers splayed across a muscular chest.

"Excuse us. Jo promised me this dance."

Jo numbly followed Rider as one of his hands surrounded hers that was holding the clutch and the radio, keeping them from falling to the floor as they moved to the soft music.

She didn't know what was worse: the monster behind her, or the predator whose arms she found herself trapped in.

Hysterically, she thought of the old saying *Trapped between a rock and a hard place.*

The monster behind her could be taken down. His burly body was more fat than muscle. The same couldn't be said for Rider. He had won the chase of cat and mouse.

The hard place she had futility sought not to end up in was exactly where Rider wanted her. Right in his arms.

12

"You look beautiful tonight." Rider forced his arms to loosen his hold on the trembling woman who had turmoil written all over her face.

"Huh?"

"I said, you look beautiful tonight." He patiently turned her so she could no longer see Curt.

"Are you high?"

"No, I'm not high." Rider smiled down at her.

"Did Greer sell you some bad weed?"

His grin deepened. "No. Why do you think I have to be high to compliment you?"

"Because we don't like each other." She tilted her head proudly as she frankly admitted that.

The stubborn set of Jo's jaw showed he wouldn't be able to handle her as easily as he handled other women. But he had already known that. That was why he had never made a concentrated effort to lure her to his bed. That had changed the minute he had caught a whiff of her perfume and seen the femininity that he could have sworn she didn't possess.

He didn't mind a woman who could bust his nuts. What

he had no intention of becoming involved with was one with no sex appeal. Jo had hidden her appeal under flannel shirts, tasteless colors, and even with the god-awful coveralls. He was willing to bet the jeans she wore were men's. A man could only light a fire in a woman's pussy if there was something to work with. She had adopted men's mannerisms until they were so ingrained in her that he hadn't wanted to explore the forest for the trees. The way she looked and was acting tonight showed he had some kindling to work with.

Rider kept his hand lightly on the small of her back, just underneath her jacket, experimentally stretching his thumb upward, rubbing her back over her dress in a circular pattern to slow her rapid breathing.

"I offered to take you out when you moved back to town. I've also asked you out a couple times since then. Would I have done that if I didn't like you?" Rider kept his thumb just below her bra, being careful not to set the skittish woman fleeing.

"You thought I was gay when I refused."

"You're not gay."

"And how have you finally reached that conclusion?"

Rider lowered his head to whisper in her ear. "You really don't want me to answer that question, do you?" He lifted his head to see her swallowing hard.

"No."

"Where do you want to go for our date tomorrow night?"

Rider saw her searching his eyes at the change of subject.

"Rosie's."

"I was thinking of something more romantic. How about the Pink Slipper?"

"No, Rosie's will be fine, and I'll pick you up."

"I didn't plan on showing up on my bike."

"I prefer driving."

"So, if you get called out, you can leave me stranded?" Rider could practically see the plan forming in her mind.

"I wouldn't leave you stranded. I'd drive you home first."

"If you get called out, I'll ride along with you. It would be a new experience for me."

"I bet you don't get many of those anymore."

Rider could hear the ice dripping off her tone, warning him away from the razor's edge.

"Not many, no." His grin faded. "But that doesn't mean I can't appreciate them when they come along."

Jo's forehead puckered in a frown. "Don't expect any new experiences from me. You'd be bored to death in under an hour."

"Then let's hope you don't get called out."

"Rider, this isn't a date, date. You know that, right?"

"Are you trying to spoil the date"—he emphasized the word *date* smugly—"before we even go out? Maybe you'll be surprised, and we'll have a good time. Enough that you'll go out with me again." He lowered his head, taking another whiff of her heady perfume.

With Jo's free hand, she reached out, trying unsuccessfully to push him away.

"Why do you keep smelling me?"

"You smell good. What's the name of the perfume you're wearing?"

"None of your freaking business," Jo snapped.

Why didn't she want to tell him the brand of her perfume? Usually women would immediately tell him if he complimented them on it.

"It has to be sold somewhere you don't want me to know you frequent." Rider used deductive reasoning to figure out the answer, taking another deep breath like a wine connoisseur inhaling the aroma of an expensive vintage. "Most department stores or drug stores sell perfumes. If you had bought it from one of those, you would have told me straight out."

"Maybe it's from the drug store, or it's a knockoff from an outlet store," Jo countered.

"Nope, you wouldn't be embarrassed to tell me that it came from the drugstore, and the closest outlet store is in Lexington."

She gave him an exasperated look. "You're being weird."

"Am I? Sorry."

"You don't look sorry."

He wasn't, but it was irritating that she knew it. He must be going soft if she had so easily looked through him.

His brow furrowed in a frown as he thought of the places she could have bought her perfume. Suddenly, a light dawned on him.

"You bought it at Sassy Vixen's, didn't you?" He laughed so hard that his shoulders shook.

At his guess, he felt a stinging pain on his chest. The woman had pinched him right under where he was holding her hand pinned.

"Shut up! Everyone is staring at us!" she hissed.

"You bought your perfume at a lingerie boutique. Did you buy anything else while you were there?"

"It. Is. None. Of. Your. Business." Jo sucked in a deep breath. Rider could tell she was trying to calm her temper before she continued in a quieter tone. "What I bought is and will never be any concern to you."

"Damn, that hurts."

"I barely pinched you."

"I don't mean that. I meant that you think it's never going to be any of my concern. Woman, if you believe that, then you don't know me."

"No, I don't. And you know something else? I don't want to!"

One second, he was holding her, and the next, he was holding air.

In the military, Rider had learned when to attack and when to retreat. It was time to retreat and give Jo breathing room.

He followed her slowly, watching as she left, wanting to make sure she got into her truck safely.

The cold air hit him as he went out the door, making him wish he had taken the time to grab his jacket. He could see the indentations of her heel prints in the freshly fallen snow. He tracked them with his eyes until they fell on the crumpled heap on the sidewalk.

"Fuck!" Rider started running, but his dress shoes were just as inadequate as Jo's high heels. Unable to stop, he slid into her and toppled over her.

"Ouch!" Jo yelled out from underneath him. "Get off!"

"I'm trying to. Give me a second." Rider managed to lift himself off Jo, then lean down to help her to her feet.

He reached down, patting her dress down to get the snow off her, and when he raised his head, he saw tears glinting in her eyes.

"Are you hurt?" he asked in concern. He went from patting her down to kneeling to reach for her ankles.

She took a step back, nearly falling again.

Quickly rising, he managed to catch her. "Where are you hurt? Is it one of your ankles?"

"I'm not hurt." Jo sniffed, brushing her hair from her face.

"Then why are you crying?" Rider reached out, wiping a glistening tear from her cheek.

"Because it's been a sucky day."

Rider didn't know what to say, considering he had paid out the ass for a date with her.

He picked up her radio and purse she had dropped, and as he did, her purse fell open, spilling its contents onto the snow-covered ground. He had to blink twice at what he was seeing.

As his fingertips touched the handle of the gun, Jo beat him to it, grabbing the gun and taking the purse out of his hand. Shoving the pistol back inside the purse, she started to leave.

Rider reached out, taking her arm. "Why in the fuck are you carrying a gun?"

"I forgot it was there. I was going to put it back in the glovebox when I came out of the house. I forgot."

"That still doesn't explain why you carry a gun." He narrowed his eyes at her.

"I carry it for protection."

"Who do you need protection from?"

"So I can protect myself if I need too." She obstinately narrowed her eyes back at him.

"Let me phrase it another way. Why do you feel the need to have a gun for protection?"

"I just do."

"Jo ..."

"I work all day and night. I would be stupid not to have a form of protection when I get called out to some of the back roads. I also live in a junkyard, where some people think they have free rein to steal parts they need."

He had never thought about Jo being alone in the massive junkyard.

"Does it happen often?"

"Enough that I have a gun." Jo rolled her eyes at him.

"Have you recognized any of them?" he asked conversationally as she started walking toward her tow truck.

Rider felt her sidelong glance as he took her elbow when her foot slipped on the icy ground.

"No."

"You're lying."

"It doesn't matter if I am. I deal with it the same way my dad did when he caught them."

"What did Lyle do?"

"Ask them what part they're trying to steal and give them a discount. Now, they pretty much just come for the discount. Saves them nearly getting their asses shot."

"Your mother doesn't want to move in with you so you won't be alone out there?"

"I'm a grown woman; I don't need my mother to hold my hand."

"She remarried?"

Unhappy that he had figured out why her mother hadn't returned to Treepoint at her father's death, she jerked away from him as soon as she touched the door handle. She didn't like discussing that her mother had washed her hands of her when she had decided to return to help her father. Rider let her go so she wouldn't knock his head off when she opened the door.

"Engaged."

The sound of thin ice cracking had him about to warn her, but it was too late. Jo had already lifted a foot onto the floorboard, nearly sending her face first into the side of the seat.

"Dammit to hell!" Jo bellowed in aggravation. "Mother-fucking son of a bitch of a biscuit eater ..."

Rider smothered his laughter at her irritation as she lifted her dress to better see the offending heel. Tossing her purse and radio onto the dashboard, she then grasped his arm to balance herself as she lifted a foot, taking one shoe off. One delicately arched foot went down onto the snow.

"You'll get sick," Rider warned, wincing when the heel she had removed went sailing inside the cabin of the truck.

"Shut up!" she snarled.

When she raised her other foot, Rider took matters into

his own hands. Taking her by the waist, he hefted her onto the seat, removing the shoe from the dangling leg.

Her blue, storm-tossed eyes glinted at him. He could practically count the ways she was mentally killing him in her mind for witnessing the embarrassing situation.

Rider reached out, preventing her from closing the door after she righted herself on the seat. It became a tugging match.

"Pleasure."

Jo stopped trying to shut the door. "Huh?"

"The brand of perfume you're wearing."

"I didn't take you for a man who shopped at Sassy Vixen's." She ran her eyes over his large body as if gauging his size. "I didn't think they would have anything that fits you."

Amused at her tart mockery, he held the door open with one hand, holding her shoe with the other. "A couple of women from the club like to shop there. They ask me to go along to give my opinion. Pleasure is one of my favorite perfumes."

"You're being a dick. You know that, right?" Jo reached out, jerking her shoe out of his hand and throwing it to the side.

"I'm being upright and honest. A few of the brothers have gotten in trouble after not saying straight-out that they have sexual relationships with the women in the club. Since we're about to go on our first date, I just wanted to put it out there that I do."

"Thank you for clarifying theirs and your relationships—"

"No relationships, just sex. As plain and simple as that."

A gurgling came from her chest. "Since you're being so upright and honest, let me clarify mine. We're not going on a real date tomorrow. It's an act of charity for those less fortu-nate. It's as plain and simple as *that*."

"Just so you know, I'm planning on changing your mind."

"Good luck with that. You'd have a better chance of riding Ferguson's old bull that he keeps pinned up behind his house."

"I might surprise you." His lips pressed together in a confident smile. "I love a wild ride."

13

Jo was stupefied as Rider shut her truck door. Turning on the engine, she cranked the heat on high and started her windshield wipers. The window was covered in fine snow, and it took several swipes before she was able to see out it. And when she could, what she saw was Rider watching her from the sidewalk, his hands in his pockets, and his shoulders hunched from the cold wind.

Shivering, she got the hell out of there, not waiting for the truck to warm up. She could practically see her breath in the cold air. She needed to find a place to change her clothes before she froze to death. The diner and the gas station were closed. That left only one other option if she didn't want to go home, which would be a waste of time. As soon as the partygoers hit the slick roads, she would spend the rest of night working.

Her choice made, she drove to Rosie's. Come hell or high water, Mick would keep the bar open until four.

The parking lot was covered in snow, so she parked to the side of the bar and pulled in longways. Pushing her seat back, Jo slipped her feet into her boots, not bothering to lace them before gathering her change of clothes and getting out of the truck, leaving it idling to warm up.

"How was the auction?"

Mick's greeting put her teeth on edge. "Don't ask. You mind if I use your restroom to change?"

"Help yourself. I'll make a fresh pot of coffee for you."

It didn't take her long to change. She was sitting at the bar before the coffee was finished brewing.

"You want me to fill your thermos for you?"

Jo blew on the steaming coffee as she slid her thermos across the bar. "I'd appreciate it. It's going to be a long night. I'll plow the parking lot for you. Call me when you're ready to go home, and I'll give you a ride."

"I can drive," Mick argued.

"Not on those roads. Besides, why take the chance when I'm perfectly willing to give you a ride home and bring you back tomorrow when you're ready to open?"

"Okay, okay. I know better than to argue with you." Mick went to the other side of the bar, taking out a small canvas bag he had stored under the counter. "I packed you a small dinner."

Jo stared at the nylon bag, a lump forming in her throat. "You shouldn't have ..."

"I knew with the weather forecast that you might get too busy to eat, and I didn't think you would eat much at the auction. Was I right?"

"Yes."

"Then I don't have to worry about you getting hungry. You don't take care of yourself."

Jo gave a wry twist of her lips. "It's not like I'll starve to death if I miss a meal."

Mick studied her critically. "If you don't get the fridge and oven fixed, I'm going to see they get fixed myself."

"You worry too much," Jo scoffed. Taking her dress, the

meal Mick had made for her, and her thermos, she stood. "Put them on my tab. I get paid this week, and I'll pay what I owe."

"You don't owe me a dime. I told you that we'd take it out in trade. You keep my parking lot plowed, and I'll keep feeding you."

"And I told you that doesn't work for me. You let me pay you, or I'll stop coming in."

"You're a pain in my ass."

"You love me anyway."

"Yes, I do. I couldn't love you any more if you were my own daughter."

"I love you, too. I better get busy plowing your lot before those Last Riders come in, wanting their nightcap."

"You're not leaving until you tell me who won the auction for a date with you."

She nearly left without telling him. If she didn't think one of The Last Riders would tell him when they came in, she wouldn't have. Mick liked the bikers, and Jo didn't trust herself not to complain about who had won.

"Rider did."

"Rider won?" Mick gaped. "He said he wasn't bidding. You sure he won?"

"Yes, Mick, I'm sure."

"Damn, I wish Moon or Dustin would have. I can see you and Dustin getting along. He's a good boy. Even Moon isn't bad. But Rider? Can you get out of it?"

"I wish. Why? What's wrong with Rider?"

"Nothing. I like Rider. I just can't see you getting along with him. And I just wish Dustin would have won." Mick picked up a bar towel, running it along the length of the counter.

"Spill. What don't you like about Rider?"

"I do like him. He livens the place up when he comes in. It's just that ..."

"Mick ... just tell me."

Mick sighed. "I hear the other Last Riders talking to each other when they think I'm not listening. I'm not going to repeat anything, but he's not a one-woman man."

"That's it?"

"That's all I'm saying. I don't want to see you get hurt."

"I'll tell you the same thing I told Rider. It's not a date, date. It's an act of charity."

Mick laughed so hard his shoulders shook. He even reached for a napkin to wipe his tears.

"What did he say when you told him that?"

"He said that he planned on changing my mind."

"I take it back. You can handle Rider. I wish I could be a fly on a wall and watch you—"

Her radio blared out, interrupting the rest of what Mick was about to say.

"You there, Jo?" Knox's voice came through.

She pushed the button on the side of her radio. "I'm here."

"Gabe can't get the snow plow working. Can you plow the main roads?"

"It depends. My rates went up after dark."

"Just do it. I'll make sure you get paid if I have to do it myself."

"Give me ten minutes."

Jo clicked her radio off. "Don't forget to call me when you're ready to go home," she reminded Mick as she hurried toward the door.

"Be careful out there. That truck doesn't make you invincible," he called out.

The falling snow was blanketing the parking lot. Trudging through it, Jo felt more confident on the icy ground in her boots and coveralls. No longer hampered by her dress and heels, she had no problem jumping into her seat. The toasty warmth of the cabin was a shelter from the wintery storm. She was back in her element, where she belonged.

Pushing the button that would lower the snow plow, she made quick work of scraping down the snow and moving the pile into a corner of the parking lot, giving access to Mick's customers.

When she finished, Jo blew her loud horn, letting Mick know she was done, before pulling out onto the road. Instead of heading directly to town, she drove farther up the mountain, scraping the road. Passing The Last Riders' clubhouse, she didn't stop until she reached the turnoff for Rachel and Cash's home.

Turning down the cutoff, she raised her plow an inch, being careful not to hurt the driveway. Then she turned around in the front yard of the cabin and went over the driveway before returning to the road.

As she neared The Last Riders' clubhouse and factory again, she turned, plowing the parking lot and piling the snow to the side. Satisfied that all the women would get home safely, she drove back toward town.

Her headlights shining on the lonely road highlighted the solitary existence she lived. She missed her father's company; the ache in her heart magnified by the holidays being near. She hadn't even bothered to put up a Christmas tree this year. She missed the things that she had taken for granted before his death like restocking his existing wardrobe or the small gifts she would buy just to put a smile on his weathered face.

Her mother had complained her entire life that her father hadn't been much of father to her, too worried about his next drink and work to care about them, but Jo saw it differently. He had flaws—she wasn't saying he didn't—but his failings had never canceled out the love he had given her every day of his life.

She had been blessed with her father's love, and with the affection Mick was giving her now that her father was gone.

Her thoughts went back to what Mick had been saying before her radio had gone off. A mischievous smile gleamed in the dark cabin.

She was going to give Mick an early Christmas present.

14

"You're dressing up two days in a row?"

Rider tucked his dress shirt into his new jeans as he watched Jewell throw herself down on his bed, making herself comfortable.

"Got a date tonight." He buckled his belt, shifting it lower to hit him around his hips.

"No shit. The whole town knows you're going out with Jo tonight." Tucking a pillow behind her head, Jewell lifted a thigh, making her T-shirt hike to her waist.

Going to his dresser, he picked up his comb, running it through his damp hair. "What are you planning on doing tonight?"

"I'm planning on having a better night with Moon and Rush than you're going to have with Jo."

"Jealous?"

"Of Jo? Hell no."

"Good." Rider shrugged his shoulders to make sure his black shirt fit right. "Should I put on another shirt that fits me tighter around the shoulders?" He wanted to show off his muscles to their best advantage.

"You look good." She raised her other leg. "You want me to show you how good you look?"

Rider laid his comb back down on the dresser, then went to his closet to shrug into an expensive black leather jacket.

"You're really pulling out all the stops to impress her. Are you going to go through this much trouble when you go out with Aly?" Her lips pursed in a moue of disappointment as she flopped back onto the bed.

"No." Rider went to his nightstand for his wallet, sliding it into his back pocket.

"So, Jo's special?"

He stared down at her directly. "She could be. We'll see, won't we?" Snagging one of her feet, he pulled her off his bed. With a soft smack on her ass, he then turned her toward the door. "You shouldn't keep Moon and Rush waiting. You know how Rush gets when you do."

"You're throwing me out of your room?" Jewell's astonishment had her freezing and Rider nearly bumping into her.

"I don't want my bed messed up in case I convince Jo to come back with me."

"Yeah, that's not going to happen."

"You never know."

"Yes, I do. If you're expecting Jo to come back here to fuck you, you clearly don't know her at all. The woman hasn't been on a date since she came to town."

"That's because the right man hasn't asked her." Giving her a gentle push, he got her moving again.

Closing the door behind them, he locked his door, making sure it would be empty when he returned. Each of the brothers had their own room, and most of them wouldn't enter his room unless the door was open, but if he was able to convince Jo to come back with him, he didn't want to chance that it would have someone in there fucking, waiting for his return. It was a habit he would have to break if his date with Jo went the way he planned.

Rider felt Jewell tugging on the sleeve of his jacket as he was about to go down the steps.

"Haven't you asked her out yourself?"

"That's water under the bridge."

Jewell's hand fell away as he started down the steps.

"Rider," she yelled down the landing.

Rider looked up to see she was leaning over the rail. Jewell seemed about to say something, then changed her mind.

"Have a good time," she finished when he kept staring upward at her.

Hearing the pinging of his cell phone, he took it out of his pocket. The text was from Jo, telling him she was outside.

Returning his attention to Jewell, he could see the concern she couldn't hide.

"Jewell, nothing is going to change our friendship. You know that, right?"

"I remember Razer telling me the same thing."

"And you're still friends with him."

"We are, but it's different now. Just like with Knox, Lucky, Cash, and Viper. It's not the same."

"Nothing stays the same. One day, you might wake up and decide to leave. Any of us could. They might not fuck you anymore, but that doesn't mean that none of us wouldn't die for you. Just like you will always be there for any of us if we need you."

Rider knew how hard it had been for Jewell to switch from lover to friends with the other brothers. The men had gone through the same thing when Evie and Bliss had fallen in love.

"I just never expected you to fall in love again."

"I'm not going to fall in love with Jo. That would be

impossible." Rider saw the relief she couldn't hide at his admission. "I'm not looking for love from Jo."

"Then what are you wanting from her?"

"I'll know when I find it." Rider couldn't explain to her any more than he could explain to himself. "I have to go; she's waiting. We good?"

"Yes. When you get home, let me know how your date went."

"I will." Rider opened the front door, giving a hurried nod toward Moon, who was watching the door. He then went down the long flight of stairs to the parking lot, seeing Jo's headlights glowing in the dark. The lights were so bright he was halfway down the steps before he realized Jo wasn't in the large tow truck she normally drove. It was only when he was walking to the passenger door that he saw it was Cash's.

Opening the door, expecting to get inside, he was dumbfounded to see Mag already there. Cash's grandmother was bundled in a coat with a blanket wrapped around her legs.

"Scoot over, Mag," Jo urged the old woman.

Rider wanted to toss Mag out of the truck. Instead, he got inside and closed the door.

Placing an arm along the back of the seat to give himself more room, he tried to wrap his mind around how Mag had ended up going on his date with Jo.

"How you doing tonight, Mag?"

"Was better before we had to pick you up."

"You know you love me. Don't be so standoffish."

The demon woman's eyes glowered at him.

He shouldn't have expected Jo to give in gracefully. Jo had lived up to her word, not taking their date seriously—the clothes she was wearing said as much. Her thick sweater and old jeans wouldn't be seen on anyone trying to make an impression. Rider couldn't imagine anyone he regularly dated wearing them on even the fourth or fifth date. At least she wasn't wearing the coveralls. She didn't even look his way as she backed up and started driving toward town.

"Rachel and Cash asked me to stay the weekend with Mag. They want to get an early start on their Christmas shopping. I hope you don't mind."

Rider didn't think she would care if he did, so he didn't answer. "I made reservations at both the Pink Slipper and King's. I didn't know which one you would prefer—"

"Mag wants to have dinner at Rosie's. I thought you would agree since you spend a lot of time there, and it'll be easier on your wallet after you bid so much on our date."

"Saturday nights at Rosie's can be a little rowdy, but I'm game if you ladies have your hearts set on it."

"We do." Jo flicked her blinker before turning into the parking lot.

Rider opened his door as Jo opened hers. From the lights on in the parking lot, he could see Jo lower the tailgate and the wheelchair resting in the bed.

Going to the tailgate, he lifted the chair down, opened it, and then pushed it toward the door he had left open.

Mag had swung her legs to the side so they were hanging down from her seat. Knowing he was facing a smackdown, he still bravely opened his arms.

"May I be of some assistance?" Courteously, he waited for the smack to come. Instead, Mag gave him a curt nod, her hands going to his shoulders.

"Did you climb into the truck by yourself?" Rider asked, lifting the woman down and turning to place her gently in her wheelchair.

"Cash helped," Jo said as she reached inside the truck for Mag's blanket. "He said you would help get her out."

"He did? That's interesting."

"Why's that interesting?" Jo swung him a sidelong glance as he pushed Mag's wheelchair toward the bar.

"He didn't tell me his great-grandmother was coming with us tonight when I saw him at lunch."

"Didn't you get my message?" Jo walked farther ahead so she could open the door for them.

"Was Cash supposed to tell me?"

Rider didn't miss the faint blush that filled Jo's cheeks as he and Mag went inside. He thought it was because of guilt for letting Mag tag along with them without asking.

Closing the door, she placed her hand over his, preventing him from going farther into the bar. "I'm sorry. I tried to call. When you didn't answer, I called the factory. I spoke to Jewell. She said you were busy. I explained that I promised to take Mag to Rosie's when Rachel and Cash went to Lexington. She was sick when I made the promise, so I haven't been able to keep it. Rachel's been tired of being cooped up because of the weather, so Cash and I convinced her to go tonight and tomorrow. I tried to reschedule our date, but Jewell said she was sure you wouldn't mind and said she'd pass on my message that, if you wanted to reschedule, to call me. When you didn't, I assumed it was okay with you." Jo started to grab the handle of the wheelchair from him.

He hadn't answered her call earlier in the day because he thought Jo had been trying to break their date. That Jewell was responsible for their date taking a detour was something he would have to talk to Jewell about when he got home.

"I get the company of two beautiful women, so I'm not angry." He twisted his hand under hers, averting her from pulling Mag away from him.

"I'm settled. Can I order a hamburger now, or are we going to stand here all damn night?" Mag snorted, reaching down to wheel herself.

"I got it, Mag." Rider laughed as Mick came from behind the counter.

"Mag! Cash and Rachel finally let you escape?"

"Like I was going to let them stop me." The old woman raised a frail hand to Mick, who ignored it to reach down and give her a bear hug. "You trying to kill me?"

Despite her words, Mag stared up mistily at Mick.

"You look younger every time I see—"

"Cut the bullshit and fix me a hamburger. I want a beer, too. Make sure you put extra onions and mustard on it for me."

"I'll take the same." Jo moved a chair from one of the tables.

As Rider started to roll Mag to the table, Mag stopped the wheels from moving.

"I want to sit at the bar." She obstinately swiveled the wheelchair backward.

"Okay." Rider patiently pushed the chair toward the bar, where most of the stools had already been taken.

Maneuvering it between two stools that were empty, he stopped, looking down to see what Mag would do next.

"What are you waiting for? Help me," she brashly demanded.

"Mag, maybe you would be more comfortable at the table," Jo tried to divert Mag from sitting at the bar, staring uneasily at the high stool.

"If you want to go sit at a table, go ahead, but I want to sit here."

"I don't blame her. I like sitting at the bar, too." Lifting the fragile woman from her chair, Rider placed her on the stool. Folding the chair, he then guided it between two stools. "You take the stool next to her," he said to Jo.

"Where are you going to sit?"

"Carter doesn't mind giving up his seat, do you?" Rider laid his hand on Carter's shoulder, staring down at him with the threatening gleam in his eyes that he had perfected in the military.

"No problem." The middle-aged school janitor immediately got off his stool, took his mug of beer, and moved to the table Mag had snubbed.

"That wasn't nice." Jo turned from checking on Mag to him, then gave Carter a sympathetic glance.

"Mick, put Carter's tab on my bill. I'll take the same as Mag and Jo to eat." Assessing if she was still irritated at him for asking Carter to move, Rider waited for her to give him another reprimand.

Instead, Jo slid the bar nuts toward Mag, saying, "Thanks, Mick."

"I'll get them on the grill." Mick gave them each a beer before heading back to start the grill.

Rider took a drink of his beer, listening to the blaring music. The beer was still poised at his lips when he spotted Curt Dawkins at a large table on the other side of the bar. Curt caught his eyes, too. Using his beer bottle, Rider acknowledged the wave Curt gave him as his friends turned to see who Curt was waving to.

Fucking hell. Rider hoped Curt wouldn't make a move to approach them. That was all he needed for his first date with Jo to become the dumpster fire that Jewell had stoked by not relaying the message Jo had given him.

When Curt remained seated, Rider gave silent thanks to the man upstairs.

"How's it going with your car being redone?"

"Carl's not really saying. His texts are few and far between. I'd be worried, but Train said that was the way he acted when he re-did Killyama's car."

"Has Train given it to her yet?"

"No, he's waiting for Christmas."

"It's a nice gift. I'm sure she'll love it." Jo tried to take a few of the bar nuts from the bowl. Receiving a glare from Mag, she pulled her hand back.

"She should have joined the military," Rider joked, reaching for a bowl near him and moving it within her grasp.

"Thanks."

Taking a few nuts for himself and popping them into his mouth, he chewed them thoughtfully as they waited for their burgers.

"When's your date with Aly?"

Her question had him wishing he hadn't eaten the nuts when they clogged his throat.

"Sunday."

"You and Aly will make a good match. Neither of you let any grass grow under your feet."

"That's about the only thing we have in common. Every time I see her, she's talking about clothes or shoes."

"When has she talked to you about clothes and shoes? Aly's been gone from Treepoint so long I didn't realize she had resumed her old friendships."

Rider felt like he had just strayed into a hidden minefield.

"Some of the women from the club shop at the store she works at."

"Is that how she met you?"

Rider took a long swallow of his beer, wishing Mick would hurry up with the food. However, when he saw Mick flip the burgers over on the grill, he knew he wouldn't be able to use that as an excuse to keep from answering the question.

"Moon introduced me to her when she came to the club."

Rider held the bowl steady when she almost flipped it over.

"Aly's partied with The Last Riders?"

"I wouldn't say she's partied with us, but she has been there." He was breaking a rule about not discussing the comings and goings of those who entered the club's doors. Then again, one thing he had learned from the relationships of the other brothers was secrets inevitably came out. He was already starting behind the eight ball of Jo's opinion of him. If they did develop a relationship in the future, Rider wanted all his bases covered.

"What are you two whispering about?" Mag bellowed from Jo's other side.

"We're talking about if we should let you eat that burger with all those onions on it." Jo smiled at Mick as he set their basket of food down in front of them.

Mag snorted, reaching for the mustard. "That's not what it sounded like to me."

"Were you eavesdropping?" Rider left out the "old bitch" he wanted to add to his sentence.

"Everyone thinks I'm deaf or senile. I have a perfectly good pair of ears on my head. You were talking about The Last Riders' parties. I tried to get Cash and Rachel to take me a couple of times, but they said it would be too strenuous for me. Like it takes any energy to sit my ass down in my wheelchair."

Rider lost his appetite when she snorted into her beer. His date was going from bad to worse. He had to keep reminding himself how Jo had looked and smelled the night before without the battleax sitting next to her.

"The next time they tell me no, I'm going to call you, Rider," the battleax demanded with a domineering glare.

"You do that." Rider wouldn't be answering any calls coming from Mag on a Friday night, or any other night of the week.

He had to give Cash props for not giving the Grim Reaper a helping hand in the old bitch's demise.

"Where are our burgers, Mick? We ordered ours before them."

The voice behind them had his date going from a dumpster fire to a raging inferno as Jo dropped her burger into the plastic basket.

Curt settled his arms companionably over both his and Jo's shoulders as he squeezed between their stools. "Do I need to come over and sit with them to get waited on?"

His disparaging tone had Mag twisting on her stool. She waved her veined, purplish hand in his face as her eyes snapped out at him. "Be gone, Satan's helper, before I get Mick to give me that shotgun he keeps under the counter and I give you a return ticket to where you were spawned from."

15

"You old crow, you aren't strong enough to pick up that burger, let alone that shotgun." Curt eyed the woman as if he didn't take Mag seriously.

"Try me, you little pissant. I'll wrap that barrel around your motherfu—"

"Calm down, Mag. Remember your blood pressure." Jo jerked out from under Curt's arm, using her elbow to jab him in his ribs.

"Go sit back down." Mick reached over the bar to catch Mag's arm when her hand came dangerously close to hitting Curt. "You ordered your burgers well-done. They'll be done in a minute."

"If I knew it was going to take this long, I would have ordered it rare."

"Like the taste of burned food, huh? You're going to get a lot of it when you get to hell, you son of Satan!"

"You keep running that trap of yours, when you finally die, I'm going to be the first one to piss on your grave."

"I don't have to worry about that; you won't be able to find my tombstone. You'd have to be able to read to do that."

Jo used her elbow to jab Curt again. "Just go, Curt."

Curt wasn't about to be interrupted from arguing with Mag.

"You self-righteous hag, I can read better than you! What grade did you get to before dropping out? Fifth? I'm college educated, and I'm smart enough to know how you bought that house you're living in by selling liquor and that stank-ass pussy of yours."

Jo was reaching for her beer bottle to brain the man she hated more than anyone else in the world, but before she could, Rider stood, and Mick came around the counter.

"Curt, Cash isn't going to be happy you're bad-mouthing his grandmother. I would watch your step before you can't remove your foot out of your ass, where Cash is going to shove it when he finds out."

The menacing bully hiked his jeans up his sagging belly. "Me and Cash are friends."

"Cash and I are friends, and I know better than bad-mouthing Mag."

"You and I are two different kettles of fish. I didn't have to pay for Jo's company. She gave it to me for free."

Fury blinded her. Rage she had never believed herself capable of had her nail's coming out to scratch the smug smile off his ugly face. Her nails only found air, though, as Rider had already used Curt's T-shirt to jerk him toward him.

As he heaved him over the counter, Jo was watched in amazement as Curt landed on the other side.

"Rider, I'll handle this." Mick tried to stop a coldly furious Rider she had never seen before. The sexy Rider from last night, and the charming one who had been casually flirting with her like a schoolboy, was replaced by a vengeful biker who didn't need the club's jacket to instill fear.

Jo stood on her tiptoes to look over the bar, seeing Curt

staring up at the ceiling in a daze. Justin and Tanner came running over to look, too.

Mag's laughter only made the situation worse.

Rachel and Cash would kill her if anything happened to the woman while she had promised to take care of her. There was no way Rider would be able to fight off three men.

Her hand went to her radio to get Knox to come to the bar, but before she could press the button, Rider and Mick went behind the counter.

Rider callously yanked Curt to his feet, pinning his arm behind his back and almost planting his ruddy face against the hot grill.

When Justin and Tanner tried to come around the counter, Mick lifted his shotgun out from its hiding spot. The sound of cocking the rifle stopped Curt's cousins in their tracks.

"Hold on, boys. This is between Rider and Curt. He doesn't need your help."

"Shh …" Jo unsuccessfully tried to get Mag to stop laughing.

"That boy has more balls than I gave him credit for," she heckled.

"Mag, please … you're just making it worse." Jo tried again to shush the woman.

"How am I making it worse?" Mag gave her a gleeful smirk. "Go ahead and fry that son of a bitch, Rider. I like my meat with a little pink showing."

"Go sit back down, Tanner and Justin. Curt doesn't need your help, do you?" Rider coldheartedly held his captive over the burgers that were sizzling under his nose, lowering Curt's face another centimeter toward the grill as loose tendrils of his hair curled at the heat.

"Go sit down!" Curt screamed out when Rider twisted his arm behind him higher.

The two men reluctantly returned to their table. The rest of the bar watched, but made no move to stop or interfere.

They weren't the only ones afraid to interfere. She was, too. Other than flipping Curt over the counter and holding the man over the grill, Rider didn't exhibit any anger. She had heard of stone-cold killers, but she had never expected to meet one.

The handsome-faced, laidback man who she had seen driving around town with women, cutting up, often acting like a clown when his friends were near, wasn't the man she was fearfully staring at now, about to maim a man without getting grease splatter on his shirt.

"Mick is going to fix your food to go, which I'm going to pay for you and your family. You are then going to leave without another word to either of those women. Do you understand me?" Rider unemotionally waited for his answer.

"Yes," Curt choked out.

Rider released Curt's arm, allowing him to rise.

Jo read the hatred on Curt's face at his humiliation, and Rider's inflexible expression. While Rider might not have any visible expression, his body was taut and ready for any move Curt might make.

Curt was the first to move his gaze away. "I lost my temper. I'm sorry."

Jo didn't believe his apology for a second, and neither did Rider.

"That's not the only thing you lost. Send Tanner to get your paycheck on Monday. You're fired."

"You can't fire me. Jewell's the manager. What I do on my off time isn't reason to fire me. I'm a good worker. I'll sue."

"Jewell may be the manager, but I'm one of the owners, and I say you're fired. You want to sue, go ahead. You won't win. Look over your contract. In the fine print, you'll see that The Last Riders have the right to end your employment at any time. I'll clean out your locker and give the contents to Tanner when he picks up your paycheck."

Shoving Rider aside to go around the counter, Curt threatened, "You'll be calling me Tuesday to apologize, and I'll be back at work by Wednesday. No one treats me this way and gets away with it—no one." With the counter safely between them, Curt's bravado had returned.

"Mick, pack their food to go. They'll be leaving."

"I don't want the fucking food. It's slop anyway. Tanner, Justin, let's go. We'll eat at the diner. You'll be calling me, Rider; you'll see."

"I won't."

Jo shakily sat back down on her stool as Rider took his, and Curt's minions flanked each side of his back as they moved toward the door.

"Let the door hit your ass on the way out!" Mag cackled.

"You prune-faced bitch, you're going to get what's coming to you, too!" Curt snarled, ducking when a beer bottle came sailing through the air, breaking on the wall an inch from his head.

Jo grabbed her beer bottle when Mag would have thrown hers, too.

The three cousins took off at a run when Rider stood up at Curt's insult. Jo grabbed the back of his belt, yanking his ass back down while also shoving Mag's burger closer to her.

"Both of you eat. Forget about them." Her fingers trembled as she forced herself to take a bite of the cold burger.

Mick took the burgers off the grill, throwing the charred meat into the trash before coming to stand in front of them. "He means it, Rider. Curt is a vindictive son of a bitch."

"I'm not worried about Curt."

"You should be," Jo seconded Mick's opinion at Rider's unconcern. "When I didn't give him a tow the other day, he had his cousins egg my house."

Rider turned his head sharply to look at her. "Why didn't you file a report with Knox?"

"Believing it and proving it are two different things."

"Next time something like that happens, I want to know. That's how Curt is getting off scot-free, because no one files a police report."

Jo opened the bag of chips that came with her burger. "Really?" She raised a sardonic eyebrow at him. "I reported that he and his friends raped me when I came back to town. Nothing was done. I reported when he ran me off the road and totaled my car. Nothing was done. I reported my house being broken into three times and that Curt had a pair of my panties hanging from his rearview mirror. You want to know what was done about that?" Jo asked rhetorically, not giving him time to answer. "Nothing. Every time I try to bring charges against Curt, one of his cousins working for the state police or one working at the courthouse stops the investigation."

"Give me another beer, Mick." Mag's appetite hadn't been affected by Curt's behavior or Jo's angry outburst. "I told you to borrow my handgun. One bullet is all it would take. That dumpling is filled with so much hard air it would take a week for the stench to clear."

"I don't want to kill him. I want him behind bars where he deserves to be."

"Why didn't you tell me that your house has been broken into three times?"

Jo could tell that Mick's feeling had been hurt because she hadn't confided in him.

"You worry about me enough as it is. I just installed cameras. If they do it again, I'll have a tape to prove it."

"You don't have a tape of them egging your house?" Rider shoved his food away.

"No, I only had enough money to buy cameras for the

inside. They hadn't done anything to the outside before. I think they were worried a customer would drive onto the lot and see them. Curt must have been so mad when I refused the tow that his anger got the best of him, and he didn't care if his cousins were caught."

"He's escalating, thinking he's untouchable. In the morning, Train and I will come by to install a new security system."

"No, thanks. I'll buy the cameras when I get paid." Jo quickly refused his offer.

"I wasn't offering," Rider stated firmly. "You want Curt behind bars, this is the way to do it. I'll wire it so that Knox can see and dispatch a car before you'd have to call."

Jo bit her bottom lip. She really didn't want Knox capable of seeing the comings and goings at her junkyard, but it would make it easier to catch Curt and his cousins.

"If it happens again, I'll let you know, and then you can install your security system. I may be blowing it out of proportion. It could have been teenagers out for a good time."

Rider wasn't happy with her decision. She could tell he was going to keep arguing unless she distracted him.

"Are you going to ask me to dance, or are we going to sit here all night?" Getting off her stool, Jo cautiously offered her hand.

She hadn't willing offered her hand to a man since she had been raped, too worried they would misunderstand and take it as an overture she didn't mean. She was smart enough to know that not all men were like Curt. She just hadn't been willing to take the chance they were.

Rider looked down at her hand, somehow sensing she didn't do it often. The inflexible expression that had been on his face since Curt had appeared at their backs lightened, returning to the one she was more familiar with. "You like to dance?"

His fingers tightened on hers when Carter stumbled toward the bar and nearly barreled into them. Helping her dodge him, Rider moved her safely away.

Lowering her eyes to the floor, she felt safe for the first time in so many years she had lost count. It seemed like fear and terror had been trailing behind her like a dark shadow, waiting for the opportunity to strike when she least expected it.

"I do, but I'm afraid I'm not very good at it," she confessed, dropping his hand to turn toward the small sectioned-off area that Mick had formed into a dance floor.

"You did okay last night when I danced with you."

"That's because it was a slow dance." The song blasting out from the old speakers hanging on the walls was anything but slow. Not knowing what to do, she basically just shifted her weight from one leg to the other.

"Mick, play some slow music!"

She gave Rider a dirty look at his yell that had all the men staring at them. "Where's your sense of adventure? You could have taught me some moves."

Sin was in his eyes and in his grin as he took her hands and pulled her closer to his body. Her nipples pebbled when she found herself plastered against Rider's chest.

Releasing one of her hands, he brought his to her ass as he parted his legs until she was straddling a long thigh wedged between hers.

"Is this adventurous enough for you?" he mocked, watching her reaction.

"Are you making fun of me?" Jo scrunched up her face in a pain-filled mask.

Rider lost his amusement, straightening away from her and dropping his hands from her.

Jo burst out laughing. "Sucker. I was just joking." She took the step he had put between them, laying her hands on his chest and making sure she gave herself breathing room so she could restore her raging hormones to a manageable level. One that didn't freak her the hell out.

"Damn, I never expected you to have a sense of humor." He moved her slowly around the dance floor, keeping the distance she had initiated.

"I guess we both have things to learn about the other." She mischievously waved toward Mag when she caught sight of her. "You should ask her to dance. She would love it."

"Is that another attempt at humor?" He stopped moving, staring down at her suspiciously.

"No. Come on; it would make her night," she urged.

He seemed to be considering it for a second, making her think he was a really nice guy and that she had underestimated him.

"No."

"Come on; be brave."

"I'm afraid of her."

"She wouldn't hurt you. She's all talk."

"That's what I'm afraid of. I'm afraid that mouth of hers would make me want to wring her neck."

"That's not nice."

"It is what it is."

As a new song started, Jo tried to return to the bar, but Rider didn't release her, still dancing.

"I'll make a deal with you. I'll even give you two options, because I'm a really nice guy."

Jo continued to dance with him, curious about the deal he was offering.

"I'll dance with Mag. I'll even make sure she's invited to a Last Rider's party ... if you go out with me on another date."

"What's the other option?" Jo warily prepared herself.

When Rider wanted something, he could be as charming as a snake handler. However, she had to give him the same consideration he had given her when she had asked him to dance with Mag.

His easy smile showed his even, white teeth. "You can give me a good night's kiss after I help you get Mag back inside her cabin."

"I'm not crazy about either of those choices."

"Then I guess Mag isn't dancing."

Jo looked to where Mag was talking to Mick at the bar. She hadn't seen the woman so happy since Jo was a little girl and Mag was running drunks off with her broomstick.

"I'll go out with you again," she relented. It would be a gift to Rachel and Cash, too. The woman would quit moaning about being ready to die, at least until after she went to one of The Last Riders' parties.

"Are you still joking?"

"No, I'm serious. I'll go out with you again."

His smile disappeared at her capitulation. "I should have made myself clear before you agreed. I'm not dancing a slow dance with her."

It was her turn to smile. "I wouldn't expect you to. She'll be happy with a fast one."

"Cool. We're on the same page. You sure you won't be jealous?" he teased.

"I don't think I have anything to be worried about. Mag doesn't wear perfume. She wears Bengay."

16

" **G** ood night, Mag."

Rider stood outside the bedroom door, listening to Jo and Mag after he had excused himself to go back to Cash's truck for her wheelchair.

"You sure you don't want me to sit in the living room until Rider leaves?"

"No, I want you safe and snug in your bed while I drive him home. I'm going to take him as soon as I walk out of your door, so you don't have to worry."

Rider could hear her sarcastic snort from the other side of the door.

"That bastard only needs a second to get in your panties. How do you think Cash caught Rachel? It's how my husband caught me, God rest his soul. Don't underestimate that no-good son of a bitch."

Rider almost reached for the doorknob, wanting to strangle the bitch. She was calling him names after rolling over his toes with her wheelchair numerous times when he was dancing with her, and he suspected he felt a hernia growing inside him from carrying her most of the night. The least Mag could do was put in a good word for him.

"Is Rider related to Cash and your husband?"

"No."

"Then I'm good."

Rider heard the sounds of the bed creaking and Jo moving around the room. When he saw the doorknob turning, he hurried into the living room, managing to sink down on the couch as the bedroom door opened.

"I'm coming. I'm just putting the wheelchair where Mag can reach it," Jo called out.

"Take your time," Rider called back. "I'm not in any hurry." He knew that would set the old witch off again.

When the door snapped closed again, he knew he was right. Tempted to go eavesdrop again, Rider controlled himself, too afraid he wouldn't be able to restrain himself from giving Mag the answers to her prayers.

"I'm sorry it took so long. I'll drive you home."

Rider rose from the couch, seeing the subtle hint of fear lurking in her eyes.

Giving her space so he wouldn't brush against her, Rider turned to the other side of the couch. It had been a long time since he had been a gentleman, but he did remember how.

Going to the door, he opened it, politely waiting until she went through it before going outside. He also opened the driver door for her before going to the other side and getting inside.

"It's cold tonight." He started the conversation to relax her. With Mag and Mick so near her at the bar, she had loosened up, laughing and joking as he had whirled Mag's wheelchair around the dance floor. Now, unless he could get her to relax around him while alone, he wouldn't have a chance with her.

Jo might have blown off Mag's comments, but deep

down, it had only strengthened her reservations about him.

"If you ever need company on nights when you have to work, text me. I get insomnia at night, and it would give me someone to talk to instead of talking to myself." He leaned comfortably back on the seat, turning to the side where he could study her.

Jo sent him a searching look as she made the turn onto the road that led to The Last Riders. "You have insomnia?"

Rider knew from experience that, to get other another person's guard down, you had to reveal something about yourself while withholding the whole truth.

"Many servicemen and women do."

"Rachel said you and Cash served in the Navy together."

"I served with all the original members of The Last Riders."

"The original members?"

"You know them all. Viper, Cash, Razer, Knox, Lucky, and Train." He didn't mention Gavin. So far, he hadn't been seen in town.

Rider didn't know how much Rachel had told Jo about The Last Riders, so he took the middle ground. It would keep him out of trouble with Viper while giving insights into the club that would correlate with anything Rachel had told her.

"Of course, Knox is no longer a member."

"Of course," Jo mimicked his answer, but Rider could tell she didn't believe the gossip The Last Riders had spread around Treepoint.

"How does Monday sound for our second date?" he asked as the truck rounded the curve to the clubhouse.

"Wednesday sounds better. You have a date with Aly tomorrow night, and you always go out with Carly on Monday nights. Tuesdays are reserved for Claire. I wouldn't want to step on her toes. She's the only cashier at the gas station I like. She lets me fill my thermos for free."

"You don't mind stepping on Kelly's toes?"

"No, I don't go to the jewelry store enough to worry about it. I'll have to take the heat when I see her at church, but she'll get over it by the next week."

"Living in Treepoint does have its disadvantage." He didn't make a move to get out of the truck when Jo brought it to a stop at the bottom of the steps that led to the clubhouse.

"Sometimes, but I love how close everyone is. My mother's and father's family lived here their whole lives. I'm the only one left now. It makes me sad that, when I die, there won't be any Turners left.

"You're still young enough not to have that worry."

Rider could see her sadness as she stared out the windshield.

"Not only is my family not very prolific, they usually married at a young age."

"It's too cold and dark to have that depressing thought." Rider wanted to reach out and touch her cheek, but he knew it would be rebuffed.

Jo gave a shaky laugh. "You're right; it is. Thank you for dancing with Mag. She didn't say anything, but I know she appreciated it."

Rider doubted it. It certainly didn't keep the witch from bad-mouthing him.

"I didn't do it for Mag. I did it for you. You're beautiful when you smile."

He expected her to laugh off his compliment. Instead, she did something entirely different that tugged at his heart-strings.

"Rachel and Cash told me that you were joking around about losing your chance to buy Willa's candy during the auction because you spent all your money on the date with me." She opened the glove compartment and took out a small

178

container, handing it to him. "I had Willa make me some this morning."

Rider took the container, shocked at the simple gift. "I hope you didn't have to pay the same price for it as Moon did."

"No, she took it out in trade. I'll be plowing the church's parking lot the next snowstorm."

"Like you wouldn't have done it anyway. You have a soft heart, Jo." To keep himself from losing the ground he had gained with her, he got out of the truck, taking his candy. "I'll see you Monday. I don't see Carly anymore."

The light from the interior of the truck highlighted her surprised reaction. "Why not?"

"A couple of reasons."

"Any of them to do with the way she talked to Jewell during the auction?"

"Jewell doesn't carry tales."

"She must not carry messages either. Night, Rider."

Rider wanted to swear rather than close the door, but he didn't. Stepping away from the truck, he cursed under his breath as he watched Jo drive away.

Getting close to Jo was like getting near a lava pit; you never knew when a spark would scorch you.

Her barb reminded him he needed to talk to Jewell, but he had someone else he needed to talk to first.

Seeing Viper's lights were still on, Rider walked across the parking lot. He then went up Viper and Winter's steps and knocked on the door. It took a couple minutes before the door was opened and Viper let him enter.

"You have a second to talk?" He kept his voice lowered, not wanting to disturb Winter and their daughter.

"It can't wait until morning?"

"I'd rather get it over with tonight."

Viper nodded, shutting the door behind them and leading

him into the family room .

"What's up?"

"I fired Curt tonight."

"Why?"

"He disrespected the woman I was with."

Viper's face hardened at Rider's brief explanation. "That woman being Jo?"

"It doesn't matter who it was. She was with me. Curt went too far. I'm fucking tired of waiting to find shit out on him. I'll take care of him myself."

"One of the reasons we've had to wait is because Jo would want to know what happened to him if he suddenly disappeared."

"She'll be glad he's gone. Why haven't you or Knox told me and the other brothers that he broke into her house?"

"We have. You must have had your mind on something else and weren't paying attention."

"Well, I am now. That shit's going to stop."

"Why?"

"Doesn't matter. If I deal with Curt, it gets him out of your hair and Jo's."

Viper planted his feet in a firm stance, crossing his arms. "And how are you going to accomplish that? We can't have any more disappearances connected to us with us taking out Crash and Candi."

"The Last Riders weren't responsible for Candi's disappearance."

"Anyone searching for her will find the connection between The Last Riders and the Destructors."

Rider shoved his hands into his jacket pockets. "I've never used my position as one of the owners to exert my influence. I've been content to let you and Shade runs things, but Curt's made his last dime working for us."

Viper stiffened. "Anything else you want to change?"

"No. I'm pretty cool about everything else." The fire crackling in the fireplace had him seeking the warmth. Staring down into the glowing embers of the wood, he thought of home.

"You've never had a problem leaving me to take the lead. Why now?"

"It's going nowhere waiting for Curt to slip up. He isn't going to spill any secrets about any of his affairs with underage girls. None of his family or friends will either. They're too afraid of him." His gaze stayed on the embers, his mind far away in another state and place.

"You're going home next month for the holidays, and we'll be the ones stuck with the repercussions of firing Curt. He's not going to take it without retaliation."

"I hope there is. I won't be taking my vacation. If there is retaliation, I'll be ready for it."

"You're not going home?"

"No. What we've been doing hasn't been working. Maybe this will shake Curt enough that he will make a mistake."

"I wouldn't build any castles on hopes and prayers. And for fucking sure I wouldn't pin any hopes that Curt will give Knox something to charge him with."

"Maybe so." His leather jacket tightened as he shrugged. "But I'm the only hope Jo has of getting any justice."

"We all want to see Curt pay. He's turned his wife into a walking zombie with the medications she's been given. None of the students who have graduated are saying a word, despite Winter's pleas. Curt thinks he's untouchable, and his family's connections are proving him right."

"The thing about people who think they are invincible is that they always have one fatal flaw. You want to know what it is?"

Rider could hear the smile in Viper's voice as he answered, "You."

17

The tow truck packed the slushy snow down as Jo navigated the back road. Turning the wheel, she turned onto another dirt road that was barely visible, low hanging trees scraping the roof of the truck. No one in town came in this direction, unless they were hunting game or scouting out a location to grow their pot plants.

"Damn," Jo swore out loud when an overgrown brush scraped the paint on the side of her truck.

A quarter of a mile farther ahead, the road widened into a clearing. Bringing the truck to a stop, she waited as the late afternoon sunlight turned to dusk. She should have gone home to change into her coveralls before coming to the scheduled meeting.

Rachel and Cash had arrived back home late, apologizing for the delay by saying they spent too long talking to Tate and Sutton when they had picked up Ema. Jo had waved off their apologies, not wanting to miss her meeting.

Feeling grouchy that she could have taken her time and gone home to change, she was about to reach for her phone to send a text when she saw headlights in her rearview mirror.

The blue car went around her tow truck, the driver pulling alongside her.

Rolling her window down, she waited for the woman in the car to do the same thing.

"I was about to leave. You were supposed to be here twenty minutes ago," Jo vented, glancing at her watch to confirm how late it was.

"Willa came into the store as I was closing my register. She wanted to give me advice on what I should and shouldn't do when I go out with Rider tonight." Aly rolled her eyes heavenward.

"I guess being late for your date wasn't one of them." Jo settled back on her seat, resting her arm on the door.

"It was weird as hell. I know without a doubt the advice she gave would irritate Rider, like I haven't already figured him out since hanging out there. If I hadn't heard The Last Riders were trying to hook you up with him, I would have fallen for it. Kind of made me disappointed in Willa, her being a Christian and all."

Jo's lips tightened at Aly's sarcasm.

"Willa is a Christian. You should get off your couch sometime. You would see her working late at night, fixing lunch bags for the school children for the weekends, or—"

"Okay, I know you like Willa, so I'll keep my mouth shut."

"Please, that would be great."

"I thought you would be in a better mood after your date with Rider last night. How did it go?"

"Fine. That's what I wanted to talk to you about. I think we should come up with another plan ... I don't feel comfortable doing this anymore. I didn't want to do it in the first place, and now that I spent a little time with him, I think we're making a big mistake."

"We're sticking to the plan. It's working. Why would we change it now?"

"I'm getting a terrible feeling that Rider isn't the man we think he is. He's creeping me out."

"Rider is creeping you out? What did he do?"

"He hasn't done anything creepy." Jo tried to think of a way to explain the vibe that Rider was more dangerous than they believed him to be. "Something isn't right. I'm afraid Rider's not as easygoing as he pretends to be."

"Rider couldn't act his way out of a paper bag. He has his mind on two things: sex and food. As long as he has a steady amount of both, he's an open book."

"I think you're wrong," Jo argued.

"I'm the one who would know. I've been learning everything about him since I started going to the club with Moon. All I have to do is talk about shoes and my discount, and they tell me anything I want to know about him. I don't care that you're getting cold feet. The only way we're going to get even with Curt is by making it personal with The Last Riders. That will get them to take care of our problems. Anyone who makes the mistake of fucking with one of The Last Riders' women disappears or dies with a bullet between their eyes."

"That's gossip. If it could be proven, they would be locked away in jail."

"Yeah." Scorn filled her voice and face. "We know how well the judicial system has worked for us. I know Curt is responsible for my parents' deaths. If the only justice I can get is to get The Last Riders to avenge their deaths, I'll take it."

"You know Curt is responsible without a doubt?"

"My parents were scared of Curt. He was trying to get them to sell their property to him. A week later, they're both dead. The coroner didn't find a medical reason for my father to go over that hill. I know Curt did it. Just like I know he raped you. I don't have any proof of that either, but I believe you," she said reasonably, as if Curt's death shouldn't bother her.

It did.

As much as she hated and despised him, she didn't want him murdered because she had lured Rider into committing the crime. She might not be the one to pull the trigger, but she would be the one to put the gun in his hand, unless she could talk Aly out of the plan they had devised.

"How many people does Curt have to destroy before he's stopped? Besides, we don't know if Rider would be the one to do it. It could be Shade, Viper, Moon, or the one who stays in his room. That could be why he stays out of sight when I go to the club."

"You don't know who he is?"

"No, and when I try to get the women to talk about him, they quit talking or leave the room, which is why I quit asking. So far, I've been able to get out of fucking any of them by keeping the women occupied with things I bring from the store. I've been hiding under their radar, so I don't want to alert the men that I'm not there to be a member. I'm on borrowed time as it is."

"No one has become suspicious yet?"

"Jewell has. That's why I bid on Rider. She keeps her eagle eyes on him. I knew she would be upset that Rider bid that much for you, so I didn't set her radar off. I was right, too, from what you texted me. She didn't tell Rider about your message. She wanted to jack up your date. Hopefully, I can mislead her that our date goes well enough that she'll worry about me more than you."

"If it goes well, you won't need me anymore. I never wanted to do this anyway. I'll pay back the money my father borrowed from your parents. I only need a little time—"

"There's not enough time in the world to pay back the

money your father borrowed. Rider will never fall for me. He hasn't fallen for any of the women at the club. You're the type of woman The Last Riders fall for. They just fuck women like me."

"According to you, they haven't."

"That's only because they're trying me out to see if I can keep my mouth shut before asking me to become one of their women members. Shade gave me another foot in the door when he asked me to discount the clothes you picked and paid the difference."

"I still don't understand how he knew I would go in there to shop."

"He led you there with those flyers. I bet he gave Lily the suggestion. It was like leaving scraps for a starving dog with a bear trap at the end."

"Thanks a lot. I really don't like being compared to a hungry dog," Jo said before trying another tactic. "I'll sign over my property and truck to you."

"Shade has a lean on your truck, and that land is more of a landfill than a property. Your house needs to be bulldozed, which is why you don't try to fix anything." Aly gave a long-suffering sigh. "Help me, and I will tear up the note your father gave mine. I'll even pay off your truck. You'll be debt free."

Jo stared back at her. Aly wasn't going to change her mind. She had no choice other than to warn Rider or Curt about Aly. After last night, she just couldn't bring herself to warn Curt. Plus, it would set his target on Aly. She was becoming just as afraid of Rider, but in another way.

Curt was dangerous but, deep down, she felt like she could handle him. He wouldn't be dealing with a fifteen-year-old girl now. Rider, however, brought the fine hairs on her arms standing. When she had seen him around town, he had done nothing to raise her fears that he was as lethal as her instincts were screaming he was. Could it be a guilty conscience? Was she making more of the feelings he was invoking than they really were?

"I don't have any other alternative. We should go to Knox and—"

"I've been to Knox. He told me to wait for the state police to issue their final accident report. When it came back accidental as the cause, he said his hands were tied. His might be, but mine aren't."

Her last resort squashed, Jo had no other suggestions that would change Aly's plan. Truthfully, she did believe Curt had something to do with her parents' deaths. He had made an offer to Aly for her parents' land before their caskets could be lowered into the ground. Two other offers had been made, each with a higher amount.

The property sat alone, without any homes nearby. Aly and she had discussed why Curt would want the property so badly, yet neither of them could up with one that would get Knox to take Aly's fears seriously.

"There's no need to stay here talking if I'm not able to change your mind. You don't want to keep Rider waiting." Jo's fingers went to the button to raise the window.

"I've been looking forward to it. If he gets away with killing Curt for us, I might have a change of heart about joining The Last Riders."

"You'd seriously consider having sex for votes to belong?"

"I've always had a soft spot for bad boys. The hard thing would be deciding which six."

Jo couldn't bring herself to have sex with one, much less six.

"I know which one I would pick—the door."

Aly's nose crinkled. "I can tell from your expression you haven't ever fantasized about being with two men."

"No, and certainly not letting six different men touch me just to get voted to become a Last Rider."

"Ember may have been giving me false information to see if I say anything to anyone in town. I've only been there a few times. We will see."

"We won't. You will. Trying to get Rider to fall in love with me is as far as I plan to go. I'm sick at myself that I agreed to that. If I had known what you wanted when you showed up at my door, I wouldn't have answered."

"You'd rather let Curt get away with murder?"

"I'd rather we didn't have to pretend that I didn't know you were back in town. Then Knox would have figured out what we were doing, and it would take this plan out of my hands."

"I made my mind that, if you didn't help, I was going to take you to court to get my father's money back. He shouldn't have lent it to your dad in the first place. It was too easy for him to use the money for his drinking and keep that lost cause of a business going."

Each of Aly's harsh words was like having a stake driven into her heart.

"You've changed since we went to school together."

"Having your parents murdered will do that to you."

Jo grimaced as she pictured the scenario in her head. She hadn't been pushed to the edge by her rape, or Curt's breaking into her house. She didn't know how she would react if she thought he was responsible for the death of someone she loved.

She was going to have to see how her future date with Rider played out. He could lose interest just as quickly as it had developed, giving her a way out of the mess she had found herself in. Other than the auction, she hadn't done anything that could make herself attractive to him.

Jo felt as if a coin had been flipped into the air, and her

conscience depended on where it landed. If Rider fell in love with her, she would have Curt's death on her shoulders. If he didn't, Aly would have to admit she had tried and it was no fault of hers, and allow her to make payments on her father's debt.

She sat on the lonely road long after Aly had left. The road ahead enticed her to take her anywhere but Treepoint.

"Just leave."

The empty silence offered no pearls of wisdom, leaving the choice to her.

Starting the engine, she drove up the winding road.

"Leave." Again, Jo spoke out loud, inwardly knowing she wouldn't. She had run once before; she wasn't going to do it again. Whichever way the imaginary coin she had flipped landed, she would be in Treepoint. It was the only place her heart yearned to be. For all its disadvantages, it was home.

18

Rider went into Jewell's office without knocking, shutting the door behind him.

"Why didn't you give me Jo's message the other day?"

"Did she leave a message? I must have forgotten."

As excuses went, Jewell's was lame.

Jerking herself out of her office chair, she went to the filing cabinet to put away a folder. It only took two steps into the small office for him to block her attempt at ignoring his angry presence.

"What you did wasn't cool, and I don't appreciate it. You were gone when I got home and didn't come back. Where were you?"

Jewell shoved him out of her way, filing the folder then closing the drawer with a snap before going back to her chair. "I was there. I just didn't answer my door. I wasn't in the mood to fuck you after your date."

"You didn't answer your door?" Rider planted his hands on the front of her desk, leaning over it, exasperated at her actions.

"Nope. I watched *Game of Thrones* all weekend. I enjoyed the time to myself."

"I wasn't in the mood to fuck you either," he snarled. "You've never had trouble telling the brothers to leave you alone when you're not in the mood to fuck. Why stay in your room and make us worry about you?"

"Who was worried? Name one man who was worried."

"I was, and Viper, Shade, and Moon."

Her stiff expression fell as he called out the brothers' names.

"You didn't worry about me enough to miss your date with Aly."

"You've never given a damn about who I dated before. Why now?"

"We spent all summer together, running after Greer's clues, and now you can't give me the time of day after you convinced me to let Crazy Bitch find them."

"I wanted Gavin to have his bike back. We knew Crazy Bitch would do the right thing. I gave you the money we would have won and your choice of bikes, but you didn't want it."

"I didn't want the bike. I prefer riding behind you."

Rider straightened off her desk, going to the window to stare out at the parking lot. "I'm not in love with you. I can't love anyone."

"I know you're not, but I didn't expect you to ignore me for a new piece of tail. If you're not able to fall in love with Jo, why did you pay so much money for a date with her?"

"You're mad because I didn't fuck you before I went out with Jo, and I spent too much money on a date with her?"

"You've never put a particular woman over your dick and stomach before."

Rider gave a bitter laugh. "My stomach and my dick have never let me down."

Turning, he reflected on the time he had spent with Jewell. She had fallen in love with him over the summer, while the time spent with her had increased the shallowness of his life.

"I've never let you down, have I?"

"No, you haven't." He looked up at her. "Tell me something truthfully. If you answer me honestly, I'll never see Jo again. Can you be faithful? Never have another man or woman between your legs, never wonder what it's like to fuck them?"

"You know I can't." Jewell began fidgeting with the papers on her desk.

"That's why Jo. She's a one-man woman."

"Since when have you cared about that?"

"Since I've seen how happy Shade and the other brothers are."

"They love their wives. You'll never be able to love Jo the way they do their wives."

"Maybe not, but I'd be creating a family." Rider's eyes went back to the parking lot. "It's hard to watch them when they're together. I want a piece of that pie for myself."

"Jo isn't going to be able to replace what you've lost."

"No, she won't, but she can give me a new start. We all have to play the cards we've been dealt, but that doesn't mean I can't fold and deal a new hand."

"You'll be miserable. You're not the same man who joined the Navy. You love sharing with the other brothers. The sweet, little innocent you're wanting will have you bored to death in a month. What happens then, Rider? You going to break Jo's heart the way yours has been?"

Rider removed his eyes from the window to stare coldly at Jewell. "You think I would be unfaithful?"

"No, but as good at pretending as you are, a woman knows

the difference between affection and love. Jo's not stupid. She'll know you're not in love with her. One hour with Lily and Shade, or Viper and Winter will show her the fucking difference."

"She'll never know; I guarantee that." His lips curled into a sensuous smile.

Jewell shook her head. "She'll know, but I can see you're determined to find that out for yourself. I'll be waiting when she divorces your ass."

"I'm not chasing Jo to put a ring on her finger. Marriage doesn't keep a woman from straying or betraying you."

"If you think you're going to get Jo without a wedding ring, you're delusional. Jo's not a motorcycle you can lock away to make sure no one smudges the wax job, especially not without a commitment from you. What if she decides what you can give her isn't enough?"

"Then I move on like I always do. Like I said, I'll play the cards I'm dealt. What I don't want is someone who's not invited into the game sabotaging me."

Jewel lifted her hands in the air. "I'm out. You want Jo, you can have her. You want Aly, you can even have her." She dropped her hands to the desk, using them to brace her weight as she rose to confront him. "You want a woman who would rather give you a tow than give you a blowjob, you have my sympathy. When you want to fuck Ember or Stori, I'm out. The other brothers will be keeping me busy, so I won't even know you're gone."

"The catty side of you isn't very attractive."

"Get back to work. I have better things to do than listen to you tell me I need to suck it up, that you're going to be with Jo. It hasn't happened yet, and it probably won't. Either way, I no longer give a fuck."

"That's all I wanted to hear." Rider ignored Jewell's furious outburst, leaving the office and closing the door behind him, giving her time to compose herself before anyone could see.

She might think her heart was broken, but it wasn't. Jewell wasn't in love with him. As much as he knew he was no longer capable of the emotion, it didn't mean he couldn't remember what it felt like. That was why he was going to make an allowance for her this time. If she interfered again, though, he wouldn't be so understanding.

Jewell liked being his old lady. It gave her preferential treatment within the clubhouse, just like being the manager of the factory did. Jewell liked being the top dog over the other women, taking Evie's place when she had married King.

That was what Jewell felt threatened about, not him. He had never told Jewell that she was his old lady, keeping their relationship sexual, and now he was glad he hadn't.

If he married her, Jewell was domineering enough to create friction between the wives. He might never trust his heart to another woman, but he cared enough about the brothers to want one who would fit in harmoniously.

It was another reason he had decided to pursue Jo. She was friends with the wives, and she wouldn't upset the balance between him and the other brothers.

Confidently, he went back to work, filling the orders. He wanted to finish early so he would have enough time to change and dress before he picked Jo up.

He had filled three more orders when Justin came into the factory, his weak jaw jutting out, making him look like a bulldog. Curt's cousin was shorter and half his size, wearing a Stetson hat since he and his cousins had gone to the rodeo. Curt and Tanner had bought ones, too, but they had stopped wearing them after a month. Justin still hadn't given up the ghost of pretending to be a cowboy, wearing his Stetson with a swagger that had Rider wanting to laugh at him.

Rider met him before he could go to the office.

"I'm here to pick up Curt's money."

He had told Curt to send Tanner, who was the least abrasive. Holding true to form, though, Curt had sent the larger of his two cousins, trying to intimidate him into reconsidering firing him.

Rider reached into his back pocket, pulling out an envelope. Giving it to Justin, he then went to a bag sitting by the door and also gave it to him.

Justin snatched them out of his hands.

"I need you to sign for them." Rider had the clipboard ready, giving it to him to sign.

"You sure you don't want to rethink firing Curt? He's willing to let bygones be bygones. Take my suggestion; you should accept his offer." Justin's jaw jutted out farther.

If Justin thought he would buy his bulldog expression, he was going to be disappointed.

"I can't say the same. Curt comes near the factory, he'll be arrested for trespassing. If he tries to harass Mag or Jo, I will personally see he will regret it."

"We ain't afraid of you or The Last Riders." Justin's voice rose, making the employees stop working to listen. Sprawling his signature on the bottom of the release, he pushed the clipboard back to him.

Rider didn't respond to his threat, taking the clipboard. "You got what you came for. You can show yourself out."

"Fuck you." Justin stormed out, slamming the door so hard that Jewell came out of the office and Train left his worktable.

At his hard look, the employees busied themselves, returning to their jobs.

"What was that about?" Jewell asked.

"I fired Curt. Justin came to pick up his check."

"Why wasn't I told?" Jewell snapped.

"I must have forgotten to tell you."

Jewell shot him a glare before going back to her office.

"It's Jewell's turn to cook tonight. I'd eat at the diner if I were you."

"I'm taking Jo out tonight."

Train blew a low whistle. "Jo's going on a second date with you? She enter another auction?"

"Very funny." Rider snorted at Train's attempt at humor. "Make yourself useful and double-check the list Shade made to monitor the security system. I want two brothers on duty at all times. One to monitor the club and factory, and one to monitor the new system we put up at Jo's yesterday."

"Jo buy the excuse Cash and Rachel gave her for being late coming back from Lexington?"

"Cash said he thought so."

"What are you going to say if she finds the cameras?"

"She won't find them," Rider assured his friend. "If she does, I'll worry about it when it happens."

"Brother, I wouldn't want to be you if she finds out. Jo's more likely to shove your explanations up your ass than listen."

"Jo isn't Killyama. Curt isn't going to take being fired without reprisal. He's a sick fuck. I had enough of playing his friend to get dirt on him. I'd rather gargle with kerosene than see his sorry ass come to work one more day."

"I won't miss him, though he came in handy when we needed someone to work overtime. Still, I'd rather work a couple extra shifts than use him to complete the orders."

"You won't have to. Viper sent for Diablo and Trip to come back. He doesn't want to hire new workers until Curt strikes out at us."

"Curt's related to half the town, so that's a good call. Most of the other employees can't stand Curt either, but they're afraid of him. If Curt tries to get them to sabotage any of the orders or trucks, I wouldn't trust that they won't cave."

"Me either. With Diablo and Trip here, we don't have to worry." Rider went to the door, opening it partway to see it had started to snow.

"It's supposed to be bad tonight. The weather report is calling for eight inches." Train moved to his side, staring out at the swirling mess that was going to put a damper on his evening plans.

"Let's hurry the workers along. I want to get as many orders as we can finish before two. I don't want the driver trying to make it down the hill when the roads get bad."

"Drake is supposed to be buying a new snow plow to help Gabe out during bad weather. He said at the auction the city council has been stymying him." Train zipped his jacket, pressing a button on the wall that would turn the heat up another three degrees.

"Curt's father and nephew sit on that board. They don't want Drake buying the truck because they know Drake will hire Jo to run it."

Rider hated small-town politics. Bliss's husband was trying to make a difference, but so far, it was like chewing glass for Drake to get anything done. Curt had the benefit of his father's and mother's family connections to the Dawkins and the Demaris, Curt believing he was untouchable. He had been ... until Rider decided to stop that shit.

Train left to check the security details as Rider worked diligently to fill the orders. He didn't take a break for lunch, and when he carried several orders to the mail cart, he saw various employees had remained on the job.

Shade carried a cup of coffee to his station, setting it down. "If I knew you could work this hard, I would have made you manager."

"You tried. I didn't want the job. Jewell deserves the job."

"She does, but she can't motivate the workers like you can. Anyone who wants off, she gives it and then takes off with them. A manager needs to accept responsibility when shit doesn't get done. She makes excuses."

"Then talk to her."

"Viper and I both have. The orders are lagging behind two to three days before they are shipped. She has to get better or Viper wants me to take over the job again."

"If you're trying to make feel guilty, it won't work. I don't want the job, and I won't take it away from Jewell."

"You want me to be the bad guy," Shade stated.

"Better you than me. I'm not Jewell's favorite person right now. If we demote her, she might want to go back to Ohio."

"Would it matter?"

"She's a friend, so yeah, it would matter."

"Train said you're going out with Jo again."

"What's more surprising, that I asked or she agreed?" Rider used the hand roller to tape a box closed.

"I'm not going to answer that question." Shade's lips quivered in the semblance of a smile. Taking his jacket off, he went to the order board, taking several to be filled.

"You pitching in?" Rider asked, astounded, not that he was ready to lend a helping hand, but that he would leave Lily alone. Her due date had come and gone, and Shade hadn't left her for more than a couple minutes since.

"Her friends arrived last night. She's in good hands. Sawyer and Vida are helping Lily re-organize the nursery."

"What are Colton and Kaden doing to keep from pulling their hair out?"

"Kaden is using the opportunity to write a new song, and Colton hasn't had time to unpack. Several of the brothers have been waiting for him to come and give them tattoos. If you want one, you'll have to get in line."

"I'm good for now." Colton was a master tattoo artist.

Being inked from Colton gave the brothers in Treepoint bragging rights over the ones in Ohio.

"I bet Diablo and Trip will hit him up when they get here."

"They already texted him as soon as Viper called and told them to come back."

The men grew silent as they worked, both focused on getting the orders finished. It was after two before Rider was able to wheel the last cart to the truck.

Viper was standing on the bed, moving swiftly despite the bulky jacket he was wearing. Train and Razer started removing the packages, laying them on the bed so Viper could stack them. When he tied the last ones down, he jumped down, then pulled the sliding door closed.

Rider went to the side, giving the driver a thumbs-up to leave.

"That was close. Stuart shouldn't have any problems with the road; Gabe just went by with the salt truck." Viper tugged his collar closer, his heaving breaths easily seen in the cold air. "Rider, Train, get the bikes moved to the garage. Jewell, send the men home."

Jewell hurried inside to follow Viper's order as Rider and Train moved the motorcycles. Each of them had an extra set of the brothers' keys.

His ass was practically numb as the temperature dropped.

"That salt isn't going to do any good if it gets much colder," Rider said, getting off Moon's bike.

"Worried about your date?" Train gave him a sideways glance as he got off Gavin's.

"No. I'm not letting Jo out of it, no matter if the snow is ass-deep. It's the perfect excuse to snuggle together and get warm."

"You try to snuggle with Jo, make sure she doesn't have anything handy to brain you with."

"You have no faith in me."

"Until you can walk on water or feed the hungry, I'm good with saying you're not going to get lucky on a second date with Jo," Train joked.

Coming out of the security room, Shade and Viper overheard the joke. Both took the opportunity to dig at him.

"He could calm the storm; make it easier if Lily goes into labor and we can't get her to the hospital."

Rider winced when Shade nudged Viper. At one time, the three men had felt his own barbs when they had started dating their wives.

"He could change water into wine. Save me a trip to the liquor store," Viper teased.

"Fuck all of you." Rider took off one of his gloves, throwing it at Train for setting the brothers off.

Train caught it and tucked it into his jacket pocket. "You're going to regret that when you get the deep freeze from Jo."

His remark set the men off again.

Rider lifted his nose high in the air. "Keep it. I don't need it. Don't you know I can perform miracles?"

19

"Will you stop fiddling with that?" Jo wanted to smack Rider's hand when he turned another dial on her CB.

"Does it work?"

"Rider, you were in the Navy. I know you know how to operate a CB." Jo couldn't keep the sarcasm from rolling off her tongue. He had been irritating for the last ten minutes after she had stopped by to tell him she couldn't keep their date because Knox had asked for her help. Despite her arguments, he had gotten in the truck to tag along.

She should have texted him. She would have if she hadn't seen him coming down the steps as she was plowing The Last Riders' parking lot.

"I thought you worked till five?"

"Usually, I do," Rider explained as he turned another dial. "We closed the factory early. It was a lucky break to see you cleaning the parking lot."

Jo rolled her eyes. "Yes, it was."

"Breaker, breaker …"

She held the steering wheel with one hand and jerked the microphone out of his hand with the other. "Behave."

"Why do you need the radio you carry and a CB?"

"Knox gave me the handheld one so he could reach me in an emergency. I use the CB to listen to the emergency channels and truckers. Plus, some of the RVs traveling through town have had trouble, and I can respond if they need help."

"Where are we heading?"

They had just finished plowing Rosie's for Mick. She had tried to get him to stay there, but he refused, saying he would be bored with everyone in town being holed up from the storm.

"The church, then the diner. You want to go inside and say hello to Carly?"

"No thanks. You going to share that coffee?"

"No, I don't have an extra cup."

"You afraid of my cooties?"

"What I meant is, my thermos is empty. I'll need to gas up when I finish the diner so I can refill it there. You can get a cup there, too."

"I should have run in to grab a thermos before going with you. We have a couple of good ones."

"Good for you. I like mine. It was my father's."

"I can tell. It looks as old as the CB."

"If it works, don't fix it."

"I have the same philosophy myself. We can go to the diner and get Carly to fill it," he suggested.

Jo brought the tow truck to a stop at the red light. A lamp beaming down into the interior of the car showed the expensive clothes he was wearing.

"You look nice tonight."

He gave her a hundred-watt smile, making her wish she had kept her opinion to herself.

"Thank you. A compliment from you was worth ironing my pants."

"You ironed your jeans?"

"I left them in the dryer too long and they were tangled up with Ember's bra. And before you get wrong the impression, we take turns doing the chores."

"Why would your jeans being tangled with Ember's bra give me the wrong impression?"

"I didn't want you to think me and Ember are a couple and we do each other's laundry."

Jo wanted to grit her teeth rather than listen to him explain his relationships with the each of the women in the clubhouse.

The light changed. Inching up the road, she turned into the church parking lot, lowering her shovel before resuming their conversation as she drove around the lot.

"Rider, do you think I'm stupid?"

"No ..."

"It doesn't take a genius to know you've been with all the women at the club, and most of the single women in town, as well as a few married ones. I'm going to tell you something about me. I don't get jealous."

"Every woman gets jealous. It doesn't have to be over a man. It could be over a purse, their job, or the car they drive."

"Not me."

"You've never been jealous once in your life?"

"Not once."

"I don't believe it."

"Believe it. It's the truth. Why don't you think I'm telling the truth? You don't seem the jealous sort yourself."

Rider gave a self-effacing laugh. "I get jealous all the time. I get jealous of a particular motorcycle I want and don't have. I get jealous of some of the brothers' clothes or boots. I get jealous of someone eating Willa's candy when I don't have any."

"Okay, you win. You're jealous-natured."

The church's lot cleared, she drove across the empty street to the diner, her plow making a path in the snow on the road that Gabe hadn't plowed.

She was going to hate herself, but she was going to ask the burning question she couldn't get to go away.

"You ever get jealous over a woman?"

"Twice." His good humor vanished as he stared out of the windshield.

"I'm sorry. I didn't mean to get personal."

"It's cool. It was a lifetime ago."

"From your expression, it doesn't seem so long ago."

"It was, so … You never answered my question. Why don't we go inside the diner and refill your thermos there?"

"Because I don't trust Carly not to spit in it when my back is turned."

"Carly wouldn't spit in your coffee. She's more likely to wipe a booger on your burger the next time you order one."

Jo gave him a horrified glance, which had him doubling over in his seat.

"You should see your face."

His laughter had Jo smiling despite herself.

When she was done with the diner's parking lot, she drove down Main Street to the gas station, her plow still down.

"Gabe isn't going to be happy you're doing his job for him."

"Gabe and I have an understanding. I help him out when he needs help, and he returns the favor."

"I can see how you're helping him out, but what does he do for you?"

"He takes once a month off and lets me earn the money for plowing the streets."

"One hand washes the other. That's nice you help each other out."

"He had the same deal with my father. I inherited it."

Jo signaled and turned into the gas station. The owner owned a small bobcat and had already cleared the snow to let customers refuel. Parking her truck, she grabbed her thermos before turning the truck off.

"You can stay here. I'll get the coffee." She got out of the truck without waiting for a reply.

She was at the front of her truck when she heard the door opening on Rider's side.

"I was going to get you one—"

"I have to use the restroom." He lifted a curious brow at her insistence that he remain in the truck.

Jo lowered her head, trying to keep the blowing snow from hitting her in the face. Her cheeks were burning, and not because of the weather outside.

She quickly moved to the side to pretend interest in a bag of chips on display so the clerk behind the counter wouldn't know she and Rider were together. Peering over the display, she hastily grabbed two large bags, not paying attention to what flavor they were.

As soon as Rider walked into the restroom, she went to the fountain area, hurrying to fill her thermos. She didn't bother screwing the lid back on as she reached for a large plastic mug and filled that one with the other pot. Jostling the hot coffees, lids, and the chips, she then strode to the counter.

"Hi, Jo," Claire greeted as she started picking up the chips to ring her purchases up.

"Hi, Claire. I'm kind of in a hurry. I forgot my radio in the truck."

The bubbly blonde loved to chat, and Jo would usually spend the evening talking to her when she was waiting for a call to come through, but she wanted to be back in the truck before Rider came out of the bathroom.

A small display of cakes caught her attention, and she placed two on the counter next to the chips.

"Haven't had time for dinner yet?" Claire asked, ringing the cakes up as Rider strolled out of the restroom.

Lowering her eyes, Jo reached for the cash in her coveralls.

"I'll take care of it," Rider called out as he went to the fast treats section next to the side of the counter. "What do you want on your hot dog, Jo?"

Her mouth grew dry when Claire looked up from the register to stare at her accusingly.

"Uh … uh …" Jo looked away from Claire to Rider. "Mustard, onion, and relish. Plenty of onions." Her gaze returned to Claire. "Rider is helping me out tonight."

Feeling like an idiot for explaining, she clutched her cash as she saw Claire ring up the coffee. Rider's presence with her had assured that her free refills would no longer be forthcoming.

Busted, she put the lids on the coffee as Rider made their hot dogs and carried them to the register.

"You forgot the onions."

"No, I didn't." Rider picked the sour and onion chips up and moved away from the counter.

"What are you doing?"

"Switching the chips. I like plain better."

"I prefer …" Miserably, she shut up when Claire's stare went from accusing to angry. "Fine." Snatching the bag out of his hand, she grabbed her hot dog and coffee and went to the door, leaving him behind to pay.

"Excuse her, Claire. Jo takes her job seriously. How's your night going?"

Jo wanted to throw her hot dog at him. Instead, she went out the door and refueled her two tanks.

"If he doesn't come out by the time I'm done, I'm leaving his ass," Jo said out loud, seeing Rider standing at the register, talking to Claire through the window in the store.

Jo stopped watching them to look at the numbers clicking off on the pump, not understanding why she was becoming piqued that Rider was staying longer than necessary in the store.

When the handle of the gas hose clicked off, she was shoving the nozzle back into the pump when she saw Rider walking across the parking lot.

Stepping on the step of her truck as she opened her door, Jo looked across the hood. Rider had opened his door, placing the coffee and hot dog inside.

"You sure you don't want to stay here with Claire?" Jo wanted to bite her tongue when he gave her a satisfied look.

"I'm sure." Bending his head, he got inside, then snapped the door closed.

Jo turned the heat on high as soon as she got inside. Then, pulling to the side of the parking lot, she reached for her hot dog and took a bite.

Rider opened the chips, placing the bag between them to share with her. Taking two sodas out of his jacket pockets, he gave her one. "I thought this would go better with our dinner."

"Thank you."

"How's your hot dog?"

"It would have been better with onions."

"I saved you from getting sick. Claire told me the toppings aren't fresh. The owner hates to throw anything away."

About to take another bite of her hot dog, she stopped and looked at it suspiciously. She was about to put it back down when Rider laughed.

"You're safe. Claire throws the old hot dogs away when the owner goes home."

"Were the chips old, too?" Jo asked, reaching for one.

"No, that was a matter of preference. With the storm, it's going to be a long night, and I need to keep my strength up. If you want, you can open the barbecue." He set the other bag of chips closer to her as he demolished the last of his hot dog.

"The plain is fine."

They sat in companionable silence as they finished eating, the heat in the cab encasing them in a warm cocoon.

"It's beautiful, isn't it?"

"Yes. It's why I came back to Treepoint. Nothing else is like it."

"No, it isn't."

Jo backed out of the parking lot, scraping Main Street before making a turn at the red light. She waited for Rider to ask her where they were going. When he didn't, she realized he was enjoying being out.

"Weather like this makes it hard to ride your motorcycle."

"Yeah, I usually keep myself occupied with work, but after a couple days, I'm ready to ride, whatever the weather. That's why I keep cars for when I get stir-crazy."

"Do you miss being in the Navy?"

"No, I like the men I served with, and they're all here."

Edging onto a private driveway sideways, she plowed the snow from behind a closed garage door as she felt Rider's gaze on her. When the front porch light came on and a tall man came outside, she stopped, rolling her window down.

"Jo, I told you I have a snow blower."

"Evening, Dr. Price. I was in the neighborhood and didn't

want you having to worry about getting your car out of the garage if you get called in for an emergency."

Dr. Price folded his arms across his chest. "The hospital's blocks away; I could walk there."

"It's too cold to stay out here arguing with me. Besides, I'm done."

"Jo, you're so hardheaded you could play for the Broncos."

"Nope, I don't like football. Get inside before you take a cold. I'll see you in church."

Rolling her window up, she went farther down the street, doing the same to another driveway. This time, she honked her horn when the porch light came on.

Doing an arc in the cul-de-sac, she plowed the other road.

"That was Dr. Matthews' house, wasn't it?" Rider asked in the dark interior.

"Yes."

"He's Lily's doctor."

"I didn't know that. You learn something new every day." Reaching for her thermos, she took a sip of the hot coffee as she turned back down Main Street.

Jo heard him lift his own coffee. Then she took her eyes off the road when she heard him rolling the window down to spit it out.

"How can you drink that stuff? It tastes terrible," he complained, setting his mug back down.

"Oh, sorry about that. It's decaf." She took another sip of hers. "I was trying to hurry and there wasn't enough in the caffeinated one."

"But you had enough to fill yours?"

"I'm the one driving." Jo tried to hold back a gurgle of laughter, not succeeding. "I need to be alert."

"It tasted like sludge."

"I don't imagine many customers buy decaf." She was wiping her tears of laughter away.

"Try none."

She laughed harder when he opened the barbecue chips to take the taste away.

"That shit could grow hair on your chest. Want to see?"

Jo stopped laughing, reaching out to punch him lightly on his arm when she saw he was about to take his jacket off.

"Stop! I don't want to see your hairy chest!"

Jo braked sharply, turning into the gas station and pulling alongside the front so he could get out.

"Go pour your mug out and get another cup."

He didn't get out as she expected, but gave her a curious look she couldn't interpret.

"You're ditching me, aren't you?"

"Don't tempt me." Jo stopped the engine, giving him the key. "Hurry. I need to plow the hospital parking lot. You can flirt with Claire on Wednesday night."

Rider took the keys, then started to get out, but he couldn't resist giving her a gloating smile.

"Do I hear a spark of jealousy?"

"What you hear is my stomach growling. Get me another hot dog when you're in there."

THE LAST RIDERS

Rider took the steps two at a time toward the clubhouse. If he rushed, he would have enough time to shower before Jo showed to pick him up.

Gaining the front porch, he saw Moon on duty.

"What did you do to get guard duty?"

"Nothing. Viper and Shade want to talk to you. They're in Gavin's room."

When Moon didn't meet his eyes, Rider knew it was bad. Was he the one in trouble?

He had spent each evening driving around with Jo. He had badgered her with texts each day until she would agree to let him go along. He was in a good mood, having only needed to send her three today before she had given in and told him she would be there at six.

Had Curt done something? Lily hadn't gone into labor yet or Shade wouldn't be waiting to talk to him with Viper.

He knocked on Gavin's door, opening it when he heard Viper's voice.

"You want ...?" Rider broke off when he saw Gavin seated on the couch at the other side of the room. The brother's change of appearance had him standing at the door with his mouth hanging open.

Gavin had cut his hair, and not only had he shaved it, but he had shaved one side clear off. The cleanly shaved part was tatted with ink that completely covered where his hair had been going down to the side of his neck and shoulder.

"Jesus, brother, that's a sick tattoo." Rider didn't know what else to say. He took a step toward the couch, wanting to see the details closer.

"Close the door, Rider."

Viper's order had him turning back to do as told.

"You wanted to see me?" he asked, still unable to take his eyes off Gavin.

"Have a seat. We need to have a talk."

Rider took the empty chair beside the desk. When Shade stepped away from the desk to go sit on the couch next to Gavin, a feeling of dread rose up.

Viper's mouth opened and closed as if he was trying to find the words to begin. He had served in the military with the men and spilled blood with them and for them. To know they were leaving it to Viper to discuss in the privacy of his old bedroom, it wasn't going to be good.

"Just spit it out."

"Jo's playing you."

"Bullshit." Rider felt the room spin around him, his mind plucked back to the past, while his body still sat in Gavin's room.

"Brother, I would rather rip out my tongue than lie to you about this." Viper's jaw clenched as he pushed a button on the computer at the desk.

Rider saw the security footage of the camera he and Shade had planted on Jo's property. Four separate screens showed the outside of Jo's house, the inside, the entrance of the junkyard, and her metal garage.

Viper pushed another button, changing the footage. Rider didn't say anything as he watched.

The footage showed Jo driving into the junkyard. Rider looked up at the date of the recording before watching Jo get out of her truck and go inside her house. Viper sped the recording until Jo was moving around in her living room, doing dishes, and sweeping her kitchen floor. Viper stopped the footage when he saw her reach for her phone.

Whoever had called Jo must have upset her from the expression on her face. She kept shaking her head *no* before she slammed her phone down on the coffee table and put her boots back on. Grabbing her coat and phone, she left in a rush.

Viper stopped the recording.

"Moon was watching the footage and called Shade."

"Why didn't Shade call me? I was the one who wanted the cameras placed to watch her."

"Shade felt it would be better for him to handle it in case it was Curt trying to lure her out. He was afraid you would take Curt out without our permission."

"Where did she go?" Rider had no doubt Shade had followed her.

"She went to a back road behind the lake. I almost didn't find where she had made the turn. I had to hike to keep them from hearing my bike."

"Who'd she meet?" Rider grabbed the arms of his chair to bring his mind back to the present.

"Aly."

"Aly?"

"I was as surprised as you. When I asked her to discount Jo's clothes for the auction, she acted like she didn't know Jo that well. She's been telling all the women in the club she wants to be a member, but so far, if any of the brothers make a move to talk to her, she's more interested in discussing shoes than fucking."

"You asked Aly to discount Jo's clothes? Why?"

"Because we're dumb as fuck." Viper kicked the leg of his desk. "We wanted you focused on Jo, not our wives."

Rider nodded at Viper's confession.

"Could you hear what they were talking about?"

"No."

"Any ideas?"

"They met for almost an hour. Jo seemed to be trying to convince Aly into something." Shade shrugged.

"Shade, you and Viper have already been talking about it, or you would have filled me in that it went down. What do you think they were doing?"

Shade laid his forearms on his thighs. "Both women have only one thing in common as far as I can see. Knox said that Aly pressured him to investigate her parents' deaths. When the report came back that nothing was suspicious, she stormed out of his office. Aly could have contacted Jo because it's not like it's a secret what Curt did to her. They could have teamed up to try to bring Curt down."

"How?" Rider already knew, but he wanted his dark thoughts confirmed.

"You. Ember said that Aly's asking questions. When I asked Winter what she thought of Aly, she said she and Jo went to school together. She also said Georgia was a friend of Aly's. She said that anytime Aly went to visit her parents, she always hung around with Georgia."

That Aly was friends with Georgia before Shade had taken her out while she was in prison didn't bode well. Georgia had been a bully who had made Willa's life miserable before she had married Lucky. She had also nearly taken out Shade and Lily when she had set a fire in the basement of the clubhouse.

"That's not all." Viper pushed the button to run footage on another part of the computer screen, showing Jo at the large metal garage at the back of her property.

Rider looked at the date and saw it was from this afternoon.

"We only placed cameras on the inside and outside of her house to catch Curt. After I saw the meeting with Jo and Aly, I went back to put more cameras in and around the garage in case they've met there. Knox was able to freeze her camera system until I could get in and out."

Rider started laughing bitterly. "I'm a fucking fool."

He was staring at the mysterious car he had caught sight of a couple times.

He scooted forward on his chair, not believing his eyes. The car he had trusted Carl with was also sitting in the middle of the garage, raised high on a lift. He sat, watching as she worked on it with meticulous care.

The brothers watched with him for a good twenty minutes before Jo wiped her hands, then touched the tire as if she was promising a lover she would be back soon.

"Train was taken in, too. None of us expected Jo wasn't being honest with you. To tell you the truth, I hope we're wrong. I like Jo. She's had a shitty deal, and still has one.

"Knox isn't happy with the accident report and asked for an independent assessment from the state. We were already suspicious that Aly was so gung-ho to hang around the clubhouse, which is why we told everyone to watch their steps around her. Ember's doing kitchen duty for the next two months because she ignored my orders and told Aly how she could become a member."

"Don't blame her. Aly has been manipulating her. Not enough to fool Shade, but Ember is too nice. She wouldn't recognize a lie if it hit her in the face." Rider picked up a ruler on the desk, sliding his thumb along the length.

"I'm sorry, Rider," Viper spoke when it became obvious he wasn't going to say anything else. "We can handle it any way you want."

"Don't be sorry. It's not your fault." He laid the ruler back down, standing. "Spread the word not to let Aly in the club-house anymore. Make it seem like we're on lockdown because of something Curt's done. I'll take care of Aly and Jo."

"What are you going to do?" It was the first time Gavin had spoken since Rider had come into the room.

"I'm going to make them believe they're in Disneyland and all their wishes are going to come true." Rider strode out of the meeting. He wasn't angry, his emotions too numb for that reaction.

Going to his bedroom, he took off his shirt and twirled it before making it taut and hitting the mattress instead of the woman he wanted to feel the pain of his lashes.

"If you're in the mood to take your anger out on someone, I have some free time," Jewell said, coming up from behind him.

He had used his foot to shut the door without waiting to see if it had closed. Jewell had taken advantage of the open door, prancing inside with only a pair of string panties to cover her pussy.

"Get out. Now."

Rider didn't look to see if she left. Jewell had the survival instinct of a cat. She knew when to draw her claws and when to retreat.

Leaving the mess he had made of the clothes he had laid out this morning to wear tonight, he walked back to his door, using his booted foot to slam it shut. Shirtless, he then went to his dresser to take out clean clothes and socks before going to the bathroom and taking a shower. Naked, he wrapped a towel around his hip and went out into the hall.

"Hey, sexy!" A feminine voice from the landing had him turning.

Sasha was skipping down the hall toward him.

"When did you get back?" He grinned, lifting her until her thighs gripped his hips.

"Two nights ago. You've either been out or working." She playfully hit his shoulder, then twined her arms around his neck to give him a hug. "I missed you ..." As he held her lightly, his towel fell to the hall floor. Sasha's eyes widened at the flesh he was exposing. "Soo much."

"I missed you, too, brat." Rider set her back on her feet, then reached for his towel, wrapping it around his hips.

"Since when have you been shy?" Sasha followed on his heels as he went inside his room.

"I'm going out."

"Again?" Sasha sat on the side of his bed as he tugged his jeans and black T-shirt on. "What's a girl to do to get any attention from you? Drive a tow truck?" she teased.

"I'm sure you're keeping yourself occupied." Rider pulled his T-shirt down, covering the muscles of his abdomen before sitting down next to her on the bed to put his boots on.

"True, but baby, they aren't you." She placed her hand on his thigh, sliding upward to cup his cock.

Rider twisted sideways, catching her lips in a demanding kiss. When she started to respond, though, he broke away, raising to shove his keys and cell phone into his jeans pockets.

"I have to go. I'll be back in a few hours." Walking back to the bed, he intimately slid his hand between her thighs, cupping her pussy. "Save some for me."

"You know I always save some for you," she crooned as he grabbed his jacket, then strode out of his room.

Going down the steps, he heard the pinging from his

phone that he was receiving a text. He didn't bother looking at it—Jo was right on time. If she said she would be there at a certain time, she would be there. It was one of the things he had liked about her.

Nodding at Moon, who gave him a searching glance, he went down the flight of steps to the parking lot.

Opening the passenger door of Jo's truck, he climbed inside. He received the same searching glance from Jo as he shut the door.

"Am I too early?" she asked, backing out.

"No. Why?"

"Nothing. It's just … you've been wearing dress clothes when we go out. Not that it matters," she hastened to add.

Rider met her eyes, staring deeply into them. "I decided that clothes don't make the man any more than clothes make the woman."

"No, they don't."

"Careful," he warned as she was about to pull out onto the road. "There's a car coming."

Jo slammed on the brakes. "Sorry, I didn't see it."

"No, you didn't. That's two of us."

21

"The roads look like they're clear."

Jo nervously kept her eyes glued to the road. "They are. The sun melted off what was left today."

The vibe that Rider had been putting off since he had gotten in the truck had her discreetly watching him from the corner of her eye.

"So, what's our plan tonight? Another hot dog at the gas station?"

"I was going to do better than that." Pulling into the church parking lot, she found a parking spot that would let her face the road in case she was called out. "Willa is fixing dinner tonight for anyone who volunteers to wrap Christmas presents for the kids."

When Rider just sat there without getting out, she looked down to see what he was staring at, realizing she had been unconsciously twisting her hands together.

Rubbing her sweaty palms on the coarse material of her coveralls, she cleared her throat. "If you'd rather not, we could go get a burger at the diner, and I can take you home afterward."

Jo couldn't understand the thick lump that had formed in her throat. It was like she had lost a friend and didn't know why. The last few days with Rider had shown just how lonely her existence had been.

She had people she called friends in town and church, but she had maintained a distance that kept them from being termed "close friends." Rider had been breaching the gap. Experiencing that distance from him, and not at her own making, shook her to her very core.

She had called Aly to meet with her the other day to tell her that she wasn't going to go through with the plan to entice Rider to take Curt on. They had argued, and Aly had left threatening to sue her for the money her father had owed.

As Jo watched, Rider's expression became shuttered. Then she tensed when he reached out to cup her cheek, running a gentle finger down it. Frozen at his touch, she stared, hypnotized by the sensuous curve of his lips.

"Willa's a good cook. If she made that offer, most of the town will show. Let's hurry before all the toys are wrapped." Dropping his hand, he got out of the truck.

It took Jo a second to realize he was waiting for her outside.

"Ninny, you're making a fool of yourself." Gathering her scattered wits, she got out, bowing her head at his knowing smirk.

Not taking the hand he held to her, she rushed past him, nearly skidding on slushy pavement. Rider managed to catch her around her waist.

"Careful. You don't want to fall."

Jo grabbed his biceps, feeling the muscles bunch underneath her touch.

"Rider ... I ..."

"Hi, Rider."

Jo dropped her hands from Rider as Aly approached them on the sidewalk.

"Jo," Aly greeted as she curled her hand familiarly around Rider's arm. "Do you mind, Rider? I don't want to fall in my heels."

"I'm always willing to lend a helping hand to a pretty girl." Placing himself between the two women, he offered his other crooked arm to Jo.

"I'm fine." Jo walked ahead, leaving them to follow behind her.

She was torn between anger and tears when she heard their soft voices behind her yet couldn't hear what they were saying.

Opening the church door, she went inside, uncaring if they followed.

Inside, Willa and Lucky were talking to Cash and Rachel.

Breaking away from the small group, Willa gave Jo a flustered frown. "I was worried that you would get called out. I have plenty of help. Unfortunately, though, most of the parishioners are too busy to stay long." Willa gave Rider and Aly a smile as they came in the door behind Jo. "I'm hoping to get most of the presents wrapped before they start making excuses to leave. I've organized the toys by age groups. Rider, you and Jo can take the three-year-olds' Bible study room. Aly, you can work with Rachel and Cash in the five- and six-year-olds' room." With that, she briskly led them to their respective rooms.

Jo could only stare as she shut the door behind them, leaving her and Rider alone in a toy-filled room.

"What got into her?" Jo closed her gaping mouth at Willa's demanding attitude.

Rider laughed, shrugging out of his jacket, then placing it on one of the small tables. "That's nothing. You should see her when she gets mad. We all take cover to get out of her path."

Jo wouldn't have believed it was possible, but doubt flickered through her at Willa's no-nonsense approach to get the gifts wrapped.

The little furniture left no place to sit; even the table wouldn't be able to be utilized. Rider came up with a solution.

Taking a roll of wrapping paper, he sat down on the carpet within easy reach of a stack of toys and began wrapping.

There was no way she was going to be able to get comfortable in the bulking confines of her coveralls. Unzipping it, she started peeling it off, exposing her pink Henley fleece shirt. She had to sit down to remove her boots, revealing her pink socks. Then she stood up to kick off her coveralls. Her jeans were old and faded, hugging her hips and making her feel self-conscious that she wasn't dressed up like Willa, Rachel, and Aly were.

Taking a seat on the carpet across from Rider, she began wrapping a cute doll with ponytails.

Rider had wrapped three before she had finished her first one.

"I've never seen anyone wrap that fast."

Rider reached for another toy. "I have plenty of experience. Willa ropes me into doing this every year."

"Now I feel guilty. You didn't volunteer this year—"

"I told Willa when she asked me that I would convince you to help me. You saved me the trouble." He finished wrapping a small plastic truck, setting it aside to pick up another toy. With his head lowered, he couldn't see her watching him.

"I'm sorry."

He raised his head at her sudden apology. "What for? I just said—"

"That I misjudged you. You're a really nice guy, Rider." She restlessly switched her weight to her other hip, trying to make herself more comfortable on the carpet.

"You think I'm nice?" Rider looked at her the way she had looked at Willa when she had authoritatively taken control of who was going to wrap which presents.

"I believed you only had one thing on your mind, and truthfully, I had no intention of getting to know you better. I was wrong. You gave an outrageous sum of money for a date with me, which is how Willa was able to buy so many toys. You were kind to Mag, despite me springing her on our date. Not only that, but you've kept me company for the last few days and made the nights go by so much faster. Thank you for becoming a friend."

"You think I've been trying to become your friend?"

She shyly fumbled with the bow she was trying to stick to the top of the present she had wrapped. "It doesn't matter what your intentions are. It's how I think of you."

"Is it?"

Jo nodded, not raising her head. "I've never considered a man a friend before." She was exposing a part of herself she had never let anyone see before, man or woman.

"Not even before ..."

Jo raised her eyes as he delicately broke off the question he was about to ask. She had never talked about her attack to anyone, other than her mother and father. When Aly had convinced her to get Rider on their side, she knew she would have to break and tell him to make him empathic to her cause. It was one of the main reasons she hadn't wanted to do it, never believing it was possible to discuss the events of that traumatic night, especially if it would lead an act of violence against Curt.

Now that she was being honest with Rider, that she considered him a friend and had bowed out of helping Aly seek her own brand of justice, it made it much easier to talk to Rider about it. It all came down to the simple reason that she wanted to finally put it behind her, in the past, where it belonged.

"Not even before I was raped." Jo stopped wrapping the presents. Raising her knees, she rested her head on them to keep from meeting his eyes. "It was the first time my mom let me go to a football game alone. My dad had promised to drop me off and pick me up right after. I had never been interested in going before.

"Curt was in my Algebra class, and I had a huge crush on him—all the girls did. I was too shy to actually talk to him during class, but that day, he stopped by my desk when the bell rang and asked me if I was going. I told him I was. I felt so happy that he had asked if I was going." Jo lifted her head off her knees to stare up at the ceiling as she fought back the hatred, not at Curt, but at herself. "I was so gullible.

"He waited until the rest of the students had left the room before he talked to me, but I didn't realize it at the time, so thrilled that he had noticed me. It took me most of the afternoon to talk my mother into letting me go. She even offered to go with me. I told her I didn't want to go if she went with me. I thought I was too old to need my mom trailing after me.

"When Dad dropped me off, I sat in the bleachers alone. I had gotten there early enough that I got a front-row seat near where the players would be standing. When Curt walked out onto the field, I waved at him ... I waved ..." Jo buried her face in her hands, taking deep breaths before she could compose herself. When she did, she lowered her hands, finding a small tear on the knee of her jeans and worrying it.

"During the last ten minutes of the game, Justin came to

sit next to me and told me that Curt wanted me to meet him at the outbuilding where the equipment was stored. I told him I couldn't, that my father was coming to pick me up. He said Curt would drive me home, and Curt would wait in case I changed my mind.

"I still remember waiting for my father, keeping an eye on my watch as everyone left the field. Two minutes before the thirty minutes were up, I went to the storage building. I was just going to ask to use Curt's cell phone. I wasn't even planning on letting him give me a ride." Jo could see the tear on her knee widening as she picked at it. "When I knocked on the storage building, Curt, Jared, Tanner, and Justin were inside.

"You want to know the stupidest thing I did?"

"No ... stop. Jo, you don't have to tell me anything."

She lifted her eyes, inexplicably wanting to share with him what had happened to her that terrible night. "I don't have to ... but I want to."

She took a deep, fortifying breath. "When I asked to use his phone, Curt raised it up over his head, so I couldn't reach it. He had a beer and said if I wanted to use his cell phone, I would have to finish it. I was smart enough to try to run, but I wasn't smart enough to fucking scream. I should have screamed my lungs out.

"I didn't scream when Curt ripped my top off, or when Tanner blocked the door. And I didn't scream when Justin held my hands behind my back so I couldn't fight. I didn't scream when Curt raped me, or Jared, or Justin. I was too terrified that someone would open the door and see me with four boys in the storage building.

"They left me, torn and bleeding on the floor, like I was trash. But before they left, Curt warned them to keep their mouths shut. He wasn't worried they would tell someone that they had raped me. He didn't want anyone to know that he had touched a piece of trash like me."

"How did you get home?" Rider's hoarse voice had Jo reaching for a pretty Barbie doll, and then she cut enough paper to wrap it.

"When I finally managed to get dressed, I walked back to where my father was supposed to meet me. I waited another hour for him to show up. I cried all the way home, telling him what happened.

"When we got home, my mom took one look at my face and knew something had happened. I went to my room and listened to my parents scream and yell all night. My mom wanted to go to the police; my father didn't. My mother and I left town the next day."

"I would have killed them if—"

Jo shook her head. "I don't blame my father. Curt and the other boys would have turned it around on me, that I had enticed them. He was trying to protect me in his own way. Curt didn't turn out the way he is without help. His family is just as bad as he is, they're just smarter at keeping a low profile. I was more concerned about my reputation being ridiculed by small-minded townspeople than screaming to the rooftops that I had been raped. Curt and his cousins had already raped me. I couldn't bear experiencing the same thing over and over by everyone in town doing it too from their snide remarks. Curt was the star quarterback, Jared was just as popular, and Tanner and Justin's side of the family came from money. Meanwhile, I lived in a junkyard. I still do."

Jo lifted the Barbie doll, the plastic representation of what she would never be—clean and new, untouched by human hands. It had her wanting to change places with the unemotional toy.

Rider used his booted heels to slide across the space separating them. He reached out, using her hair to tug her head to his shoulder.

"You're not trash, Jo. You weren't then, and you're not now."

"It's okay. I don't believe it anymore. Not really. Times have changed. I wasn't ashamed to tell anyone that Curt had raped me when I got back to town. The whole town knows now. Curt might not have gotten any jail time for it, but it was enough to make him change his last name to his mother's, and I like to think it cost him his job at the high school."

"Why are you telling me this tonight?"

"Because I haven't trusted anyone in a long time, but I do you." Jo lifted her head, giving him a trusting smile. "Besides, I don't want you to feel guilty if you want to blow me off for Aly." She didn't want Rider thinking he had to stay in the room with her if he really wanted to help Aly.

Using a twisting motion in her hair, he raised her head from his shoulder. "Where did that come from?" His unfathomable gaze stared back at her. She gave him a self-effacing one in return.

"If I were a guy, I know which one I would prefer."

"Maybe I'm not a normal guy."

"I'm the one who's not normal. That's what I've been trying to tell you. I want to be upfront with you, not lead you on that there's more between us than friendship, because there isn't."

"There isn't?"

Jo started trembling at the sensual way he was rubbing the back of her neck.

"I'm asexual."

She expected him to refute her claim, or ask any number of questions. What she didn't expect him to do was fall back on the floor, laughing.

"It's not funny. I am."

"You're not asexual."

"Are you me?" She glared down at him. "I think I know myself better than you. Even my therapist agreed with me."

"Was your therapist a woman?"

Jo wanted to pinch him to make him stop laughing.

"I'm asexual."

"Jo, you just told me less than ten minutes ago you weren't."

Her forehead furrowed in confusion. "I didn't—"

"You told me that you had a crush on Curt before he raped you. If you had been asexual, you wouldn't have had a crush on him. What you are is repulsed by sex because of a traumatic event. Not that I can blame you. If I had been forced to have sex with Curt, I would have been repulsed, too."

"That's not funny!" Her eyes watered at the thought of him taking her confession so lightly.

She tried to stand, but Rider tugged her back down onto her butt, using the motion to raise himself from his sprawled position.

"It's easier to laugh than to find Curt and beat the hell out of him for making you believe that about yourself."

"It's not a belief. It's a fact." She folded her arms over her chest stubbornly.

"I can prove to you that you're not."

Jo rolled her eyes. "How? By having sex with you? Forget I said anything. You're being a jerk—"

"Calm down. I was merely offering to kiss you. Friends kiss all the time. If you meant it—that you trust me—what's the harm in a small kiss? I'll even make it easy for you." Rider scooted sideways, sitting on his hands, closing his eyes, and pursing his lips. "I won't lay a finger on you, I swear."

"You look ridiculous," she told him, having no intention of kissing him.

"Come on … Don't keep me hanging."

"Quit. I'm not going to kiss you. Besides, you don't look attractive right now. You look silly."

"Then that should make it easier for you … Come on, Jo. Be brave. Just a little smooch, and I'll believe you're asexual. Have you even kissed anyone since that night?"

"No, I've never kissed anyone," she admitted.

Rider's eyes flew open. "Then, how do you know for sure? Come on, Jo. What have you got to lose?" Rider closed his eyes again, pursing his lips for the kiss he was daring her to give.

She stared back at him, letting her guard down now that he wasn't watching.

What did she have to lose?

Jo could answer that question with two words: her heart.

22

Rider watched Jo through his lashes, seeing the indecision on her face. Not moving a muscle, he let her walk blindly into the trap he had set for her. One good trap deserved another.

He believed her sudden outpouring of the night she had been raped had been deliberate. Trusting him as a friend had been planned to garner a protective attitude from him. Going along with her was his own plan of turning the sword back on her. Revenge was double-sided, and he didn't like being anyone's patsy, though Curt more than deserved being taken out.

He didn't believe for one second that Jo wasn't telling the truth about what had happened to her that night. And if she had come right out and asked him to kill Curt, he would have done it without hesitation. He still might if he could find a way without drawing attention to The Last Riders. Anyone who hurt a woman that way didn't deserve second chances, and certainly after the tactics he had used to harass Jo.

However, he wanted to see how far she would go to convince him. It wouldn't be the first time a woman had tried to manipulate him. Viper and Lucky had been the ones to warn him then, and he hadn't listened. He would never ignore their warnings again. He had paid dearly for not listening then.

He was about to raise his eyes when he spotted her inching closer. Closing his lids tighter, he listened for her movements, holding his breath.

The moment her lips brushed his, Rider had to hold back a groan. Like a perfume that never smelled the same way on another woman, no two women kissed the same.

Her lips quivered against his. They tasted like salty tears and fear.

His dented pride that she had been lying to him about his car, and why she was letting him ride along with her was sucked out of him when she then trustingly laid her hands on his chest and pressed her lips more firmly against his.

A woman could lie with words, deeds, and her eyes, but they couldn't lie with their kisses. At least, Jo couldn't. She wasn't pretending the fear, nor was she pretending the small spark of response she felt at their kiss.

Rider let his lips part slightly, giving her the option to further the kiss, waiting for her to retreat. With iron-filled determination, he kept his cock from rising when he felt her tongue entering his mouth, rubbing along the inner skin of his bottom lip. Opening his mouth wider, he touched his to hers, enticing Jo farther inside.

The sound of a cell phone had them both opening their eyes.

"It's yours," Jo said, scooting away and reaching for the Barbie. She began wrapping it as he answered his phone.

"Lily went into labor." Knox's voice had Rider getting to his feet immediately.

"On my way." Rider grabbed his jacket, shrugging it on as he returned to Jo. Hunkering down, he lifted Jo's embarrassed face to his. "I have to go. Lily's in labor." Without giving her time to protest, he pressed a firm kiss to her lips. "We'll pick this up another—"

"There's nothing to say. I proved my point."

"You did? I must have missed that. It felt very sexual to me."

"It didn't."

Rider pressed a finger to her lips. "Don't lie. It's very unbecoming, especially when we both know it isn't true."

"I don't know …"

Rider dropped his hand, brushing his knuckles against her nipples and perking them up even more until they were blatantly thrusting out at him.

Jo turned her face stubbornly away from him. "I thought you were in a hurry."

"I am. I'm just not going to let you lie to yourself about what just happened, even if it makes you feel better."

"A gentleman wouldn't gloat."

"Sweetheart, I'm no gentleman." Giving her another kiss, he rose, then strode across the room. Opening the door, he saw Rachel and Cash coming from a room farther down the hall, their expressions just as intense as his.

"You can ride with us. Willa called and said she and Lucky already left. They wanted to make sure you had a ride."

"How long has she been in labor?" Rider asked as they hurried outside and piled into Cash's truck.

"You know as much as we do," Rachel said, holding on to the dashboard as Cash peeled out of the parking lot.

As they drove to the hospital, headlights glowed behind them. From the side-view mirror, Rider could see motorcycles making their way to the same place.

Moon, Trip, and Gavin were getting off their bikes as Rider, Cash, and Rachel were getting out of the truck. Rider was surprised to see Gavin there. He preferred being alone during the day and would ride alone during the night, despite every attempt he and the other brothers made to include him, or tried to ride with him.

Rider fell into step with him as they went through the sliding glass door and down the hallway to where Willa had texted Rachel they would be.

"Where's Shade?" Rider asked Viper when Gavin sat down next to him.

"In Lily's room with her."

"That won't last long." Rider sat down next to Gavin, forcing his presence, though he could tell Gavin wished he had picked another place to sit. "Shade doesn't do well with Lily in any type of pain." Stretching his legs out, he waited for the fireworks to begin.

It only took two minutes before the elderly doctor came into the waiting room.

"Viper, may I speak to you privately?"

Rider grinned when Dr. Matthews lifted a handkerchief out of his pocket to mop up his sweaty forehead.

"Here we go." Rider used his elbow on Gavin as Viper left with the doctor.

"Something could be wrong." Gavin shifted away, out of reach of his elbow.

"If something were wrong, we would know. Shade goes apeshit over Lily."

"You exaggerate."

"Think so? Cash, Gavin thinks I'm exaggerating about Shade going apeshit over Lily when something goes wrong."

Cash hooked an arm around Rachel's shoulders, leading her to Viper's empty chair. Sitting down, Cash tugged Rachel down onto his lap. The waiting room was filled to capacity with The Last Riders.

"An ape would have more common sense." Cash grinned. "He's more like a psycho on steroids. Isn't that right, Vixen?"

Rider could sympathize with Cash's wife as she could only sit and stare at Gavin. He was a fearsome sight with his new haircut and tattoo.

"I should go call Holly and ask if she and Greer can spend the rest of the night with Mag and Ema." Excusing herself, Rachel moved away to the farthest edge of the room.

"I don't think Rachel likes your new haircut," Rider teased his friend.

When Gavin stood up and strode out of the room, Rider watched him leave with a heavy heart. At one time, he and Gavin had been closer than he had been to Viper. They had become friends the first day of basic training. It had even been their idea to start The Last Riders.

He could sit there and let Gavin have time to heal, but since getting to know Jo better, he realized that old wounds didn't heal themselves. They just made them more dangerous.

Rider watched as Gavin walked down the hall then went into a room to the side.

Walking down the hall himself, he was about to go into the room when he saw Stud, Calder, and their wives coming from around the corner. Calder stopped to talk to him as the others hurried into the waiting room.

Rider's eyes went to the side, watching Gavin get a drink then sit alone by the window. About to say a quick hi, he was determined not to let Gavin be by himself.

Calder's eyes also went to the side, seeing Gavin. Then he turned back to him.

Rider expected him to go inside and talk to Gavin, but he was surprised when Calder took his arm, leading him back toward the waiting room.

Rider jerked his arm away, stopping. "I was going to talk to Gavin."

"Gavin doesn't want to talk right now. He wants to be left alone."

Rider liked Stud's brother, but he was man enough to admit to himself that he was also jealous of him. He had the relationship now with Gavin that he had once had. He had been trying to break through the sheet of ice Gavin had placed between them without any success.

"He stays locked up in his room most of the day. He rides alone. The only time he talks to one of us is when he's working out." Rider raised his voice deliberately, wanting Gavin to hear his frustration. "I want—"

"What you want and what Gavin needs are two different things." Calder kept his voice low and steady.

"Memphis betrayed him; the rest of us didn't."

"Gavin knows that. That's why he's still here."

"Then why the silent treatment?" Rider dug his heels in when Calder's jaw tautened, and he motioned him to go into the waiting room. He wasn't going anywhere until he had it out with Gavin. If he blamed him for not being there when Memphis had kidnapped him, he would readily accept the blame. He deserved it. He had let Gavin down.

"It's not about you, Rider. It's about Gavin." Calder raked his hand through his hair. Moving to the side, he then braced his back against the wall. "You're trying to re-connect with a man who doesn't exist anymore."

Rider felt as if Calder was chipping away at his heart with an ice pick. He hadn't believed he had enough of his heart left to hurt anymore. Calder was proving him wrong.

"You know what makes Gavin tick? He lost years of his life and the woman he loved. Only two things kept Gavin strong. One was his fiancée, and the other was The Last Riders."

"We're here." Rider clenched his fist, then hit himself on his chest.

"Are you? Gavin hasn't left. He's staying at the club."

"What are you trying to say?"

"I'm not trying to tell you anything. I can't. I'm Gavin's sponsor." Calder stared meaningfully into his eyes. "You served in the military with Gavin, didn't you?"

"Yes. Why?"

"Viper said that Gavin was highly decorated. That true?"

Disconcerted by what he felt Calder was trying to tell him, he answered, "Yes."

"It takes a special kind of man to become decorated."

"Yes. Gavin did the Navy proud."

"I imagine Viper and Ton were proud of him, too."

"Gavin lived to make Viper proud. It's why he went into the military. Gavin hero-worshiped his big brother. It's why he wanted to expand the factory. He wanted to prove that The Last Riders weren't just a motorcycle club, but that they could make a difference in people's lives. That's why he chose Treepoint. It was economically depressed. When Shade's father told him about the people here, he wanted to help."

"That's the kind of man he is." Calder nodded, his eyes delving into his.

Rider stared back. Calder was trying to tell him something without revealing any of Gavin's secrets.

Rider emotionally stepped back, thinking about his friend logically.

Gavin hadn't interacted with The Last Riders since his return, maintaining his distance from the brothers and the women, with two exceptions: Knox and Diamond. Why would he make an exception for them and not Viper or him? He and Train had been closest to Gavin before his kidnapping. What made Knox and Diamond special now?

Taking into account what made Gavin tick, what Calder was trying to tell him finally clicked.

He reached out to the wall to steady himself, closing his

eyes as a burning agony seared his soul so deeply he couldn't catch his breath. Only one time in his life had he experienced a pain so excruciating that it cut him off at the knees.

He had to talk to Knox.

Gathering his strength, he started for the waiting room to find the man, when Calder caught his arm again.

Jerking away, he nearly punched him to make him let go.

"Later, Rider. Tonight's not the night. Tonight is for the joy of birth, not reliving old nightmares."

Rider nodded.

This time when he made to go into the waiting room, Calder let him.

Finding a seat, he started thinking, racking his mind as to what could be so bad that Gavin felt unable to talk to him and Viper. He was still sitting there when the sun began to shine through the blinds and Shade came out to tell them that he had another son and that Lily was fine.

Rider stayed apart as the brothers and women came forward to congratulate him. Gavin stood stoically to the side, watching Shade for the same reason.

It wasn't often that Shade let his emotions shine through. As unemotional as Shade was, he was a good father and husband. His small family was his weakness, but it was also his strength. His family made him human and not the assassin the military had trained him to be.

Shade's harsh features were softened with a love that shined brighter than the sun outside. He had weathered many storms with Lily and would inevitably weather many more, but the constant that would see that their marriage would survive was love.

It was something Rider had forgotten how to do or believed himself incapable of doing again. Shade hadn't given up, hadn't retreated. It had been possible for him because, from the second he had seen Lily, he had fallen in love with her.

Gavin stood alone, surrounded by people who loved and cared for him, just as Jo did.

Jo ran around town, helping anyone who needed her, yet she kept herself separated, using her truck as a barrier from taking part in their lives, handing out small parts of herself to keep herself from being hurt again.

Gavin and Jo had been victims, both unable to see past their private horrors. They couldn't take the one constant that could free them from their nightmares.

Rider was given his nickname in the military because he didn't stop. He would ride through a shitstorm to complete a mission. He could take on Gavin, who he loved like a brother, and Jo, who, while he didn't love her, could give him the future he wanted. It just depended on if he wanted to.

It wasn't a question where Gavin was concerned. With Jo, it was.

Standing, he went to the cord to raise the blinds. Looking out, he saw Jo's tow truck drive into the parking lot. Curious, he watched as she stopped and got out of the truck. Then she went to the passenger door, opened it, and reached up, holding her arms out for the small boy who jumped into them. Grinning, she set him down as Sasha climbed out. Sasha then took Shade's son before going toward the hospital entrance.

Rider narrowed his eyes as Jo took one step toward the hospital, then stopped. The myriad of expressions on her face were easy to interpret as she argued with herself over whether she should go inside or not. It was clear she wanted to, but instead of doing what she wanted, she got back in her truck and drove off.

It was the yearning on Jo's face that made his decision for him where she was concerned. It was the same yearning he felt every time he was with Shade and Lily, or the other married brothers. It was why he would steal time away with the wives when their husbands were gone.

The yearning of one day having that slice of heaven for himself.

Raising the blinds, he let the sun pour into the room. It wasn't the only thing he allowed inside. Calder had been right the previous night. This time was about birth, and with birth came hope.

Rider felt the first flickers of hope that he hadn't experienced in a long time. If he was lucky, maybe he would be able to make a start in healing. Not only with Gavin and Jo, but find a small piece for himself.

23

J o snuggled under her blanket, trying to get warm. Lying sideways on her couch, she was too tired to get up and turn her space heater up higher. She rested her head listlessly on the arm of the sofa, trying to stop shivering. She should have just stayed in her truck. It would have been easier to keep warm.

She had spent Christmas Eve towing cars that wrecked, thanks to the sudden snowstorm that the forecasters had said would miss them. She had stayed out on the roads until the wrecks had been cleared.

Fighting exhaustion until the snow had stopped, with the beginning of the flu, she had come home, determined to get a few hours' sleep before she was called out again. Hopefully, everyone had gotten to where they were going and stayed there until the weather cleared.

Shivering harder, she started to cough. Her full bladder had her braving the cold room, moving out from her cocoon.

Swaying, she had to rest her hand on the back of the couch as a spasm of coughing overtook her.

Placing the back of her hand to her forehead, she felt the heated warmth of a high temperature.

Finally, she gained momentum to make it to the bathroom.

Turning on the bathroom heater, she took a shower, trying to lower her fever. Getting out, she put on her favorite flannel pajamas and her mother's old robe.

In her bedroom, she found a thick pair of socks, and a thicker blanket and a pillow.

She flipped her space heater on high and curled back down on the couch, tucking the blanket close to her face, she sniffled into it, feeling miserable.

She wondered what Rider was doing. After the night she had kissed him, he had been trying repeatedly to invite himself on her tow runs. That had been over a month ago. However, she had refused his offers, as well as the many invitations that Rachel and Winter had issued.

The hardest invitation she had refused was from Lily, who had wanted her to come for dinner to meet her new baby, who they had named Clint. The adorable baby in the pictures that Lily had texted her had her aching to hold him.

"Clint looks just like Shade and John. Please come, Jo."

Jo had made the excuse that she wasn't feeling up to the weather and didn't want to expose the baby to her germs. God was punishing her for lying.

Her sniffles and another round of coughing had her sitting up and reaching for the cough syrup that was as old as she was. Shaking it, she saw that the black goo was so thick she could see clumps dancing inside it. She would rather take the coughing than drink that. Besides, it was probably a cold. She would feel much better after she got some sleep.

Jo had no time for being sick. Aly had kept her promise to take her to court for the money her father had owed. The official letter was still sitting on her coffee table, where she had left it to motivate her. She only had until January fifth to pay the outstanding balance. If it wasn't paid, a lean would be placed on the property, or worse. The judge could order her father's property be sold to pay the money back.

Reaching for a pen and paper, she wrote out her expenses, cutting and slashing what she could to come up with the money.

Tired, she closed her eyes. She tried to force them open until she could tabulate the columns of numbers. However, the pencil slowly slid from her grasp as both pencil and paper fell to the floor.

Jo WHIMPERED IN HER SLEEP, feeling like she was on fire. She kicked her foot out to kick the thick covers off.

"Shh ... Go back to sleep."

As cold water was placed at her lips, she opened her eyes.

"What are you doing here?" Jo winced at the raw tinge of pain she felt when she spoke. Taking a long drink of the iced water, she would have drunk it all, but Rider pulled it back, making her take small sips.

"Knox got worried when you didn't answer his call, so I volunteered to come check on you. It's a good thing I did. Your fever is over 102."

Jo tried to move the glass of water away with her hand while trying to sit up in bed. "I need to get back to work."

"You're not going anywhere. Train borrowed your truck to answer Knox's call. He's also going to make your rounds, so you can relax and go back to sleep."

"Train can't operate that truck. It's a complex machine, not like a regular truck."

"Train can land a helicopter during a sandstorm or as bombs go off; I think he can handle your tow truck."

Jo felt tears of frustration at her inability to get out of bed and to kick both his and Train's asses for doing what she should be able to do herself.

"Why are you crying?" Rider lifted her, giving her tablets to take before giving her another drink of water.

"Because I feel bad."

"You're crying because you're sick?"

"Yes. I'm never sick, and this couldn't be a worse time to be sick."

"You told Lily over a week ago you were sick, and that was why you couldn't visit her."

"I lied. God's paying me back."

"God's not making you sick to pay you back. The flu has half the people in town in bed. Mick had to close the bar late last night he was so bad."

"Mick is sick?" Jo tried to get out of bed again. "I need to go check on him."

"Beth is with him. He's in better shape than you are, and he's twice your age."

Jo cried harder. "That doesn't make me feel any better."

Rider pushed her back down on the bed. "Jo, you're exhausted. You've been working yourself to the bone for the last six months. The flu took the last reserves you had left."

"I just need a couple hours. When I wake up, I'll feel better." She took the washcloth out of Rider's hand and scrubbed her tear-soaked cheeks.

"Unfortunately, Dr. Price disagrees. He was here two days ago—"

"I've been sleeping for two days?" Jo's screech ended in a spasm of coughing that had Rider reaching for a bottle of cough syrup.

"Take this," he said, pouring a spoonful.

She took it only because she had no alternative if she wanted to breathe.

It took several minutes for her coughing to settle. Lying back on the pillows Rider had punched up for her, she sighed in defeat.

"I'm sick."

"No shit, Sherlock."

"Gloating is very unbecoming in a man," she mused, tucking the blankets tighter around herself.

"Is it? I'll have to remember that. I gloat a lot." He smiled as he gathered the empty glass and dirty spoon to take to the kitchen.

She dozed off when he was gone, waking during the night with the urgent need to go to the bathroom.

She threw her covers off and was trying to rise when an arm around her waist tugged her back down.

Screaming bloody murder, she struck out in the dark, striking something squishy that had her cringing in disgust.

"Goddammit! Stop screaming, Jo. It's me." Rider turned the light on, nearly blinding her with the suddenness of stark brightness.

Jo gaped at a shirtless Rider sitting on her bed under the same cover she had been under.

"You have two seconds to explain why you're in my bed."

When his lips opened, she changed her mind.

"Forget it. I don't care. Get out!" she screamed, pointing a finger at the door.

Rider moved his hand away from his rapidly swelling eye to stare at her. "There isn't anywhere else to sleep."

"You can sleep on the couch. Or better yet, you can go home. I'm sure you have numerous beds to sleep in there."

"The snow's over thirteen inches outside, and Train is sleeping on the couch. I'm not going to wake him when he just got to sleep. He hits harder than you do."

Jo wobbled out of bed, going to the window. The lamp-post in the middle of the yard showed her how massively high the snow was outside.

Jo laid her forehead on the cold window. "Only I would get sick on one of the few money-making days of the year. Do you know how much money I'm missing out on by being home?"

Rider searched through the covers on the bed, coming up with a familiar yellow pad of paper. "I don't have to guess. I know."

Jo went to her bed, snatching the pad out of his hand. "This is none of your business."

"I made it my business when I found it ... and the letter stating Aly is suing you."

"I need to go to the bathroom." Jo needed time to think.

"Then go."

Swearing under her breath, she went into the bathroom, used it, and then brushed her teeth, unable to bear the taste in her mouth.

She was getting about to get back under the covers, so focused on what she was going to say that she forgot to order him out of her bed.

"Get out! Go sleep with Train. Or, better yet, walk home." Yawning, she climbed under her blanket, tugging the majority of them away from Rider. Then she stopped when she became worried he might be naked. "You better be wearing pants." Glowering at him, she tossed half an inch back toward him.

"I found a pair of your father's pajama bottoms."

"You went in my parents' bedroom? Is there any part of my house you didn't snoop around in?" Coughing, she reached for the cough syrup. Not seeing the spoon, she opened it and simply took a large drink.

"That's prescription strength."

Ignoring his warning, she took another sip for good measure.

"I want to go to sleep."

"Then go to sleep. I'm not stopping you." He settled back on the bed, turning the light off.

"Are you being serious?" She felt her forehead in the dark. Was she more feverous than she had thought? Was she delirious and didn't know it?

"I've been taking care of you for the last three days. I'm tired. The roads are too bad for me to leave. If you don't want to sleep here, you can go sleep on the couch with Train. He sleeps like a rock, so he probably won't know you're there. On the other hand, Killyama might kill ya if Train tells her. The fucker couldn't keep a secret if he tried."

Despite herself, Jo snuggled back under the covers. She couldn't remember the last time her house was this warm. Even the bed felt toasty. Either that or that cough syrup was stronger than she had thought.

"Keep to your side of the bed." Her eyelids felt like they weighed a thousand pounds each. She groggily tried to lift them, then decided she was better off with them closed when she heard Rider shifting on the mattress.

"Don't worry; I'm not anxious to catch your flu cooties."

"I don't have cooties. I brushed my teeth." Her eyelids flew open at her words. It had made her seem like she wanted him to kiss her.

"I'll take your word for it. Unlike you, I'm not asexual. Unlike you, Train will deck me if I try to share the couch."

"I'm not asexual," she admitted, snuggling back onto the mattress. She didn't know why she was admitting it to him in the middle of the night, when he was inches away from her in the bed. Only that, if she died from the flu in her sleep, she didn't want to carry that lie to her grave.

"I'll keep that in mind for when you're feeling better. Night, Jo."

She was asleep before the last two words were out of his mouth, sinking into the mattress she'd had since she was a teenager. The indentations worn through time curved around her.

Subconsciously, she slipped into a deep slumber, knowing she was safe and warm, listening to the sounds of the night, twigs breaking from the weight of the snow, the floorboards creaking. After her father's death, she had jumped at every sound in fear. It was easier to get sounder sleep in her truck than her bed.

With Rider beside her, she didn't have those fears and could find a deep sleep, subliminally aware of the gentle hand going to her forehead, checking for fever, or soothing her when her body was racked with spasms of shivers, pulling her close to share his body heat with her.

Consciousness tried to beckon her forward. Not experiencing the tender touches from another human being since she was a small child, she resisted the pull. In her fever-induced haze, it wasn't another Christmas night that she wouldn't have to spend alone. As Christmas presents go, she hadn't asked for Rider, but when given this particular present, it was better not to ask God why, and just enjoy.

Jo wrinkled her nose under the covers. Poking her head out, she sniffed. Her stomach growled at the aroma.

It took her several seconds before she could get her wobbly legs under control as she got out of bed. Finding her robe, she put it on, knotting it around her waist. It was when she was slipping her house shoes on that she realized the floorboards were warm, not giving her the cold rush of reality she usually dealt with most mornings.

She took the time to brush her hair before leaving her bedroom.

Her eyes went around the living room, finding it empty and Rider in the kitchen doing the dishes. The smell coming from the stove had her moving forward, seeing Rider watching her in amusement as she stood over the steaming pot.

"It's chicken soup. Rachel dropped it off with the cough syrup Greer sent over."

Jo spotted the bottle sitting on the kitchen counter. Picking it up, she saw it was blacker and thicker than the one she had found in the medicine cabinet.

"Rachel said to only take a small sip every four hours."

"Uh … no. I'd rather die."

Rider laughed. "I can't say I blame you. Rachel told me how Greer makes it. You're better off with the prescription Dr. Price gave you." Rider moved her to the side when she sniffed the soup again. "Sit down. I'll fix you a bowl."

Jo eagerly went to sit at the small table to the side of the kitchen. Pushing the curtain aside, she looked outside, telling Rider, "I need three bottles of it. That stuff was the bomb. I don't remember anything after I took it."

"That was the codeine in it," he said, setting a steaming bowl of soup down in front of her.

"You're not having any?" Jo swirled the homemade noodles in the broth with her spoon, then took an appreciative taste, savoring the flavors.

Glancing up, she caught a strange expression on Rider's face.

"I'm hungry," she excused, self-consciously taking a smaller bite.

"You're very expressive when you eat."

"I am? I like it." She shrugged. "We have something in common. I like to eat, too."

"Most people do."

She was about to take another bite of her food when she realized her truck was gone. "Where's—"

"Train and Moon went on a call. The brothers are fighting to see who can go with him next."

"No one. I'm going to shower, and then I can take over again—"

"No, you can't. You're still running a high temperature. You're not going anywhere for at least a week, and that's only if Dr. Price gives you a clean bill of health."

"It's not up to you."

"We'll talk after you finish your soup."

"There isn't anything to talk about … at least where my work is concerned. What I want to talk about now is how my furnace is working."

"You were too sick to be left alone, and I couldn't take my balls freezing off, so Train fixed it."

"Is there anything Train can't do?"

"I may have been exaggerating about him flying in a sandstorm."

Jo had to hide her smile by taking another spoonful of soup.

"I don't know how he managed it. I've been saving up for another furnace."

"Save yourself the money. It would be cheaper to bulldoze your house down and start over."

"That's not nice."

"The truth hurts. You're a big girl. I think you'll be all right." Taking her empty bowl, he refilled it before sitting down at the table across from her.

She knew he was waiting for her to finish eating before he said anything else. Contrarily, she took her time, savoring each bite until his eyes narrowed on her suspiciously.

"Even if you eat the whole pot of soup, you're not going to get out of what I want to talk to you about."

"There's nothing to discuss, other than how much I owe Train for working for me and fixing my furnace and stove."

"I fixed the stove. Your wiring is shit. You blew a fuse. And save yourself the trouble from adding to the list of bills to be paid." Rider stood, going to the living room, then returning with her yellow pad and the letter saying she had to appear in court. Rider then fixed himself a cup of coffee and her a glass of juice before sitting back down.

Her appetite deserted her when he set the pad down on the table.

"I'd rather have the juice."

"You'll be lucky if you keep the juice down."

"You fixed my fridge, too?"

"It was on the same circuit breaker."

Jo wanted to bury her face in her hands, embarrassed that she hadn't been able to fix something so simple. "I didn't think to look. My dad usually took care of things like that."

"You would have figured it out if you hadn't been driving yourself to the point of exhaustion to pay bills you don't have a chance in hell of paying."

"I'm making progress."

"You were until ..." Rider pointed to the large sum of money that was what her father had owed Aly's father. "I take it this is the money Aly is taking you to court for."

"This isn't any of your business."

"It actually is. The money Shade lent you for the tow truck was company money, and I'm one of the owners of the company. The Last Riders wouldn't have lent you that money if they had known the extent of your debts."

The soup she had just eaten threatened to come back up. Taking a drink of her juice, she forced it back down.

"Let's see if you can be more honest with me than you were with Shade." Rider trailed his finger over to the name of the month she had written down with the figure. "Is this when you found out about your father's debt? Or did you know before?"

"I didn't know about it before," she croaked out.

He trailed his finger down the columns of numbers. "I don't see you paying any of Aly's debt off but here." Rider pointed to where she had crossed out several bills that she was going to ignore in order to make a payment to Aly. "Why were you trying to come up with the money the day before Clint was born when you knew about the loan your father owed since Aly came to town?"

"Rider, I'm not feeling well. I need to go back to bed." She shakily started to get up.

"Sit."

Jo's butt hit the chair, although she wanted to go back to her bedroom and bury herself under the covers until he left.

"We couldn't come to an agreement on how to pay the money back. That's why she's taking me to court."

"How did you originally think you could pay her back? You only started to find the money last week."

"It doesn't matter."

"It matters to me. Depending on your answer, I'm going to help you out of this mess."

"I don't need your help."

"You'd rather lose your home and business than accept help from me?"

She stared out the window. To anyone who came into the yard, they would just see old cars stacked on top of each other, but it meant a lot to her. Some of those cars had been put there by her grandfather. She could even remember when the old blue Ford was stacked on the red L.T.D. with the white vinyl roof that was placed on top of it by her father.

"What do you want to know?"

"Explain." Rider pointed to the large sum she owed Aly.

"Aly wanted me to pay the loan back other than by using money. I agreed at first, because I didn't have the money to pay it back."

"How did she want you to pay it back?"

"By getting me to convince you to go after Curt Dawkins." She felt so ashamed of her actions. She didn't expect Rider to speak to her ever again. When he told The Last Riders, they would all hate her, too.

"How did Aly think you would accomplish that?"

Jo flushed, keeping her eyes on the window. "Not by

using sex—I wouldn't have agreed to that—but by trying to get you to like me. I mean, in a romantic sense."

"I know what you meant."

Her flush deepened at his sardonic jibe. She felt foolish for ever having agreed to Aly's plan.

"Yes, well, I went along because I thought it would give me time to come up with the money. I thought I would win the bid to garage the state's vehicles. It's the perfect location, only three miles away from the State Police headquarters and the government offices."

"Except, you didn't win the bid."

"No, they decided it was cheaper to build their own, and they awarded the money to one of Curt's cousins to build a new garage."

"Tough luck. You shouldn't have counted on it anyway."

"I know that now."

"Why did Aly want you to attract my attention?"

"She thinks Curt's responsible for her parents' deaths. When Knox couldn't find any proof of wrongdoing, she wanted to get The Last Riders involved. They have a bad reputation around town, in case you didn't know."

"We know."

"They do?" She shook her head. "Anyway, Aly said some of the people who had hurt women belonging to The Last Riders had disappeared or ended up dead. Aly wants Curt dead, and she wants you to do it."

The stark truth coming out of her lips had the color leaving her face. She was so cold that she shivered underneath her robe.

She tearfully stared out the window, hearing Rider scoot his chair back as he got up. She couldn't blame him for leaving. She hated herself for agreeing to go along with Aly's plan for so long.

She was startled into tearing her gaze away from the

window to look up at Rider when he placed a blanket around her shoulders.

"Why did Aly choose you? She could have tried to get my attention herself."

"She did. She said that's why she started hanging out at the club. But when she heard some of the women members joking that the men were trying to fix you up with me, she decided she would have more luck with them becoming involved if I were the one in a relationship with you."

"Aly has a devious mind." Rider's face didn't reveal what he was thinking.

"Yes, she does," Jo agreed. "I tried to talk her out of it, but I felt bad for her, too. Both her parents are dead, and I can understand why she feels that Curt is responsible. Curt has a worse reputation than The Last Riders."

"And how was Aly going to get me onboard with her plan?"

"Actually, she came up with the idea when Shade asked her to pretend to use her discount to pay for a nice dress, and he would pay the rest."

"Really? I'll have to thank him for that."

Not missing the small tick of a muscle on the side of his forehead, she pulled the blanket tighter around her.

"Whose idea was it to use the perfume? Aly or Shade?"

"Perfume? I don't …" The muscle ticked harder. "Aly." Jo raised her blanket to cover her scarlet cheeks, mumbling through the thick material, "The women in the club told Aly that you … uh … uh … like it when they buy new perfumes."

If she had been offered a million dollars, she wouldn't have been able to look at Rider. It had been embarrassing enough when Aly had told her many of Rider's secrets, much less confessing to his face what she had been told.

"Why are you so embarrassed?"

Despite herself, she looked toward Rider, curling her

fingers into the thick blanket. Slumberous eyes watched her reaction with the intensity of a panther stalking its prey.

"I admit I have a thing for sexy perfume. Just like I think a woman wearing pink is sexy."

Jo tucked her pink socks under the hem of her robe and surreptitiously tightened the knot at her waist, forgetting he had seen her in her pink Henley last night.

"Sex involves all the senses: touch, sight, smell, taste … even the way a woman says my name can be a turn-on."

"I think we're getting off track." Jo cleared her throat before taking a sip of her juice.

"I think we're just getting to the best part. Who picked the perfume?"

"I did. Aly said your favorite is Chanel. I googled the closest matches and came up with the one I chose."

"Which woman told Aly my favorite perfume?"

"I don't remember. Aly must not have told me."

Rider's lips quirked. "I'll leave that alone for now. So, why did you scratch out the bills you were paying and move that amount under the amount you owe Aly?"

"After you won the auction, I tried to back out, but she wouldn't let me. I met her about a month ago and told her I wouldn't do it, that she would have to come up with another plan or get your help herself."

"What did she say?"

Jo picked up the court letter and tossed it toward him. "That's what happened. She's suing me."

"Why did you back out?"

This was the hardest to explain. Jo tried to come up with a different explanation, other than the truth, deciding at last to be completely honest and let the coin fall where it would land.

"I was afraid of you. I told Aly that I thought you were more dangerous than you pretend to be."

"That was smart of you."

"Not too smart or she wouldn't have sued me. I should have played along with her until she realized you had no interest that way."

"Why didn't you?"

"You wouldn't stop riding along with me. Then I worried you might actually hurt Curt after the night at the bar. It was easier to just tell Aly no and stop letting you ride with me."

"Why did you tell me about the night you were raped?"

"I didn't know what Aly would do. I already told her I wouldn't help her, and I didn't want her using Curt's attack on me to ever factor in you hurting Curt. It happened to *me*, and I had finally let go of the fact that Curt got away with it, that it was left for God to deal with him."

"I see. And you really feel that way?"

"Yes, I do. I never wanted Curt killed. I wanted him behind bars. It would kill his pride if everyone in town knew where he was, and his family wouldn't be able to cover for him anymore."

"What about Justin and Tanner?"

"I feel the same way toward them." She gave a bitter laugh. "I imagined them sent to different prisons so they would be alone and couldn't depend on each other. That would have been worse than hell to them. Justin and Tanner can't tie their own shoes without Curt."

Rider picked up the letter that had fallen onto his lap and set it on the pad of paper. "Are these the bills you owe?"

Jo shrugged out of the blanket, going to the coffee table and pulling out a thin drawer. Grasping the mound of bills that she had hidden from sight because she couldn't pay them, she walked back to the table and set them on top of the stack Rider had created.

Sitting down in her chair, she waited expectantly for him

to tell her that he couldn't help her, when he arched a brow at her.

Confusion turned to understanding when he reached forward and lifted the blanket over her shoulders, folding it closed in the front.

"Are you ready to hear how we're going to solve your problems?" He stared at her the way he had the night of the auction.

The last time she had listened to an offer of help, she had regretted it and ended up deeper in debt.

"Do I have to?"

"Yes. I think it will be better to get it over with now."

"Then, can I have my cough medicine? I think I'm going to need it."

25

"No, I'm going to make this painless." Rider slid the bills to the side, then tore off the yellow paper until he came to a clean page. Picking up the bills, he folded the sheath of papers and bills together, placing them in his jacket pocket that was hanging off the back of his chair. "You now have a clean slate."

Rider rose, getting Jo another glass of juice, then setting a prescription bottle down by it. "Take one. It's an iron supplement."

Jo took the pill, staring down at her juice. "I can't accept your help. I called Drake after I received the letter. He's having an appraisal done on the garage and most of my land. I should be able to make enough to at least keep the house."

"What the appraisal showed was that you would be lucky to pay off half of what you owe."

"How would you …? Drake *told* you?"

"That would be unethical, wouldn't it?"

He didn't deny nor admit it, but she must have figured it out when her head fell to the table.

"Lord, kill me."

Rider couldn't help laughing. "You've been spending time with Mag."

Jo lifted her head to glare at him, which had him laughing harder.

"You don't like her, do you?" she accused.

Rider reached out to remove a stray noodle that was stamped to her forehead, using the opportunity to see if she was running a fever. He was barely able to snatch his hand back before she tried to swat it away.

"I can't stand the bitch," he admitted.

"That's just mean."

"I can be mean when I have to be." He shrugged, picking up his coffee cup. "In this case, I think everyone in town would agree with me."

"Everyone in town loves Mag."

"Name one." When he saw she was going to name several, he cut her off. "Name one who isn't related to her."

Her mouth snapped shut, then opened. "Me. I love Mag, and I'm not related to her."

"Name one besides you."

When she didn't immediately, he couldn't help but smirk at her.

"Cat got your tongue?"

"I'm thinking," she bit out, then snapped her fingers under his nose. "Mick loves her."

"You think so? Let's ask him." Rider took out his cell phone, pressing Mick's number.

"You're not seriously calling him."

His answer was another smirk as Mick answered.

Rider put it on speaker phone. "Mick? I have a quick question. Do you love Mag?"

"You high, Rider?"

"No, I'm not high. I'm not drunk either. I'm with Jo. I told her that I don't like Mag, and I told her that no one in town loves that old bitch, other than those related to her. Well, except Jo. She said you do. I disagree with her. So, do you love Mag?"

The static crackled across the line as Mick hesitated. "I like Mag, but I wouldn't go so far as saying I love the woman."

Rider jerked the phone out of Jo's reach when she tried to take it from him.

"Calm down, Jo. Me and Mick are just kidding around. Mick, you want to help Jo out? Can you think of anyone in town who loves Mag?"

"Do they have to be breathing?"

"Mick!" Jo yelled over Rider and Mick's laughter.

"Jo, are you really there with Rider?"

"Yes!"

Rider couldn't resist grabbing the tail end of the blanket she had wrapped around her when she got up to go toward the coffee pot. Tugging it, he made her sit back down.

"I was just joking. Me and Rider cut up all the time," Mick tried to explain through a coughing fit. "I need to go and take my medicine ..."

"Traitor!" Jo then, as if unable to help herself, asked, "Are you doing okay?"

"I will be with Beth and Razer looking after me. Greer brought me some of his cough syrup, so I'll be back at work tomorrow night."

"You're actually taking it?"

"It knocks that flu right out of you. He makes a batch every winter. He uses horehound candy, rock candy, and 100% Kentucky Bourbon. I don't have much left, but I can call Greer and get him to bring you some."

"When did Greer give it to you?"

Rider's shoulders started shaking when he saw Jo looking at the large bottle he had sent her.

"About an hour ago..."

"Mick, you're only supposed to take a sip every four hours."

"You have some? If you have any left, can I have it? You know, just in case I'm not feeling better by tomorrow. The first bottle is free. The son of a bitch charges thirty dollars after that, and it's half the size of the free one."

Jo shrugged the blanket off her shoulders and started rubbing her face. She was getting upset, so Rider decided to put her out of her misery and end the call.

"Thanks for your help, Mick. I'll have Train bring over what Jo has left." He disconnected the call to see Jo staring at him angrily.

"That stuff is going down the drain."

At first, Rider thought she was laughing. When he saw tears sliding out of the corners of her eyes, he realized she wasn't. When she saw that he could see her tears, she couldn't hold her sniffles back.

"I feel like crap!" she wailed, reaching for the discarded blanket to hide her face again. It was either that or she was trying to use it as a tissue.

Rider immediately stood. Bending down, he lifted her into his arms, and her head fell to his chest as she cried a storm of tears that he would never have imagined her capable of.

"I hate being sick."

"I know, baby. It's the flu, and you're not going to bounce right back."

Rider tucked her back into bed, giving her the medicine the doctor had given her to relieve her fever. Sitting on the side of the bed, he then handed her several tissues and waited until she had her tears back under control. He didn't have to check to see if her fever was spiking again. Her flushed face showed that it was.

The blue smudges under her eyes told him how sick Jo was. She had been working herself to exhaustion for so long that the flu had been able to strike with a vengeance. It was going to take a good deal of care to see her restored to full health.

"Can I get you something, except for coffee?"

"Can I have another glass of juice?"

"I'll be right back."

At her nod, he left her to make a glass of cranberry juice. She had finished the last of the orange juice. He would text Train and have him run to the store before bringing the truck back.

When he returned to the bedroom, he found Jo sleeping. Setting the juice down on the bedside table, he left the bedroom, closing the door behind him.

He used the time she was sleeping to make a grocery and pharmacy list for Train. When he was done, he called Viper.

"How's it going?" Rider asked without preamble as soon as his president answered.

"Moon and Diablo installed cameras on Aly's property."

"How is she?"

"Mad. She lied and said Jo made it all up when Shade and I confronted her. Then, when I told her Jo wasn't the one to tell us, she blamed Ember and Stori. Said they were the ones who gave her the idea."

"That bitch is a piece of work. I can see how she and Georgia were friends. She going to do what we tell her?"

"Yes. She may be a cold-hearted bitch, but she loved her parents and wants to find out the truth—if they were murdered or not."

"Shade figure out why Curt wants that property?"

"Not yet. He gave that job to Greer. Shade has his hands full with the baby. John and Lily both have the flu."

"Shade is taking care of the baby all by himself?"

"Yes. Most of the clubhouse is down with it, too. You, Moon, Train, Gavin, and I are the only ones who have escaped it so far."

"Take plenty of videos of Shade waiting on everyone—"

"No, I like my new phone. Besides, Shade's not letting anyone inside his house."

"When did you get a new phone?"

"When Shade broke my last one after I videotaped him watching *Dirty Harry* with the baby while Lily was at church with John. I was stupid enough to say I was going to show her."

"That wasn't bright. Even I wouldn't have been dumb enough to do that," Rider gloated before realizing Viper had hung up.

He made sure to delete his own video of Shade mimicking Clint Eastwood with a cigar in his mouth. He had filmed it when Shade had come back to get Lily and the baby some clothes after Clint had been born. The brothers had all shared cigars together before Shade had gone back to the hospital. He hated to lose the video, but he loved his phone more.

Looking at his watch, he hurried back to Jo's bedroom door, opening it slowly to make sure she was still sleeping. Then he closed it when he saw she was.

Going to the old refrigerator, he held his nose as he removed the only thing inside—the bottle of cranberry juice —setting it on the counter.

Heaving the refrigerator to the side, he then unplugged it before scooting it away from the wall. He had just finished when he heard a truck outside.

Opening the door before the delivery driver could knock, he signed his name on the electronic pad. Rider then stood on the porch as two men unloaded the new fridge he had ordered over the phone.

He had to go inside to grab his jacket when the wheel of the dolly went through one of the rotted boards of the steps. It took all three men to get it on the porch. Then Rider prayed the entire time they brought it inside that it wouldn't sink through the sagging floors.

The delivery drivers were leaving with a generous tip when another truck pulled in next to the appliance truck.

The electrician got out of his van, going to the side to open the sliding door and coming out with a toolbox.

Rider took him inside to show him the fuse box.

"You don't need an electrician. You need a match and a good insurance policy."

"My old lady is attached to this house."

"I'd get a new woman. You can have mine. My alimony payments are killing me."

"Can you fix it or not?" Rider was getting worried that Jo would wake up and see what was going on behind her back.

The beady-eyed electrician looked like a shark that could smell blood in water. "How much are you willing to pay?"

"You related to Greer Porter?"

"No, but I know him. We share a beer every now and then."

"We're friends. He told me you'd give me a good deal."

"You're lying. Greer doesn't have any friends."

Rider could see the price going up every time he opened his mouth. Wisely, he knew when he was beaten. "Just fix it."

"You got cash? I don't take checks."

"You take credit cards?" Rider had to bite his tongue. The electrician might not be related to Greer by blood, but they certainly were by greed.

The electrician set the toolbox down. "With my alimony payments? Believe it."

He was congratulating himself for his iron control when he heard Jo call out from the bedroom.

Rushing to it, he opened the door to see Jo getting out of bed.

"You shouldn't get out of bed!"

"I have to go to the bathroom."

Rider took her arm, letting her lean on him as they walked out to the bathroom. He tried to stop her from seeing the man who was in the small closet, working on the fuse box, but Jo was sick, not blind.

She came to a stop. "Who's he?"

"The electrician."

"I thought you said you fixed the fuse?"

"I wanted to get a professional's opinion."

"I can't pay for an electrician. Do you know how much they cost?"

As Jo's voice rose, the electrician's beady eyes met his.

"You paying or not?"

"I am." Rider sent him a warning glance.

The electrician nodded, going back to work.

Rider heard Jo cursing under her breath as she went to the bathroom. He leaned back against the wall outside, waiting for her to come out. When the sound of water came through the thin walls, he took the opportunity to go back to the closet and warn the electrician to keep his mouth shut about money.

"It was supposed to be a surprise. When you're done, I'll go outside and pay you."

"She didn't look happy at her surprise. She looked like my ex, which is why I dumped her ass. We must have the same taste in women."

"You and I are completely different." Rider was so frustrated by the electrician that he was tempted to shove the expensive toolbox up his ass.

"You can say that again," he mumbled into the breaker box as if it would agree with him.

Fed up, Rider was close to throwing out the electrician and calling the number that had promised emergency and prompt service. One that didn't remind him of Greer with every word coming out of his snarky mouth.

The sound of water being turned off had him returning to his position by the bathroom door.

"Better?" he asked solicitously.

Her hair was damp under the towel she had wound around her head. The sight of the gray pajama top peeking out of the neckline of her robe showed she had also changed her night clothes.

"I need another glass of juice."

"Go back to bed. I'll get it."

Not listening, she moved toward the living room.

Groaning inwardly, he tried to redirect her back to her room. Other than picking her up and carrying her there himself, he was left with no choice but to follow her.

"What is that?"

"What?"

Her widened eyes narrowed angrily at him as he went around her to take the juice out of the fridge.

"Where did it come from?"

"I bought it." Pouring her a glass of juice, he then nodded in the direction of her room. "Go ahead. I'll bring it."

"I can carry a damn glass of juice myself," Jo snarled. "What was wrong with the other fridge if you fixed it?"

"It had an odor."

"Then don't open the darn thing." Jo pointed at the new refrigerator. "It's going back."

"No, it's not. I paid for …"

She became so furious he could see her visibly shaking.

"I don't need you to come here and fix things! I don't need you to pay my bills!" Jo jabbed a finger to her chest. "Me, not you."

Rider saw the hurt pride in her flushed face. "I agree. That's why I'm keeping a tab on what you owe."

"Huh?" Jo's jaw went slack at his words.

"The money you owe Aly, your bills, the electrician, the fridge—all of it will be added to the loan The Last Riders are giving you."

"*The Last Riders* are loaning me the money? I thought you said The Last Riders wouldn't have lent me the money for the tow truck if they had known how deep in debt I was? The money I owe Aly is nearly twice that amount, and that doesn't include my other bills."

"That was when you had no way of generating a new income. The Last Riders are willing to lease your garage. We need to expand the factory. Rachel's work with hydroponics needs more room at the factory than we're able to give her. It requires her to be close to monitor the plants and equipment. We can't give her that room now. But if we use your garage to house our vehicles and bikes, we could use that portion of the factory for her.

"You and Shade can hammer out a deal that will benefit both you and The Last Riders. Of course, we will take out the money we're going to lend you out of whatever deal you agree on."

Expressionless, he waited for her reaction. He could practically see the wheels turning in her head as she considered the offer.

"Not only would we rent the garage, but Train and I were talking about how convenient it would be to hire your services exclusively for The Last Riders."

"Doing what?"

Rider carried the juice to the coffee table, not answering her question until she sat down on the couch. Going to the bedroom, he then grabbed a blanket before going back to the living room and laying it across her lap.

"Basically, doing the same thing you're doing now, except being paid for it. Plowing the clubhouse and factory's parking lot, Rachel and Cash's driveway, the church's, and Dr. Price and Dr. Matthew's. You wouldn't have to answer calls at all hours of the day and night. You could work normal hours."

"Winter only lasts a few months; what am I supposed to do the other months of the year?"

Rider sat down on the coffee table and stared at her before saying, "I know, Jo."

A puzzled frown crinkled her forehead. "Know what?"

He waited in silence for her to figure out what he was talking about. When she still looked confused, he prompted, "I know what's in the garage."

Jo looked down at the blanket in dismay. "You know?"

Rider could barely hear her whisper.

"How?"

If he wanted honesty from Jo, he was going to have to give her the same in return, or partly.

"Before offering you the loan, I thought I should check the garage out to make sure it would work with us housing our vehicles there. When you were sleeping, I took your keys and went inside. You have a cool setup there. It has plenty of room."

"You saw your car, didn't you?"

"Yes. I can't lie and say I wasn't surprised." The lie rolled off his tongue so expertly she didn't blink. That was always a good sign. Going slow, he lured her to the path he wanted her to go. "Does Carl use your garage to work on cars?" He knew damn well who was working in that garage, and it wasn't Carl. He was testing her to see if she would tell the truth while withholding it himself.

"No, I do. I was going to tell you when I felt better."

"Why didn't you tell me when we were sitting at the table?"

"I was too embarrassed about talking about my involvement in Aly's plan ... and showing the number of bills I have to confess to that, too. I'm sorry."

Rider looked away from her bluebonnet eyes and her mortified expression, steeling himself to get the rest out of her.

"You've been rebuilding my car?"

"Yes, and I did Killyama's, too."

"Who owns that sweet ride I saw in there?"

"I do."

"You rebuilt that one, too?"

"Yes." She brought her hand out from under the blanket, waving it toward the junkyard outside. "It's not like I don't have a yard full of spare parts."

"I saw the setup for where you can even paint cars. That must have cost a pretty penny."

"It did. I was hoping if I got the contract with the state vehicles, I could charge for repairs if any of the cars were in wrecks."

"Why didn't you just open a business working on cars?"

"How many men do you think would hire me to work on their cars in town?"

"I know several, in fact. Do you know how to work on motorcycles?"

"Yes. I may not know how to fix a fuse box, but I can do anything mechanical."

"Train and I both hate working on our machines. We'd be glad to hand that job over to you. I have two bikes I've been wanting restored. Moon has one, and so does Cash. He wants the bike he crashed restored. It was his favorite ride."

"They'd let me do it?"

"Without a doubt. That would give you something to do when it's not snowing. You'll even be able to use the tow truck to bring the bikes down from our Ohio chapter and bring them back afterward. You could do something you enjoy instead of sleeping with one eye open, waiting for Knox to call."

"I could do both. That way, I could pay the loan back faster—"

"Whoa … That's not up for debate. You either work exclusively for The Last Riders, or it's no deal. You're so exhausted Dr. Price doesn't want you to go back to work for a while. You can't burn the candle at both ends. It's slowly killing you."

"It's just the flu. I'll—"

"Either/or, Jo."

"Who will do it if I don't?"

"You'll be forcing the council to hire someone else who can help out. You'll also be giving someone else the chance to open their own tow truck business. Let them be the one having to sleep in a truck and respond to fatalities. Don't you want a normal life?"

"To me, it's normal."

"Give it a chance. What have you got to lose? You may find out you love working in your own garage without the long hours. You would be creating a normal for yourself." He paused. "Sometimes you have to step away from one life to discover a better one."

Jo sighed. "What I'm doing now isn't working, so I'm going to give it a chance. If Shade and I can come to a deal, then I'll do it."

Rider hit the palm of his hand against his thigh. "Good girl. Now, get back to bed."

She stubbornly didn't move. "Are you going to be one of my bosses?"

"Why?"

"Because I'm already getting tired of you bossing me around."

"I won't be your boss, but you're going to wish I were," he taunted. "You're going have the same one I have … Viper."

"He can't be any worse than you."

"I'll remind you of that when you start working for us. Now, if I ask nicely, will you go back to bed?"

"Why? Is someone else going to show up to fix something while I'm sleeping?"

Rider smiled. Standing, he reached out to help her up. "No, I just want you to get better so you can take me out for a drive in your car."

"Can I drive?"

"No." Jo grinned, feeling happy to be out of her house.

She expertly shifted gears as they left the outskirts of town. The muscle car's tires glided over the pavement, cutting through the water on the road like a knife through butter. Most of the snow had melted, leaving traces of water as if it had never been there.

She turned her eyes from the road long enough to see Rider rolling his window down and putting his hand out. His enthusiasm had the memory returning of how he'd looked the night of the auction.

The loneliness that had been weighing down on her shoulders since her father's death was gradually lessening, replaced by Rider's companionship. His friendly and no-nonsense approach toward her sickness had her feeling as comfortable with him as she would with a nurse. The only snag—well, two, actually—was her suspicious nature telling her that Rider wanted more from her than friendship, and her own growing physical attraction to him. He had even offered to blow-dry her hair when she had been too weak to do it herself. She had promptly taken the dryer from him after a few minutes, unable to bear his gentle touch as he had run his callused hands through her hair.

She had finally talked him into going out for a ride, despite his concern that she would have a setback, by tempting him with the promise of a ride in her car.

Jo breathed the fresh air in, not concerned about the chilly air. Rider, however, turned the heat on high.

She was unused to the care he was always exhibiting toward her. It was what heightened her fear there was more going on between them than friendship. She was scared silly that it might already be too late to prevent her burgeoning feelings for him from deepening.

It was a frightening thought, one that had her going even faster, as if she could outrun the feelings she was secretly beginning to feel for him.

He only left the window down for a few seconds before he was rolling it up again.

"Leave it down!"

"We can when the weather gets warmer."

Jo stuck her tongue out at him, then hastily put it back in her mouth when his eyes narrowed at her in warning.

Embarrassed, she kept her attention focused on the two-lane road, speeding around another curve.

"You're lucky Knox hasn't pulled you over for having your windows tinted so dark."

Jo gave a joyous laugh. "He has to catch me first."

When they reached Jamestown, they picked Sonic to eat at. Pulling into an empty parking space, they placed their order. Jo grinned proudly as the customer in the next space gave her a thumbs-up as he pulled out.

"People will be doing the same to me when you finish my

car," Rider boasted. "Mine is going to make yours look like a Volkswagen."

"Do I hear a hint of jealousy in your voice?" she teased.

"Maybe."

His pout was adorable, but she wasn't about to tell him that. Instead, she tugged the mirror down to smooth her tousled hair. Taking it out of the ponytail, she quickly pulled it back neater.

"Why don't you just leave it down?"

"It gets in my face."

She was reaching for her wallet as the waitress approached on skates, when Rider shot his hand out before she could get her cash.

"I'll be right back, sweetie."

Jo knew the woman with the tight black leggings wasn't referring to her. Giving Rider his burger and fries, she opened hers after stealing a fry from him.

She was about to steal another one when the waitress came back. Instead of coming to her window, though, she went to Rider's side, giving him the receipt and his card back.

"Cool car," she gushed, bending over until her face was level with Rider's. "It's nice of you to let her drive it."

"It's mine," Jo smarted off, forcing herself to take another bite instead of ripping the woman's head off the way she wanted to.

"It is. I've been trying to get her to let me drive it." Rider gave her an amused look, moving his fries to his other hand and out of her reach. "Can you bring me another order of fries?" He held the card out again.

"Sure thing, sugar. Don't worry about it; it's on the house." She gave him a wink, not taking his card as she went back inside the restaurant.

"I wonder how the manager would like her giving food away."

"Stop wondering. Daryl knows Missy likes her customers happy."

"You know her?"

"I come to Jamestown a couple days a week," he said, tossing his empty hamburger wrapper into the bag at his feet.

"What days? Wednesdays and Saturdays?"

"You keeping track?"

"Do you take a rest on Sundays?"

Rider shook his head, laughing. "I never rest. There's enough time for that after I die."

Jo winced at the old saying. "Now who sounds like Mag?"

"Bite your tongue. That old—"

"Don't you dare say what you're about to say. I'm not sick anymore, and I'll leave you to hitchhike back home."

Rider raised his hands up in surrender as the waitress came back with his fries.

"I brought you another burger. I knew one wouldn't be enough to put a dent in your stomach."

"Thanks, Missy. I appreciate it. You coming to the club-house this weekend?"

"I wouldn't miss it. You going to be there? I missed you last week."

"I'll be there. I'll see you then. Thanks for the burger."

Any enjoyment she'd felt on the drive was gone. She focused on eating the rest of her burger as Rider rolled the window up and started eating it.

"You could have told me you wanted another burger when I asked what you wanted."

"I was trying to watch what I ate. I haven't been working out lately. I was barely able to button my jeans this morning."

Not thinking, her eyes went to his crotch. Then she jerked them away when she caught him staring.

She had been embarrassed many times in her life, but being caught staring at his crotch had to be the worst.

"You want some of these fries?"

"No, thanks."

Starting the engine, she pulled out, heading back to Treepoint. She was kicking herself for ever suggesting driving to Jamestown in the first place. She didn't want to know that Rider was going to The Last Riders' Friday night party. He had spent last Friday watching a movie with her, as he had the last two weeks.

It dawned on her that she was better and there was no longer any need for him to stay with her.

The thought wasn't as welcome as she would have thought. She was going to be alone in her house, listening to every sound and movement it made.

With that thought, she didn't drive as fast on the way home as she did going, every mile bringing the time they had spent alone to a close.

"You happy with the deal Shade offered?" Rider broke the silence.

Shade had come to her house that morning with the legal papers that would get her out of debt if she accepted the offer she and Rider had discussed when she was sick. It was more than she had expected, and she still didn't quite believe she would be starting over without the insurmountable financial worries that had dogged her footsteps for the last few years.

"What's not to be happy about? I'm debt free, and I can start work on Monday. He even told Knox already that he needs to find another towing service."

"You don't seem happy."

"I guess I'm scared of the unknown. I don't deal with change easily. That's why I came back to Treepoint."

"I was scared when I went into the military. I was scared

shitless the first time I went on a mission. I was scared the first time I was married."

Jo nearly jerked the steering wheel. "You've been married?"

"Twice. Once to my high school sweetheart. The second time to a woman I met overseas."

"You've been divorced twice?" She hadn't expected him to have been married once, much less twice.

"Divorced once. My second wife died."

Jo glanced over to see him staring ahead at the road. "I'm sorry."

"Thank you."

"Do you have any children?"

"No, I haven't been blessed with any so far."

"You want children?" She sounded as incredulous as she was.

"Is that so surprising?"

"I'm sorry. I ... You just seem pretty happy as a bachelor."

"I am happy. I won't stay where I'm not. That's why I joined the military when I turned eighteen."

"I didn't mean to be nosy."

"You're not. I was the one who started the conversation. You're a strong woman, Jo. Probably one of the strongest women I've ever known. You've been able to face Curt, Justin, and Tanner, despite what they did to you. Starting a new job will be a piece of cake for you."

"You think so?"

"I know so. I have every faith in you."

"I didn't take you for a religious man," Jo teased, the enjoyment of being with him returning. "I never see you in church on Sundays."

"The only religion I believe in is football."

She scoffed. "I don't believe you."

"Believe it." He gave her a crooked grin as she crossed the

county line into Treepoint. She hated to see the turnoff to her home.

Winding through the old cars toward the garage, she pressed a button on her visor to raise the door. Driving inside when she had enough room, she parked it in the back of the garage, then looked around the almost empty space. In four days, it would be filled with The Last Riders' motorcycles and cars.

She was about to get out of the car when Rider reached up, took the garage door opener, and put it in his pocket.

"What are you doing?"

"I wanted to have it handy for Shade when he comes in the morning to put the security camera up."

Frowning, she got out of the car and walked outside with him, waiting for him to close the door with the opener. "I could have given it to him myself."

"Shade wants to get an early start. There's no need to wake you up. You haven't been getting out of bed until ten. Enjoy what free time you have left. I'm anxious to get my car finished, almost as much as Cash wants his motorcycle restored."

She nodded at his explanation as they walked to the house. She wanted to argue, but she wouldn't if that meant he was going to stay another night. She couldn't explain to herself why she wanted him alone one more night, too afraid to look inside herself to find the answer.

Rider hung his jacket up on the peg on the wall before sitting on the couch, propping his feet on the coffee table, and nabbing the television remote before she could.

"What are we going to watch tonight?"

Jo sat down on the other side of the couch. "*Zombie Apocalypse* is on Netflix."

"No, let's watch something else."

"Like what?"

"I don't care as long as it's not dead people wandering around, looking for something to eat."

"Are you scared?" she said in a sing-song voice.

"No, you are."

"Me?" She looked at him in astonishment. "I love zombie movies."

"They give you nightmares. Let's watch *Smokey and the Bandit.*"

"How do you know they give me nightmares?"

Rider dropped his legs to the floor. "I'm getting a beer. You want some juice?"

"Yes, you can get me some after you answer my question."

"You cry out when you sleep."

He went to the kitchen, coming back with a glass of juice and his beer.

"So, is *Smokey* good for you?"

"It's fine," she said, distracted by trying to think back to any memories of nightmares. "I really have nightmares?"

"Every night, except for the nights we didn't watch horror films."

"I love horror films."

"I love onions, but they mess with me."

"Really, that's why you don't like onions?"

"Yes. I hate the taste they leave in my mouth," he said, starting the movie.

"What else do you love to hate?" Jo folded her legs on the couch, sitting cross-legged.

Rider laid the remote on the arm of the couch where she couldn't reach it. "I love to eat on dishes, but I hate to wash them," he joked.

"I love working on cars, but I hate waxing them." Jo got into the game she had started.

"I love buying new boots, but I hate breaking them in."

"Ouch." Jo laughed. "I love popcorn, but I hate the kernels."

"I hate electricians."

"You're supposed to say what you love about them in comparison."

"I don't love anything about them." Rider propped his feet back on her coffee table.

"That reminds me. When Shade and I itemized the bills The Last Riders are paying off, the electrician's bill wasn't there."

"I must have forgotten."

"Don't worry about it. I called his company and added it to the list Shade has."

"How did you know the name of the company?"

Jo shook her head in exasperation. "It was printed on the back of his coveralls."

"Oh. Good thinking."

"I thought so." She beamed proudly at him, pleased she had outsmarted him. Not much got past him. "I also had him add in the groceries you had Train bring to the house."

"How did—"

"I got Train's number from Shade. And I also had him figure out how many hours he worked when I was sick."

"What did he say?"

"He told me the amount of the groceries, but then hung me up on me when I asked him about the hours, so I guesstimated them."

"I bet you did."

"Are you being sarcastic?"

"What gave you that clue?" Rider turned the volume up on the movie. "Sometimes people want to help without anything in return."

"And sometimes people don't like to take handouts."

"It wasn't a handout. How long is it going to take you to pay back the loan with everything added in?"

"A few years."

"More than a few. Will you at least be able to retire before you're ninety?"

"Yes, The Last Riders offered me a very generous sum for the lease and to work for them."

"Cool. You want to start work early and get me another beer?"

Jo threw a small pillow at him. "I hope you're joking."

"I am. Can I watch my movie now? I love watching movies, but I hate when people talk during them."

"Jerk."

They were twenty minutes into the movie when Jo decided she wanted something to nibble on. Going to the fridge, she grabbed two sodas and a bag of popcorn out of the cabinet. Setting one down for Rider, she opened hers, then sat down cross-legged again, opening the popcorn.

"I hate when people get something good to eat, and don't offer to share."

She tilted the bag so he could take a handful. "You don't know when to stop, do you?"

When he didn't answer, she looked over, catching him watching her.

"I know when to stop when I want to."

"Your jokes are as bad as Jackie Gleason's." Jo turned the popcorn's opening back to her. "I have to buy some more of this popcorn." It was a mixture of cheddar cheese and caramel. The two flavors together were one she had never tried before.

"It's my favorite. I like sweet and salty."

About to take a drink of her soda, Jo looked over the top of the can to see him staring at her again. "What?"

Rider gave her a mysterious smile. "Nothing. You in the mood for a pizza? I can order us one."

Jo groaned out loud. "I love pizza, but I hate my fat ass after I eat it."

Rider reached out, taking the popcorn bag away from her. "I love fat—"

Jo squealed, bending over on her knees to press a hand to his lips. "Don't you dare ..."

With that mischievous look, Rider stared back at her from over her hand, his shoulders shaking with laughter. Then he reached up, pulling her hand away.

"I was going to say, I love fat ... crusted pizza."

"Really?" She stared at him skeptically.

"What did you think I was going to say?"

"Never mind. I'm sorry I misjudged you."

"S'all right. Can I have the popcorn back? By the way, your ass looks fine to me."

E very time she felt herself nodding off, she forced her eyes back open. Knowing it was the last night Rider would be staying, Jo hated to go to bed. She wanted it to last.

The damn pizza had done it. She had eaten two slices. Now full and content, her body just wanted to sleep while her mind fought it.

"Jo, go to bed."

She felt his hand on her shoulder, jerking her awake.

Raising her lids, she saw he had changed the movie.

"What are you watching now?"

"*Gumball Rally.*"

Jo stood up, stretching. "Good night, Rider."

"Night, Jo."

She sleepily made her way to her bedroom door.

"I'm glad you're feeling much better."

The sound of his voice as she was about to go into her room had her turning around to face him. A chill went up her back when she saw the way he was looking at her.

"Thank you. I am, too," she said, not taking her eyes off him until her bedroom door was safely locked behind her.

What in the hell was that? The frantic thought raced around her mind as she paced her bedroom.

Tearing the rubber band out of her hair, she tried to calm herself. Had she imagined the sound of promise in his voice? Or the way he had looked at her, the same way he had the night of the auction?

Taking a steadying breath, she concluded it was her overactive imagination. Meanwhile, her inner voice screamed to barrage herself in her closet.

Reasoning came to her rescue. Rider had been alone with her for almost two weeks and hadn't done anything to deserve the fear coursing through her body. He had been a gentleman every inch of the way, had found a solution to her problems, and he didn't want anything in return … so far.

Psyching herself back up, she got ready for bed, dressing in old red flannel pajamas and its matching top.

About to get in bed, she felt the need to go to the bathroom. She tried to ignore it, but she knew she wouldn't be able to go to sleep until she relieved herself.

"Dammit, I shouldn't have drunk those sodas." Padding to the bedroom door, she silently unlocked it, trying to sneak out of her bedroom and into the bathroom without Rider seeing her.

"You're not asleep yet?" He was standing behind the couch, a beer bottle at his lips.

Her eyes widened when she saw he had removed his shirt and boots, standing only in his jeans that rested on his hips. Her mouth went dry, feeling as if she was trying to talk past a clump of cotton.

"I need to go to the bathroom." Feeling like an idiot, she fled into the bathroom.

After using it, she didn't want to go back out, then she grew embarrassed for taking so long.

"Jesus, I am an idiot," she muttered, washing her hands before exiting.

"Good night again." This time, she was smart enough not to look at him, her feet flying over the floor to her room.

"Night again."

His amusement had her wanting to catch another glimpse of him before she shut the door, but she didn't want to chance it.

She had seen his chest briefly the night he had slept in bed with her, but the sight of him when she wasn't sick had her wishing for a magic wand to erase the memory. It was the dead of winter; how did he even have that sun-burnished glow? The numerals tatted across his chest had her wondering about the significance to him.

Turning her light off, wide awake, she tossed and turned, trying to get comfortable. Feeling hot, she began to think she was catching the flu again.

Thumping her pillow repeatedly until she was satisfied, she finally settled into a fitful sleep that took her until dawn to finally fall into a deep one.

She was sprawled on her belly with her pillow over her head when she was awoken by the sound of a knock on her door.

"Jo?" Rider's voice came from the other side of the door.

"Go away. I'm still sleeping," she mumbled.

"Can I come in?"

"No."

"Are you okay?"

The sound of his voice beside her bed had her jerking around, rising onto her elbows.

"I didn't say you could come in!"

"Sorry. I hated to wake you, but I was worried about you." He pressed his hand to her forehead, checking for a fever.

Jo swatted his hand away. "I'm not sick. I was sleeping."

"It's almost one o'clock; I wanted to see if you wanted to eat some lunch."

"It's not one."

"It's five till."

"Jesus, I slept like the dead." Jo pulled the blanket around her. "Get out and I'll get dressed."

"Your wish is my command," he told her, moving away from the bed. "How does a grilled cheese sandwich with tomato soup sound?"

"Like heaven. I'll be there in a minute."

When he closed the door, she jumped out of bed, finding a clean pair of jeans and a blue sweater she had bought at the thrift store. She was dressed and in the kitchen as he was sliding the grilled cheese onto a plate for her.

"You cooked; I'll do the dishes," she said before taking a bite of the gooey sandwich.

Rider gave her a mug of the tomato soup before sitting down at the table across from her. "I'll take you up on that."

"Did Shade get the cameras installed?" she asked, using her tongue to twirl the gooey cheese inside her mouth.

"Yes." His strangled reply had her looking toward him to see him drinking his soup. "Moon and Train also started filling the garage. Cash wants to get started on expanding Rachel's area."

"That's nice of him. I'm anxious myself to see what cars and bikes you brought," she said excitedly. "I hated being nosey when I dropped off Killyama's car."

"We'll go when we're done eating," he promised.

"Thank you so much, Rider. You've helped me so much." Placing her sandwich back down on the plate, she reached across the table to place her hand on his. "I don't deserve it after I went along with Aly's plan. You could have ended up hurt or in jail. I hate myself for agreeing."

Rider turned his hand over, returning her grasp. "That's water under the bridge. Forget it. I have."

"You showed me the last two weeks what you're made of. I want you to know I consider you a friend. Now, if there is any way I can repay you, I hope you'll let me know."

"Depend on it. I'll remind you of that next time we go out on a joy ride and you won't let me drive."

Jo smiled at him sincerely. "Anytime you want to drive my car, the keys are yours."

After lunch, they walked to the garage. She looked around for the cameras Shade had installed.

"I don't see the cameras," she remarked as Rider raised the metal garage door.

"They're there." Rider pointed to three different areas facing the garage.

Jo turned to where he pointed at three different cameras. One was directly behind them that could see the door, one was to the right that would see anyone walking toward it, and the last one was at eye level that could see anyone leaving.

"Shade placed some all along the driveway, too. On the way back to the house, I'll show you where they are. That way, if you need to move any of the cars or need to disturb any of them for parts, you tell Shade and he can put them somewhere else."

"I expected them on the side of the door."

"This gives a clearer picture of their faces and a view of license plates."

"Are there any inside?" she asked as they walked in.

"Five." He motioned to the four corners of the garage. They were mounted high on the walls. "There's also one over here that has an electronic beam that will give an estimate weight and height."

"Can I turn that one off before I go through the door?"

"No. Relax, the feed goes directly to your new laptop. No one else will see it."

"That's reassuring. Wait. I don't have a new laptop."

"I must have forgotten to mention it." Rider went to a workbench, showing her the laptop.

"Am I paying—"

"No, The Last Riders are. The only way Viper would agree to the lease was if he knew our vehicles were safe. This gives him peace of mind."

"I can understand that." Jo looked around her garage in appreciation.

Ten motorcycles rested in a neat line. There were also two cars that had Jo giving a drawn-out whistle of lust as she walked closer.

"Who's are these beauties?"

"Mine."

"Both of them?"

"Yes."

Both cars had her itching to drive them. The Bugatti was completely black, and the Ferrari was a steel gray with a white stripe down the hood.

"Where are the keys? Just in case I need to move them."

"If you need to move them, call me, and I will."

Jo tried sticking her bottom lip out while thinking of a movie that had brought tears to her eyes. She had never pouted before, but if there was time to discover her feminine wiles, this was it.

"Do you need to go back to the house to use the bathroom?"

Jo jabbed him with her elbow. "I was trying to pout."

"That was your pouty face? Jesus, don't do that. It's scary."

"Thanks a lot. I know I don't have your expertise. You've got it down to an art form."

"Yes, I do. It's taken a lot of hard work."

"I bet. How many pieces of candy have you begged for before Willa just gave up and made you an entire batch?"

"Several, but I've never been afraid of a little hard work."

"How you have that flat stomach with as much as you eat makes me want to throw my scale in the trash."

"You noticed my stomach?"

She gaped at him, realizing too late what she had said. "You'll have to show me how to log on to the computer." She tried to distract him by opening it.

"You don't want to talk about my flat stomach anymore?"

"No."

"You're a killjoy."

"Rider …"

"Okay, okay. I'll show how to log on. Then I can show you the camera in the driveway before I leave."

Jo kept her face blank as he quit joking around, showing her how to log on and how to monitor the security cameras. All the while, she felt sick to her stomach that he would be leaving soon.

"You got it?" Rider repeated his question when she didn't answer.

"Got it."

Satisfied, he closed the computer. "Keep it where you can see it in the house or the garage. If you see anything suspicious, hit the red button I showed you and stay put."

"Yes, sir," Jo smarted off.

"Careful, Jo. That sounds good on your lips."

Jo was stunned at his innuendo. For a split-second, she thought lust had shone in his eyes. However, the next second it was gone.

"I may like being one of your bosses if I get that term of respect from you."

"I thought you said you weren't my boss." She followed

him out as he closed the door, then handed her the remote opener.

"I'm not. You're basically your own boss, Jo. I was just kidding. The loan papers are signed, and you have your own copy. As long as you don't break the agreement, you can set your own hours and do the jobs you want to do for The Last Riders. Those you don't, hand them over to Train or me if they aren't too complicated. That's why you were hired, so we can concentrate on other things, other than oil changes or spark plugs."

"Like what?"

"Train is working on an underwater navigating system. And right now, I'm trying to develop a voice-controlled robotic arm."

"No shit!"

"No shit."

"You're that smart?"

As they walked back to her house, he showed her the cameras. However, Jo barely paid attention, stunned he was working on a robotic arm.

"I'm insulted you don't believe I can build a robotic arm, yet you believe Train can develop an underwater navigating system."

"I didn't mean it that way. Just that … I mean … You really don't seem to take things as seriously as Train. For God's sake, your favorite movie is *Home Alone*."

"That's true. I love comedies."

As they went up the porch, he showed her the new doorbell that would take a picture of anyone coming within a few feet of the door.

"It's like I'm living in Fort Knox," she said as they went through the door. She set the laptop on the kitchen table.

"Not hardly, but as close as you can without getting there.

You won't have to worry about anyone egging your house again."

"That'll be a relief. It was a mess to clean." She watched as he went to the couch and picked up his duffle bag. A lump formed in her throat. He was about to leave. Not only that, but it was a Friday night.

She wanted to ask if he wanted to watch a movie, or play another game, go for a ride—anything other than him leaving. Instead, she stood still, tongue-tied as he went to her fridge.

"You mind if I take the last unopened bag of popcorn? It'll give me something to snack on tonight."

"It's yours. Take it. I can get some more when I finish the bag we ate out of last night."

"Cool. Don't forget to keep that computer within sight. Don't worry after dark. We have a security man who watches it until 7:00 a.m. You'll get a text message if he sees something, and he'll send Knox."

"Wow. Shade thinks of everything."

"Yes, he does." With his duffle bag over his shoulder and his popcorn in his hand, he walked toward her. "I'll be going. If you need anything, just call. I guess I'll see you Monday morning. We're going to paint my car, right?"

"Right." Jo licked her dry mouth. Going to the door, she opened it for him. "I'll see you Monday."

"Bye, Jo." With a smile, he was gone.

She had to force herself to shut the door instead of watching him get on his motorcycle. She jumped when it started, the loud sound booming throughout the house until the roar of his motor died away.

Jo looked around the empty living room and kitchen, at the old, worn furniture, the kitchen table that wobbled, the stove that only had two working burners. She should turn her television on or play some music. Anything was better than the silence that was creeping slowly back inside. It had been held at bay when Rider had been there. Now that he was gone, it was back with a vengeance.

Carrying her laptop to the coffee table, she set it down so she could watch it. The remote control was where he had left it. Turning it on, she flipped to Rider's favorite movie, playing *Home Alone*.

"Macaulay, how do you feel about leftover pizza?"

Rider juggled his drinks and the popcorn as he went into the security room.

"You bring us some snacks?" Moon grinned, looking up from the security screen.

"Nope. I'm giving you and Diablo the night off. Go have fun."

Diablo rolled his chair back from the monitors he was watching. "You don't have to tell me twice. I'm out."

Rider was taking his chair before Diablo was out of the room. Glancing at the screen Diablo had been watching, he opened his popcorn.

"Viper said two of us has to be on duty."

"That's when you goofballs are on duty. I've got this. Go. I cleared it with Viper."

"Then I'm gone, too." Moon stood.

"Don't tell anyone I'm here. I don't want company."

Moon raised a brow. "Not even Jewell?"

"Especially not Jewell."

"Why especially not Jewell?" Moon leaned a hip against the desk that held the monitors.

"Brother, the party is waiting. You rather stand here shooting the shit with me or get laid?"

"If you don't want to answer, all you have to do is say so."

"So." Rider reached for another handful of popcorn.

Moon straightened off the desk. "You want me to bring you some dinner when it's done?"

"No, I'm good."

"Later."

Rider leaned back in his chair after Moon left, propping his feet on the desk within reach of the popcorn and his soda. His eyes traveled from one screen to the next, seeing Missy and Daryl arrive and walk up the front steps to the clubhouse porch, remaining there until Nickel opened the door for them.

Seeing the front and the back of the clubhouse was empty, he looked at the cameras that showed Cash's house. Seeing Cash's bike and truck, and Rachel's car, he knew they weren't coming to the party tonight.

When he saw no movement in Cash's yard, he focused his attention on Jo's property. The yard showed no movement along the driveway or the garage.

Raising a hand, he pushed a button on the computer that would activate a screen that had been dark. At his motion, the screen grew bright, showing Jo sitting on her couch, eating a piece of pizza and watching *Home Alone*.

Grinning to himself, he sat watching the movie with her. Every few seconds, his gaze would flick back to the other screens, keeping track of Cash's house and the clubhouse.

His eyes returned to Jo when he saw her jump on the couch, seeing her look over her shoulder toward the door.

Rider sat up, his eyes going to the screen showing the outside. There was nothing there that should have startled her. She must have realized that, too, because she looked toward the cameras on her computer screen and relaxed back on the couch.

Rider frowned. He had told her that she wouldn't have to watch the security feed after dark. His gut churned when it dawned on him she was watching it because she didn't feel safe alone.

"Fuck." Rider closed his bag of popcorn to watch the screen closer, still keeping track of the other cameras.

An older model black SUV pulling onto the parking lot had him watching to see who was getting out. It was Claire and another woman Rider didn't recognize.

Rider texted Nickel that he could let them in when they arrived at the club's door. Claire had told him that her cousin was visiting from Jamestown and asked if she could come with her to the party. Rider had asked for her name and address, and Shade had cleared it yesterday. Claire's cousin could come.

Seeing the women go inside, he studied the other monitors before going back to Jo's. She was still watching *Home Alone*. Jo had finished eating her pizza and had lain down on the couch. Every few minutes, she would raise an arm, looking at her watch.

Rider looked at the time on the screen, wondering why she was concerned with the time. She never closed the computer either. Was she waiting for someone?

As the time grew late, she put on *Smokey and the Bandit* when *Home Alone* ended. He was surprised she hadn't chosen another movie. She had complained when he had played it last night.

Periodically, she would rise to a sitting position as if she had heard something, before settling back down.

It was near ten when she got up to go to the bathroom. The camera he had placed in Jo's living room only gave him a view of the front portion of her house, not of the bathroom or the small hall that led to the two bedrooms.

He had investigated the room when he had placed the camera while she had been staying with Mag. Any guilt he had felt died when he had been monitoring her feed and saw she was sick. Nor had he felt guilty for picking her lock, finding her burning up with a fever and nothing but a small space heater to warm the room she was in. It was a miracle the old heater and wiring hadn't burned her alive when she had been too sick to get out.

He had paid for a new furnace to be installed the next day. The prompt service the electrician had promised meant Jo would never know he had been there and wouldn't be able to add that amount to the loan he had given her.

Shade would never let him live it down that he hadn't wanted Jo to know the loan was from him under the guise of one of the companies Viper managed for him.

Monitoring the clubhouse's cameras, he saw Beth and Razer walking from their house to the club. He waited until the back door was shut securely behind them before switching his gaze to Jo again.

She had returned to the living room and was watching *Space Balls*, and instead of lying back down on the couch, she was pacing. Opening an energy drink, he watched her pace back and forth, occasionally looking at her watch.

"Who's she waiting for?" Rider was getting angry. Was there someone in town she was seeing who he didn't know about? Had Aly contacted her? If that bitch showed up, he would snap her fucking neck.

He kept waiting for whoever Jo was waiting for to show. At first, Rider believed her increased pacing was because of a late showing, but when Jo sat down on the couch and drew her knees to her chest and started rocking herself back and forth, laying her wrist down so she could look at it without lifting her head, he touched the screen, zooming in to see her expression. He could see her lips move, but he couldn't hear what she said.

"Dammit." Taking his phone, he texted Shade.

He watched the other camera as he waited for Shade. He was about to call when he heard the door to the room open.

"What do you want?"

That the brother wasn't happy he had asked him to come was an understatement. A dark shadow of beard was on his jawline, and the dark look he was giving as he took the other chair at the desk had Rider wishing he didn't need the brother's particular skill.

"I need you to tell me what Jo said." He rewound the tape to where Jo said something out loud so Shade could watch.

"You're shitting me?"

"No. I want to know what she said." His jaw clenched. "It'll only take a second, then you can go back to bed."

"I haven't had a good night's sleep since Clint was born, and you woke me up because you want to know what Jo said?"

"Chill. I'll pull your shift in the morning so you can sleep late."

"You're going to pull my next two shifts." Shade moved his hand away from the mouse, clicking to rewind the tape again. "If you had used the camera I told you to use, this wouldn't have been necessary."

"I wanted to give her some privacy."

Rider ignored the exasperated sound his friend made.

"If you're going to watch her, do it right the first time."

"What'd she say?"

Shade removed his hand from the mouse. "She said she hates you."

"She didn't?" Was the brother jerking his chain for getting him out of bed?

"She did. She's obviously mad at something you've done."

"I haven't done shit, other than come home." His mind went back to earlier today. What had he done to piss Jo off to say she hated him? Had he forgotten to put the toilet seat down?

"Guess she didn't want you to leave. We done?"

"Yes, thanks." Confused at being hated on for no identifiable reason, he backtracked, trying to remember if she had shown any hint of her anger before he had left. He was sure he had put the seat down …

Shade nodded, going to the door. "Oh, she also said she hopes one of the women bites your dick off when they give you a blowjob and that the surgeon can't reattach it. Your woman has a vicious temper."

Rider grinned at Shade's retreating back. "Yes, she does. Night, Shade."

He didn't take it personally that Shade didn't respond. The brother was an asshole, especially when his sleep was disturbed.

Satisfied that he knew why Jo was so uptight, and why she was keeping an eye on her watch, he leaned back in his chair and reached for the popcorn again.

"My old lady is jealous," he gloated to himself.

Throwing the empty bag of popcorn away, he yawned, rolling his computer chair over to make a fresh pot of coffee.

He had dropped any plan of revenge against Jo when he had seen how sick she was. She had been working herself toward an early grave, not only physically, but by going along with Aly's plan. If he hadn't found the notepad where she had tried to make her money stretch to repay the loan her father had owed Aly's father's estate, he wouldn't have contemplated backing down on the revenge for her and Aly.

Then again, his doubts about her ruthlessness of using him

to take Curt out had begun to surface when he had seen her in the parking lot the morning of Clint's birth. She had wanted to come inside, yet had been afraid she wouldn't belong during the momentous occasion. Rider had seen in her the same desire he had been trying to attain since he was eighteen.

As the coffee brewed, he rolled back to the monitors, his eyes flicking over the screens with laser intensity.

They were moving from the screen of the parking lot to the one behind Viper's house when a red light glowed in the corner of the screen. Grabbing his cell phone with one hand, he used the other to lower the steel shutters on Viper's house.

"What's up?" Moon answered on the first ring.

"One of the fence alarms behind Viper's house went off. Take Diablo and check it out," Rider ordered, keeping the camera pointed to where he had seen a flash of movement.

"On our way."

Rider disconnected the call, pressing another button to send a mass text to all the brothers. It didn't require him to use any words; it was a simple yellow sign to warn the brothers to be on alert. Rider then scooted his chair closer to the desk, checking the other cameras to make sure there was no activity while maintaining his focus on the camera behind Viper's.

Moon and Diablo were nearing the house, their guns drawn. Diablo stealthily broke away to slink into the shadows of the front porch, reaching the backyard from a different direction.

Two minutes later, his cell phone rang. Rider answered Moon's call.

"We didn't see anything. Probably a deer."

Rider put the call on speakerphone, zooming the camera to search the dense woods, seeing nothing. There was nothing there, but Rider didn't tell the men to stand down. The alarm had gone off for a reason.

"Set up a perimeter until Shade gets there. Something feels hinky." Disconnecting the call, he called Shade. The brother answered it immediately.

"Report."

"I sent Moon and Diablo out to check a sensor alert behind Viper's house. Moon said it's all clear, but I know I saw something."

"I'm on my way. Send Train to my house and notify Razer to keep anyone from leaving the club until I call."

"Already done. I texted Viper. He has Winter and Aisha in the safe room."

Rider set the cell phone down on the desk when Shade hung up, his fingers flying over the keyboard, repositioning cameras, then flipping another switch that would hit the recording feature. Shade would want to look back on what Rider had watched that made him send out the alert.

Rider could only sit and watch as Shade, Moon, and Diablo searched Viper's backyard and the woods beyond until they were out of sight. When he saw Cash coming out of his house on the camera feed, he knew Shade must have found something.

He watched until Cash got in his truck and squealed out of his driveway before sending a text to Knox that Cash was heading to the club. Knox would send a deputy car to watch the place until Cash returned.

Cash drove into the parking lot three minutes later. Getting out, he ran toward Viper's backyard, disappearing into the woods where the other men had gone.

It drove Rider nuts not being able to do anything other than watch the screens, but the one on duty wasn't allowed to leave. They had to coordinate the brothers into a deadly force that kept the women and children safe.

When Viper came out, going to the woods with his gun and locking the door behind him, Rider knew they were tracking something or someone. He wanted to call Shade to ask what was happening, but he didn't, keeping his eyes pinned to the screens to make sure the others remained safe from harm.

His eyes flicked to Jo, who had fallen asleep on the couch with the television on. Assured she was safe, he waited for Shade to call or the men to reappear.

In the military, one of the most nerve-racking things to do was wait and watch as his brothers-in-arms went out on a mission. It was no easier to do so now that they were out of the service.

The Last Riders had formed a bond that would never be broken. It went beyond blood and tears, to the deep core of trust they held for each other. That no matter what secret they had confided, not even threat of death would force them to repeat it.

Rider watched as the brothers came out of the woods, leaving Moon and Diablo to guard Viper's house while the others made their way down the hill toward the factory. He knew they were coming to examine the footage.

Rider automatically opened the door, saving them time opening it themselves.

"Show me," Shade said, taking a seat next to him as Viper and Cash stood over their shoulders.

He already had it ready, so he set the footage running.

"See?" Rider stopped the tape and then pushed it again at Shade's sharp nod.

"What did it look like to you?" Shade turned his head to ask Cash.

"Like someone's head wearing a baseball cap."

"That's what I thought." Rider continued to let the footage

run until Moon and Diablo appeared, then he let the camera go back to real time. "What did you find?"

"I found where a trip wire had been cut." Shade pulled a fine wire out of his pocket.

"Fuck. I was hoping I was wrong."

"You're never wrong. That's why I was already dressed when you called," Shade said grimly. "Moon and Diablo will watch Viper's house until Cash and I can repair it in the morning. I want to make sure whoever it was didn't find our other sensors."

"Any ideas who it could be?" Viper poured himself a cup of coffee that Rider hadn't had time to drink.

Rider got up, pouring himself a cup, thinking aloud. "Whoever cut that wire had to have come from the woods. I didn't see anyone else on the other cameras."

"It could have been a hunter, and he could have realized he had set off a trip wire and took off." Cash rewound the footage on another screen at least three times before he stopped it.

"I don't think it was a hunter, and I think there were two of them. I'll know more in the morning when I can go back out in the light."

"I don't want you going alone. Take Train and Shade with you," Viper ordered, setting his cup down on the desk. "It could have been Curt or one of his cousins. Shade and I were talking yesterday. We're surprised he has yet to pay you back for firing him."

"Curt would come after me, the factory, Mag, or Jo before he would go for you. Whoever was out in the woods was targeting *your* house," Rider said as he resumed watching the monitors.

"I agree with Rider." Shade rubbed his eyes tiredly, his weariness becoming more apparent. "I still think someone deliberately opened those gates at the rodeo, and Knox never found out who broke into the church's office three months ago. The Porters never found out who lured Logan away from his house. They thought it was the Hayes, but what if it wasn't? Something is going on, but damn if I know what it is."

At that, Rider took his eyes away from the monitor. "What if Aly is right and someone did kill her parents, but it wasn't Curt? We could be looking in the wrong direction."

Viper nodded in agreement. "Then I suggest we start looking in the right direction before one or more of us end up just as dead as the Warrens. Knox has been trying to get an independent opinion on the accident. Let's get our own. Shade—"

"What's that?" Rider pointed to a camera showing Aly's home. He hadn't taken his eyes off the cameras as Viper had talked.

Just as he cut off what Viper was saying, a bright light flew from out of sight of the camera to land on the porch, igniting it in flames.

The brothers ran out of the security room, leaving him to watch them pile into Cash's truck.

Before they could get out of the door, Rider was already calling Knox, relaying the information, then calling the fire department.

After The Last Riders' homes were shut down under steel shutters and the brothers were mobilized in their emergency positions, Rider watched as Aly ran out of the back of her house screaming, with F.A.M.E following.

Aly had warned them that whoever had killed her parents would be after her to get their property, and she was right.

The fire spread across the porch like kindling wood, greedily lapping up the exterior and spreading toward the roof. Before the fire department could get there, it was completely encased in fire.

Rider spent the rest of the night monitoring the cameras.

It was dawn when Viper escorted Aly to Cash's truck, and the brothers climbed into the back to head back to the club-house. Rider knew Viper would keep Aly under protection until they could find out who had firebombed her house. It was a decision Viper had to make.

Whoever had burned Aly out of her house was working with the same ones who had cut the wire to distract them from mobilizing the brothers in force, making them waste time before searching for whoever had thrown the Molotov cocktail.

Rider looked at the screen showing that Jo was still asleep. When she found out Aly was staying at the clubhouse, she was going to assume Aly was fucking one of them, thanks to all the gossip Aly had told Jo.

Rider shrugged the thought off. He was tired of playing nice guy. It was time to turn up the heat with her.

He had given her a subtle warning the night before and again yesterday. The new year was going to bring a lot of changes for Jo, not all of them good ... and some were going to be downright naughty. He had to get a start on getting on the naughty list again this year, and Jo was just the woman to help him do it.

29

J o carried her thermos as she walked toward her garage.
It was strange being able to walk to where she would
spend her day instead of driving the tow truck that was
standing alone in the yard.

Opening the garage, she sat the laptop down on the
workbench, opening it and placing it so she could see it
easily from most areas of the garage. Opening her thermos,
she then poured herself a cup of coffee, reminding herself
she should buy a coffeepot the next time she went into town.
Now that her business was in the black, she could splurge on
necessities, and a coffee pot was definitely a necessity.

Jo glanced at her watch, seeing it was only seven. She was
itching to get started on painting Rider's car.

Withstanding the temptation, she went to the scrambled
heap of metal in the corner of the garage, taking a drop cloth
with her. Spreading the tarp out, she started removing the
parts, placing them on the tarp.

Blowing a tendril of hair off her face that had escaped her
ponytail, Jo carried the carburetor to the workbench. She
had to talk herself out of ordering a conversion kit to make

Cash's motorcycle fuel injector, knowing Cash would have a heart attack if she suggested it.

She was breaking it down when she glanced up at the laptop and saw Rider entering her driveway. It was only eight. She hadn't expected him until noon.

Jo kept working on the carburetor, masking her features with a friendly smile as he walked into the garage. She refused to search for signs that he had spent the weekend in bed with a variety of women, one of them being Aly.

Rachel had texted her Saturday morning as she was about to go to the grocery store that Aly's house had burned down from something that had been thrown on her porch. Knowing Aly had been right about Curt not stopping until he had her parents' property was terrifying. She only hoped Knox would be able to prove that Curt was the one responsible.

Rachel had also told her that Viper had offered to let Aly stay until she found another place to live, or until she could rebuild her house. Or until she decided she wasn't going to stay in Treepoint.

Jo hadn't bothered to call or text Aly after finishing her talk with Rachel. They had never been friends, and after her refusal to help talk Rider into eliminating Curt, they had only talked through letters. One from a lawyer stating she was being sued, and the other one she had sent through certified mail with a check paying off her father's debt.

"Good morning," she said as Rider came up behind her to stare down at the carburetor.

"Morning. I see you're hard at work." Grimacing, he poked at the metal. "I won't miss having to work on one of those."

"I almost ordered him a conversion kit."

"Bite your tongue. Cash would have fired you on the spot."

"That's what I thought, which is why I'm going to try to fix this one or pull one off one in the graveyard."

Rider hopped up to sit on the bench, watching her. "You have a good weekend?"

"Sure did. You?" She concentrated on what she was doing to keep from looking at his face.

"I've had worse, but I've had better. We need to get a coffee pot in here."

"I was thinking the same thing this morning." Reaching for cup on a shelf above her head, she set it down next to his thigh. "Help yourself to my thermos. When we need more, I can go to the house to make some.

"Miss the good old days when you could go to the diner?"

"Not yet, but I'm sure I will. Old habits are hard to break."

"That's for sure. I miss waking up to fix you breakfast and having someone to watch movies with."

Startled that he had missed her, she looked up, flushing. "I didn't miss you," she tried to joke, needing to recover from her embarrassment. "I fixed myself a hamburger last night for dinner and ate two slices of onions. I even ate it with sour cream and onion chips."

Her joke backfired when he leaned forward, making her stiffen when she felt him run his nose along her neck, stopping at her ear.

"I would have never known if you hadn't told me. You smell like my perfume."

Her head flew back like a hot wire had poked her. "I'm not wearing perfume."

Rider laughed, leaning closer, then leaning back. "Quit shooting those sparks out of those bluebonnet eyes of yours. I'm just joking."

"You wouldn't know a good joke if it bit you on the ass." Fuming that he had succeeded in making her take his joke seriously, she moved her thermos to the other side of the table.

"Try me."

Her mouth dropped open at the look he was giving her. Blinking at the crazy image that appeared in her mind of her actually biting him on the ass, she grabbed a cloth to wipe her hands off.

"You ready to paint your car? Or do you want to spend the rest of the day bugging me?"

"Do I get a choice?"

"No." She was already heading toward his car.

Sliding inside, she backed it up slowly, driving to the area she had sectioned off for painting. Getting out, she then went to a locker that held the supplies, giving Rider one of the plastic suits to wear before taking one for herself.

"Suit up."

"Damn, I've been waiting most of my life for someone to say that to me."

"Today's your lucky day, then."

Not able to resist his charming excitement, she unzipped the plastic suit and stepped into it, pulling it up her thighs before it got stuck at her waist.

"Let me." Rider squatted, helping her lift her heavy boot to get it through the tight opening.

"I've got it—"

"You can return the favor in a minute." Using his shoulder to brace his weight, he maneuvered the boot out then lifted the other foot to do the same. Standing, he then tugged the sides of the suit upward. "Raise your arms."

"I can—" She gave in, raising her arms when he didn't move away. When her hands slid into the armholes, he went to the zipper. "I can do that—" The zipper was closed before she could get her hands through the other side.

"My turn."

Jo had to restrain herself from knocking him on his ass, regretting that she hadn't painted the car before he had arrived.

"What's the holdup?" he asked, shaking a foot to get her to help him the way he had done for her.

"I was waiting to be asked. Unlike you, I prefer to be asked for help before I get all touchy-feely with someone else's body."

"Bluebonnet, you don't have to ask for permission to get all touchy-feely with my body."

Jo went to her haunches, nearly ripping the thin plastic of the suit as she jerked his big foot through the opening before jerking herself back to her feet.

"You can do the rest yourself. I wouldn't want to catch any cooties from your weekend activities."

Disdainfully raising her nose in the air, she unrolled the thick plastic sheets that fell from the ceiling to keep the other vehicles from getting accidentally sprayed with paint.

"Aly told you about the parties?" He raised a brow as he zipped up his suit.

"She did. Not that I wanted to listen," she hastened to add, turning on the ventilator before going back to the locker, where she took out two masks, handing him one. "I found it too disturbing to listen to, so I told her she could keep that to herself."

She had already prepped the sprayers, so she was able to simply aim the long wand at his car and pull the trigger.

"What did you find disturbing? That women want to get laid? Or that they waited to be fucked by me in particular?"

At his question, she was startled into turning toward him at the same time she pulled the trigger. Horrified, it took a couple seconds to pull her finger away.

He was covered in candy apple red, even his goggles.

Jo covered her mouth, unable to prevent the gurgling

laughter that had Rider rising the goggles to stare at her wrathfully.

"That was just mean."

Laughing harder behind her hand, she shook her head in denial. "It was an acc—"

She stopped trying to explain to drop the wand and take off at a run. She would apologize when he calmed down and she could stop laughing.

Jo slapped at the heavy plastic, trying to get away from him, then found herself entangled within the folds.

"You need some help?" Rider plucked her from the floor, shouldering his way through the thick curtain and lifting her to his shoulder.

"You're getting paint on me." She squealed in laughter. "Hey, go back. I missed your back."

"Hardy har har … You're just full of it today, aren't you?"

Jo found her ass on the worktable with Rider glowering down at her.

"Seriously, it was an accident—"

"You want to know what I did this weekend? All you have to do is ask."

"I don't want to know." Her amusement vanished in a heartbeat.

When his mouth opened, she pressed her palms over her ears so she couldn't hear what he was saying. Undeterred, he took her wrists, lowering them to her sides.

"I spent the weekend monitoring security footage. Someone tried to break into Viper's house the same night that someone torched Aly's house."

"It had to be Curt."

"Knox paid a visit to Curt, bright and early Saturday morning. He had spent the night with Carly. She said he didn't leave her apartment the whole night."

"Then it had to be Justin or Tanner."

"That was who Knox visited next. They said they spent the night in, getting drunk."

"They alibied each other? How convenient."

"Maybe, but Knox can't arrest them without proof."

"Of course, they're going to get away with it again."

"Sooner or later, they'll screw up."

"Just not last weekend."

Rider shrugged. "It is what it is."

"I hate that answer."

"I'm a realist. Sometimes, there isn't an easy solution. Like you and me."

"There isn't a you and me."

Jo tried to hop off the bench, but Rider placed his hands on the table on either side of her thighs, keeping her from jumping off.

"Okay, we're friends," she conceded.

"We're more than friends. I feel more than friendship for you, and I think you feel the same for me."

"No, I don't. You're too arrogant. You have women lined by the day."

"I have several days open."

"You jerk—"

Rider lowered his head, covering her mouth. "You can have Monday," he said, raising his lips a hairsbreadth away. Then he lowered them again to kiss her longer the second time while she refused to open her mouth, even when he nipped on her bottom lip. "And Tuesday," he whispered, his breath stealing hers. "Wednesday is yours, too." With one hand on her jaw, he lifted her gaze to his, drowning her in his depths. "I already penciled you in on Thursdays."

"What about Fridays?" Jo asked with a shudder, gripping the front of his plastic suit, trying to keep herself from being swept away. She gripped him harder when he moved his mouth to the side of her neck, running the tip of his tongue up to her ear.

"That one is definitely yours. Saturdays, too," he whispered seductively.

"And Sundays?"

"I might need Sundays off."

"To be with other women?" She twisted her neck from his reach.

"I watch football on Sundays."

"I like football." She allowed him to turn her face back to his.

"Then you can have Sundays, too."

Jo let him have her mouth back, let his tongue enter her mouth in a rush of sensations that she had read about but had never believed possible for herself.

She inched her hands up his chest to twine around his neck, nervously following his lead. When he parted her lips wider, her burgeoning arousal disappeared. She pressed her lips firmer against his, trying to bring it back.

"Jo, stop. You're trying too hard."

She pulled her mouth back, trying not to cry. "I told you I'm no good at this—"

"If you get any better, you'll be scraping me off the ceiling."

Tantalizing her with whispers and touches, Rider unzipped the plastic suit and pulled her arms out. Then he unzipped his and shrugged out of the top half before removing his T-shirt.

Taking her hands, Rider placed them on his bare chest.

"I feel like I'm in a *Dexter* tv show."

Seductively, he brought his mouth back to the base of her throat. "That reminds me of something." He shut down the cameras from the laptop before closing it.

"Did anyone see?" Aghast, Jo tried again to jump down.

"No, security gets off at seven."

"That's a relief," she said, seeing Rider reach for the remote control, sending the garage door down.

"Yes, it is, since I'm the one who worked it all weekend."

"Who usually does it?"

"Depends on who Viper puts on the list. All the brothers take turns."

"That's fair."

"We think so. Jo, you mind if we stop talking for a few minutes?"

"Do we have to?"

"No, but I would rather be kissing you."

"I'd rather talk."

"Let's compromise. You can listen, and I'll talk."

"I'd rather be the one tal ..." She trailed off at the words that came out of his mouth.

The foreign words and the way he said them were like a blowtorch thawing out frozen pipes to get the water running again. She couldn't understand and would die of embarrassment if she did, but it forced her not to concentrate on his words and what his hands were doing, but to just *feel* the emotions behind them.

Since Curt, Tanner, and Justin had touched her, she had never been able to bear the thought of a man's hands on her. However, she was now unconsciously scooting closer to the edge of the worktable, trying to get closer to Rider.

"Say that again," she demanded, burying her hands in his thick hair.

When he did, with the same thick, nasally accent, she felt herself dampen in her jeans, as her legs went around his waist, as her mouth reached for his.

His sensuous words sank deep within her soul, removing the traces of the other men's touch, replacing their ugly comments with the beauty of his words. She didn't feel self-conscious or belittled; she felt wanted and needed as he took off her T-shirt, finding a lacy bra cupping her breasts.

Each syllable of his words soothed her raw nerves, creating a newfound world she hadn't known existed. Each of his hands neither crushed or grabbed, merely moving the bra away from her heated flesh until he could take a nipple into his mouth.

A gasp escaped her at the gentleness he used to tempt and provoke the nub to tauten and beg for each swirl of his tongue.

"Do you like it when I lick your nipples?"

It took a second for her mind to realize she could understand what he was saying.

"Yes," she mumbled, tugging his hair so he would kiss her again.

"I know something you'll like better."

She felt the air move as he lifted her off the table before turning her so her back was to him and her belly was pressed again the cold metal of the tool bench. Then Rider took her hands, placing them at each end, stretching her out until her bra-covered chest lay flat on the table.

"Rider …"

He went back to speaking in words she couldn't understand and didn't want to, trusting his actions wouldn't hurt but give her a pleasure she never wanted to end.

Jo laid her cheek down on the table, listening to his movements. Her stomach fluttered when he slid his hand around her waist and dipped into her jeans, inching his fingers inside her panties to find her damp flesh.

Jo bit her lips when he found her clit, rubbing it in a circular pattern that had her squirming in his grasp.

"Oh …" Jo panted, then moaned when he burrowed his face under her hair to kiss her neck, pulling her flesh into his mouth to bite down. "Rider … please."

"More?"

She could only nod as she licked her dry lips.

When he parted her flesh, sliding a slippery finger inside her, Jo closed her eyes tightly, nearly seeing stars he felt so good. When her butt pushed back at him, wanting more, Rider gave a sultry laugh, pulling his hand away to unbutton her jeans.

She felt the heated air hit her body as he tugged down the plastic suit, her jeans, and her panties, leaving her lower body bare to his gaze.

Thankfully, she couldn't see his face, even if she opened her eyes. She made no move to raise herself from the table, giving him the access he wanted.

When she felt him release the patch of skin he had left his mark on and lifted his chest off her back, she held her breath, waiting for what he would do next.

Then hands parted her ass, and she jumped, her breasts rising off the bench.

"Don't move."

His order had another rush of heat spiraling toward her core, making her ache for something she had never dreamed was possible to want.

"Can we …?" Jo couldn't bring herself to say the word.

"Fuck?" Rider cupped one of her ass cheeks, spreading her farther apart.

Jo nodded, holding the table so hard her knuckles showed white.

"We're going to when I'm sure you're ready."

"I'm ready," she whispered.

"Let me be the judge of that. I may not be your boss at work, but when we fuck, I'm the one in charge."

Jo gave a small scream when she felt his tongue slide through her fleshy lips, finding her clit and sucking it into his mouth.

"You can be in charge."

He clenched his fingers on her ass, raising her to her toes to give himself better access.

"Oh, my God … I can't believe it feels so good."

She cried out again when he slid his tongue inside her opening, the sensations so exquisitely sensuous she felt new and stronger cravings for Rider to fulfill.

He finally released her ass, sliding his hands up to the curve of her waist as he used her body to lever himself back to standing.

"You know what, Jo?" Satisfaction dripped from his voice, sending chills up her spine.

"What?" She nervously waited for his answer. Was he about to change his mind and not have sex with her?

"You're ready."

30

Rider took his time unzipping his jeans, seeing the goose bumps rise on her arms. Having Jo under his control and begging for his touch appealed to his masculine pride, which he admittedly had too much of, but Jo's eager surrender was more than he had expected of her. Her willingness after her initial hesitation showed how starved for human affection she was.

If he were a nicer man, he would ease her slowly into having sex with him, but he wasn't a nice man. In fact, he was the furthest thing from nice a man could get without letting the darkness in his soul overwhelm him.

He used sex to keep him grounded to reality. You always knew where you stood with a woman when your dick was buried in her pussy. With Jo, though, it was different. He was using her to create something more. He was using her to make a family. To achieve his piece of happiness that the other brothers had found—his own home with his own bed to sleep in, a table that had his own chair, a couch that he watched movies with Jo on. He knew what he was getting with Jo, unlike the women he had married.

Jo was strong, hardworking, gentle. When Jo loved, she was loyal to a fault. How she could love the sorry excuse of a father she still missed was a mystery to him. She hadn't even been able to clear out his bedroom after his death, dusting and cleaning it as if he would miraculously come back.

She even loved the old bitch who he was still hoping Curt would take out for him. On the other hand, if she could love Lyle and Mag, then she could learn to love him, and he was damn determined she would.

Taking a condom out of his back pocket and rolling it on, he caught her peeking at him before closing her eyes tightly again.

Moving closer to her, Rider swirled his condom-covered cock against her damp pussy before going to her opening.

"Do you feel how ready you are for me?"

"God ... yes." She stifled a whimper with her hand.

"That's not where I put your hand. Put it back."

"Okay."

"Say *yes, sir.*"

Her rebellious bottom lip poked out, giving an adorable pout that had him holding back his own groan, imagining her sucking his dick.

"I'm waiting, Jo. Perhaps you're not as ready as I thought."

"I am ... sir."

"That's all I wanted to hear my bluebonnet girl say." Sliding intimately closer, he allowed the head of his cock to work inside her tight pussy, hissing at the feeling of her flesh parting, allowing him entry. It had him leaning over her back to bite her earlobe.

"You wore my perfume, didn't you?"

"Yes."

"You lied to me, didn't you?"

"Yes. I'm sorry."

"I hate women who lie, but I do love to fuck bad girls, so I forgive you."

Jo gave a startled laugh. "Only you could make me laugh when you're ..."

"Fucking you. You have a real problem with that word, don't you? It can be sexy when it's used the right way."

Rider released her earlobe to rest his forehead between her shoulder blades. "You're so tight. I'm trying not to come."

"You are?"

Rider could sense her insecurity. Raising his head, he started placing kisses across her shoulders.

"You're beautiful when you look at me with those blue eyes, and I've never felt a woman clench around me harder."

"I love men who give compliments, but I hate when they compare women to others."

"Touché, mon cher."

"Maybe we'll be better off if you keep using that language."

"You like it when I speak French? I can speak six others fluently, but I can say *fuck* in nineteen."

He started counting them off in his head to keep himself from climax as he moved inside her, at first shallowly, thrusting to stretch her, then driving deeper with hard strokes that had her holding on to the table as she loosened, relaxing into his trust.

He unclasped her bra, seeing the indentions from the tight elastic. Following the marks with his tongue, he started fucking her harder, still repeating *fuck* in different languages.

When he came to nineteen, he started moving faster, hearing her gasping breaths as he pounded into her.

"I'm going to teach you how to fuck me the way I like it. Your pussy is going to be sore until you get used to it. If it becomes too uncomfortable, you're going to tell me, and I will give it a break until it doesn't hurt. If I find you're not honest with me, I'll get mad. And Jo, you don't want me mad. You get what I'm telling you?"

"Yes," Jo gasped.

"Yes what?" Rider stopped moving, leaving her feet held off the floor, using his hips and cock to hold her in place.

"Yes, sir. I understand."

"I like to play games sometimes when I'm fucking. Other times, I don't. You don't like playing it at all, you'll tell me that, too."

"I will."

"I like safe words that are simple. Red will be yours. Red means stop. Whenever you use it, I'll stop whatever we're doing."

"Do we need …? I mean, I prefer not to need them. Unless it's a thing you need from another woman …"

Rider jerked his cock out of her pussy. Turning her around, he lifted her back onto the bench so she could look at him. When she tried to look away, he locked eyes with her.

"I like playing games, but I would never do anything that makes you feel uncomfortable … ever. You don't want to play games, we won't. I told you I'm a realist, and I meant it. With being one, I can understand not all women are into the same sex games. I can deal with it if you aren't. I also believe in putting my cards on the table.

"I like you. I'm trying to form a lasting relationship with you. If you're on board, I will be completely faithful to you. That means not fucking other women who can give what you can't."

"I'm on board."

Her shy response had him giving her a hard kiss.

"With parts or all of it?"

"All of it. I'll tell you what I don't like."

"That's what I want to hear from my old lady."

Rider scooted Jo to the end of the table, where his cock

was waiting. Jo wiggled her hips, offering him what he wanted.

"I hate that term. I like bluebonnet better."

He released her hips to place his hands down on the table, using the leverage to build the speed up again. "I won't call you old lady again if you shut up and tell me to fuck you."

"Rider, fuck me … hard."

Hearing the dirty word coming out of her mouth had his balls about to explode.

"Fuck." He delved between her thighs, reaching for her clit to put them out of their misery. Rubbing the little button, he felt her start to tremble and shake.

Her screams vibrated off the steel walls.

When her head fell to his shoulder, he pulled Jo closer to the warmth of his body, running soothing hands across her back. Each of his actions was designed to draw her closer into his world. Creating an intimacy between them was the key to making her fall in love with him and would put him in the position he needed to achieve his goals.

Slowly releasing her, Rider took her bra off the table, placing it on her chest before nimbly fastening it at her back without having to turn her around. Then he reached down, tossing the plastic suit to the side and giving Jo her jeans and shirt.

Awkwardly, Jo dressed, avoiding his eyes as he fastened his jeans and put his T-shirt on.

"I have another set of clothes in my saddlebag. Let's go to your house and shower. Cash and Train will be bringing some more bikes in an hour. I don't want them thinking we killed someone and hid their body."

Jo shakily laughed. "We should leave your suit out, and you could hide."

He grinned. "Make them think you killed me when I showed up this morning?" Opening the garage door, he burst into laughter, swinging an arm around her shoulders. "Woman, I like the way you think."

Walking toward the house, he was aware of Moon and Diablo watching them from the security room.

When they reached her house, he let Jo go first into the living room, politely holding the door open for her. Behind her back, he came through the front door, lifting his hand in a sweeping motion across his throat, giving the signal to kill the camera.

"I won't be long," Jo said, heading toward the bathroom.

"I'm the one with the most paint on me. I should go first." He moved around her, beating her to the door.

Jo stopped. "You go ahead—"

Rider snaked his hand out to grab her hand as he opened the bathroom door, drawing Jo into the small room with him. "I don't mind sharing."

"I'd rather wait …"

"Are you sure?" He took off his shirt, setting it down on the edge of the old-fashioned tub before removing his boots. "My handprints are on your back and ass. You're not going to be able to reach them." Without shame, he unzipped his jeans. "You got paint on my shoulders and back; how am I supposed to reach?"

Her cheeks flamed red. "I'm sure you'll manage."

Rider stepped into the tub, reaching for the curtain. "You sure?" He slowly started to close the shower curtain. "What if I get scared? This shower looks like the one in *Psycho*."

"No, it doesn't."

"It feels like it. I'm scared." He showed her the way a pout should look.

"For God's sake, I could have been showered and dressed in the time you're taking." Frustrated, Jo started to remove her clothes.

Not wanting her to feel self-conscious, he started the water, letting it heat up.

"Fuck!"

"What's wrong now?"

"The water is colder than a witch's tit."

Jo got inside, closing the curtain. "It takes a little time to warm up."

"No shit. It would be quicker to fly to Alaska, shower, and come back before your water gets hot. You need a new water heater."

"No, I don't. You were in the military; where are your balls?"

"They're shriveled into acorns. I won't be able to have kids."

Jo's giggles made him smile. It was one he didn't have to pretend to feel. Her laughter shone a light on a part of his soul he hadn't felt in a long time.

Taking a step back in the tub, he moved her in front to deflect the cold spray from him.

"Tell me when it's warm." Reaching for a washcloth, he started washing her back, seeing her goose bumps.

"Asshole," she grumbled.

"One thing I learned in basic training was when to retreat and let someone else take the cold water."

"You didn't learn that in the military."

"No, but I did learn the value of a good water heater, and baby, yours sucks."

THEY MANAGED to shower and change before Cash and Moon arrived. Rider sat on one of his motorcycles as Jo inspected the ones the brothers had ridden in on to store. She looked like a kid in a candy store.

"You want to go for a ride?" he offered when she touched the handlebars on the one he was sitting on.

"I should be working. We need to paint your car, and—"

"It can wait until we come back. We can take a quick ride and be back in twenty minutes."

She tried to resist, and as she looked toward Cash and Moon, he realized what was holding her back.

"It'll be on the clock. I want you to listen to my motor. It's lagging." He invented the excuse for her.

"Oh … then I should go with you, just so I can hear when it's doing it." Jo turned red when Moon held a helmet out to her.

"We're heading back to the club. F.A.M.E is here to give us a ride back," Moon told him as Jo circled her arms around Rider's waist.

Rider nodded as they left, raising his hand to F.A.M.E as he rode out of the garage and saw him sitting outside in Cash's truck.

Turning in the direction of town, he watched his speed, being attentive when her arms would relax or tighten as he drove. Being the first time he rode with her at his back, it was important for both their safety to take it easy and get her comfortable riding with him. It was why he loved riding a motorcycle—it was the closest he could get to sex without actually fucking.

It was a high he didn't have to smoke, and he could let any problem fly away on the wind that rushed past them. There was only one experience he likened to it, and that was no longer available to him. Riding his bike was as close as he could get to it now.

"How you doin'?" He turned his head when he stopped at the red light in town.

"It's terrific! Let's go on the road to Jamestown. You can

go faster," she urged him excitedly, shaking the motorcycle as she bounced on the seat.

If he let her talk him into riding toward Jamestown, he wouldn't be able to keep the promise to be back to the garage in the twenty minutes he would have Jo back in.

"No, some other time."

"I dare you to run the light." She kept bouncing her ass as she tightened her arms around his waist, trying to coerce him into breaking the law.

He narrowed his eyes at her disappointed expression. His old lady was learning to pout a little too well. He would save that for later when he taught her how to give him a blowjob. He was a firm believer of a need-to-know mentality. When it benefited him the most, she would need to know. He would play whatever cards were dealt to him. At the same time, there was no need to stack the deck against himself.

"If you want to go to Jamestown, we'll go."

"What changed your mind?"

"Blue eyes, whenever you want to be bad, I'm never going to say no."

Grinning, he turned back around, seeing the light was still red. Releasing the throttle, they took off.

He was in the game to win Jo's heart. She just didn't know it. When she did, it would be too late.

"Fucking hell. I'm going to tell Cash myself it's impossible to restore this piece of crap."

Ignoring Rider's rant, Jo tried not to give in to her misgivings as she tried to fit a salvaged fender that she had taken off a scrapped motorcycle onto Cash's wheel frame. "No, you're not. I'll fix it. You just have to be patient. I told you I don't need your help. Don't you have something to do at the factory?"

Repairing Cash's motorcycle had been consuming more time than she had anticipated. When she became too frustrated, she would set it aside and work on another job. She had just finished working on Gavin's bike before going back to Cash's. She already wished she had started on F.A.M.E's when Rider came in to witness her failure.

Rider gave Cash's motorcycle an impatient glance. "No. You trying to get rid of me?"

Jo shrugged. "I just thought you might have something better to do than drive me up the wall."

He put an arm over her shoulder. "That's not the way an old lady should talk to her old man."

Jo jabbed her elbow into his flat abdomen. "I told you not to call me old lady."

"If the shoe fits, wear it."

He hunched over at his attempt of humor resulting in another jab.

"I need to work."

"Okay." He moved away from her. "I can see when I'm not wanted. I need to go anyway."

Jo's stomach sank when he mentioned leaving, although she had just told him to go.

Wiping her hands on a rag that was sticking out of her coveralls, she grimaced at the grime that had worked its way under her short nails.

"Are you working tonight?" she asked as if she wasn't interested in his reply, though butterflies were filling her stomach.

In the last three weeks, they had spent the majority of their nights together, Rider coming by after he got off work and leaving in the mornings, except for Fridays and Saturdays. He was at the clubhouse those nights, coming over during the day to spend time with her. She never asked what he did those nights, keeping her fears to herself that he was using them to be with other women.

She tried to blame it on their newfound intimacy. That was what women her age did, right? Well, that was what she told herself. She didn't want to pressure Rider into talking about his feelings for her, whereas she kept finding it difficult from expressing hers to him. She was afraid of scaring him off, trying to combat her fears that he was becoming more entrenched in her heart.

Sexually, she was sure she was more repressed than some of the women he had been with, but he had never shown that he wanted more than she could give him when she had shyly broached the subject. Instead, he had assured her that she more than satisfied him. However, deep down, she wanted him to experience more than satisfaction when they had sex. She wanted to blow his mind. Because of her inexperience, she didn't know how.

The thought of spending another Friday unable to sleep and watching horrible movies had her voicing her thoughts. If he was with other women, she would rather know the truth than be kept in the dark.

"I had lunch with Rachel today."

"I know. I was here when you left." He raised a brow at her comment.

"She showed me a dress she's wearing to the party tonight."

"And?"

"Is Aly still there?"

"Since you had lunch with Rachel, I assume you already know the answer to that."

Jo nodded miserably, not knowing how to get the question out without making a fool of herself.

"Come here." Rider went to the workbench. Jumping on it, he tugged her between his thighs. "Look at me."

Jo raised her eyes to look at him, placing her hands on his jean-clad thighs. Every time she did something as simple as touch him, she felt the newness of their relationship.

Rider made no secret of their relationship, referring to *his* woman within hearing every time one of The Last Riders stopped by. They had eaten out at several of the restaurants in town, and even gone to dinner at Rachel's together.

"You know the parties get pretty wild, right?"

"Rachel goes. So do Lily, Beth, Winter, and Willa."

"Occasionally."

"It can't be too bad if they go." She lowered her eyes to her hands on his thighs, feeling a possessiveness for him that was at the root of her problem. "I can't see Lily or any of them going if—"

"Jo, you do know Lily and Shade have sex? That Willa and Lucky do, too?"

"I'm not stupid." Hurt, she started to turn away, but his hands covered hers, keeping her in place.

"I don't think you are. I'm just trying to be delicate. Bluebonnet, your friendship with the women blinds you to the fact that they share a very healthy relationship with their husbands. A relationship that you may not understand, but it works for them."

"I know Lily, Willa, Beth, Winter, and certainly not Killyama had sex for votes to become members."

"There are different ways to get votes."

His evasiveness neither confirmed nor denied how to become a member.

"I could do the other ways."

"Are you trying to ask me to take you to the party tonight?"

"Only if you want to, and if I don't have to have sex with any of The Last Riders."

"That can be arranged. You good now?"

She couldn't understand his wide grin, chalking it up to her not asking how he had spent his time during the parties while they had been together.

"I'll come back and pick you up in a few hours." He hopped down from the bench.

"Wait. What should I wear?"

"Wear the dress you wore to the auction." He gave her a quick kiss before trying to leave.

Grabbing his jacket sleeve, she stopped him. "Be serious."

"I'm sure what you have on under those coveralls is fine."

Jo flushed, looking away.

"Let me see."

Jo smacked his hand away when he tried to unzip her coveralls.

"I washed all my jeans. They're in the dryer."

"Unzip it and go climb on top of the hood. I want to take a picture," he ordered, taking his cell phone out of his pocket.

Jo threw the dirty oil rag at him. "Go! Before I—"

"Sheesh. It was just a fantasy of mine and all red-blooded men in the universe."

"They make calendars for men like you."

"Really? Will you buy me one?"

"I'll buy you a new pair of boots, because I'm about to shove the pair you have up your ..."

He was smart enough to leave before she could finish her threat.

Her smile disappeared when he was out of sight, now wishing she hadn't agreed to go. Was she moving too fast with Rider?

Jo worked on Cash's lighting kit until she saw it was almost four. Closing the garage, she went to her house to search her closet for something to wear. The dress Rachel had shown her wasn't overtly sexy or provocative. She had also seen how Aly had dressed one night before going to one of their parties.

In the back of her closet, she found a sweater she had bought at the thrift store without unfolding it. When she had gotten home and planned on wearing it, she had been surprised to find the arms laced up, exposing the skin underneath. It was blue—the color of her eyes.

Taking her favorite pair of jeans out of the dryer, she then took a shower, using a nail brush to clean her nails. Blow-drying her hair took longer than expected. Then, after dressing, she had to rummage through her closet to find a pair of boots that had a small heel that she hadn't worn since high school, praying they still fit. Dressed, she tapped her foot as she turned to see herself in the mirror.

Running a brush through her hair, she tugged the back of the sweater to raise the front higher. The deep V was lower than she had expected. Thinking about finding something else to wear, she was going toward the closet when she heard Rider knocking at the front door.

"I'm coming," she yelled toward the door, making a pit stop at the bathroom to spray herself with perfume. Waving her hand to dissipate the smell, she then opened the door.

"I was going to make us something to eat before we leave." She nervously fiddled at the ties at her wrist. "Or, if you want, we could eat at the diner."

"We can eat at the club." Bending, he kissed her, then rubbed his jaw along hers. "You smell fantastic."

"Thank you."

"If you're ready, we need to go before the food's gone. Willa cooked tonight."

Jo grabbed her coat, then stepped outside to see he had arrived in style. "You drove your car."

"I thought you could drive us to the clubhouse." He took the keys out of his pocket.

She snatched them away before he could change his mind. "I'll be gentle," she teased.

"If I didn't believe that, you wouldn't be driving it."

She looked at him from over the roof of his car, catching his expression as he was about to get inside.

"Is something the matter?"

"No. Why?"

Jo got inside the car. "Nothing. I must just be nervous."

"There's no reason to be nervous. We'll eat dinner and hang out at the club for an hour before I have to work."

"You're working tonight?" She frowned, starting the car and backing out.

"I work every Friday and Saturday. They're the nights the brothers hate to work, so I volunteered to take them. Then I don't have to be scheduled for the other days of the week."

Relief filled her at his explanation. She wouldn't have to spend the weekend nights imagining him partying with the women anymore.

The short drive to the clubhouse wasn't long enough. She wished she could talk him out of going to the party and spend the night experimenting to see how fast his car could go. She knew it was a forlorn wish when he gave her an encouraging look as they got out the car.

"Bluebonnet, you're not going to the doctor's office. It'll be fine. Have I ever let you have a bad time?"

"No, but I don't want tonight to be the first. I don't really fit in at parties."

"You'll fit in. If you hate it, we can leave. Cool?"

"Yes."

Jo smiled at the man standing at the front door when they reached the porch. Awkwardly, she tried to pull her hand out of Rider's clasp, but he just held it tighter as he gave a brief introduction to the man who opened the door for them.

"F.A.M.E, meet Jo. Jo, F.A.M.E." Rider then led her through the doorway before she could respond.

"That wasn't nice."

"You'll see why."

She wasn't given time to take in the entryway that had another flight of steps going upward before she was forced to quicken her steps to keep up with him. They went through a large room that had a bar with stocked shelves behind it, two pool tables, and several couches and chairs placed in different areas in the room. Taking it all in, she nearly walked into Rider's back when he pushed a swinging door open. She couldn't even fit in the room with the long line reaching around the expansive kitchen.

She peeked over his shoulder to see a table that was already full.

"Maybe we should go to the diner."

"It doesn't take long. Now you see why I was rushing." He placed his hand on her back to move her to stand next to him so she wouldn't have to stand in the door.

She had known there were quite a few Last Riders and several women in the club, but seeing them all together ... there were more than she had assumed there would be.

"Are Rachel and Cash here yet?" she asked out of the corner of her mouth.

He looked over the crowd critically. "I don't see them. Why?"

"Just curious."

"Jo, you don't have to whisper. No one else is. You don't need Rachel and Cash to be here either to make you feel more comfortable. I'm standing right here, and I'm not going anywhere."

"All right. I know I'm being silly."

"Relax. The food here is better than the diner, and it beats yours."

"What's wrong with my cooking?"

"I didn't want to hurt your feelings, but I'm tired of eating pizza and burgers."

"I can cook. It's just easier to order pizza or grill a burger."

"Bluebonnet, you don't grill your burgers; you obliterate them."

"See if I grill you another one," she mumbled, staring at the man's back in front of them. She didn't recognize him from the back, and she certainly didn't from his strange hair-cut. Half was long, reaching his black long-sleeved shirt, while the other half was completely bald and covered in tattoos.

"The cows of America thank you."

At his joke, the man in front of them turned around.

Dismay and fear had her shaking in her boots. His tatts extended to his neck and face, leaving one cheek unmarked. She could see the startling beauty of how handsome he was. However, the other side with the tatts made her afraid to be in the same room with him.

As his expressionless eyes looked her over, she unconsciously took a step back, bumping into a woman who was trying to come through the door.

"Watch it."

Jo recognized her from the auction, remembering her name from the night she tried to excuse herself.

"I'm sorry. I didn't hear you come in."

Calculating eyes swept past her to Rider's, then to the man who had turned toward them.

"They're sick, aren't they?"

"I wouldn't describe them as sick."

"It's just an expression." The woman turned her nose up at her, raising her hand to her own cheek. "I'm thinking of getting a few on my cheek myself. What do you think, Rider?"

"I think you're going to do whatever you want. You always do."

Jo looked at Rider, seeing the warning glint he was giving Jewell. The smugness he received in return showed Jo that Jewell had received whatever message he had sent her.

Ignoring the byplay between the two, she held her hand out to the man who was silently watching the interaction between them.

"Hi, I'm Jo."

"Gavin." He didn't take her hand, turning around to move along with the line that had finally began moving.

Letting her hand drop to her side, she tightened her lips when she saw Jewell's curl in a smile.

"Behave, Jewell." Rider's cold voice cut through her thoughts of pretending to have a headache so she could leave.

How Lily and Willa could survive this hostile environment shocked her. Rachel, she could understand. Her friend had three brothers. She had learned how to survive nasty comments. Even Beth, being a caretaker for several elderly patients, would be able to hold her own. Killyama, she was pretty damn sure could have made them frightened of her. Winter was used to dealing with troubled hoodlums, so even Jo could understand that. But poor Lily and Willa? It must have been like leading sheep to the slaughter.

"Or what? You'll punish me?" Snide dripped from her lips.

"No, that doesn't interest me anymore."

She knew from the catty way Jewell's gaze darted toward her that she was going to be the next target to show her anger at Rider's shutdown.

"Aren't you going to introduce yourself to me? Or don't I matter because I don't have a dick?"

Rider took a step toward Jewell, but Jo placed a firm hand on Rider's chest, unaware Gavin had swung around at Jewell's malicious question.

"I can understand how you're missing your boy toy, but he's mine now, and I don't share. If you have a problem with that, we can settle that after dinner. I really don't want to get out of line to rip those extensions out of your head, but if I have to, I will."

"I have a problem." Jewell pushed forward, using her breasts as battering rams.

Jo's mouth dropped open in shock that the woman would pick a fight in front of everyone in the kitchen. Then her temper turned into a blinding rage. She was going to yank every extension out of her head and strangle the bitch with them.

"Titty fight!" a loud voice shouted from the front of the line.

Reacting without thinking, Jo sprung herself at Jewell, then found herself lifted off the floor and held against a firm chest. Blowing her hair out of her eyes, she saw Jewell being held back by Rider, his grip around her waist.

"Let her go, or I'm walking out that door," she snarled, seeing his hands on the woman inflaming her rage.

Rider held his hands up in the air, moving away from Jewell.

"Jo, you can get in front of the line with me." Lily's small hand touching her arm brought her back to her senses.

Gavin released her at Lily's touch, placing himself between her and Jewell.

"Thank you, Lily, but I would rather take my turn in the order I came in. Maybe Jewell would like to accept your generous offer?"

With the whole room watching, Jewell started to move around her.

Jo couldn't explain to herself why she said what she said next, other than she saw the hurt the woman was trying to hide by being so hostile toward her. "This isn't easy for me either." Jo shot a quick glance toward Rider, then back to her, giving her a pitying look.

"Don't feel sorry for me. Save that sympathy for yourself. You're going to need it more than I will."

Jo turned around to find the line had moved forward and everyone had lost interest when there was no fight. She tried to get Gavin to get back in front of her. However, he just motioned to her to go ahead and got in line behind Rider.

Her pretend headache became a reality as the woman in front of her gave her a friendly smile.

"I'm Ember. Just ignore Jewell. You'll like her once you get to know her."

"I'm sure I will," Jo lied, sure she wouldn't. She wouldn't say that to the pretty woman who had tried to take the sting out Jewell's harsh words, though.

"There're usually not this many here." Taking a plate and setting it on the counter, Ember gave it to her before taking one for herself. "It's just because it's Friday." Jo liked the woman even more when she gave her a worried glance. "You do know Fridays can get rowdy here, right?"

"Rider told me." Jo nodded, taking a scoop of mashed potatoes, then a slice of ham that had a mouthwatering sauce to go over it.

"That's good. The first time Lily came, it was a disaster. Although, that was a mistake—she hadn't been invited." Ember rolled her eyes toward Lily, then hastily lowered them when Lily caught her staring.

"I'm friends with Lily," Jo said, leaving the small bit of macaroni left when she saw Rider take three slices of ham and three rolls. Gavin would be lucky to find a crumb left after getting in line behind Rider.

"You are?" Ember lowered her voice. "Forget I mentioned Lily's first time here. We don't talk about it."

"I won't," Jo whispered back.

"Thanks." The woman moved away, going through an archway leading to another part of the house.

As she came around the corner of the counter, Lily waved from the table that Beth and Razer were also sitting at. Looking at Rider, he nodded at her silent question.

As she took the seat that Lily had motioned her to, Rider set his plate down next to her before walking away, then returning with another chair.

"Did you get enough to eat?" Jo teased, seeing the amount of food on his plate.

"Not yet. Willa hasn't put the desserts out. I need something sweet with my food."

"Then try the ham. It's going to rock your world."

Jo took another bite of the ham as Gavin came from behind the counter after fixing his plate.

Viper, who was sitting across the table, started to get up. "Sit here. I'll grab another chair."

"No, I'll sit in the dining room." Gavin walked toward the archway as Viper stared after him, sitting back down.

It was an uncomfortable moment that Jo had no idea how to fill. Fortunately, Rider didn't have the same problem.

"Get your plate, Jo. We're going to sit with Gavin."

Jo stood, grabbing her plate, as Viper, Winter, Beth, and Lily did the same. The six of them went through the archway and into the dining room that had twice the space and was filled with tables. One of which had Gavin sitting by himself.

She took the seat across from Gavin, who wasn't happy at having been invaded. The fearsome man had given her pause when she had seen him in the line, feeling terrified of him, but he reminded her of the times she had eaten alone in the school cafeteria and had refused to let anyone sit with her. It was a form of protection to keep others from getting too close.

Placing her napkin on her lap, she grinned at the face that was glowering back. "You're riding your clutch too much."

His glower turned into a confused frown. "What?"

"I said, you're riding your clutch too much. Cool it, or you can fix your own bike next time."

32

"I'm not riding my clutch—"

"Since I'm the one who had to fix the cable for it, yes, you are." Jo cut another piece of ham with her fork.

Gavin silently chewed his food, staring her. "I thought you only worked on cars."

"I work on anything with a motor."

"Then why didn't you work on your furnace?" Rider scooted his chair closer to the table to reach for the salt.

"Did you see where the furnace was? I've been afraid of that basement since I was a kid. The only thing I tried to fix and couldn't was my refrigerator. I think the bastard had it out for me."

"You can fix anything mechanical, but you couldn't figure out a fuse box?" Spearing the last of his ham, Rider gave her a doubtful gaze.

"I was afraid of being shocked again. It hurts."

"You were shocked?" Gavin's eyes went over to her as if it had just happened.

"Put me on my butt. After that, I used space heaters and an ice chest. It was more aggravating but less painful."

"Are you adjusting to not giving tows anymore?" Lily questioned.

"I think my truck misses me more than I miss it."

"You think your truck misses you?"

"Lily, haven't you ever talked to your car?"

"My old one, I did. I used to beg it to start."

"Did it ever answer?" Shade asked, coming to the table.

"No, of course not."

"Your truck ever talk back to you?"

Jo laughed, shaking her head.

"Then I think it's safe to sit at the table with you. What do you think, Gavin?" Shade asked, sitting next to his wife.

"I think I should have eaten in my room."

"I thought I should have stayed home when I got here," Jo said, sympathizing with him. "But my headache is gone now."

"Jewell is still here. She's in the clubroom."

At Winter's mention of the source of Jo's headache, Shade looked at her sharply. "Jewell said something to cause you a headache?"

"No, that wasn't what I meant."

"Jewell isn't happy Jo is with Rider."

"I told you I would say something to her." Viper gave his wife a censoring look.

"Please don't," Jo begged. "I would prefer you didn't."

Viper tilted his head to the side. "Why not? She was rude as fuck to you."

Jo winced. "It will create harder feelings toward me."

"She hates your guts. How much worse can it be?" Gavin's sarcasm didn't go over her head.

"I'd rather know her feelings than her hide them and be nice to my face. She's honest. I can appreciate that. It's better than what I tried to do to Rider."

The whole table, except for Shade, was surprised at her admission.

"I apologized to Rider, but I owe your club an apology, too," she told Viper. "I should have told Shade or Rachel that Aly suspected Curt and was trying to get The Last Riders involved. I'm sorry. I wasn't going to say anything until Aly was here, but I don't see her."

"She isn't allowed to attend the parties. I gave her the room in the basement until she decides what she wants to do with her property or finds a job out of state." Viper's harsh features reminded her of Gavin's. The similarities hadn't been immediately apparent, but they were enough that it had her staring at the two men.

"Are you and Gavin related?"

"We're brothers."

Gavin's chair scraped across the floor at Viper's acknowledgment as he left the table.

Jo looked at the various expressions on those left sitting.

"I'm sorry. Should I not have said anything?"

"It's cool." Rider placed his hand on her thigh under the table. "Gavin doesn't like to be reminded he's Viper's brother."

Jo licked her lips, debating whether to say anything. Deciding to let the subject drop, she turned to Lily.

"I haven't seen Rachel and Cash yet. I hope Rider left them enough food to eat."

"Rachel didn't mention coming tonight when I asked her if she could babysit John and Clint."

Jo frowned. "At lunch, Rachel told me she was coming."

"I hope I didn't ruin her plans by asking. I'll call." Lily reached for her cell phone worriedly.

"Greer was bringing Logan when I was there to drop off John and Clint. The boys must have gotten together for a sleepover."

Lily laid her cell phone back down. "I hope our boys won't be too much trouble for her."

"Rachel can handle ten kids. Quit worrying," Shade assured her. "Clint will sleep the whole time, until he's ready to be fed again. And before you ask, I filled the milk bag. Relax. This is our first night away from the kids since we had Clint."

"I will, I promise."

"I'm going to hold you to that," he warned, giving Lily a look that had Jo blushing and glancing away from the intimate gaze the couple were sharing.

When Rider tightened his hand on her thigh, she raised her eyes to him.

"I'm going to get some dessert. You want some?"

"No, I'm good."

Jo had expected to feel uncomfortable once Rider stepped away from the table, never having been good at small talk, but Lily and Winter made it easy for her. And when Willa and Lucky returned with Rider, carrying their plates, she enjoyed the easy banter that flowed back and forth between Rider's friends. They were still talking when they walked in the main clubroom after carrying their plates into the kitchen.

Going to one of the large couches that had two chairs placed next to it, Shade pulled Lily down on his lap as Lucky tugged Willa down on his. Viper let Winter take one of the chairs, sitting down on the arm. Rider took her hand and started to sit down on the other chair, but Jo pulled her hand out of his grasp, sitting on the arm.

"You'd be more comfortable if you sat on my lap."

"I'm fine right where I am."

"We could sit on the chair, and you and Rider could sit—"

"No, they can't."

Lily looked at Shade. "Why not?"

"Because I'm comfortable."

Jo was studying the room curiously when she spotted

Jewell playing pool with Moon. Jewell's leather leggings were so tight they showed how small she was. Jo wouldn't have been able to wear legging like that if she had dunked herself in motor oil first. And her flesh-colored halter top showed her breasts every time she took a shot.

Another woman joined the game. She recognized her as Sasha from the night Shade and Lily's son had been born.

Jewell must have said something because Sasha looked to where they were sitting but didn't come to say hi to her. When she had been in high school, the popular kids had looked at her the same way.

"Anyone want a beer?" Lucky asked everyone as he shifted Willa so he could stand.

The men all took him up on his offer, but Lily and Willa didn't ask for anything, so Jo shook her head when Lucky glanced at her.

"We have some bottled drinks that Shade buys for Lily when they go to Cracker Barrel." Rider put out a hand, stopping Lucky. "I think there's limoncello, grape, root beer, and we even have diet root beer, strawberry-orange, Big Red, and of course Ale-8"

"I'll take a Big Red. I haven't had one since Mick stopped carrying them. They used to be ice-cold, and I still remember the taste."

"Shade, when you take Lily to Cracker Barrel, stock up on enough Big Red for Jo," Rider teased. "I'll even get Mick a couple to keep in his cooler for you."

Jo didn't know what flustered her more: that Rider expected her to come to the clubhouse regularly, or that he was thoughtful enough to give Mick the bottles to make her happy.

"You want to go to Cracker Barrel for Valentine's Day?" Jo heard Shade ask as she took the bottle from Lucky.

"I can enjoy the food without the work," Lily admitted.

"I've never eaten there," Jo admitted.

She was taking a drink of her soda when a woman's squeal caught her attention. Jewell was sitting on the pool table and using Moon's T-shirt to pull him toward her while also untying the halter at her neck. None of the people on the couch turned around at the sound.

Jo switched her gaze to Lily's, whose hands started twisting on her lap.

Shade twined one of Lily's dark curls around his finger. "You ready to go home?"

Lily jumped up at his question. "Yes, I want to call and check on the boys. Now that you're better, Jo, I hope you come by and see the baby. I love showing him off."

"I will," she promised, keeping her eyes glued to Winter after Lily and Shade left.

"We should be going, too, Lucky. I want to say good night to Gideon before he falls asleep."

Jo said goodbye as they left, about to pretend her headache was coming back when Rider stood, reaching for her hand.

"I need to get to work. Come on, I'll show where I'm going to be spending the rest of the night."

Jo nodded goodbye to Viper and Winter, relieved to be leaving the room. Someone had started the music, and several of the members were now dancing.

Rider took her out the back door, and as they walked down the path, she admired the way the houses behind the clubhouse couldn't be seen from the road.

He took her to the security room from the garage. There were still five bikes left. The majority of the space was now being taken up by boxes and plastic sheets that she couldn't see through to what was under them.

"That's the equipment Rachel will be working with. We're just waiting for the tables to come in. Then we can set it up."

"I'd like to see it when it's finished."

"I'll let you know when it's done," he said, opening a door at the back of the garage and ushering her inside.

"You're late," Train commented, not taking his eyes off the several monitors that were set up in a large half circle around the table.

"Sorry. I'll make up for it tomorrow night." Rider pulled out an empty chair. "You can sit, Jo."

"Hi, Train. I'm sorry he's late."

"Not your problem. He's always late, but he makes up for it later," he said, turning the chair so Rider could sit down.

"I'm not always late," he retorted, scooting in under the desk. "Besides, he's late just as often as I am."

"How was dinner?" Train reached out, taking his jacket off the hook on the side of the door.

"Great. Willa saved some for you and Killyama in the oven for when you get there."

"I saw Lucky and Willa leave. I'll fix her a plate, and we can eat when she gets here."

"Killyama babysat for Willa and Lucky?" Jo curiously looked at the cameras.

"We all have to take turns doing the club jobs. Cooking is one them, babysitting is another. Killyama chooses babysitting over cooking."

"I would choose babysitting over cooking, too."

"Not me. I'd rather cook," Rider said without taking his eyes off the screens.

Jo was surprised at his focus. He hadn't turned the whole time Train and she were talking.

"We would rather you babysit. You're a terrible cook. Gotta go or Killyama will beat me."

"Bye, Train." Jo used her foot to push herself around in the computer chair. "This is so cool. I feel like a spy, ready to rush in and save the day."

"You watch too many movies. It's boring as hell. Three to five a.m. is the worst. You get tired, and all you want to do is sleep. That's why, unless it's Shade or me working, the other brothers only pull four-hour shifts."

"Have you ever fallen asleep when you're watching the cameras?"

"Fuck no. Viper comes in two to three nights a week. Believe me, you don't want to be asleep if he catches you."

"I'll take your word for it. Viper is one person I wouldn't want to get angry at me, or his brother."

"Yeah, you should definitely put Gavin on the don't-fuck-with list."

"Winter never mentioned Viper's brother. Are they not close?"

"No one is close to Gavin anymore."

At the tone of his voice, Jo turned the chair to look at him. "Do you and Gavin get along?"

"We used to be best friends, but that was a long time ago. I've tried getting close to him again, but he won't let me in. It's the same with Viper and the rest of the brothers."

"How about the women?"

"The same. He wants to be left alone. He goes out riding alone and doesn't say where he's going. One day, I think he won't come back."

"Don't say that." Jo reached out, giving him a comforting touch on the arm. "Find out what's keeping him from getting close again."

"I've tried. The only one he confides in is Calder, and he won't say. The only other people he's been talking to are Killyama, Knox, and Diamond, and they won't talk about it either."

"Then the only thing I can suggest is to keep asking until … Is Jewell giving Moon a blowjob in front of everyone?"

"Yes."

"Can you shut the camera down?"

"Sorry, no."

"You don't look sorry."

"Bluebonnet, the brothers and the women aren't shy about having sex where everyone can see. To tell you the truth, they probably prefer everyone watching. If anyone doesn't want to watch or participate, they can go to their room and shut the door. But they usually leave the door open."

"Did Aly—"

"No, she's usually holed up in the bedrooms, talking to Ember or Stori about clothes and makeup."

"I can see why Willa and Lily left. Where are Winter and Viper going?"

"I don't know. Do you want me to call and ask them?" he joked, then saw her aghast expression answer for her. "They're going to spend the evening with Gavin. He doesn't come down for the parties, and they're worried about him spending so much time alone."

"Do they know—"

"They *all* know."

"Even Rachel?"

"Even Rachel."

"O.M.G. Turn the camera off. Beth and Razer are in the hallway."

"I'm not turning the camera off."

"O.M.G. Everyone can see what they are doing!"

"Where they are, no one in the clubroom can see."

"*I* can see."

"Then look at another camera if it bothers you," he advised.

"Can you call Train and ask him to drive me h— Is that Train and Killyama getting in the whirlpool? Jesus, doesn't anyone in the club believe in having sex behind closed doors?"

Rider laughed, reaching out to swing her chair to face him. Taking her hand, he pulled her from her chair to his, tugging her onto his lap. "When the action slows down, I'll get Moon to take over so I can drive you home."

Her nose wrinkled at the scene she was watching on the camera. "Make him take a shower first."

Jo's hand went to her mouth when Jewell pulled her mouth away from Moon's cock before leaning back on the pool table. Jo could only watch, spellbound, as Moon then took her leggings off.

"That was a miracle." Jo snorted.

"What was?"

"Moon getting Jewell's leggings off," she answered distractedly, peering closer at the screen to see what he was doing. "There is no way ..."

"What?"

"There is no way Moon's thing is that big."

"My thing is bigger."

Jo didn't even care his voice was filled with amusement, too busy watching Moon rolling a condom on. "You wish."

"I can prove it ..."

She felt him trying to unzip his jeans.

"Don't you dare." Jo turned on his lap, seeing Rider was no longer amused. "You're right; you're bigger."

"Damn right." He sulkily looked over her shoulder at the camera.

Seeing he was seriously peeved, she laid a hand on his chest. "Much bigger."

"Okay, now you're just pandering to my ego."

Jo laughed, her head falling to his shoulder. "A little."

"That's cool. I'd rather you do that than give my dick a complex."

"Dick's don't have complexes."

"If you can talk to your truck, my dick can have a complex."

"You always have to one-up me, don't you?"

"You know it. That's what having a small dick will do to you."

"You don't have a small dick. It's just not as big as Moon's or"—she darted a quick glance over her shoulder before turning back around to him—"Razer's, but yours is definitely bigger than Train's."

33

When she burrowed her face into his shoulder, Rider felt a clenching in the area of his heart he had never experienced before. He combed his fingers through her hair, releasing the ponytail holder that kept it back. It fell in silky waves, framing her oval face.

Her blue eyes shone back at him, her lush eyelashes curving against the fair complexion that had a faint scattering of freckles you couldn't see unless you were as close to her as he was.

Her reaction to what was going on on the screens was typical of Jo. Her no-nonsense attitude had peeled away to expose the private woman she was. She was extremely shy yet hid behind false bravado. She concealed to her friends how she felt by making sure they were taken care of. It was why she had been talked into doing the auction, why all her clothes were bought at the thrift store, why she constantly volunteered at the church, even though she had worked herself to exhaustion to pay bills her father had convinced her to assume.

Placing his thumb under her chin, he lifted her head out

of the crook of his neck to place featherlight kisses against her lips. Jo responded by immediately kissing him back, giving him what he wanted.

"It isn't how much you have, but how you use it."

She gave a sweet laugh, mingling her breath with his. His dick grew and thickened in his jeans.

Adjusting her into a more comfortable position that didn't make his nuts feel like they were being scrambled, he deepened the kiss, letting his tongue slide inside searchingly, ratcheting Jo's desire from slumbering into a red-hot flame.

Using his foot, he turned his chair so he could watch the monitors as he felt her clutch the material of his shirt.

"You don't seriously believe that, do you?"

"Are you trying to make my confidence take a hit? Because it's working."

"I couldn't dent your ego with a sledgehammer."

"You dent it every time I look at you. And I ask myself how fucking lucky I am to have you in my bed."

"Technically, I haven't slept in your bed. You've been sleeping in mine."

"We need to change that. Your mattress sucks."

"No, it doesn't. Each of those lumps conforms to me and provide me with well-rested sleep."

"While those same lumps are hell on my back. And the only reason you haven't bought a new one is because you're waiting for the one you want to go on sale."

"See if I take you shopping with me again."

"I can pay for the mattress, or at least let me go in half. I sleep there enough that I should pay my part."

"I'll think about it."

"You saying you're thinking about it is another way of saying no." He moved his chair again to watch a different a camera.

"Are you making out with me at the same time you're watching the cameras?"

"I can do two things at once. I'm ambidextrous."

"Jesus, you're so full of yourself."

Rider caught her taking another peek over her shoulder before pressing her lips back to his.

"*You're* doing two things at once. You're getting me horny and you're watching those cameras, too."

"I am not."

"Are, too," he teased. "Your cheeks are as red as my car."

When she sneaked another peek, he raised a brow at catching her and couldn't help but laugh.

"Who are you staring at? Moon or Diablo?"

When she turned around to see what Diablo was doing, she didn't turn back to him as quickly.

He grabbed her waist, turning her on his lap so she could see the screens without getting whiplash.

"Jewell's letting them ..."

"Yes, she is." Rider didn't remove his hands from her waist while keeping his eyes on the other monitors.

With one hand, he slid down intimately between her thighs. When she didn't pull his hand away, just gripped his wrist as if torn between removing it or letting it stay, he rubbed her clit through the material of her jeans, making the decision for her.

He used his chin to move her hair to the side so he could nuzzle her neck, using his tongue and his teeth to tantalize the sensitive flesh.

When her thighs clenched his hand hard against her, he used his other hand to stealthily unzip her jeans, sliding underneath her panties to find her damp pussy.

Her head fell back on his shoulder as he fingered her opening and freed his trapped hand to spread her thighs, placing one leg over each of his to give him better access to the creamy flesh he wanted more of.

His eyes flicked to the monitor she was captivated by, seeing Moon had switched places with Jewell. He was on his back on the pool table with Jewell riding his cock. Moon's hands were on her ass, spreading her cheeks so that Diablo could fuck her, too.

When Diablo grabbed Jewell's hair to hold her in place, Rider felt another rush of cream lubricating his fingers.

"Have you done that with a woman?"

His cock nearly exploded in his jeans at her question.

He slid his finger deeper inside her before answering, "Yes."

The walls clenched on his finger as if she was still trying to decide if she wanted it there.

Moving his mouth to the skin below her earlobe, he bit down, stoking her fire enough to make another decision for her.

"A lot?"

"A few times," he countered, wanting to tell her the truth yet not wanting her to jerk off his finger.

He slowly started pulling her jeans down, when she gripped his wrist tighter, stopping him.

"Someone could come in."

"No one can come without the red light coming on here." Rider straightened up on his chair for two purposes. One, to get her to release his wrist, and two, to drive his finger higher inside her. When he regained the use of his wrist, he pointed to a button on top of the middle computer. "I can also delay them from entering for sixty seconds."

"That's not much time." The soft plaintiveness of her hesitation had his cock feeling like it was in a noose.

He started to tug her jeans off again, and this time he succeeded, now able to play with her pussy unfettered.

An aroused moan spilling from Jo's lips had him going to his own jeans when he tossed hers aside.

"Is that Missy?"

Rider saw the couple walking through the door.

"Yes, and that's her boyfriend, Daryl. He's the manager."

Missy and Daryl were regulars at their parties.

The couple coming in had Razer using his back to cover Beth as they went deeper into the shadows of the hallway that led to the dining room. Even through the screen, you could see the arousal on their faces when they saw Moon and Diablo fucking Jewell.

Ember, who was sitting on F.A.M.E's lap, waved at them, drawing their attention to her.

"I like Ember. She's very friendly."

"Yes, she is." Rider grinned against her neck.

He heard the suck of Jo's breath when Ember grabbed Daryl's belt and pulled him toward her, quickly unbuckling it and his jeans to reach for his cock.

"You said that's Missy's boyfriend ..."

"He is. They have an open relationship."

"Oh, God, she's giving him a blowjob right in front of her!"

"It seems that way."

Rider saw a lone woman parking her car, then walking up the steps to the porch. While Jo wasn't paying attention, he grabbed his cell phone and texted Trip a stop sign. He sped up his finger-fucking as the uninvited, disappointed woman went back down the steps.

F.A.M.E slid Ember off his lap to sit next to him on the couch, replacing her with Missy. The woman placed her hands on his shoulders as she straddled him, messy hair falling forward and keeping them from watching them kiss.

"Have you ever"—Jo cleared her throat—"been with Missy?"

"Don't ask questions you don't want answered," he growled into her neck as he took his cock out behind her. Moving his hand away from her pussy, he brought her down on his cock.

"In front of Daryl?"

"Missy doesn't fuck men unless Daryl is there."

"I need to go home." Her head fell back against his chest as her hands instinctively went to his thighs, gripping him tighter.

"You want me to call Moon?"

"We can wait, then."

"Okay."

He shifted his eyes from left to right, taking in each detail of the outside cameras before going to the one she was fascinated with. He could tell by her accelerated breathing that she was about to climax.

"Don't come."

"I can't help it!" A faint moan escaped her when F.A.M.E pulled up Missy's red mini-skirt to show she wasn't wearing panties. She took F.A.M.E's cock out, her knees on either side of his legs widening as she placed a condom over him before poising herself over his cock. Then she slammed herself down on him.

Jo's eyes went back to Jewell, Moon, and Diablo as both men sped up their thrusts.

"If you start to come, I'll stop." He moved one hand under her sweater, sliding it under her bra to grasp her breast, roughly pinching her nipple.

"That isn't fair." Jo started shaking. He felt her stomach muscles tensing as she fought her orgasm.

"I'll stop, then."

"Please ..."

Rider kept thrusting inside her. "You're being such a good girl." He moved the hand that was at her waist away to bury it in her hair, raising her mouth for a passionate kiss that had him in trouble of climaxing.

Switching to her other breast, he plucked at her nipple until it was a hard nub in his palm.

Breaking the kiss, he bit down on her shoulder, then went to play with her clit as he fucked her.

"Can I come, please?"

Rider saw that Moon and Diablo had almost hit their limit.

"Every time Diablo thrusts inside Jewell, count. When you see it eight times, you can come."

"What if I can't?"

"Then I'll stop, and you'll have to stand beside my chair for an hour before I have to start all over."

Whimpering cries were torn from Jo's lips as they watched Diablo's muscles tighten as he almost pulled out of Jewell, then release as he pumped back inside.

"Have you ever thought of fucking two men at once?"

"No!" she screeched out. "I wouldn't want to."

"Not even if it was me and Moon?"

"No!"

"How about me and Diablo?"

"No!"

"How many has that been?"

"Five!" Jo sobbed out.

"I only counted four."

"It was five!"

"To be fair, we need to start over."

"Rider ..."

"How many?"

"Seven!"

"Just one more ..." he crooned to her as Diablo's ass flexed again.

Rider surged into her pussy at the same Diablo did into

Jewell ass, gripping Jo's breast so tightly he wouldn't be surprised if he left handprints.

"Eight!"

Her sighs had him hooking one of her legs over his arm to place it on the desk as he rammed his cock higher until he felt the strong tugging sensations while she was climaxing.

Regaining control of his body, he lifted both her legs, turning her to the side so she could curl against his chest. He stroked her thigh until she quit shaking from her orgasm.

Putting a long arm down to his side, he was able to reach for her sweater and help Jo back into it. Snuggling her to him, he started the pattern of watching the screens, then reversed it as she traced her fingers over the tattoo on his chest.

"Are you cold?"

His mouth quirked. "I'm hot-blooded. I don't get cold."

"Rider, I don't … ever want to be with two men."

Glancing down at her, he could see the concern in her blue eyes. "When I asked if you ever thought of being with other men, that was playtime to get you wet. What we have going on is serious. I would never mix the two, nor would I want to." His eyes darkened possessively. "No one will touch you but me, so you can give that fear a rest. Have you ever seen any of the brothers riding my motorcycles or driving my cars?"

"No."

"And you won't. What is mine is mine, and stays that way."

"Can I ask you a personal question?"

"Shoot." He lifted his eyes, returning to the monitors, expecting her to ask him about his marriages, or a variety of questions about the women they were watching fuck in the clubroom.

"What do the numbers on your chest mean?"

"4-20. Blaze it up, brothers." He lived life the way he wanted to.

Her eyes widened. "Do you smoke pot often?"

"I wouldn't say often, but I do occasionally." He watched the cameras as he answered her. There were some things he preferred not talking to her about. Sex and pot weren't one of them.

"I saw you smoking pot the night I was swimming in the lake. You thought I was Rachel."

"I knew you weren't Rachel. I saw your bike leaning against the tree."

"So, you weren't trying to …? You weren't trying to hit on Rachel?"

"No, I was trying to hit on you. The brothers dared me to see if I could score with you."

"You failed."

Rider felt her chuckling against his chest.

"No shit. I knew I would when I took the dare."

"But you tried it anyway."

"Bluebonnet, a man has to do what a man has to do, or he's no man."

His carefree enjoyment of teasing was cut short when she dug her short nails into the firm flesh of his chest.

"So, you knew it was me?"

Wincing, he tried to remove her claws when they sank in even deeper. "I just said I did."

"If you knew it was me, then where are my panties?"

Jo stared down at the drop cloth that had rows after rows of bike parts splayed out on them. Picking the engine parts out to work on, she carried them to the worktable.

"What are you doing out here?"

Startled, Jo turned to see Rider coming inside the garage.

"What are you doing up? I thought you would still be sleeping." She had left him sleeping in her bedroom. She had ended up falling asleep on his lap in the security room last night, with him nudging her awake in the morning. After his shift had ended, they had come back to her house to crash in her bedroom. It was only twelve, so she had assumed he would be sleeping much longer.

"Why didn't you bring your computer?"

She frowned at his annoyed expression. "I didn't think I needed it with you sleeping in the bedroom."

"I wouldn't be much help sleeping if Curt, Tanner, or Justin showed up."

"I wouldn't need your help anyway. I keep my gun in the

garage now that I'm no longer having to keep it in the tow truck."

"I'm going to schedule you for a conceal and carry license."

"Don't bother. I won't carry it. The thing gives me the heebie-jeebies."

She felt him coming up behind her as she arranged the engine parts. Then she leaned back against him when he slid his arms around her waist and rubbed his rough cheek against hers.

"Go back to sleep. I'll wake you before you have to go to work."

"I'll never get back to sleep. Want some help?"

"Depends if you're going to pick on me for the way I do things."

"Would I do that?" Giving her a lingering kiss, he moved to the side to stare down at that mangled parts.

"Constantly. You can't help yourself."

She enjoyed working beside him, to have someone to bounce ideas around with, and especially when he helped her scavenge for the parts she needed. She wished she had more motorcycles in the graveyard to work. She decided to take one day next week to go through the junkyard in Jamestown. It could be fun picking through another yard like hers.

"You want me to fix you some breakfast?"

"No, I ate some cereal."

"Which ones? The Froot Loops or the Cap'n Crunch?"

"The Cap'n Crunch. The Froot Loops box was empty."

Jo gave him a censoring gaze. "That's because you put it back in the cabinet instead of throwing it away."

"Me? I'm pleading the fifth."

Jo rolled her eyes. "It's just not fair that you look so good when you eat like a garbage disposal."

"What can I say? Genetics."

"Does your family look as good as you?"

"Better."

"Of course they do. Life is never fair. Do you get to see your family often?"

"Often enough. We should go to the grocery store. I finished off the Cap'n Crunch."

She took the change of subject in stride. He kept any discussion of his family to a minimum. She had almost asked Rachel several times if his parents were living, and if they were, where did they live, but then had decided against it. If he wanted her to know, he would tell her. She didn't talk about her mother. Not that there was much to say. They had grown distant since her remarriage had her growing closer to her stepchildren than to her.

It was two hours later when they stepped back to survey the work they had done.

"You want to fire it up to see if it works?" Rider asked, wiping off his hands.

"No, I'll wait until tomorrow. Why spoil the rest of the day if it doesn't? I'm going to fix us some lunch. I'm starving. You coming?"

"In a minute. I want to check it over again and make sure we didn't miss anything."

"You're going to see if it works, aren't you?"

He grinned.

"Then I'll leave you to it. Just don't tell me if it doesn't."

"Coward."

"Nope. I'm about at the point of telling Cash that it can't be fixed. I'm giving him another day of keeping the hope alive."

"Okay," he drawled out. "That's a little nutty, but I won't say anything if it doesn't work."

"I'd have to be a little nutty to love you," she said, reaching up to kiss his cheek. "Don't take long. I'm making steaks and potatoes."

She turned on her heel, rushing toward the open garage door.

"Whoa!" he yelled out. "You can't say that to a man, then take off running!"

"Say what?" Assuming an innocent expression, she poked her head back inside the garage, keeping her body outside.

"You just told me you love me."

"Did I? Do you want yours medium or well-done?"

"Yes, and I like it rare."

"Cool." She hurried away, this time not stopping when she heard him swearing inside.

After taking a quick shower, she put the steaks on the grill and checked on the potatoes she had put in the microwave before getting dressed. She was putting them on the plates when Rider came in the door.

"Smells good," he complimented, going to the sink to wash his hands.

"It does." She stared proudly at her accomplishments. The steak and potatoes looked picture-perfect.

Rider enthusiastically sat down at the table with her.

Sliding the butter close to him, she watched his face as he cut his steak. Her shoulders dropped when she saw he was having trouble cutting it.

"I may have gone past the rare stage."

"Bluebonnet, you blew through that stage and went to the charcoal stage again," he said with laughing eyes.

"I'm sorry."

"Don't worry about it; my teeth need the workout."

She threw her napkin at him. "It's not that bad—" She broke off what she had been about to say when she saw he was having a problem opening the potato.

"You like your food well-done, that's for sure."

Jo covered her mouth with her hand. "I'm sooo sorry."

"No worries. It's nothing that a lot of ketchup and butter won't make better."

"I need to add that to the shopping list, too." Miserably, she promised herself she was going to learn to cook, even if she had to buy a new stove.

He earned another piece of her heart when he cleaned his plate and asked if there was any more.

Jo went to the kitchen cabinet, digging into the back. She took out a small box of Cookie Crisp cereal.

He gave her a disappointed expression. "It's a sad day when your old lady has to hide your favorite cereal."

"It's self-preservation for when you get on my nerves," she said, reaching for the milk jug and a bowl for him.

"How do I get on your nerves?"

"When you call me old lady, and when you eat the last of the Cap'n Crunch."

"That's only because they're my favorites."

"Judge, I rest my case." Joking, she stole one of the cookies from the box before giving it to him.

Rider ate two bowls before patting his stomach. Taking his cell phone out, he glanced at it. "That should tide me over until morning. I need to be going, or Train will kick my ass for being late again."

"I agree. He didn't seem happy last night." She tipped her chair forward, stealing another cookie. Then she stood up to put the box back in the cabinet, but Rider caught her arm before she could move away from the table.

"You want to come and keep me company again tonight?"

She had been dreading him leaving, though feigning unconcern. She didn't want to appear too eager to spend the night with him instead of watching another boring movie or trying to read a book she had no interest in.

"Are you sure?"

"I am sure." He gave her a tender grin that had her giving the cereal box back. "Give me five minutes to change."

He plunged his hand back into the box, taking out several cookies. "You don't have to change."

"I'll just be a second." Dashing into her bedroom, she changed her sweater to a flannel shirt, then grabbed a sweater for added comfort, buttoning it closed.

Rider stood up, laughing when she came out of the bedroom.

"How many layers did you put on?"

"A few," she answered primly.

"Damn, woman, you're taking the fun out of spending the night with you."

"That's the plan." She went into the kitchen, grabbing an empty grocery bag from the drawer to pack his favorite popcorn and what was left of the cereal. "I'm ready."

"You didn't put in any snacks for yourself?"

"Jerk, you'll be lucky if I share one kernel with you and don't ask you to swing by and pick up Mag. She keeps asking when you're going to keep your promise to me."

"You can tell her the truth. That hell will freeze over first."

JO MUNCHED on her popcorn as she swung her foot back and forth, watching the cameras.

"Do they ever give it a rest?"

Rider was sitting on the computer chair next to her, turning his head at her voice.

"No."

"You could have humored me and lied."

"How could I lie? You have a bunch of cameras in front of you, telling you that I was."

"Ember is being friendly again."

"When she isn't, I'll get worried," he said matter-of-factly.

Her elbows on the desk, she propped her jaw on her hand.

Ember was standing on the bar, dancing as the men egged her on, all except for one man. Moon was sprawled out on the couch with his mouth buried in a woman she had seen sitting at a table with the night before. F.A.M.E was standing beside the arm of the couch as the woman fucked Moon while giving the other man a blowjob.

"I saw her last night."

"Who?" Rider looked at the camera she was watching.

"The woman on the couch with Moon and F.A.M.E."

"That's Mercury."

"Mercury is her nickname?"

"Yes."

"Who gives the women their nicknames."

"The brothers do."

"I see." Biting her lip, she watched Mercury's experienced mouth that made her embarrassed at her novice efforts when she had given Rider one. "How do the men make up their nicknames."

"Don't ask questions—"

"I want to know."

"Stori got her nickname because the brothers had a story each time they fu—did her. Ember got her nickname because she set them on fire when—"

"I get the picture." She cut him off. "What's Rachel's nickname?"

His expression became guarded. "You trying to get my ass kicked?"

"I won't tell anyone, I swear." Jo mimed zipping her lips and throwing away the key.

"Vixen."

"What's Winter's?"

"Pretty Girl."

"Lily's?"

"Angel."

"Willa's?"

"Siren."

"Beth's?"

"Kitten."

At the rapid questioning, Rider swung his chair toward her.

"I call you Bluebonnet. Don't you like it?"

"It's better than old lady," she mumbled into her hand.

"What's wrong with it?"

"Nothing."

"I answered your questions; the least you can do is answer mine."

"It isn't sexy. It isn't special like Angel, or Kitten, and for sure isn't Vixen."

"It could be worse. It could be Killyama. And I think you're sexy when your bluebonnet eyes get all murky when you give me a blowjob."

"Do I look that gullible?"

"A man can only hope."

She wasn't amused by his wiggling eyebrows.

"Well, it's only going to be a forlorn hope until you come up with a better nickname."

"Well," he mocked wickedly, "I may need some inspiration."

Jo glumly watched Mercury sucking F.A.M.E's cock like she was determined to keep the men's attention on her instead of Ember dancing on the bar. The thought had her swinging her chair around to study him.

"I keep meaning to ask. Is that monitor broken?" She missed the start he gave at her question to check out if he was getting excited from what was going on in the clubroom.

"Yes, I have a new one ordered. It hasn't come in yet."

"Oh, is it one of the cameras at my place?"

"Yes, it's not an important one. It just shows the side of the garage."

"That's good to know."

Damn, she couldn't tell if the bulge in his jeans was the normal size or not. She promised herself to check him out when they were watching a movie at her house.

"Are you staring at my dick?"

Flushing, she swung forward. "No."

"You were." His laughter filled the small room.

Giving him a dirty look from over her shoulder, she admitted, "Okay, I was. I was trying to see if you were getting hard watching Ember and Mercury."

He kicked his chair out from under the desk, leaned back, and held his arms to the sides. "Come and find out."

Mercury and Ember didn't have a problem making their desires known. When they wanted something, they reached out and took it. None of the men on the cameras had made a move on the women that hadn't been initiated by them. Now she could understand how no one had hit on Aly when she had been pretending interest in becoming one of The Last Riders' women. She had never initiated the contact.

She could sit here and wonder if Rider was getting excited, or she could be brazen enough to find out in a way that might earn her a new nickname.

Sliding out of her chair, she dropped to her knees, falling between Rider's thighs. Then she slid her hands up his thighs to audaciously unbutton his jeans and pull out his soft cock. As she stroked his length, it became aroused.

Wetting her lips, she leaned down, giving small breaths to provoke the response she wanted. As his cock stiffened, straining upward to his belly button, she let her tongue come out to trace the veins that began appearing, following the most prominent one that led to the helmet of his cock.

She explored the head as if she had never given him a blowjob before, and truthfully, she had been so nervous she hadn't given him the attention he had deserved. She made up for it now, searching the front before investigating the back. Then she sucked the head into her mouth, letting her salvia wet the spongy tip as it rested on her bottom lip. Blowing her breath on him again, she couldn't resist giving him a smug look when she felt his cock jerk.

"Personally, I think your nickname is too tame."

"You do?" he hissed out between clenched teeth. He might have been watching the cameras, but his body was giving her all his attention.

"I do ... I would have nicknamed you something more legendary." Sucking his cock into her mouth again, she curled her tongue so she could encase him in the warmth of her mouth.

"Like what?"

She didn't answer him, moving her head forward and sucking his cock farther back into her mouth, like the way she had seen Mercury do. Bobbing her head over him, she mouth-fucked him, using her fingers to gauge how deep she was taking him. Each time she went down, she was determined to take him in deeper and suck harder. When he clenched a fistful of her hair, she knew his desire was escalating.

Needing oxygen, she released his cock with a *pop*, using her hand to mimic what her mouth had been doing.

"Something like Dragon or"—she rubbed the head over her bottom lip, watching him from lowered lashes —"Titanium."

Twin emotions of conceit and doubt crossed his face. It was priceless to watch him try to decipher if she really believed what she was saying or just heightening the pleasure of his blowjob.

She might not be a bubble-headed blonde or a sexy siren, but she knew one quality Rider had in abundance was conceit.

Playing to his puffed-up ego, she tried to think of another nickname that would boost his pleasure. The only one she could come up with in her blank mind was Thor, and she didn't think that even Rider would believe she thought of him as the Viking god.

Deciding to quit while she was ahead, or until a better nickname came to her, she sucked him back into her mouth. The velvety softness of his cock was aided by a thrust from him. Taking her cue, Jo moved her mouth over his cock rhythmically.

She slid her free hand inside his parted jeans, reaching for his balls and squeezing them softly, afraid she would hurt him. Hearing a low growl from him, she began squeezing them with firmer pressure.

"Stop. I'm about to come, and I want to finish in your pussy."

"What if I want you to come in my mouth?" Letting his cock slide out, she moved her hand faster over his slippery length.

Another growl escaped him. "I'll make you a deal. I'll come in your mouth, but if your panties are wet, you have to stand by my chair for an hour, then let me fuck you."

"You're going to lose that bet."

Clicking his tongue, he increased her punishment. "Make it two hours."

"If I win, you have to keep your promise to let Mag come to a party, a much tamer party. And you have to pinky swear to keep it."

"Deal."

Grinning, she increased her assault on his cock, determined to win. Rider tangled his fingers in her hair, dragging her head back down and setting the speed he needed to climax. It worked for her. The sooner she could make him come, the better. She had been fighting her own arousal, trying not to remember how good it had felt last night when he was fucking her.

Trying to find something to distract herself, she removed her hand to pinch her thigh.

"That's cheating."

She hastily went back to squeezing his balls, counting backward as she worked her hand and mouth to wreck his control. Then it hit her.

"Give it to me … Steel."

She had to hurriedly encompass his cock as it throbbed and jerked in release while his eyes practically rolled back in his head. When it quit moving, she slowly dragged her mouth off him, seeing lust flaring in his eyes as she licked her bottom lip.

Pulling her hand out of his jeans, she gently patted his thigh before regaining the other computer chair.

"Are you forgetting something?" Rider's eyes went to monitors as he shoved his cock back in his jeans, then pushed his chair back under the desk.

"I don't think so—"

"Stand up and come here."

His stern voice had her reluctantly standing, moving to the side of his chair. His eyes caught hers as he unbuttoned her jeans.

"I'm not wet."

"Excuse me if I don't take your word for it." He moved his hand inside her panties. It didn't take him a second to find the creamy warmth she hadn't been able to control. Fastening her jeans back up, he gave her a gloating look.

"It's fine where you're standing." Ignoring her standing by his side, he went back to scanning the screens.

When he reached for her popcorn, she took a small step forward.

"Uh-uh ... you're not allowed to move. Back up to where you were."

Backing into the position he had put her in, she stood still as he started eating her popcorn.

"You know I'm going to pay you back for this, right?"

"Uh-huh. But not before I finish this popcorn, that box of cereal, and before you fuck me."

SHIFTING her weight from one foot to the other, Jo watched as Shade approached the outer garage. She gave a silent prayer of gratitude that she had asked Rider to use the restroom, thankful she had straightened her hair.

His eyes flickered over her then to Rider, who was watching the screens, as he strode into the security room.

"Jo, how are you doing tonight?"

"Fine."

"I was going to ask Rider if he needs anything, but I see he's been taken care of."

Flushing, it took her a second to realize he had been talking about the snacks Rider was happily munching on.

"Thanks anyway," Rider said, not turning around. "Have a seat. If you have time, I want to make sure these sensors are back in line."

Shade walked to the other computer chair. "You sure you don't want to sit down? I can stand."

She felt her cheeks redden under Shade's scrutiny.

"No thanks. I'm tired of sitting. I'm just trying to stretch my legs."

"You sure?"

"Positive." Her fingers curled over the back of Rider's chair, tempted to upend his ass in front of Shade.

She listened as they ran a series of tests before both were satisfied the sensors were working.

"You want some popcorn? I have plenty."

Shade shook his head. "I just ate."

The men turned to look at the camera pointing at the parking lot. A car that Jo easily recognized came speeding in, then braked sharply. Lucky got out of his car and, with furious strides, made his way toward the garage. When the door didn't open, he pressed a button, and then Lucky's angry voice filled the security room.

"Let me in, Rider."

Rider pushed the button he had shown her last night that delayed entry.

"So, you came by to see if I needed anything, huh?" Rider gave Shade a skeptical look. "Why's Lucky so mad?"

"You don't know?" Shade's voice turned silky.

"That was two days ago. He's still mad?"

"He's outside, isn't he?"

Rider released the button, letting Lucky come in.

Jo had never seen her pastor so angry, the metal door clanging as it hit the wall when he slung it open. Her eyes went round at Lucky's fury.

When she moved protectively closer to Rider, Lucky stilled.

"Jo."

"Pastor."

At a sound Shade made, she gave him a censoring look before staring Lucky down again.

"You're up late tonight with church being so early in the morning," Jo commented.

"I was about to go to bed when I couldn't find something

Rider promised to return to me when I talked to him yesterday."

"I forgot."

Jo wanted to hit him on the back of his head for pricking Lucky's temper even further.

"You didn't forget; you just don't want me to have them."

"Those pants cost me four hundred dollars. Buy your own."

"I had my own pair until you accidentally washed them. You shouldn't have been washing my clothes anyway."

"I was trying to help Willa out."

"You were trying to get her to make you some candy!" Lucky's voice rose to a shout.

"Those pants were too small for your fat ass anyway. Buy another pair."

The angrier Lucky got, the more amused Rider became. She didn't know a lot about men, but she knew enough to know that Rider was walking on thin ice.

"Motherfucker, you told me you would give me yours or buy me another pair!"

"I changed my mind."

Jo screamed when Lucky jerked Rider out of his chair, sending the wheels rolling. Shade's arm came out of nowhere, moving her out of the way.

"Stop!" Screaming, she tried to break them apart, but Shade held her back, not bothering to get out of his chair.

Lucky threw Rider against the metal door that had swung closed after Lucky's furious entrance, sending the monitors shaking on the desk.

"Watch it! Any of the computers get broken, you're paying for them!" Shade snapped.

Lucky held Rider pinned to the door with one hand and turned the knob with the other, sending Rider flying backward out of her sight.

Jo tried to catch a glimpse of Rider to see how he was doing, but she couldn't because Lucky blocked her view as he went out the door after him. She could hear a heated struggle as the door slammed shut after them.

"Aren't you going to stop them?" she screeched out, yanking her arm out of his grasp. She opened the door to look out, seeing Lucky and Rider rolling around on the floor, pummeling each other.

"No. They'll stop when they're tired."

His calm voice had Jo starting to go out the door to do it herself.

"You better not break any of those glass tanks out there, or Cash will kill you both!" Shade shouted, keeping his eyes on the different screens.

Her mouth dropped open when Shade dug into the popcorn, taking a handful. Placing a few in his mouth, he chewed thoughtfully as the fight between Rider and Lucky raged on.

Halfway out of the door, Shade's comment of "Damn, that's pretty good" had her turning around.

"They're killing each other, and you're just going to sit there and eat popcorn?"

"It's Rider's turn," he said, taking another handful of popcorn.

"*What!*"

"Every few weeks, the brothers let Lucky blow off some steam."

"*Let?*"

"Okay, we help Lucky blow off some steam. It's Rider's turn. Son of a bitch nearly broke Moon's jaw last month. It was my turn this month, but Rider owed me a favor."

"You're not serious? Rider could get hurt!"

"You see any blood?"

Jo turned back to the fight. "No."

"Then he's good. Have a seat. They'll stop when they're tired."

Jo looked closer at the two men. Lucky was pounding Rider's stomach and shoulder like a punching bag, fierce concentration on his features that she had never seen on her pastor's face before. Rider was laughing up at Lucky.

"Is that all you got, motherfucker? Willa hits harder than you." Pushing Lucky off him, he then threw himself on top of him, pounding him back.

After watching the crazy interaction between the two men, she went back to the spot she had been standing in before Shade's arrival, looking at the time on the clock.

Shade took his eyes off the screens to raise a brow when she didn't sit.

"I'm not tired." Blushing, she winced when she heard cursing come from the other room. "How long do the fights usually last?"

"Depends on what the brother did to piss Lucky off. Rider ruined Lucky's leather pants, so it could take a while." Shade picked up the bag of popcorn, holding it out to his side. "Want some?"

"Thanks." She took a handful, and they watched the monitors until Rider returned to the security room.

Taking his chair, he soothed a hand over his jaw, wiggling it back and forth experimentally.

"Are you okay?" she asked in concern over his battered face.

Rider gave her a reassuring smile, then gave Shade an accusatory glance. "The fucker's been working out."

"Has he? I didn't know."

"Bullshit, you know every stink set off in the clubhouse."

"Not everyone." He cast Jo a glance as she remained standing next to Rider's chair. "I better go. Lily will be wondering what's taking me so long."

"Good." Rider grimaced as he ran his hand over his ribs.

"Night, Jo."

"Good night, Shade."

Shade went out the door, but before it could close, he poked his head back inside. "Rider, I forgot to mention, she moved to the door for three minutes. Later."

Blushing furiously, she glared at the closed door. "Prick." She was so mad she could spit. Lily had her sympathy.

"Welcome to my world."

Jo sat cross-legged on the floor as she watched Clint play. Lily's baby was adorable, wiggling on his back with drool escaping out of the side of his mouth as he swatted with his baby arms at the miniature gym that had little stuffed animals and rings.

"Can I take him home with me?" Fascinated at the little creature, Jo only half joked with Lily as she walked around the living room, making sure Jo would have everything she needed to care for Clint while she and Shade went out for Valentine's Day.

"Shade might have something to say about that."

"I thought I'd try. Lily, he's adorable."

Lily proudly beamed down at her child. "He is beautiful, isn't he?"

"Yes." Jo leaned forward, using a burp cloth to wipe the drool away. "I see a lot of Shade in him, but he has your eyes. He's gorgeous."

Lily's face glowed with health and the joy of parenthood. "I'm truly blessed with my children, and with Shade, too."

"Yes, you are." Jo looked away from the baby to her as Lily

took a seat on the couch, waiting for Shade to come downstairs.

"You're very happy, aren't you?"

Lily stopped jiggling a playful elephant at the wistfulness in Jo's voice that she hadn't been able to hide. Her violet eyes rose to hers. "So much that I get afraid sometimes."

"Why?"

Lily gave a graceful shrug. "That Shade will wake up one day and realize he doesn't love me, that another woman can give him what I can't." As she talked, she looked down and ran a hand over the delicate tattoo of forget-me-nots that was on the underside of her forearm. "It's kind of surreal how happy I am. It can't last forever, can it?"

Jo didn't think that Lily was talking to her anymore, but to herself.

Shade came into the room, breaking the moment. Carrying Lily's coat, he held it open for his wife.

Shrugging into it, Lily gazed up at her husband lovingly.

"We can go somewhere else if you prefer. Maybe we should eat somewhere closer?"

"I'm craving Cracker Barrel. Jo has this, and Rider is coming over when he gets off work."

Leaving Lily to button her coat, Shade went to John, who was putting a puzzle together at the table, easily lifting the boy to kiss his son's cheek.

"Dad, I'm too old for that."

"I'll have to remember that. You look out for your baby brother until we get back. Can you do that, little man?"

"Yes, sir!"

Shade set John back in his chair as Lily went to kiss him next. Squatting down, he carefully moved the gym to the side to lift the baby into his arms. "Since John doesn't want my kisses anymore, that means more for you." Kissing both cheeks, the baby squealed in delight at his father's appearance.

John jumped off his chair, running to Shade to pat his father on his back to get his attention. "I didn't mean it, Daddy. You can kiss me."

Shade cradled Clint in one arm and gathered John in his other, alternating kissing each of his sons before handing Clint to Lily. When the boys were settled, Shade opened the door for Lily.

"We won't be late," Lily assured Jo.

"Take your time. I'm glad to help out." Jo stared at the couple, seeing the closeness apparent between them. "Lily, I didn't have a chance to answer your question. I don't think you have a darn thing to worry about. And yes, I do. I can't think of another person who deserves it more."

Lily gave her a tearful nod before leaving. Shade gave her a discerning look that had her unable to look away.

"Thank you, Jo."

There was no doubt in her mind that Shade wasn't thanking her for babysitting, but for what she had said to Lily.

After he left, she played with Clint until he grew tired and cranky. Laying him in the bassinet, she made Clint a bottle from the breast milk that had been left in the refrigerator. Then she helped John find a missing puzzle piece.

She was giving the baby his bottle when Rider came in the door.

"Yo, John, what's up?" Rider tousled the boy's hair.

"Uncle Rider, can we go for a ride on your bike?"

"Your father wouldn't like it without him here. I'll ride you around the parking lot tomorrow."

"Can you help me finish my puzzle?"

"Sure thing." Winking at Jo, he sat down at the table.

Jo cradled Clint, smoothing his black hair down that was

so fine it stood on end, springing back up when she moved her fingers away.

She could understand Lily's fear of her happiness being taken away. She felt the same fear in her heart every time she looked at Rider. His good looks would always garner feminine attention. His facial structure and features would allow him to age gracefully. His body would fuel any woman's fantasies, and she'd had sex enough times to speak from experience that he gave as much as he received.

He filled the lonely life she had lived with humor and a playfulness of a much younger man, while also showing an insight into her emotional needs. It was how he had gotten past the barriers she had used to keep men out for years.

She had been waiting for a special man and hadn't even known it, believing she would die alone and unloved. She had been roaming endlessly in a dark labyrinth until Rider had strode into the maze of her own making and guided her out, only to find that the impossible had happened and she had fallen in love with him.

Clint's sucking stopped, and he was sleeping, slack-jawed, with milky drool coming out of the corner of his mouth. She tenderly burped him, waiting until she heard the unmistakable sound she was waiting for, before placing him in his bassinet.

Sitting at the table next to Rider, she watched as he and John worked on the puzzle. Scooting her chair closer to his, she laid her hand affectionally on his thigh.

Rider let John slide the last piece in place. Finished, the little boy looked for something else to do.

"Can I go play with Noah and Chance?"

Rider reached for his cell phone "Let me ask Razer."

He twined his fingers through hers as he talked to Razer. Hanging up, he gave John the go-ahead. Jo made sure John was bundled up in his coat and hat before Rider watched him from the porch until Razer waved that he had him.

"The boys are close, aren't they?"

"In their minds, they're already brothers." Rider took her hand to pull her close after shutting the door. As he gave her the kiss she had been waiting for since he had gotten there, she ran her hands over his chest to his shoulders as he parted her lips in a demanding kiss that had her nails digging into the back of his shirt. Gasping, she twisted her lips away, trying to calm the rioting desire that had her wishing they were at home in her bed.

"Happy Valentine's Day."

"You told me that this morning before I left, and when you brought me lunch at the factory before coming here to babysit."

"Just making sure." She resumed kissing him when a small sound from the bassinet had them breaking apart.

Rider went to the bassinet before she could get her brain functioning again. Jo's heart skipped a beat when he lifted the baby to cradle him in his arm.

Rocking him from side to side, Rider crooned to him, letting the baby wake slowly. Grabbing the blanket in the bassinet, he went to the chair, dexterously draping the blanket over his lap to lay the wiggling baby down.

"You're very good with babies."

"I've had my fair share of practice babysitting. It was a nightmare when Noah and Chance were born. They were born troublemakers. They never woke up at the same time, and one would wake the other up. I don't think Beth or Razer slept until they were four. I'm glad Lily asked you to babysit first. Sasha is watching them tonight. Those two hellions are going to drive her crazy."

"They're little angels in church." Jo denied his assertion about how bad they were.

"That's because Razer has raised them to respect the holy hand that spanks their ass if they misbehave."

"He believes in corporal punishment? Poor boys!" When she had children, she was never going to spank them or let their father.

"Poor boys? I give you five minutes with those boys, and you'll be tied to a chair or locked in a closet."

"I'll take your word for it."

Rider stared at her pityingly. "You're going to be suckered into babysitting for them sooner or later. May the force be with you."

Jo gurgled with laughter. "You're exaggerating."

"If anything, I'm understating them. Don't worry; I'll have your back when they try to set you on fire."

"That's good to know. I'll have your back when you need me to." Jo moved to sit on the arm of the chair where he was. Leaning against his shoulder, she nuzzled his neck. "I got you a Valentine's Day present. I'll give it to you when we get home."

"I have one for you, too. I'll give it to you when Lily and Shade get back. It's in my bedroom."

She trailed loving fingers across the nape of his neck. "Is it perfume?"

"No."

"Is it bigger than a breadbox?"

"Wait and see."

"Is it the size of a—"

"Jo, wait and see."

LILY AND SHADE came back earlier than she had expected. Then Jo and Rider left after saying a rushed goodbye to the couple. It was obvious they wanted to spend the rest of night doing what she planned to do with Rider.

It was strange how drastically things had changed. Usually, Valentine's Day was spent in the tow truck, waiting to be called when a couple had imbibed too much and listening to Rachel describe what Cash had gotten for her. For once, she was going to be able to celebrate the holiday the way it was meant to be.

She felt like skipping down the small path, excited for him to see her present.

"Slow down. What's the rush?"

She had been walking so fast she had gotten a little ahead of him.

Walking backward, she couldn't help but tease him. "I'm anxious to see my present. It's not going to be as good as mine."

A deep frown marred Rider's forehead as he sped up to match her steps. "Jo, it isn't much."

"If it's a card, it's more than I've had before."

"You've never had a Valentine's Day card from your parents or from a friend?"

"No, my mother thought it was a waste of money, but my father always took me to Mick's for Valentine's Day, and he would give me a hamburger and a—"

"A Big Red," he finished for her.

"Yes," she replied as they went through the back door of the clubhouse and into the kitchen.

Jo almost tripped over her own feet when she saw the kitchen was full. It wasn't there being so many members that made her so clumsy; it was how provocatively the women were dressed. For example, Ember was dressed in a red teddy, and Mercury was wearing a tiny red thong and a big red bow wrapped around her breasts.

Rider grabbed her hand, dragging her toward the living

room, but before going inside, he changed his mind and went to the table, pushing her down on a chair.

"Wait here. I need to go upstairs to take a shower and grab your present. If I didn't have Clint's spit on my clothes, I'd take one at your house, but the smell is getting worse."

"Go ahead. I'll keep her company." Ember sat down at the table with her.

Jo returned Ember's smile. It was only when she was raising her eyes back to Rider that she thought the two had been communicating behind her back.

She placed her hand on the table to rise. "I can wait in your room."

Rider pushed her back down. "No. Stay with Ember. I don't trust you to open your present until we're at your house."

"Hurry, then. I'm getting impatient."

Rider took off, leaving her alone with Ember.

"That color looks good on you," Jo complimented.

"Thanks. It's new. I wanted something special for tonight."

"You succeeded."

"There are a lot of people here."

"There're even more in the other room and upstairs. The brothers from Ohio decided to come and celebrate with us. I think because Sasha and Mercury are still here," she confided.

"Do the women who live here get jealous when the other ones come to visit?" Jo felt strange talking to Ember. She was unassuming, and Jo had never felt a spark of jealousy within her presence or while she had watched her on the monitors for the last month and a half.

"No, if the women get jealous, they don't last long."

If Jewell wasn't jealous of Mercury and Sasha, then why was she jealous of her? She just hoped she wouldn't see her tonight. She didn't want anything to spoil the night she had planned to have with Rider.

The swinging door opened with Willa coming in, carrying two pink canvas bags. A large group followed behind her to crowd inside.

"Get back, or I'll take it back to the church."

Moans and groans filled the air as Willa went behind the counter.

"You can all get in line and take your turn." Willa opened one bag, setting pink boxes out on the counter, then removed the lids.

Jo jumped up to help her, taking the bag as she emptied the other one. Then she went to the pantry for a big stack of paper plates and forks.

The smorgasbord of delicacies ranged from huge chocolate-covered strawberries, pink macaroons, chocolate cakes with pink filling, pink cupcakes with pink icing, and pink marshmallows dipped in chocolate. There were so many Jo felt like she had gained ten pounds by just touching the boxes.

"They're beautiful, Willa. You have outdone yourself ... in pinkness."

"Pink is my favorite color."

"I can tell. You think they'll kill me if I snatch a pink cupcake without getting in line?"

Willa took one from the box and gave it to her. "They're too afraid to mess with me. I need to run. I just wanted to drop these off so everyone can enjoy them tonight. Can you give this to Rider for me?" Reaching for a smaller pink box, she then handed it to her.

"Sure. He's upstairs now, but when he comes down, I can."

"Thanks, I'd appreciate it. Be careful, or they'll sneak it away from him."

"I'll be careful," Jo assured her.

As Willa left, everyone hugged her, finally managing to escape when Moon started arguing with F.A.M.E that he was taking all the cupcakes.

Taking a bite of her cupcake, Jo was walking around the counter when Jewell turned from the refrigerator. Her bite of cupcake settled in her throat like lead. Jo hadn't seen her enter the room.

Jewell hadn't dressed in red like the other women. Instead, she had gone for black, wearing a silk robe that came to the top of her thighs and was belted loosely at her waist. The robe was partially open, showing the swells of her breasts and her waxed privates, which weren't really private, as anyone near her could see.

Jo looked at the box Willa had given her for Rider, debating what she should do.

"You can take it upstairs if you want. He's going to want to thank Willa before she leaves. If you don't want to, I'd be happy to do it for you," Jewell said, twisting the top off a bottled water.

"Willa already left."

"She's probably at the factory. She wouldn't leave before giving Diablo and Trip any. What's on the counter will be gone before they get off."

"All right. Then I better hurry."

Jewell shrugged as if she didn't care what Jo did.

Going around the table, she managed to go out the swinging doors and into the clubroom. Keeping her eyes lowered, she tried not to look at what the members were doing, grateful when she made it up the steps. She then headed toward the bedroom that Rider had shown her a couple of times when she had stayed with him in the security room and he had to get a change of clothes before leaving with her.

As she passed the bathroom, she heard the water running.

Not wanting to assume it was Rider and seeing his door was opened a crack, she decided to check and make sure he wasn't in there. Besides, if Rider was in the shower, he wouldn't have enough time to see Willa before she left anyway.

She gave a brief tap on his door, which had it opening a bit, allowing her to see further into the room.

What she saw had her taking an unintentional step forward. Her eagerness to celebrate tonight sunk into a deep pool of ice water as reality hit her with a smack across the face.

Rider hadn't wanted her to come upstairs because he was worried she would open her present. He had wanted to open his.

Rider dried off, then wrapped a towel around his hips. Running a quick comb through his wet hair, he decided not to take the time to blow-dry it, too anxious to get back down to Jo.

As he left the bathroom, he saw his door was wide open. Whoever had gone inside would have their ass bounced out. He didn't have time …

He stopped at the threshold, seeing Jo sitting on the bottom of his bed, surrounded by the mound of presents the women had given him.

He only had a split-second before she saw him to come up with a strategy for damage control.

"You were supposed to wait downstairs."

"Willa brought you a gift. I wanted you to see it before she left." Jo held a small pink box he easily recognized.

He walked to his dresser, taking out his clothes. "Has she left?" he asked as he put on his jeans.

Nodding, he saw her hand go to the new pair of jeans that Ember had given him for Valentine's Day, holding them out.

"You don't want to wear these instead?"

"No, they need to be washed."

Jo jumped up, running for the open door.

Anticipating her reaction, he caught her around the waist, lifting her into his arms and using a foot to slam the door. He checked that it was closed before carrying her to his bed and sitting down. He let her hit his chest as she struggled against him on his lap.

"Let go of me. I want to leave!"

"I want to talk first. Then, if you want to leave, I won't stop you."

"There's nothing to talk about."

"I think there is. Your feelings have been hurt, and I can't fix it if we don't talk about it."

"I don't need you fixing anything!" she snarled, sinking her teeth into his shoulder to get him to release her.

"Red."

Jo immediately stopped biting him. "That's my safe word, not yours."

"Now it's mine, too. I didn't like the way you were biting me, and I didn't want to hurt you to make you stop."

"I'm sorry. I shouldn't have hurt you."

"You didn't. I just didn't like the way you were doing it. Anytime you want to use those sharp teeth on me when I'm balls deep in your pussy, go ahead; just not when you're mad at me. I wouldn't hurt you when I'm mad at you. I expect the same from you."

"I want to leave."

"We're not finished talking."

"I don't want to talk. I want to get the hell out of here."

"If you don't want to talk here, we can go to your house," he offered the alternative, hoping it would lessen her distress.

"No!" she yelled out, then lowered her voice when she heard how loud she had become. "I want to go alone."

Rider knew why she didn't want him to go with her. She didn't want him to see what she had gotten him for Valentine's Day. With the bounty on his bed, she now felt like hers would be just one more present without any special significance to him.

When he was nine years old, he had decorated an old shoebox for Valentine's Day. During the school day, their class had a party where all the students would walk around the desks and put their Valentine's Day cards in each other's boxes. He still remembered one of his friends whose box had been nearly empty, while his own had been filled to overflowing.

Jo's hadn't had a few cards. Hers had been empty. She had never had a Valentine's Day when she had felt singled out and made to feel that she was important.

"Then we'll stay here," he answered imperturbably.

"Fine," she snapped, crossing her arms over her breasts stubbornly. "So talk."

"I'm not the one who's angry. You are." He remained unruffled, seeking to defuse her anger by getting her to examine and talk about what had hurt her.

"Are all those presents from the women in the clubhouse?"

"No, Moon gave me the blow-up doll. It was a prank gift."

"No shit."

"A few are from women in Treepoint, Jamestown, Lexington, and Ohio," Rider continued as if she hadn't spoken. "I've never hidden the fact I had sexual contact with women who didn't just belong to the club; only that I had stopped playing around when I won the date with you at the auction."

"Then why did they give you all these presents?"

"Because, while I no longer share a sexual relationship with them, I'm still their friend."

"It's good to know we'll remain friends when you break

up with me." She dropped her arms to her sides as she sat stiffly on his lap.

"Or it could be a saving grace when you break up with me." Taking one of her hands, he twined his fingers through hers before raising it to rest on his heart.

Artfully pretending a guilelessness that couldn't be further from the truth, now that her anger was diffused, he needed to disperse her hurt feelings by switching from herself to him. Jo had a weakness that he logically used against her. When Jo loved someone, she placed their needs above her own. It was the one thing that he had every intention of exploiting.

"You think I'll be the one breaking up with you?"

He met her gaze, making sure he didn't blink or turn them away from hers. "I come with a lot of baggage. I wouldn't blame you. I've been married twice, and I belong to a motorcycle club that I'll never leave. Sometimes I'm going to have to put them first when you won't want me to. I'll never shirk the duty I've pledged to The Last Riders, but I promise that you will always come first when it counts.

"Those presents don't mean a damn thing; only yours does. I'll give them all away or return them if you want me to. I already planned on returning the blow-up doll to Moon. I plan to shove it up his ass."

Her body loosened, sinking against him as she rubbed the shoulder she had bitten. "You'd return Willa's candy?"

"Not that one, but I'll share," he compromised.

"You can keep that one." Jo nuzzled her face into the side of his neck.

His semi-erect cock beginning to strain under his unbuttoned jeans, he gently lifted her to his side so he could fasten his jeans.

"Can I give you your present now?" he asked with fake humbleness, the hardest emotion in his repertoire to fake.

Waiting for her slow nod, he went to his closet, opening it to reach inside and take the box out.

"I hope you like it." Placing it on the floor at her feet, he didn't have to fake his enthusiasm. He had given a lot of thought to her present and was excited to see if he was right.

Jo slipped to the floor on her knees. She stared at it for a minute before carefully unwrapping it.

His excitement dimmed at how careful she was being. He had expected her to tear it open. That she was using a finger so the wrapping paper wouldn't tear disconcerted him.

Going to his haunches, he started to help her.

Jo swatted his hand away. "Don't. I want to do it myself. I want to save the paper."

"Why? I have more paper in the closet—"

"It won't be the same as this one." Shyly, she paused from loosening a flap that had more than its fair share of tape. "I know it's silly, but it was wrapped in the first present you gave me."

Stunned at her reasoning, he sank onto his butt, leaning back against the bed's footboard as he watched her unwrap her present.

No punch had ever affected him as much as her embarrassed confession had. His bitter heart had frozen over when he was twenty-four, and the passing years since then had only hardened it further. From the first night he had fucked Jo, she had been chipping away at his resolve to never love another woman. He had repaired each chip, fortifying his bitterness with the same steely willpower he had learned in the military. It had saved him then, and it would save him now.

With the paper folded and placed at her side, Jo opened the box and reached inside, pulling out a big heart that was filled with chocolates.

Smiling, she placed it on the floor next to her knees, then

reached inside again, taking out a stuffed middle-sized puppy. It was sitting on its hind legs with doleful eyes, holding a red box between its front paw. On top of the box, it said *"Be Mine."* Rider didn't miss the trembling of her fingers as she opened it.

Jo took out two necklaces. Each one was gold, and one was thicker than the other. The thinner one was so fine it didn't look strong enough to hold the gold heart with a picture gazing back at them.

They had taken the picture when Jo had wanted to go to the Jamestown junkyard. Afterward, they had gone to a restaurant where they had jokingly taken selfies as they waited for their food, their faces pressed together. He had known Jo liked it when he had seen her using it as a wallpaper on her phone a few days later.

"One is for you and the other is for me." Rider took the necklaces out of her hand, showing her that, when the magnetized hearts were close together, they clung to each other. Then he opened the clasp of the necklace that held his face in the center, leaning forward to clasp it behind her neck. Giving her the thicker chain, he waited expectantly for her to put it on him.

When she was done, her hand went to the necklace she was wearing. "Thank you, Rider. It's beautiful."

"You're welcome, Bluebonnet." Dipping his head, he poised his lips over hers. "You didn't answer my question?"

"Your question?" She lifted stargazed eyes to his.

"Will you be mine?" he asked huskily, seducing her with words.

"Yes, Rider, I'll be yours."

"Forever and ever?" he prompted the response he wanted.

"Forever and ever."

He swooped down, capturing her mouth, giving her no time to think about the commitment she had just promised.

He sought out the proof he wanted, the proof that her promise wouldn't be forgotten when another man came along.

The stuffed puppy fell out of her hands when she circled her arms around his neck.

Pushing her backward, he covered her body with his, nudging himself between her thighs so his cock could rest against her pussy. His kisses became more forceful, parting her tender lips to find the passionate warmth she hid from everyone else.

He was tired of coercing her responses, determined to use his body to get the final vow he wanted from her. He had learned the hard way that marriage certificates and pledges taken in a church, in front of preacher, wouldn't ensure a lasting relationship.

He jerked her sweater upward, breaking the kiss with a swipe of his tongue on her bottom lip. Then Rider buried his face between her breasts.

"I finally found the only thing that tastes better than Willa's candy." He eased his tongue under her bra to lick the rise of her breast.

"I bet you've said that to all your women."

"No woman has reached that distinction before but you. If I could, I would give you a blue ribbon for taste." Rider dragged the cup of her bra down so he could lick her nipple, feeling it harden under his tongue.

Jo gave a sighing moan, melting into his hard body as if releasing the last of the hurt she had experienced when she had seen the presents on his bed.

Rising, he went to work on the button of her jeans, looming over her, pinning her in place as he then took her jeans and panties off.

Reaching a long arm out, he opened his dresser, taking a

condom out. Startled, he realized his fingers were shaking as he tore it open.

"Let me do it." Jo raised herself, taking it from him. "I never expected you to be nervous."

"I'm not nervous. I'm horny."

"Really?" She slid the lubricated condom over his dick, rolling it down. "I didn't notice," she teased as she lay back down, wrapping her thighs around his hips, opening herself for him.

"Bluebonnet, if you can't see how hard my dick is, you need glasses."

"Steel ..." Jo dragged her tongue over her bottom lip, wetting it. "I see it. I'm just waiting for you to use it." Jo was getting better at being seductive.

Feeling a chip of ice fall off his heart, he told himself he would worry about repairing it right after he fucked her.

Reveling as his fingers found her wet, he stroked her thigh with his other hand before raising it higher up his side. "Take your bra off. Let me see those prize-winning breasts."

She arched her upper body as she reached behind her to release the clasp.

"That's much better. When you get your nipples pierced, I'm going to buy you blue stones to match your eyes," he expertly planted the seed in her mind.

"I'm not getting my nipples pierced. You can get me earrings instead, or I'll buy them myself."

"It won't have the same effect."

"My ears aren't even pierced. There's no way I'm doing it to my nipples. It'll hurt."

Rider lightly pinched her clit. "You don't seem the type to allow a little pain to keep you away from what you want to do." Releasing her clit, he thrust a finger inside her pussy, rocking it back and forth to lubricate her.

"You're right … *when* I want to do something." Her hips arched under his hand. "And I don't want any tattoos either."

"Aly told you about the tattoos, didn't she?" Rider grinned down at her.

"That the women get tattoos when they become a member? Yes. I won't be becoming a Last Rider, so—"

Rider removed his finger so fast a small "*oomph*" escaped Jo. Before she could get her bearing, his hands were at her waist, turning her and pressing her back to his chest, her on her knees.

A hand on her breast, the other at her throat, using it to tilt her head to his shoulder, Rider said, "You're going to become a Last Rider because you're *this* Last Rider's woman." His voice went dangerously low. "You don't want to fuck to get the votes, that's cool, because I don't want you to get them that way anyway. I'd kill any man who tries to touch you, and that's a fucking promise. I'll take care of the votes, just like I'll take care of anything that concerns you. Because you're *mine*. You don't want a tattoo or get your nipple pierced, that's cool, too. What you don't have the right to decide on is saying no to being a Last Rider, because you're fucking mine."

She hadn't just chipped away at his heart by claiming she wouldn't become a Last Rider; she had taken off a big chunk, and he was going to get it back.

Rider felt her nod under his hand.

Using his chest, he pushed Jo flat on the floor. "You know what I'm going to do now?" he taunted.

"What?" Jo asked, trembling.

"I'm going to fuck you because you're fucking *mine*, aren't you?"

"Y-yes," Jo stuttered.

"Say it."

"I'm yours."

"For how long?" This was the question he waited with bated breath for her to answer.

"Forever and ever."

"You're damn right about that." Rising up, he removed his hand from her throat, using it to ruthlessly push her back down before driving his cock into her pussy in one stroke.

"Too hard?" he purred seductively.

Testing that she would stay in the position, he squeezed her ass cheek as he started fucking her with deep thrusts.

"Harder," she moaned out.

"I'm going to show you that you can handle a little pain, and you're going to be a good girl and take it."

"Yes, sir."

"I'm going to take it easy on you tonight because you were smart enough to say *sir*."

"Thank you."

"You know what to say if you don't like what I'm doing?"

"Yes, sir. Red. Except, I really don't want to try spanking."

"Then don't do anything to deserve one. Is that fair?"

"Yes, sir."

"I could fuck you every hour of the day." Squeezing her ass harder, he claimed his possession of her with rapid strokes of his cock that had Jo gasping for air every time he drove in deeper and higher.

He loosened his grip on her ass, seeing his handprint on her. He had to hold back the desire to make the mark brighter and last much longer. His bluebonnet wasn't ready to play the games he enjoyed, and until she was, he would wait.

Rider smoothed his hand over her silky cheek, skillfully parting the cheeks while moving his fingers featherlight over the rosebud of her anus. She almost jumped off his cock at the movement.

Moving downward, he traced the indention before

moving back to her ass cheek. His poor little flower was shuddering at his boldness, calming when he started squeezing it again. Rider practically read her mind, knowing she would think that if he was squeezing her ass cheek, he wouldn't go off exploring.

Jo didn't know him at all, but she would learn, and how she would learn had him moving harder.

She had lost her timidity and was rearing her ass back as he plunged into her pussy.

"You're as tight as a vise, clamping down on me." Reaching forward until he was once again leaning over her, he grabbed a pert breast, giving it the same treatment as he did her ass.

"Steel …" Jo whimpered.

"It's not going to work. I'm not ready to come."

"Rider, please … I want to come."

"Then come. I'm not stopping you." Biting down on his favorite spot on the back of her nape, he ground into her, making it impossible for her not to find the relief she was begging for.

Her whimpering moans and the contractions on his dick showed she had given in and was coming.

Rider rode her through her climax, and when she would have fallen to the floor, he found one of her nipples and gave a small twist. The pain had her arching back on his cock.

He controlled her every movement, not letting her slip into the afterglow of her orgasm, but building it into another, more satisfying one. Her fingers curled in the carpet as he rocked back and forth, each thrust more forceful than the last.

He felt her second orgasm on his cock at the same time her scream filled the room. When he released her nipple, a third climax had her clawing the carpet to get away.

"Do you want to use your safe word?"

"No."

"Are you sure?" He went to her other breast, seeking her nipple. Twisting it, he found another rhythm to wring another climax out of her.

"Yes!" Her screams grew higher in intensity, but she quit trying to claw herself away from the pounding she was taking.

"Do you want me to come?"

"God, yes."

"What are you going to do to help me with that?"

Her screaming stopped. "What do you want?"

Rider nearly laughed at her worried question.

"The next time I work in the security room, you have to stay naked for two hours."

"Do I have to stand?" she sulkily countered.

"No, you can sit."

"I can do that."

"Then"—Rider pushed her shoulders to the floor while he kept her ass right where he wanted it—"we have a deal."

He was fucking lucky she had agreed when she had. If she had held out a moment longer, she would have had her wish without having to agree to anything.

Groaning, he sped up, rocking against her hard, frustrated at himself that he couldn't last longer. He was used to sex marathons and had intended to have to carry her to his bike to take her home. Now he would be lucky if he didn't have to drag himself down the long flight of steps.

His climax rolled through him like a bomb had detonated inside him, jarring his heart more than he had intended. With Jo, he had to show a part of himself, or she wouldn't be fooled. She was too caring and tender-hearted not to recognize those qualities were missing from him. The double-edged sword had turned around on him, and she had sliced out another chunk of ice from his stone-cold heart.

Sinking to the floor, he stretched out on the carpet, trying to catch his breath as he pulled Jo to rest beside him. Curling an arm behind his head, he stared up at the ceiling as she snuggled against his side, laying her head on his tattoo. The reminder of the meaning of the tattoo and the promise he had made to himself made a mockery of the feelings that Jo was innocently arousing in the heart that beat under her ear.

"Damn."

Jo lifted her cheek, propping her chin on the hand that was covering his heart. "What's wrong?"

"Nothing. Never mind. I lost something, and I can't find it."

"Oh." Settling back against him, she placed her head back on his chest. "We can find it later," she said, yawning.

"I hope so." Rider stared up at the ceiling. He hadn't prayed for so long that he had forgotten how, but he broke that drought tonight. "God, I hope so."

38

R ider circled his arm around Jo's shoulders as they went in the front door. Her glorious blue eyes shone with the love that she was unconsciously revealing to him.

"Did you have a good time?" he asked, tightening his grip on her as she almost stumbled tipsily onto the rug in front of the door.

"How couldn't I have?"

Allowing her to break away from him, he shut the door, then made sure her back was still to him when he signaled to Trip to cut the live feed.

Jo almost caught what he was doing when she spun around, splaying her arms out to her sides as she spun around the room.

"It's been the best Valentine's Day ever!"

The giggles escaping her had him smiling as she continued to spin.

"What was the best part?" Rider asked, taking his jacket off. "That Shade had dropped your Big Red off before coming home and it was ice cold, or the two hamburgers Mick fixed you?"

"Those were good, but that's not why." She stopped spinning to grab the back of her couch, steadying herself.

"Was it the three cherry vodka shooters Mick gave you?"

"Nope. You're not even close." She haughtily placed her hands on her hips, then lost the effect when she kept tilting to the side as if she was about to fall over. "By the way, I don't know why you didn't let me have that last shot. It was soooo good!"

"I wonder why?" he mocked, reaching out to keep her from falling over the back of the couch.

"You were being a party pooper, but that's okay because I love you anyway." Her hiccup had his smile turning into a full-fledged grin.

"You do?"

"I do. But"—she put a finger over her pursed lips—"don't tell him."

"Why not?" Rider rested his tired ass on the back of the couch, crossing his arms over his chest.

"I'm playing hard to get." Trying to tap her finger against her forehead, she missed, making her ponytail even more lopsided. "I'm being smart. He's going to break my heart." Her joy-filled expression turned tearful. "And it's going to hurt like a motherfucker."

His smile disappeared. "No, I'm not."

"You're not?"

"No, I'm not going to break your heart. I'm going to make you very happy for the rest of your life."

"You are?"

"I am." He stared at her fiercely, letting his determination shine through his eyes. This, he would never lie to her about. He was being a son of a bitch about everything concerning her, but with this, he had no intention of being fake.

"That's good. You know why?"

"Why?"

"Because I love you." Jo started spinning again.

"I wouldn't do that. You're going to make yourself sick."

"No, I'm not. I can do this all night."

"You might be able to, but I need to get to sleep. You ready for bed?"

"Do I have to?" She stopped spinning, and she would have fallen to the floor if he hadn't hastily caught her. "But I haven't told you what the best part of Valentine's Day was."

"What's the best part?" Taking her shoulders, he frog-marched her to her bedroom. Turning the doorknob, they came to a stop as he looked at what she had done to her bedroom.

"You."

Her soft, heartfelt reply shook him to his core. Bracing himself against the door, he stared at the unmade bed with a big red bow on top.

"It's a new mattress. Do you like it?"

"Yes."

He had seen the mattress delivered earlier, before she had gone to babysit. What he hadn't been able to see from the camera in the living room was what was spread out on her bed that he had watched her carry in.

Going to the bed, he unfolded a new pair of jeans, clenching the material in his fingers.

"I hope they're the right size. I looked at the sizes you wear when you were sleeping."

"They're the right size." Setting the jeans down, he reached for the long-sleeved, black and gray thermal shirt. Looking at the tag, he recognized the Pro Club brand, as well as the short-sleeved black T-shirts that were stacked neatly on her bed.

Sitting down on the bed, he reached for the red Teddy bear, staring down at it.

"Do you like them?"

At the uncertainty in her voice, he lifted his head. "Where're your sheets?"

"I'll get them—"

"Just tell me where they are?"

"In the bathroom closet."

He walked by her to go to the bathroom. Finding the sheets, he came back, setting them down to carry his presents to her dresser before making up her bed.

"I can help—"

"I'll do it. Don't move."

"The comforter is in the dryer ..."

Retrieving the comforter after putting the sheets on, he spread it over the bed. Removing his clothes, he laid them on the hamper that was by her closet door.

Meanwhile, Jo remained silent as he moved around her bedroom, watching uneasily.

Going to the side of the bed, he held out his hand to her. "Come here," he ordered starkly.

Obediently, Jo wobbled across the floor to him.

"You want to know how I like my presents?"

Tearfully, Jo nodded.

"I'm going to show you how much I like them."

He took off her clothes, one article at a time, placing kisses on each curve he exposed. Her hair fell forward when he pulled her jeans down and pressed a kiss to her mound. The springy curls tickled his nose as he swiped his tongue downward to find her clit.

Raising his eyes, he watched for her reaction to see if she was too sore to fuck. When her hips pushed for more, he stood up and pushed her back to the mattress. His lips curled into a predatory smile when she bounced twice. Then Rider slid her jeans all the way off after removing her sneakers.

"I like them so much you're not going to be able to work tomorrow."

"Why not?" Jo licked her lips, staring up at him trustingly.

"Because this is the best Valentine's Day I've ever had, and I don't want it to end."

THE JARRING of the lamp on Jo's nightstand had him rolling over, careful not to wake her. Nabbing the vibrating cell phone, he put it to his ears, coming awake.

"You're late." Jewell's cold voice had him swearing.

"Sorry. I'm on my way." Disconnecting the call, he dressed in his new clothes then grabbed the rest of his presents before leaving Jo's bedroom without waking her.

In the kitchen, he wrote a brief note, explaining how he had to go to work and to call when she woke up. Placing the note on her nightstand so she could see it when she awoke, he went outside to his bike, putting his presents in his saddlebags.

At the factory, he took off the necklace before going inside, putting it in his saddlebags with the rest of his presents that he would take to his room after work. He then went to the office, knowing Jewell wanted to yell at him for being late.

After knocking and receiving no answer, he went to the work orders, taking the ones that had been clipped to his name.

He had finished the first order when Shade strolled toward his station with two cups of coffee.

"I figured you could use it," he said, giving him one.

"Thanks," Rider said absently while scanning the list on the next order, committing it to memory with one glance.

When Shade didn't move away, Rider gave him another

glance. Shade wasn't one to chat for no reason. "Something wrong? I know I'm late. I'm going to talk to Jewell when she comes back from lunch."

"Jewell won't be coming back from lunch. I'll be managing the factory until her punishment has been decided on."

"What'd she do? Let Moon off early?"

"Come in the office. We need to have a talk."

That Jewell had done something so bad that Shade didn't want to discuss it around the other workers had him preparing to come to her defense. She had always been a good friend to him, except for the one exception with Jo. Since then, she might have been chilly with Jo, but she had kept her space from her. Therefore, he had made the allowance, knowing the woman was having a hard time at the new tenor of their friendship.

Shade went behind the desk to put his coffee down as Rider shut the door. Then he took the chair in front of the desk, blowing on the hot coffee.

"Did you want Jo to go upstairs while you were taking a shower?"

Rider frowned at Shade's question. "You know I didn't. I shot everyone a mass text not to let her come up. I didn't want her to see the shit on my bed. I was going to give everyone hell for it after work."

Shade nodded. "How did Jo take it?"

"How the fuck do you think she took it? Her feelings were hurt. Luckily, I was able to smooth it over, but I'm still pissed about it. That's why I was waiting for after work to speak to the brothers and the women. Especially Ember."

Shade nodded. "Ember knew you would be mad. That's why she went to Viper's house to talk to him this morning."

"Why didn't she text or call me? I'm angry, but when have I ever hurt a woman for—"

"She didn't call because she didn't know how you would react to something she wanted you to know. Viper and I both think it was a wise decision."

"Tell me." He set his coffee on the desk.

"Ember got distracted when Willa came into the kitchen with all the treats. All the brothers and the women did, except for Jewell. Ember said one minute, Jo was there, and then she was gone. When she realized Jo wasn't in the room, she asked Jewell where she was. Jewell laughed, saying she had sent her upstairs to take the candy that Willa gave you. Jewell told her that, as soon as she did it, she regretted it. That when she went upstairs to get her before she could go in your room, it was too late. You were coming out of the bathroom, and she was afraid to tell you what she had done."

"Bullshit. She did it deliberately, then lied to Ember that she was too scared of me to tell me the fucking truth."

"I agree. I came into the office as she was hanging up on you. I'm sorry, brother. I'm glad you were able to smooth it over. I like Jo and wouldn't like to see the woman hurt. She's taken enough crap to last a lifetime. She doesn't need The Last Riders adding to it."

Rider stood up. "I don't blame the brothers or Ember. If I had been in the kitchen when Willa came in, the same thing would have happened. She should go in the military. She could probably start a war with those cupcakes of hers. Who I blame is Jewell."

"Viper knows. That's why he's sending her to Ohio after I speak to you. It's up to you if she stays in the club. It's a split vote. She either goes to Ohio, or we cast her out of the club."

"She can go to Ohio. I won't be the vote that casts her out. But she's in Ohio for good. I don't want to see her ass in our clubhouse again. She betrayed me *twice*. Once, I let it slide, but twice? Fuck no. She'll be cool in Ohio because she knows it will be her last chance. If not, I'll pull the plug and she won't be bothering anyone again."

Shade's shrewd gaze met his. "I will make the grave situation clear to her."

"Do that, because if I get near that bitch, the other bitch buried in our backyard will have company."

39

Jo woke to the urgent need to use the bathroom. It was only after she showered and brushed her teeth that she felt somewhat human. Using a towel to dry her hair, she went back into her bedroom, seeing the note Rider had left her.

Dressing, she tried to remember what she had said to Rider after they had come home. The cherry shooters had been lethal.

Grabbing her cell phone, she went to the kitchen to make coffee. When it started dripping, she called Rider.

"Bluebonnet, I was starting to get worried about you."

Jo leaned against the counter, staring out at the afternoon sunshine. "Why? You're good, but you're not that good," she teased.

"I'll pay you back for that tonight. What are you doing?"

"I'm hard at work."

"I don't believe you."

Jo raised a surprised brow. "Why not?"

"You would have called me before you went to the garage."

"Oh … I didn't think of that. Did anyone tell you that you're too smart for your breeches?"

"All the time." He laughed. "I wanted to be there with you when you woke up. I'm sorry about you seeing the presents. I didn't want anything to spoil your day."

"It's fine. I overreacted. You're a popular guy. Did you give Moon his doll back yet?"

"Not yet. I'm waiting until I get off work. That's when the others come back, too. And I'll mail—"

"Don't. Keep them. I overreacted." She traced an imaginary line on the counter. "Next year, you can tell them you're taken."

"I'll do that. What's the plan for dinner tonight?"

"Nothing. Right now, food is the furthest thing from my mind."

"Hungover?"

"A little."

"A lot from the way you sound. How about I get dinner and bring it to you?"

"I have a better idea. Text me what you want, and I'll go pick it up at the diner. It'll be nice and hot when you get here. I haven't taken out my truck in a while. It needs some exercise."

"You sure? I don't mind picking it up."

"I'm sure. Get back to work before Jewell docks your pay."

The phone went silent.

"Are you still there?"

"I'm here. You're right; I better get back to work. Bye."

"Bye," Jo repeated, hanging up.

It had seemed as if he had expected her to say something after she had mentioned Jewell's name.

Carrying her thermos, she went to the garage to work.

Razer and Moon stopped by to bring some other motorcycles that needed work done. They stayed talking longer than she had expected so that when they left, she realized she hadn't called Rider's order in.

Calling Carly, she ordered his food and a cup of soup for herself. Then she locked the garage and carried the computer and her thermos back inside her house, grabbing the keys to her tow truck.

Driving into town, she saw the diner's parking lot was so full she had to park across the street and walk back.

The restaurant was busy. It took several minutes for Carly to come to the register, where she was waiting.

"I didn't expect you so fast. Take a seat at the counter, and I'll get the order ready for you." Carly took her money before going out back.

Jo found a booth behind two men. Texting Rider that the food wasn't ready, she wasn't paying attention to the low voices of the men behind her. She was about to text Rider that they were wearing The Last Riders' colors when she tuned in to their conversation.

"I'm nervous about meeting Viper for the first time."

Jo was sure it was the younger man who had spoken. She had caught a glimpse of his face before she had sat down. He had seemed to be early twenties. The other one, she had only seen his profile and that his beard was hanging down to his chest. He seemed much older.

"Relax, we're not staying long. Just playing escort to one of the women."

"Who?"

"Jewell."

"I haven't met her yet," the younger one spoke. Jo could hear the youthful eagerness in his voice.

"Their loss is our gain. She must have pissed Viper off bad because she won't be coming back to Treepoint."

"Is he as mean a fucker as everyone says he is?"

"Worse. I served with him in the military. Hell, Viper is

the reason I'm still breathing and got to come home to my wife and kids. Viper and Crux."

"I haven't heard you mention him before."

"Not much to talk about. No one knows who he is. Most of the men I served with don't even think he existed. They think we just made him up to scare the new recruits."

"But he wasn't?"

"Fuck no. I saw him in action myself. Of course, I wouldn't know him if he were seated right next to me. That's why he was so good at his job. They said he was recruited before he even finished his SEAL training."

"What was he recruited for?"

"His job was to be a spy, going into hostile camps, finding the best way to take them out, and devising the plan for us to neutralize them.

"One night, I nearly shit myself. We'd been ordered to retake a town by the higher-ups. We'd lost three squadrons already trying to get that town. All the way there, I thought I was going to die. You ever been that scared?"

"No." The young man's awe had Jo's lips twitching as she listened.

"Well, I have. A mile out from the fucking town, we were given our orders just as the sky lit up like the fucking fourth of July."

"Why did they wait to give you your orders?"

"It was some secret shit, that's why. Viper was our commander. We lost four men that night. The squadrons before us lost all their men. He won a medal for the job we did, and he refused to take it because he said Crux deserved it more than him. Several officers Crux had saved said the same."

"Why didn't Crux get the medal?"

"Because he was a spy, asshole. You stupid? They said he could walk into a village and make everyone think he was one of them, or he would pretend to be a prisoner and take everything they gave to gather intel. They said he could charm the underwear off any man or woman. Once, he had been scheduled to die at daybreak, and he won his freedom by helping them steal a cache of guns. He suckered them into a trap. Another time I heard about, he used a shipment of food he had taken from base camp to get into a town, then stole it back the next day. A buddy of mine bragged for a fact that Crux had even married a head leader's daughter to prove his loyalty to them. Each mission, his code name would change. They called him Sphinx, Enigma, Rubik ..."

"You trying to sucker me in like the new recruits?"

"It's no skin off my nose if you believe me or not. Crux was a legend in the SEALs. He still is."

"What happened him?"

"No one knows, or ever will. If I had my guess, he's probably still out there, still saving ..."

Jo saw Carly come out from the back. Standing, the men were still talking as she walked around, taking the plastic bag from Carly, then going outside. Watching for traffic, she went to her truck, waving to Knox as he came out of the sheriff's office.

"You getting Rider dinner?" he asked as he walked her to her truck.

"Yes. I need to learn how to cook better. It'd save us a lot of money."

"You should ask Rachel, Beth, or Lily to teach you how. He used to eat at their houses all the time."

"I might have to do that. What's his favorite thing to eat?"

"Truthfully, I haven't found anything Rider doesn't like," he answered, taking the bag from her as she hopped up into her seat. She thanked him when he handed it back to her.

"When I was in the diner, there were two men wearing Last Rider vests I've never seen before."

"That must be Cam and Driver. I'll stop in and say hi. Thanks for telling me."

"I would have said something to them if I had seen them at the clubhouse before. Maybe I'll be able to meet them before they leave."

"Not unless you're going tonight. They aren't staying long."

"Next time, then. Have a good night, Knox."

"You, too." Knox shut the door, then crossed the street to go into the diner.

On the drive home, Jo started thinking about who the older biker had been talking about. She felt sorry for the mysterious man. He had to work alone to infiltrate enemy camps without any friends to turn to when he needed help. He was probably dead and no one even knew it.

The sad existence of a man she didn't even know had her shrugging the conversation off.

She had just gotten home when Rider showed up. She had taken the food out of the plastic to keep warm in the oven, setting it on a cooking sheet and wrapping it in foil. As he showered, she microwaved her soup. Then, hearing the water turn off, she took his food out of the oven and put it on a plate.

"You look tired tonight," she commented as they sat down.

"I didn't get much sleep last night." Winking at her, he picked up his double-decker club sandwich and took a bite, then promptly spit it out. "That sandwich is hard as a rock." He took off the top slice of bread, tapping it on the table. "I'm calling Carly and getting your money back. That stuff is inedible. I think I broke a tooth." He worried his perfect teeth, checking for signs of damage.

Jo frowned, reaching across the table to move his hand away, wanting to see for herself if any of his teeth were broken. "It was fine when I put it in the oven to keep it warm."

Rider pulled his hand away from his mouth. "For how long was it in the oven?"

Jo looked down at watch. "Thirty minutes; an hour max. You took a long shower."

"What degree did you warm it on?"

"Three hundred. That oven is finicky. I wanted to make sure it stayed warm."

Rider just stared at her.

Blushing, she slid her soup across the table toward him. "You can have my soup."

"That's not going to fill me up. I'll just fix a bowl of cereal …"

Jo shifted uncomfortably in her chair. "I was so busy getting your presents for Valentine's Day that I didn't make it to the store before I went to Lily's. I'm sorry. I didn't mean to ruin your food. I'll run into town, go to the store, and get you some more from the diner."

"It's … fine. I can salvage it. When we're done eating, we'll both go to the store and load up on groceries."

Rider took all the bread off his sandwich, looking around for the loaf. "Where's the bread? I can't—"

"We're out." Miserably, she had hoped that wasn't what he had been looking for.

"New plan. I'll order pizza to be delivered, then we go to the store."

"I like that plan," she agreed.

Rider threw the inedible meal away, then ordered his pizza.

She couldn't bring herself to eat her soup while he was waiting for his food.

"Why is Jewell going to Ohio?"

Rider set his cell phone down on the counter. "How'd you know she was?"

"When I was at the diner, I heard two men wearing Last Rider vests talking. One mentioned Jewell's name and that they were escorting her to Ohio because Viper was angry with her."

"You eavesdropped?"

"I didn't mean to, but I did." She was ashamed of herself, yet she couldn't help gauging his reaction to the news of Jewell leaving.

"I'll have to tell Viper that he needs to tell the brothers not to discuss club business in front of anyone who could be listening in."

Jo jumped up from the table, placing her hand on his chest while snatching his phone, holding it tightly in her hand. "Don't do that."

He raised a brow. "Why not?"

"Because the younger one is afraid of Viper."

He cupped her cheek. "And how do you know that?"

"I could just tell." She clutched his shirt tighter. "Promise you won't say anything?" she pleaded.

"I promise."

"Thank you." She gave a sigh of relief.

"Did you hear anything else while you were listening?"

"No." She didn't want herself to look worse by admitting how long she had been listening, even though she was curious if he had heard the same stories about Crux as the man in the diner had.

"I'll let it slide this time, but the brothers should have known better than flapping their lips in front of anyone."

"I shouldn't have listened. So, why is Jewell leaving?"

"Unlike those brothers, I keep my mouth shut about club business."

Hurt by his stern response, Jo placed his phone down on

the counter, going back to sit at the table. She then lifted her chin as she turned to look at him. "You said I was your woman, and as your woman, I was part of The Last Riders. Doesn't that give me the right to know?"

"I hate having an argument on an empty stomach."

She narrowed her eyes at him for the reminder that she was the cause of his empty stomach.

"Are you trying to change the subject?"

Jo caught the surprised flicker of emotion before he came to sit back down, placing a hand on hers. "It was a club decision to send Jewell to Ohio. If you want the answer to that question, you'll have to ask Viper."

"You know I won't do that." She numbly pulled her hand from under his.

"Why does it matter anyway? You don't like Jewell."

"Don't tell me who I like or don't like. You don't know. I don't know. I haven't gotten to know her well enough to know. One thing I do know is that, from watching those cameras, she's friends with everyone in the club, and those friends are going to miss her."

"I may not know if you like Jewell, but I know for fucking sure she doesn't like you."

"I know that, but her feelings about me are based on jealousy. I can understand that."

"How can you understand? You said you've never been jealous."

"I guess I never cared enough to feel those emotions before. I do now." She stared at him directly. "Aren't you going to miss Jewell?"

His jaw dropped at her question. "You don't want Jewell to leave because you think *I'll* miss her?"

"Won't you?"

"Fine, I'll talk to Viper."

"Now would be good. Knox said they were taking her tonight."

"Jo, for a woman who didn't want to be a Last Rider, you know as much as me."

"I'm a fast learner."

"I'll have to keep that in mind."

Rising, she went to answer the door. She signed for the pizza before carrying it to the table and setting it down in front of Rider.

"You don't want any?"

"No, thanks. My stomach is still a little upset after last night. I'll have my soup. I'm going to make a grocery list while you eat." Going for a pencil and paper, she talked to keep her stomach from churning at the smell. "I saw Knox as I was coming out of the diner. I was complaining how much money we were spending eating out, and he suggested asking Rachel, Beth, or Lily for help in learning how to cook. I could ask Willa to show me how to make the candy you love."

"All the women have tried to make it. It usually doesn't turn out the same, or they said it was easier to buy from Willa. Ember made it with evaporated milk one time, and it came out harder than those french fries I threw away." Rider became so animated he was gesturing with his slice of pizza. "Jewell made it with mashed potatoes. I couldn't bring myself to taste—"

"Oh, that reminds me. You forgot to do something." Sliding his cell phone next to the pizza box, she said, "You forgot to call Viper."

"I'll do it after I eat."

"Do it now. Your food will sit better in your stomach."

Getting up with his slice of pizza in one hand and his phone in the other, he gave her the pouty look he always gave women when he wanted his way.

Staring at him resolutely, she placed her hands on her hips, staring him down.

"That candy better be good."

To ensure Jewell would be there the next time she visited, she cut Rider a deal he couldn't refuse.

"If you convince Viper to let her stay, the next time I work security with you, I'll stand next to your chair for two hours wearing the new nightie I wanted to put on last night."

"Is it flannel?"

"No."

Rider took a bite of his pizza as he thought about the deal. "What if I can't convince Viper to let Jewell stay?"

"Then *you* have to stand by *my* chair naked for two hours."

"Okay ..."

Jo let him get partway out the door before she clarified, "In heels."

40

"**B**rother, I need a favor."

"Depends on what it is." Rider placed his dirty lunch plates in the sink as Moon came around the corner to talk to him.

"I've got a hot date with Nada. She's the chick who replaced Aly at the department store."

"That's fast work. Aly just started training her yesterday."

"You know I work fast."

Rider rolled his eyes. "So, what does it have to do with me?"

"I told her I'd take her out tonight, and I forgot I was on the schedule to work security."

He already knew where this conversation was going, and he wanted no part in it. "No."

"I'll work Friday and Saturday for you," Moan coaxed.

"The women are going to Jo's to teach her how to cook. I'm not missing that. I'm the taste tester."

"Brother, how many times have I done you a solid?"

Fuck, he could see his evening plans going down the drain. "Who else is on the schedule tonight?"

"Shade."

A glimmer of hope began to sprout, until Moon dashed it before it could grow.

"Shade won't work alone. He wants to be able to leave if Lily needs help with Clint."

Fuck.

"I'll pay for you to take her to King's if you put it off to another night."

"I can't call it off. You know what women are like. I might not get another chance. Trip is keeping an eye on Aly today. The fucker will scoop her out from under me."

"When has that been a problem for you?"

"Trip is a stingy bastard. He won't share until he's done with her. You going to do it for me, bro?"

"Jesus … Go. I can't stand it when you're nice to me."

Moon slapped him on back. "Don't worry; I'll be back to hating you tomorrow."

Moon left before Rider could return the slap with a much harder one to his gut.

He had been looking forward to tonight for the last month. The women had decided to make a party of it, and it had taken time to work around everyone's schedule. Jo had also wanted to wait until she could afford a new stove. Despite his attempts to pay for it, she had refused. It had been delivered a week ago, and so far, he hadn't noticed any difference in the way she cooked. If possible, it had become worse. Jo could burn water.

He had several orders to get out before it was time to be at the security desk. Moon, Trip, and the other brothers had been complaining that there had to be two on duty. Since he was the one who had suggested it, Viper and Shade were waiting for his input before resending the order.

Despite expecting Curt to strike out at him or the club, he

had done nothing. Shade had found out he had began a job as a car salesman in Jamestown.

Aly had decided to sell her place, which had sold last week. That was why she was now working the night shift, training her replacement. She was planning to leave Treepoint in the morning. It would lighten the load of someone keeping an eye on her.

Knox, who was waiting for the independent report to come back from Frankfort, was beginning to doubt Curt's involvement in Aly's parents' deaths. Especially when, instead of buying Aly's land when it had gone on the market, Curt had bought a small house in Jamestown. If he had wanted Aly's parents' house bad enough to kill for it, why burn it down, then not even bid on the land?

The young couple who had bought Aly's land had no ties to Curt or his family. Was another sick fucker like Jared running around, killing people to settle a score no one knew about?

Rider was filling the last order when Jewell came out of her office. They had been chilly toward each other since the day after she had deliberately sent Jo to his bedroom. The woman stayed out of his vicinity when they were in the club, and they kept their conversations to the bare minimum at work.

Viper had let him have the last say in letting Jewell stay in Treepoint. He didn't regret the decision. Jewell, on the other hand, knew she was walking on thin ice where the club and he were concerned.

He stopped packaging the order when Jewell approached him.

"Jo called me yesterday to invite me to her cooking party tonight. I didn't know what to tell her. I thought I would check with you."

"She called you yesterday, and you're just now asking me?" He tersely shoved the flaps down on a box.

"I needed to think about whether I wanted to go." Jewell laid a hand on the box, forcing his attention to her. "I gave Bliss a hard time when she couldn't get over Shade, and then I fell into the same trap with you. I've already told you I'm sorry. I'd like to have the same opportunity with Jo."

"Don't act like it's because you feel bad about doing it. You're tired of having to stay in your room anytime Jo comes to the club."

"Be real, Rider. Jo's not in the club enough to worry about that. She comes over two days a week to eat dinner. The only other times, I'm at work anyway, and those are the few times you've decided to stay in your room at the club after your security shift is over."

"I don't want you going. Make up an excuse; you're good at that."

She dropped her hand to her side. "I deserve that. I'll go and call her." Jewell started back toward her office.

Rider jerked the tape across the box, sealing it. "Jewell, we've been friends a long time. It's going to take time to rebuild the trust I had in you."

"Do you care about Jo?"

"You haven't rebuilt enough trust for me to answer that question."

She looked at him sadly. "I don't have to. You might like her, but deep down, you don't care about her any more than Ember, Stori, or me. You make a great lover, Rider, but as a boyfriend, you suck."

"Jo doesn't know that, and she never will."

Jewell shook her head at him. "I told her I felt sorry for her. Did she tell you that?"

Rider slapped the tape down on the worktable. "No, she didn't."

Jewell gave a look that showed she couldn't believe Jo was so gullible. "I did, and I meant it. God help her when she does find out. I'm going to pray for you, too."

"I don't need your fucking prayers." Any thoughts Rider had about forgiving Jewell flew out the door.

"I'm going to anyway. You're going to need them when you realize what you lost."

Rider was glad she was wise enough to walk away after that. It would be a cold day in hell before he would trust her around Jo again.

Looking at the clock, he put the package in the mail cart to be shipped. He had enough time to grab dinner before going to the security room.

SHADE WAS ALREADY THERE when he arrived, and F.A.M.E, who had been waiting for him, stood up and stretched his broad shoulders as Rider took his chair, pulling it under the desk.

He swept his eyes across the monitors to assess where everyone was and the vehicles outside of each home. It helped having a photographic memory. He could tell instantly when something was out of place.

"You might as well go to the diner for dinner," Rider warned F.A.M.E, absent-mindedly popping open the top of the energy drink he had brought with him. "The only thing left in the kitchen is one hot dog and a few fries."

"I wasn't planning on eating at the club. I volunteered to watch the women when you took Moon's shift."

Rider pivoted in his chair. "If you're working a double, then you can work for me and I can—"

"He can't," Shade reminded him. "It was your bright idea that no one worked a double in the security room."

"Fuck." Rider swung back toward the monitors.

"Later, brothers," F.A.M.E called out as he left the room.

"I'm going to *brother* him when he gets back," Rider grumbled.

"Why not before he leaves?" Shade turned to the side, flipping the monitor on for the inside of Jo's house.

"Don't want the women upset when he shows up with a busted face."

Rider watched the outside of Jo's, seeing three cars outside. Then he looked upward to the monitor that Shade had turned on.

"Why's Aly there? Jo didn't tell me she was going to be there."

"It wasn't planned. Aly told Trip that she wanted to go by to tell Jo goodbye and apologize for trying to sue her. Jo invited her to stay."

"You're shitting me?"

"She's there, isn't she?"

"I'll be glad when that bitch is gone. The only reason I haven't paid her back for the crap she tried to pull on me was because I've been waiting for her to disappear so no questions could be asked."

"Her new employers will know."

"They're going to think she took a different job. I don't want her in the same room with Jo. I was lucky to put out the fire Jewell started; I'm not going to put out the one I'd bet my bottom dollar that Aly will try to start. Text F.A.M.E. Tell him, when he gets there, bring her back to the club."

"Trip can bring her," Shade said, reaching for his phone. "Trip deserves a good meal. F.A.M.E doesn't."

"No. He could have let Moon work the day shift and F.A.M.E take this one."

"Moon and F.A.M.E have been sharing a lot lately."

"They're going to be sharing more than women when

they get back," Rider threatened as he stared at the monitors. It had grown darker, making it harder to discern the shadows around each house.

"I'm shocked Jo's house is holding so many. I hope Mag shows Jo how to cook chicken and dumplings. Rachel's are too dry," Rider criticized.

"I wouldn't tell Cash that."

"He knows. We've talked about it."

"He lets you criticize his wife's food?"

"He thinks it will keep me from eating there as often." Rider crushed his empty metal can before tossing it toward the trash can without taking his eyes off the screens. Not even the sound of the crushed can hitting the floor had him looking. "Who moved the trash?"

"I did." Shade didn't look at the can either.

Rider stood, walking to pick up the can and move the waste basket back into the position while dropping the can inside.

He was walking back toward the desk, scanning the screens when he started to walk faster. He put his palms on the desk, staring hard at one over Shade's head.

"Do you …?" Shade began to ask at the same time Rider hit the alert button.

"One perp; side corner of your house. Two coming from behind Razer's, moving toward the club," Rider called out.

Shade was sending the red alert on his cell phone as he scanned the screens closest to him.

"Come on … come on …" Rider willed the steel shutters to go down faster. He had given enough warning to assure the doors would be locked. Everyone was safe except for the new recruit pulling guard duty at the front door.

One of the two coming from behind Razer's cut down the side yard, taking the new recruit out before Driver could remove his gun.

Shade was getting to his feet when the lights went out.

"Those motherfuckers are dead."

Rider heard Shade going toward the door, concerned for his kids, who Ember had volunteered to babysit. She was the least prepared to handle the situation she found herself in.

"The lights will be on in ten seconds. At least wait until we can see the positions again. The shutters made it down."

As the backup generator came on, Rider immediately scanned for the perps' positions.

"Three coming from behind Viper's house ... heading toward the back of the factory."

"They know we're in here."

Shade's cold tone didn't stop Rider from focusing on the other monitors. When he got to Jo's house, his blood ran cold.

Rider opened the drawer to his side, taking his Glock out. Shade already held his, looking at the same monitor he was.

It was the most defenseless house out of all of them, the only one without steel shutters or the automatic locks, and right now, it held The Last Riders' most priceless possessions.

Cash, Trip, and F.A.M.E had been sent the same mass text. Cash and Trip were outside Jo's house, and F.A.M.E was inside, sitting at the table next to the window. The only brother who was in there with them didn't know he was about to die.

Spellbound, Rider and Shade watched as Aly walked behind F.A.M.E as he sprang out of his chair. She pulled a gun out from underneath her bulky sweater and fired two shots into the back of F.A.M.E's head.

Rider smothered down the pain of the loss. He would grieve for both F.A.M.E and Driver later. Right now, it was imperative to regain control of the situation.

With coldness and precision, Rider gave his instructions

to Shade. "I'll hit the delay button, so even if they get in, they won't expect you waiting for them." As Rider's eyes went from screen to screen, he opened the drawer to the right and took out a set of keys, tossing them to Shade. "Get on my bike. Don't start it until I start opening the garage door. There's another perp coming up from the side of Viper's house. You're going to be facing four. Go now, brother—save our women."

Rider waited until Shade was seated on the bike he had planned on moving the next day since it was in Rachel's way. Then he pushed the garage door button, listening to the sound of the motorcycle filling the air as it rose.

Shade started firing at the perps' legs as soon as the door was at their knees. He reloaded, then fired, taking out the last one standing. Shade continued firing at the four men as he rode out of the garage, making sure none of them would be getting up.

Rider watched as Shade swung his booted foot down to keep the bike from falling as he made the sharp turn out of the garage and into the parking lot.

"Faster, Shade, faster ..." Rider could only sit and watch as Shade hunched down over his motorcycle as two of the three perps ran to the end of the front porch and leaned over the banister to shoot down at Shade.

When the bike swerved, Rider knew one of the bullets had struck him. He held his breath until Shade drove onto the main road, thanking God no cars were coming as the perps ran to the other side of the porch to continue firing after him.

Rider stopped watching when he could see Shade had rounded a curve and was out of sight. Finally able to answer his phone that had been going off throughout this, he picked it up, knowing who it would be.

"Three perps are on the grounds. Two at the front." Rider

scanned the screens again. "One at Shade's back door. One moving to where I am. I'll take him. In ten, I will release your back door; you take the two on the front porch. Lucky and Razer are in the house. Lucky will take the one out at Shade's house."

As he gave Viper his instructions, he stood with his Glock in hand. Rider took another glance at the monitors as he counted out the ten seconds, then released Viper's door, locking it behind him immediately as he slipped out.

He called Lucky without looking at his phone as he began moving toward the security room door. He was opening it when Lucky answered.

"One perp at the back of Shade's, moving to the left side. He's running toward the clubhouse. Shoot him as he comes around the corner."

Rider saw his own perp trying to lift one of the men who Shade had shot. Rider lifted his gun as he walked toward him. The perp saw him and tried to raise his gun too late. Rider shot him in the heart.

Moving quickly, Rider then kicked the five dead bodies out from under the garage door so it would completely close, instantly pushing the button to close it when it was clear.

Running back into the security room, seeing that Lucky was dealing with the last of the perps, he scanned the surrounding woods to make sure there wasn't anyone in the shadows to take them out. Satisfied, he turned his focus to Jo's driveway, where Shade was just arriving.

Cash had been running for the front door last he looked, but now he had fallen back to take a position behind a car ten feet away. Rider knew why when he saw that Aly had stepped over F.A.M.E's body, going to the window next to the table. She must have shouted a warning out to Cash, threatening to kill the women.

The bitch meant it, too. She had Rachel take one of the

chairs at the table, then had Lily take the other, across from her. Staying to the side, Aly then lowered the blinds so the men outside would only see shadows, not who was who.

Seeing Lucky and Viper come to the garage door, he opened then closed it once they were through.

Rider hit Shade's number on his cell phone as the two men came through the door. When they saw he had his phone to his ear, they remained silent.

"The outside yard is clear. It's only inside. Lily is in the chair closest to the door; Rachel on the other side. Aly has the rest of the women standing in a line across the doorway along the front wall. Any shots in that direction will strike one of them. She has two guns. One a Glock 27, the other a 45. Knox is on his way with Greer. Position Knox at the beginning of the driveway. No one in or out unless it's one of us."

Rider sat down, scooting the chair forward while motioning for Viper and Lucky to help with surveillance, making sure the other houses and the club were still secure.

Putting his phone on speaker, he sat it down on the desk. Concentrating on the inside of Jo's house and her property, he left it to the other men to make sure the other members were safe.

"Shade and Greer to the black Cavalier. Circle around to the tan Cadillac that sits on top of two other cars. Make a right at the red Fiat. That will put you behind Jo's house. Let me know when you're in position."

"The area is clear here. You want me to send more men to Knox?" Shade asked.

"Moon is sixty seconds from here; send him to Shade's house and let him in," Rider answered, prioritizing who he wanted where.

He waited for Shade to get in position. Any miscalculation in his plan, and there would be a bloodbath inside Jo's house. There were only two men in the world who he would trust to save their lives.

Out of the corner of his eye, he saw the screen that kept trying to distract him.

"Lucky, call Killyama and tell her it's Hammer and Train coming. She's about to shoot one of them."

"I'm in position," Shade's voice came over the phone.

"Hold your position," Rider ordered Shade on one breath, then gave the next order on another breath. "Viper, call Gavin and give the phone to me."

Rider raised his hand in the air, watching every movement Aly made. The phone was in his hand in a second.

Rider heard Gavin answer the phone.

"You good?"

"I'm good. What do you need?" he asked.

"I need you to save my woman for me. Can you get it done?"

"Let Shade or Viper—"

"Viper is going to open the front door in ten seconds, and then you are going to haul ass to Jo's place and save my old lady. You goddamn owe it to me! *You fucking hear me?*" It was the first time since he had started his military career that he had come close to losing his cool.

"I hear you."

"Good." Rider lowered his voice back to normal. "And this time, don't fuck it up."

"If you move, I'll shoot the two next to you."

Aly's threat had Jo stiffening her shaking legs so neither Beth nor Willa would be forced to pay with their lives for her not being able to get herself under control. Gathering her courage, she tried to think of anything that could distract the woman who had two guns pointed at their backs.

The laughter that had filled the small house had turned to screams of terror when Aly had come up behind F.A.M.E and shot him, not only once, but twice. That she was capable of any violence had stunned her.

At first, she could not believe her own eyes, despite the women trying to flee toward the door. When a bullet had narrowly missed Beth as she tried to grab the doorknob, the women had frozen in place, following Aly's demand to stop. She had then ordered Lily and Rachel to sit at the table and lowered the blinds before forcing them to line up in front of the wall that had the windows facing the junkyard.

"You should run. The Last Riders are going to kill you."

Mag rolled her wheelchair around F.A.M.E's body, going to the stove.

"I told you not to move." Aly walked over to Mag, putting one of the guns to her head.

Rachel started to get up, but when Aly lifted her hate-filled glare at her, she sat back down.

"Don't," Beth whispered to her when Jo started to turn to go to Mag.

Jo stilled, not wanting to set off a chain reaction that could hurt the women next to her.

Aly hadn't missed that she had been about to intercede.

"I wouldn't let her move, Beth. The life you save may be your own."

"Unless you want to save The Last Riders the trouble of smoking us out, I need to turn that chicken off," Mag advised, not even shaking under the gun pointed at her.

"Turn it off." Aly stepped back, giving Mag room to go to the stove.

"Aly, please stop. You're not going to get away with this."

"Oh, but I am. I got away with murdering my parents, didn't I?" she bragged.

"God, Aly. Why?" Jo felt as if an abyss had opened beneath her and she had been sucked inside.

"I needed money, and they refused to give me any more. I wanted them to sell their house so I wouldn't lose my business; they refused. They were old, could barely take care of themselves; what did they need that house for? I had to sell my business, so the least they could have done was lose their house. Of course they don't know I sold it—they're dead. But they believed in the afterlife, so I'm sure they know I did and got the money from their insurance policies, too. Fortunately for me, they had a double indemnity clause for accidental deaths."

Aly mocking her dead parents sent a chill of terror up Jo's

back. If Aly could kill her own parents, she wasn't going to hesitate to kill all of them.

"What do you have to say to that, Jo? Are you finally getting the message that if you don't do what I say, I'll kill all of you?" she sneered.

"I'd say you're crazier than a tick in a room full of dogs."

Aly strode over to Mag, lifting her gun and striking Mag across her cheek.

When Mag's head snapped back at the force of the hit, all the women moved at once, regardless of the fear of being shot. Rachel screamed, and Lily caught her arm when she tried to go to Mag, jerking her back over to her chair.

Aly jerked Mag's wheelchair around so she could stand behind her, pressing both guns to Mag's temples. "Get back!" she snarled.

The women backed away, moving into the position Aly wanted them in. Rachel was the last to move. Standing by her chair, the redhead bristled with rage.

"You're dead when Cash finds out you touched her."

"Don't you stupid sluts get it? The Last Riders won't be coming to your rescue! They're all dead!" She looked at them all in mock pity. "Do you think I waited all this time to get you where I wanted you without knowing I would get away scot-free?"

Jo felt Beth grab her hand at Aly's announcement. She reached out her other hand for Willa to take. The conviction in Aly's words had her not caring if the abyss swallowed her whole. Without Rider, she didn't want to live.

"Cash isn't dead, and neither is Trip. They're right outside."

"Not yet, but they will be when Curt and his family get here. They're planning a big party for you ladies, and to renew old relationships. Isn't that right, Jo?"

"Curt and I never had a relationship. He and his cousins raped me."

"He didn't have to rape you. You were constantly chasing after him with those big cow eyes, begging him to notice you. And when he did, you started running your mouth about what he and his cousins did to you. There were no cops coming to arrest him, were there, Jo? Because it *didn't happen.*"

Her furious rant had Jo worried for Mag. The old woman still hadn't seemed to regain her senses, and her lined face was drawn and sagging.

"He didn't have to rape you. He was getting everything he wanted from me. You teased him when Justin and Tanner let you convince them to meet you at the storage building."

Jo could only shake her head at the deranged woman's delusions. "He may have told you that, but you know that isn't the truth," Jo said simply. You couldn't reason with a mad woman, and Aly was clearly sick.

"It doesn't matter anymore. I got over Curt a long time ago," Aly sneered. "I've moved on to bigger and better men. You have, too. If I didn't know what Curt had in mind for all of them, I might have decided to stay around longer. If I didn't think that it would be too suspicious to be fucking all of them so soon after my parents' death instead of being bored to tears in that fucking basement, I would have screwed their nuts off."

Aly moved the guns away from Mag's head. Jo's relief was short-lived, though, because Aly then moved her hands to the handles of Mag's wheelchair and tilted it forward, spilling the old woman into a heap next to F.A.M.E's body.

When Rachel tried to kneel next to Mag to check on her, Aly shoved one of the guns into the waistband of her pants to yank Rachel to her feet with the other gun pointed at her head.

Using Rachel's hair, she slammed her back down in the chair. "Sit!" Releasing her, she retrieved her gun to go sit down in the chair in the living room that faced the line of women.

Jo could only stare at the woman who she had never expected to carry such ugliness within her soul.

"Oh, please. Don't stare at me that way, Jo. All of you are nothing but sanctimonious hypocrites.

"Holly, you kidnapped a kid and played mommy to him as if his mother never existed.

"Rachel, you and Sutton act like you're best friends now, but when she dumped Tate to go to the prom with Cash, where was your family loyalty then?

"You all stand there like I have a screw loose, yet everyone walks around Lily like she's made out of glass. You all know she's as crazy as a looney bird."

"No, she's not." Jo tried to drop her hands from Willa's and Beth's. She'd had enough of Aly's insults.

"Yeah, right." Aly curled her lip in contempt. "Just like Diamond isn't nuts for buying an island because she's afraid of zombies. Word to the wise, Dia; if you're afraid of something, don't watch movies about them."

"Don't call me Dia." Diamond stared hard at her. "Are you having fun, Aly? Pointing those guns at us while you belittle us? There isn't a woman here who hasn't been nice to you. You blackmailed Jo to get what you wanted her to do. When your house burned …" Diamond's eyes widened as the same thought hit all of them. "You burned down your own home, didn't you?"

"I was never going to get anyone to buy that old house. At least, not for the same amount as I got from the insurance." Aly laid one of her guns down on her lap as she took out her cell phone. Then she switched the two items, putting the gun back up to point it back at Rachel and Lily.

Jo saw her darting quick glances nervously down at her phone.

"What's the matter, Aly? Curt running late?" Jo drew her attention back to her and off the other two women.

"I'm not worried. He'll be here."

"How late is he? A few minutes? An hour?"

"Shut up, Jo. Beth and Willa have kids; you don't want to make them motherless, do you?"

"They are going to be motherless regardless of whether you pull the trigger or Curt does. They have no intention of letting us live, do they?"

"That's not my problem. The last of my problems were taken care of last week when that sweet couple bought that dirt patch they're planning on building a home on."

"If that's true, why didn't you just take the money and leave? Do you have to have a whole roomful of women's deaths on your conscience? Just leave. Your car is sitting outside. We won't stop you."

"I owed Curt for helping me make my parents' deaths look like an accident, and for burning my house down. Unlike you, I pay my debts."

"I paid you what my father owed." Jo hadn't believed she could hate anyone as much as she hated Curt, Justin, and Tanner. Aly, however, had gone to the head of the list.

"You would have, if I hadn't spurred you on to get Rider interested in you," Aly taunted. "Curt and I killed two birds with one stone with that masterpiece." Aly sneered, leaned forward in the chair. "You're really going to appreciate this …"

Jo promised herself not to react to whatever Aly was about to tell her. The venomous woman was feeding off their fears and the disclosures she was revealing.

"Your father never owed my parents that money. Lyle made it *so* easy for me and Curt. He had different places he always liked to drink. Curt was smart enough not to go to Rosie's and catch him there … He liked to drink in Jamestown on the weekends. The bar Lyle liked to hole up in didn't have a Mick there to watch out for him."

"I know my father's signature …" Despite her promise, each word Aly uttered was stabbing a knife through her heart.

"It *was* your father's signature, but he was drunk as hell when he signed it. Curt and I are still laughing our heads off over that. Of course, I've had to hang on to that secret for a while for it to be any good. A couple of things had to happen first."

Both Beth and Willa's hands tightened around hers, giving her the support she needed to keep from attacking the woman, regardless of her fate. Only the reality that Beth or Willa would pay for the price had her strengthening her resolve not to let Aly know how bad the blows she was dealing her were.

"You had to wait for my father to die."

Aly nodded. "Curt helped with that, too. He rigged the brake pedal so it wouldn't work. He was the town drunk; no one even checked to see if it was a mechanical failure. You were so broke. I knew you'd have to seek help to pay the loan back, so I gave you a little nudge in the right direction. That was the good idea Curt had. He said all The Last Riders were loaded. I had to get my foot in the door to find out about the patsy that would be financing my new life. They made it so easy for me when I found out The Last Riders were trying to steer Rider in your direction."

"I don't understand. If the only thing you and Curt wanted was money, why attack The Last Riders? Why hurt the women?"

"Come on, Jo. You of all people should know why." Aly looked down at her phone again, pressing the home button.

Jo knew she was checking the time. "Because Curt is a vindictive son of a bitch, which is another reason I had to live up to my end of the plan. Which, unfortunately for you ladies, didn't originally include you or The Last Riders getting snuffed out until Rider made Curt mad by firing him. So, don't place the blame on me; blame Rider. There won't be anyone left standing when Curt gets here. They won't be leaving any witnesses. Lucky for me, but I can't say I'm sorry for any of you."

"I feel sorry, Aly. Actually, I feel sorry for both you and Curt. You've both been planning this for years while you could have been enjoying your life. Even if Curt and his family do succeed in killing every last man and woman who belong to The Last Riders in Treepoint, the Ohio chapter won't stop until they find out what happened. You, Curt, and any family member who took part in it won't be able to run fast enough."

Aly shifted uneasily in her chair, picking up the phone and pressing buttons before putting the phone to her ear.

Jo gave her the same mock-pitying look that Aly had given them when her confidence had been soaring from the adrenaline of taking them all hostage.

Disastrously for Aly, she had underestimated The Last Riders.

Jo turned the metaphorical knife that Aly had used to stab her with when she had confessed to her father's murder, using it to plunge it deep, deep into Aly.

"Curt isn't coming, Aly. He never had any intention of coming. He never does his own dirty work. He lets his family do it for him. He's probably in a bar or at a store, miles away from here, making sure he's being seen and has plenty of witnesses to back him up."

"He's coming!" Aly yelled, slapping the phone back down on her lap.

Jo feared one of the guns would go off. From the way the women's hands she was holding were shaking, she knew they had been afraid of the same thing. The tension between the women was fraught with fear. Diamond and Holly were pregnant, and the fear in their eyes for their babies' safety was evident. The women next to them had placed themselves a step forward, trying to block them if Aly did start shooting.

"Take me, Aly," Jo pleaded. "Use me as collateral. Rachel can call Cash and tell him to let us go. You can have the gun at my head. I won't fight you. Please, Aly. I'm begging you."

Aly laughed at her. "*You* as collateral? That's a joke, right? I killed one of them. Rachel said it herself. What I did to Mag was enough to get me killed."

"Cash won't know about it until we're gone. Rachel won't say anything. Will you, Rachel?"

Rachel, who had scooted her chair forward enough that she could reach Cash's grandmother's hand, looked up stonily at Aly. "I won't say anything."

Aly's face went thoughtful. "It won't work with you as my hostage." She narrowed her eyes at Rachel. "But he won't shoot his own wife, will he, Rachel?"

"No, Cash wouldn't," Rachel agreed, making no effort to conceal the loathing that she had refrained from putting in her answer.

"You're not taking Rachel. Either take me, or you can sit here until the cops come to gas you out. According to you, we're going to die anyway. There's still time to get away. Take the only chance you have left," Jo begged.

"One more word from your big mouth and I'm going to shoot you." Aly pinned her gaze on Jo as she tried to call Curt again.

When Curt didn't answer, Aly stood up, studying all the women's the faces. Jo knew she was staring into the face of death. Aly wasn't going to leave anyone alive to repeat the details of the murders she and Curt had committed.

Jo was about to look at Beth to tell her goodbye when she stopped in stunned amazement, seeing Jewell coming out of her father's bedroom, sleepily rubbing her eyes.

"Is the food ready? I'm starving ..."

At the sound of Jewell's voice coming from behind her, Aly half-turned, pointing one gun at Jewell and the other at the women by the door.

"Don't move!" Aly screamed, dropping her cell phone to the floor.

Jewell's hands went up in the air, her face a mask of terror. Jo couldn't understand how Jewell had come from her father's bedroom. She had been so engrossed in the cooking lesson that she hadn't seen Jewell come in. It took a couple seconds for her to realize that Jewell must have climbed through the bedroom window. Jo didn't know how—the window had been painted so many times that the last time she had tried to open it, she had given up in defeat.

"You've been in there the whole time?"

"Yes. I was tired, so Jo offered to let me take a nap until the food was ready," Jewell explained.

"Get over there. Stand between Diamond and Sutton." Aly watched her closely as Jewell sidled past her.

Aly moved until she was facing the women again, her back once again to the hallway. She darted her gaze down to her phone, then to the women. Just as her eyes locked on them, her cell phone rang.

Jo managed to keep her face impassive, not wanting to give away the fact that there were two men silently coming down the hallway so fast that, if she had blinked, she would have missed it.

Gavin was on Aly before she could raise her eyes. As

Shade ran by them, Jewell turned, unlocking the door, then ushering the women out of the house.

Jo only had time to see Shade jerk Rachel and Lily out of their chairs and toward the door, using his body as a shield from any bullets that Aly might get off before Jewell shoved her out the door.

Rachel didn't make it off the porch before Cash snatched her up. The rest of the women didn't make it much farther before unfamiliar, vest-wearing men surrounded them.

"Get behind the tow truck, then make your way toward the garage," Cash ordered her when he saw her hesitate to go with one of the men. "It's the Blue Horsemen. It's cool, Jo. They're friends of ours," he assured her.

She finally managed to gather enough wits to let the man take her arm and lead her to the back of the truck. The last thing she saw before the truck blocked her view was Greer running inside.

THE LAST RIDERS

J o crossed her arms over her chest, trying to keep herself warm. After tonight, she would always keep a spare jacket in her garage.

She stood to the side, unable to take her eyes off the women reuniting with their husbands. Tate had taken his jacket off, placing it around Sutton's shoulders as she cried into his chest. Cash had wrapped his arms around Rachel, practically zipping her into his jacket as she begged him to let her back inside the house. Holly, like her, stood alone, watching the couples around her.

Jo's cold hands trembled when she saw Knox storming into the garage, the large man nearly dwarfing the garage with his appearance. Jo had to look away when his searching eyes found Diamond's face, then dropped to her protruding belly as if assuring himself his baby was safe and snug, exactly where it was supposed to be. He was the one with tears in his eyes when he carefully lifted her into his trembling arms.

Lily was flanked by two of the Blue Horsemen as she waited for Shade to come into the garage. When he did, Jo knew any of Lily's fears of him straying were in her imagination. Shade loved Lily with a magnified love that Jo didn't think she understood. In the house, he had made sure his body had blocked any bullet. If Aly had killed anyone else, it wouldn't have been Lily.

Feeling as if she was evading their vulnerable moments by gawking, Jo glanced away to see Lucky come inside, kissing Willa between prayers of thanking God for her safety and telling her how much he loved her. Jo gave her own thanks to God. If Aly's cell phone hadn't rung when it had, one or more wouldn't have been in the garage among them.

"Are you okay?" Holly crossed her arms over her chest, shivering as badly she was.

"Yes. You?"

Holly nodded as Greer came into the garage. Her husband looked like he was about to vomit at any second.

"Let's go. Dustin is outside," he told Holly as he fussily wrapped a blanket around her.

"You should have sent Dustin in to get me." Holly berated, smilingly at her husband.

"I don't need anyone taking care of my wife but me." He scowled. "This is the last time you leave me home alone while you go gallivanting around." He ran a possessive hand over the mound of her stomach that was the same size as Diamond's.

"I wasn't gallivanting around," Holly protested with a tender smile as he bundled her closer to his side.

"Were you home?"

"No."

"Then you were galivanting away." Greer had the same grouchy tone of voice he always had, but the look in his eyes was pure love. "Let's go, Tate."

The two couples left.

Jo was becoming colder by the minute. Shivering, she

walked over to where Knox and Diamond were standing when his cell phone rang. Jo waited impatiently for the one-sided conversation to end before she tapped him on the shoulder.

"Knox ... has the ambulance for Mag left yet? Do you know how she is?"

"The ambulance left with her. I heard her cussing at the driver to go slower, so it's safe to say she'll make it. We can go now. Trip and Viper are waiting for the coroner van to arrive. They'll lock up your house for you."

"What about Aly? Has she been arrested?"

"Aly didn't make it. When Gavin tried to grab the guns from her, one went off and shot her through the heart."

Jo frowned, walking beside Diamond as they left the garage.

An SUV she recognized pulled to the side. Knox went to the back door of Razer's vehicle and helped Diamond inside as Razer jumped out, running to the garage as Beth came out.

The heart-tugging reaction of Razer cupping Beth's face as she sobbed at seeing her husband was one she would never forget. She couldn't hear his words when he pressed his forehead to hers, but she didn't have to. Jo knew he was telling her how much he loved her.

Knox took her arm. "You're freezing. Get inside, Jo."

She got in the third-row seat so Knox and Diamond could sit together, and once everyone was inside, she stared out the window as Razer drove by her house. Several Last Riders stood outside her closed front door. Jo was relieved she didn't have to go back in there yet. She didn't know if she could with the memory of F.A.M.E and Mag on her floor.

"Are we going to the police station?" She raised her voice so Knox would be able to hear her.

"No, we're going to the clubhouse. I'll take everyone's statement in the morning."

"But Aly told us that Curt is the reason my father died. You need to arrest him—"

"Jo, there isn't anyone left to arrest. Curt is dead. The electric company found him. He blew a transformer so The Last Riders would lose power and they could attack in the dark. He used a broom handle to blow it—"

"How would—"

"The broom was metal. It had been painted to look like wood."

Jo started to laugh, hearing the edge of hysteria in her own voice. "I told Aly he wasn't coming. I just didn't know how true that was."

"Razer, drive to the hospital. You need a sedative," Knox told her.

"No!" Jo bit down hard on her lip to make herself stop laughing. "I don't want to go to the hospital. Is Rider okay? Were any of Curt's relatives able to get into the club?"

"Rider's fine. He's working. Mercury is waiting for you at the club. She'll help you get settled in Rider's room. He'll see you as soon as he's able."

"So, no one was hurt? He's okay?"

"Rider's fine, other than being pissed he's still working when he wants to check on you."

"I don't have my phone … He can't call me."

"He can't talk right now. He's contacting F.A.M.E's family. He served in the military with him and spent time with his family. He wanted to be the one to tell them."

Jo didn't envy him the job. She remembered when she had been notified of her father's death.

When Rider's SUV came to a stop at the base of the steps, Jo gratefully accepted Knox's hand as she stepped out. Her whole body was beginning to shake.

Razer, Beth, and Diamond remained sitting inside, waiting for Knox to come back before driving them home.

Killyama had been babysitting for Willa. Jo was willing to bet she and Lucky would be holding their son for a long time that evening before putting him to bed.

Diablo started to open the door as she and Knox approached, but Mercury opened it before he could. Knox stopped to speak quietly to Diablo as Jo passed him to go inside.

"Let's get you in a hot shower." Placing a comforting arm over her shoulders, Mercury led Jo upstairs. "I've already put a pair of pajamas and a robe in there. You're freezing, you poor thing. If you need anything, let me know. I'll be right outside the door."

"Thank you." Going inside, Jo turned on the shower before undressing. When it was warm enough, she opened the shower door and stepped inside, feeling the warm water rush over her. When she lifted her face to the spray, her tears started falling, mingling with the water as the events unfolded in her mind.

She blamed herself for ever inviting that woman into her home. Hated herself for allowing Aly inside while trying to make peace with the woman she detested. The southern hospitality that had been ingrained in her since birth had nearly gotten everyone killed.

She also blamed herself for not reacting faster when Aly had suddenly shot F.A.M.E. Her guilt had made Jo second-guess herself right up until she found herself in the garage, not remembering how she had gotten there.

Sinking to her bottom, she hugged her knees, letting the water rain down on her until she heard Mercury knocking on the door.

"Jo, are you okay?"

Jo unsteadily got back to her feet, turning the water off. "I'll be out in a minute."

Toweling off, she put on a pair of pink fluffy pajamas

with Valentine hearts on them. Finding a smaller towel, she wrapped her wet hair before opening the door.

"Girl, I was getting ready to come in there after you. I went downstairs and got you some hot chocolate. I put some marshmallows in it for you. Do you like marshmallows? I do." Mercury carried the hot chocolate into Rider's bedroom for her, placing it on his nightstand. Turning the bed down, she then raised dark cherry eyes to hers. "You get to bed. My bedroom is right next door. If you need anything, throw something at the wall." She looked around as if searching for something she could give her to throw.

"I don't need anything." Jo sat down on the side of the bed.

"I know." Mercury walked to Rider's dresser. Opening the top drawer, she took out a tube of tennis balls, taking one out before putting it back and closing the drawer. "Here you go."

The woman's kind concern had Jo taking the ball from her.

"You try to get some sleep, and if you need anything at all, just throw that ball."

"I will. Thank you."

"I am glad to help." She started for the door, then came back, giving her a comforting hug. "I'm glad you're okay."

Jo gave her a watery smile as she released her. "Thank you. I needed that."

"Anytime." Mercury pointed to the hot chocolate. "You drink that. It'll help warm you."

"I will."

Jo sat listlessly after she left, making no effort to lie down or drink her hot chocolate. She was unable to comprehend how the night had gone so haywire. Unable to make sense of it, she finally reached for the lukewarm cocoa, sipping it as she took the towel off her head. Carrying it to the hamper in Rider's closet, she went to his dresser for his brush. Not seeing it, she hesitated before opening the drawer to see if it was in there. Mercury hadn't worried about opening it, so why should she? Still, it didn't make her guilty conscience feel better, but if she were to lie down without brushing her hair, it would be a rat's nest in the morning.

Sliding the drawer open, she saw the brush strewn among the other contents of the drawer. She stood, looking down at the items before taking the brush out and closing the drawer. Sitting on the bed, she brushed her hair, lost in her own thoughts.

Jo didn't know how long she sat before realizing her hair was almost dry and her cup was empty. Placing both on Rider's bedside table, she lay down, closing her eyes, uncaring that her pillow was damp from drying her hair.

Scooting over, she switched the pillows out in the dark on the side that Rider always slept on, curling into his mattress as if her heart was breaking. She lifted her fingers to the necklace she hadn't removed since he had put it on, curling it around the metal.

Burrowing her face into the pillow, she forced her fingers to release the heart, letting it dangle to the side of her neck.

Some pictures were worth a thousand words; she was going to find out what hers was worth in the morning.

JO PUSHED the swinging door open, going into the kitchen. She found more Last Riders up than she'd expected. It was barely past six. She had assumed they were still sleeping or just getting up.

Mercury looked up from scrambling eggs to run a critical eye over her. "They fit?"

"Yes. I appreciate you letting me borrow them."

"Anytime. Most of the clothes around here end up in each

other's closets. Grab a plate. The toast is done and there's bacon on the counter."

"No thanks. I'll just take some fruit."

There was a large bowl of fruit sitting on the counter. Taking a handful of grapes, she turned back to Mercury, watching her cook the eggs.

"Were you able to sleep?"

Jo nodded absently, staying beside the stove. She leaned back on the counter next to it, facing the swinging door, watching the occupants at the table as they ate.

"Viper, when you finish eating, do you mind giving me a ride to the hospital?"

Jo felt Winter's curious eyes on her at the question.

"Rider's on his way from the security room; he can."

Again, she nodded.

She responded whenever Mercury made a comment, but other than that, she stayed silent, watching the interactions between those who were sitting there.

Looking uncomfortable, Beth gave Winter a wary glance.

Taking a grape from her hand, Jo chewed it slowly, enjoying the tart juice filling her mouth.

"Are you okay, Jo? I can fix you a bowl of cereal or oatmeal," Willa offered, giving her husband a sidelong, questioning look.

"No, thank you," she answered politely.

"There's a lot to choose from," Willa tried to coax. The cereal boxes were lined up on the counter for everyone to eat for breakfast.

Jewell picked up her plate from the table. "You can have my chair. I'm done," she said, carrying her dishes to the sink.

Jo waited until she had set them down before telling her, "Jewell, I can never thank you enough for what you did last night. You saved us." Jo bit down on her trembling lip. Forcing her shoulders back to give herself strength, she met her eyes. "Aly could have shot you when she saw you. That you were willing to sacrifice your life for your friends' is a true testament to your loyalty to The Last Riders."

Jewell had a strength of character Jo had always been able to see. The woman never hid how much she cared about the people who filled the room.

"I did it for me, too. The best cooks in the club were in that house. It was self-preservation." With that, she went to retrieve her coffee cup from the table and was refilling it when Rider came through the swinging door.

Jo popped another grape into her mouth, thoughtfully watching his reaction. His eyes went around the room, latching on to hers. Walking toward the counter, he went to the cabinet to grab a bowl, giving Jewell a fist bump as he passed her to set the bowl down on the counter before coming to her side.

She stood stiffly as he pulled her into his arms. "Bluebonnet, how are you doing?" he asked, running his cheek alongside hers.

Jo trampled down her desire to melt into his arms. It was the shadow of his beard abrading her skin that gave her the strength to move away from him.

Stepping away, she reached for another handful of grapes, putting one in her mouth. "I'm fine. When you're done eating, I'd like to go to the hospital to see Mag."

"We can do that. I'll eat quickly." Rider gave her a curious look as he went back to the counter to pour out a bowl of Cap'n Crunch.

Going to the refrigerator, she set the milk down next to his bowl. Focused on him, she hadn't noticed the room had gone quiet.

"Can I ask you a question?"

"Of course." Rider nodded toward the table as he poured his cereal. "We were going to talk about last night anyway.

That's why Knox and Diamond are here. He felt it would be easier to talk here than at the station."

Jo felt everyone's eyes on them. When she looked toward them, they hastily returned their attention to their food.

Rider opened the milk, splashing it down on his cereal.

"Do you love me?"

His hand jerked, spilling the milk on the counter.

Jo looked down at the thin skin of the grapes, taking another as Rider went to the paper towel holder. Returning, he was searching her face, trying to derive from her expression what was going on behind her cool exterior.

"Let's go to my room to talk," Rider said as he cleaned the mess the milk had made, tossing the paper towels into the trash before trying to take her arm.

Jo jerked it from him. "I don't want to go to your room. I want you to answer my question."

He narrowed his eyes at her. "You had a traumatic experience. We should discuss this privately."

"Have you ever had a problem having sex in front of them?"

"No." His jaw firmed.

"Then you should be able to talk about your feelings for me in front of them. Do you love me?"

"Don't ask questions—"

"I want the answer," she stated, uncaring that they were the center of attention.

Jewell had carried her cup of coffee back to the table, retaking the chair she had offered to her. Lazily sipping her coffee, she watched the escalating tension between them.

"No," Rider finally answered.

Jo nodded. She had figured that out for herself last night.

"You know I love you."

"Yes." Rider put the bowl of uneaten cereal in the sink.

"You told me the night you got drunk, but I knew before then. You wear your feelings on your sleeve."

"Do you even like me, Rider?"

"I care about you."

She caught the flicker of something behind his eyes. She believed him. As far as she knew, whenever she asked him a direct question, he would answer it truthfully.

"Wow. Thanks. I feel so much better." Jo turned to the telephone that was sitting on the counter. Rider made no effort to stop her when she dialed the number she knew by heart.

A sleepy voice answered, "Hello?"

"Mick, I'm at The Last Riders'. Can you come pick me up? I'll be waiting in the parking lot."

"I was going to take you." Rider waited until she hung up before trying to put his arm around her. "Jo, what happened last night was a traum—"

"Quit saying that!" Jerking away, she backed away from him until the length of the counter separated them. "When I was raped, that was traumatic. Yes, last night was horrible, but I will get over it. And, God willing, I will be able to get over whatever experiences the future holds for me ..." She lifted her fingers to around her neck, unfastening the necklace he had given her for Valentine's Day. "And like the others, I will get over them without you."

Her injured feelings had her walking away from him without a backward glance.

Rider strode to the back door, blocking her from leaving.

"Jo, every person is different. Just because I don't call the feelings I have for you love doesn't mean I don't feel that."

"Don't bullshit me, Rider. I can only stomach so much. I was raised watching my father try to win my mother's love. I won't spend the rest of mine trying to earn yours." Jo turned toward the swinging door, but Rider hastily moved to block her from leaving through that exit, too.

Seeing that he was determined to get her to listen to him, she went behind the counter.

He shot Mercury a look that sent her scurrying out of the way.

Lily cleared her voice. "Shade, we should go." Standing, she was about to take John by the hand to get him moving, when Shade tugged her down onto his lap.

"I want to finish my coffee. If I pick up Clint's carrier, he'll wake up."

Rider ignored what was going on behind his back,

searching for a way to save the relationship he felt slipping beyond his grasp. "I don't understand what set you off—"

"I'm not a military mission you can fix!" she yelled at him. "You are a devious bastard."

Rider started around the counter, wanting to calm her down. The way she was looking at him was chipping away at the ice encasing his heart.

"Jo—"

"Stop it, Rider, just stop!" She had moved to the other side of the counter, both exits open to her, but she didn't try to run. She did the exact opposite. Slamming her hands on the counter, she confronted him with the counter between them. "If it's not love you feel for me, what have all these months been about? You don't do anything without a reason, so tell me what it was! Because I for damn sure thought what was between us was love."

"I want a family."

"This is about having children?" She raised her brows in disbelief.

"No, I was going to leave that to you." He realized he should have lied when he saw her skin go ashen. "I want a family, whether it consists of two, three, four, or how many you want. I was going—"

"To leave it to me," she finished sadly, looking away from him. "Why do you want a family?"

That she was delving deeper into his reasoning gave him a spark of unease, but he wanted her to know the truth, so that when or if she decided to give them another chance, she would know what to expect. It was a cold approach, but the alternative was impossible for him. He wasn't going to drop his guard and love her. He had failed twice, and he didn't have the heart to try it again.

He was about to answer when Gavin came into the room.

"What's going on?" He stopped, reading the strained atmosphere in the room.

"Jo is giving Rider hell," Jewell explained, sipping her coffee.

"Oh."

Rider raised a brow when the brother sat down at the table to watch.

"Are you going to answer me?" Jo slammed her hands down on the counter to regain his attention.

"I want what they have." He gestured to the table.

Jo snapped her head around, surveying the room. Then she heatedly came around the counter to stand in front of him. "You want me to give you what they have? You want us to have what they do?" She lifted tear-washed eyes to his.

The feelings she was making no effort to hide weren't just chipping away at his resolve. It was worse. Each blow fractured and cracked open to pierce his wounded heart.

"Yes," he gritted between clenched teeth.

"What you're seeing is love, Rider. A love that, when Cash saw Rachel, he couldn't wait to have her in his arms."

Rider stared at the couple who were sitting at the table and holding hands. Their chairs had been scooted together so no one could get between them.

Jo's words peeled away the layers of protection he had surrounded himself with when he had divorced his first wife.

"A love that can make a man the size of Knox not be ashamed for everyone in the garage to see the tears in his eyes when he saw Diamond."

Rider flicked his gaze to the couple sitting next to Cash. Knox's arm was around the back of his wife's chair; their chairs so close together she could snuggle into his side.

"A love that can make my pastor thank God for his wife's safety and tell her in the same breath how much he loves her."

Rider watched as Willa stroked her husband's cheek at Jo's description of what Lucky had done.

"A love that, when Shade saw Lily, his first instinct was to place his body in front of hers so she wouldn't get hurt."

Rider's eyes slid from Willa to Shade and Lily. She was crying into Shade's shoulder as he clutched her tightly to him.

Slow tears coursed down Jo's cheeks as she unashamedly forced him to see what made the relationships he had tried to analyze and pin down as to what would make theirs successful and why his hadn't been was love. It had a lump rising in his throat.

Love couldn't be explained, nor was it something you could lay out to measure the depths or the lengths one would go for the person they loved.

"Killyama and Winter weren't even there last night, but I bet Viper and Train made sure their wives didn't go to sleep without telling them how much they loved them."

Rider could tell from Winter's expression at the table and from Killyama, who was sitting in the family room on the couch with Train, that they had.

"That's the love you're wanting, and that's the love you're letting walk out the door." Jo wiped her tears away, then spun to the side, going for the back door.

"Don't go." The voice that came out of his throat wasn't one he recognized.

Jo grabbed the doorknob, her forehead dropping help-lessly to the door as if she was physically and mentally strug-gling with whether to go or stay.

He saw her slumped shoulders straighten as she turned her head to look back at him.

"Don't worry; you won't miss me. You have enough condoms in the top drawer of your dresser to make sure you won't be lonely. Of course, you'll have to untangle the necklace that's mixed in with them first."

Rider winced, prepared for another blow.

"You certainly won't miss my cooking or having me forget to buy your favorite cereal. You know what's really whacked?"

"What?" he croaked out.

"I love you, and it's killing me to walk out this door. And in a month, I'll feel the same way. In a year, I will still feel the same way. I'll feel the same way forever and ever because that's the type of person I am, while you're the type of person who's letting me go. Just like you almost let Jewell go. And if you're not careful, you'll lose Gavin, too." Jo wiped her tears away, then opened the door and walked out, letting the door close itself behind her.

When she was gone, Rider turned back to the room, his eyes falling on the cereal boxes. Without thought, he struck out, sending the boxes flying. Cereal scattered throughout the kitchen.

"That's going to be a hell of a mess to clean up." Shade reached around Lily to spoon out the cereal in his coffee.

"I've seen worse." Willa started to get up, but Rider stopped her.

"I'll do it."

As he went to the pantry for the broom and dustpan, he stepped on cereal every step of the way, listening to the same sounds as he returned. Everyone remained seated as he swept.

"Rider ..." Lily's soft whisper had him raising his head, exposing the expression on his face. "Go after her."

"I can't ... I don't deserve her."

"The man who saved us last night deserves a woman like that," Shade said, picking a purple Fruit Loop out of Clint's hair.

"The Rider I know, who caught Ema sneaking outside when I was taking a nap, deserves Jo," Rachel said, coming from the dining room with Cash.

"The man who saved Viper's and my sanity when Aisha had colic by singing 'This Is The Way Ladies Ride' until I didn't know which was worse—the colic or Rider singing that song—deserves Jo."

"The song," Viper said, raising Winter's hand to his lips.

"The man who saved countless lives during your time in the service, letting others take the medals you earned, deserves a woman like Jo." Train rose from the couch, as the other men stood showing a respect that was worth more to him than a million medals.

"Personally, I think he deserves a woman like Jo because she's the only one of you bitches who saw through that mother"—Killyama paused, when the men sat back down except for Gavin, picking a blue crunch berry off the cushion behind Train's shoulder and putting it in her mouth while looking at John's wide-mouthed expression—"bleeper."

Rider finished sweeping the cereal into a pile. He was about to bend down when Gavin took the dustpan from him.

He positioned it so Rider could sweep them onto it, saying, "No other man deserves to find love more than you. You've paid for defending our country in a way few men would have the courage to do. And if that wasn't enough, it demanded more when you got out. It's time to cut the ties that have been binding you all these years. You've sacrificed enough … It's time for you to live and fight one last battle for yourself."

Rider's face clouded. The happy-go-lucky man who always wore a grin or a flirtatious smile was now gone, and they were able to catch a glimpse of the despair behind the disguise he had lived with so long that he didn't know which parts of his persona were real and which were fake.

"What if I lose?" He didn't think he could live through another broken heart.

Gavin went to the trash can. Stepping on the peddle, he threw the pieces of cereal away. Then he let the can close with a snap.

"You kidding me, brother? You don't know how to lose. You're a legend."

44

Jo ran a clean shop rag over Cash's motorcycle. She wanted it to look shiny and brand spanking new ... Well, maybe not too new, but enough to make him pleased with her work.

She was about to start work on Razer's bike when she looked up from draining the oil to see Rider standing in the doorway of the garage.

"If you're here to pick up Cash's bike, get it and go. If you're here to get some work done on one of your cars or bikes, fill out a work order on the workbench, then go," she said matter-of-factly.

"I'd like to talk. Cash said you've been staying at the hospital with Mag for the last week and staying with them at night. Moon and I were the ones who cleaned your house after—"

"That wasn't one of the options I gave you." She carried the dirty oil she had dumped into the oil drum to the back of the garage, hoping he would be gone when she came back to the front.

"If you don't want to talk, then I hope you will at least listen to what I have to say."

Frustrated that he was going to give her the "let's be friends talk," she was tempted to go inside her house until he left. Only the fact that she worked for The Last Riders and it was inevitable that they would see each other around town had her giving in.

"Go ahead, Rider. Say what you want to get off your chest."

"Thank you." Rider shoved his hands into his jacket pockets. "I want to be able to say you're wrong about me, but I can't. You were right in what you said about me. I wanted you to fall in love with me, while I had no intention of doing the same with you. I'm a selfish bastard."

"So far, you're wasting my time. You aren't saying anything I don't already know."

"Did you mean it when you said forever and ever?"

"Yes, Rider, I meant it. Jesus, why'd you come here? To take what pride I have left?"

"No. I came here to tell you that, if you really mean it, then I'm in."

"What the hell does that mean?" Jo's eyes widened as she tried to understand what he wanted from her.

"It means that I never gave you a real chance to fall in love with you. I'm ready give you a chance."

Her hands went to her hips. "You are un-fucking-believable. You're going to give me a chance? You narcissistic a-hole, you can take your chance and give it to another woman. I don't want it."

"You said you love me," he stated simply.

Jo frowned. "I do."

"If I had cancer, would you love me?"

"You don't have cancer." She narrowed her eyes.

"No, but if I did, would you love me?"

"Yes."

"If I couldn't have children, would you still love me?"

"Yes."

"I'm an a-hole. Can you love me despite that?"

He was not going to make her laugh, nor was he going to talk himself back into her life.

"I won't be my father. You're too good at turning things around to benefit yourself. I'll never be able to trust that you're showing me the real you."

"I know, but I can prove to you that I can be the man you feel you're in love with. If I can do that, will you give me another chance? Give us both another chance? Please? Isn't finding forever and ever worth one more try?"

Jo made a sweeping gesture with her hand. "Fine, go ahead and prove it. If you can, then yes, I'll give you another chance. But I'm warning you now, I threw that perfume away."

Rider gave her a boyish grin and started toward her as if he was going to hug her.

"Red." She gave him a firm nod. "You haven't proven a damn thing yet."

"Okay." He stopped in his tracks. "That's cool. I didn't expect you to agree." Rider ran a hand through his hair. "I have to go back to the club to pack, and I need to get Jewell and Shade to cover my shifts." He looked down at his watch. "I'll make reservations and be back in an hour. Does that give you enough time to pack?"

"Pack? I'm not going anywhere."

Rider frowned. "You have to see the proof."

"You can tell me about it; you don't have to show me." She should have listened to her first instinct and gone into her house, locking herself inside until he left.

"Please, Jo, I'm going to show you the most beautiful place on earth, or at least, I think it is."

It was the self-depreciating laugh that had her reconsidering going. That he was showing a vulnerability she hadn't known existed in him. That he wanted her to think that the place he was going to show her was as beautiful as he did.

Rider being vulnerable left her defenseless at telling him no.

"I'll go pack." Jo locked the garage as he was leaving.

I should have gone inside the house, she repeated the refrain for the third time.

Rider was too hard for any woman to resist, and she was no exception. She was already seeing the hard, rocky road ahead of her to achieve her forever and ever.

Jo kicked a large rock out of her way. "Next time I break up with him, I'll go inside the fucking house."

HE WAS RIGHT; Texas was the most beautiful place on earth. It wasn't because of the gorgeous house that had stunned her when Rider had driven up the driveway, nor was it the sight she saw while sitting on the top rung of the fence—she could easily see ahead of her for miles. No, it was seeing Rider riding hell-bent for leather, chasing after a calf that had successfully wandered away from its mother.

"Run, baby, be free!" Jo laughingly yelled after the fleeing creature.

The man who was steadily moving the cows into their pens gave her a censoring glare.

"Sorry." Grinning, she tossed her hair over her shoulder as she stared raptly at Rider as he maneuvered the calf back over to his mother.

"Better luck next time." She couldn't help enjoying the sight of the baby bellowing out as if it was angry at Rider for cutting its fun short.

Rider's cinnamon-colored horse changed directions, turning toward her.

Jo raised her hand to cover her eyes as he approached. With her other hand, she gripped the fence to balance herself, keeping herself from falling backward as she looked at him.

Rider lifted his hand to raise the brim of his Stetson. "Having fun?"

"Yes, but not as much as you seem to be having." Jo pouted up at him, stroking the horse's muzzle.

"Then you shouldn't have talked me into taking you for a ride this morning. Your sore ass should be thanking me."

"I hate that we have to leave tomorrow."

Rider's eyes grew distant at her reminder as he rested his forearm on the saddle horn. "It is beautiful, isn't it?"

"Yes. You don't get tempted to come back and work with your father and brothers?"

"No," he answered shortly. "Come on; it's time for dinner."

Rider lifted her off the fence, placing her in front of him as his knees tightened to get the horse moving.

"I like riding with you on a horse better than a motorcycle."

"A motorcycle doesn't shit and doesn't draw flies." He rested the palm of his hand across her waist, making the butterflies circle around in her stomach again.

During the last two weeks, she had seen a new side of Rider.

When he had first introduced her to his father and step-mother, she had wanted to leave. His father had the same build as his son, but that was where the similarities ended. Ben Stiles was a cold, distant man who Jo hated being in the same room with, when he did decide to show up for the family meals.

Rider's stepmother was much younger than her husband, closer in age to Rider than her husband. She seemed to spend most of her days with friends, shopping, if the numerous bags she came home with each day were anything to go by.

That Rider wasn't close to either of them hurt her for him. When his half brothers were around, his father tried to make an appearance of a family unit, yet the young boys kept looking at the adults, as if sensing the strain between them. His stepmother was the opposite, sending Rider furtive looks when no one else was watching, making it awkward every time she was near.

Fortunately, Rider and Jo spent most of the last two weeks out on the ranch. He had shown her the vast operation his father owned, from the quarter horses he raised to be sold, to the citrus farming that Rider explained he had been responsible for starting. But it was the miles of turf that she had enjoyed seeing the most.

Rider fit in with the surroundings like a glove. The sight of him riding a horse and the way the horse followed the slightest movement of his supple body made her ache that they fit together so well. He was a natural-born cowboy, and she couldn't understand why he preferred Treepoint to the life waiting for him here.

"Can I ask you something?" Jo laid her head on his shoulder, using the brim of his hat to shield her from the sun.

"Yes." He tightened his hand on her waist.

"Why Treepoint? Don't you miss this?"

"Every fucking day."

"Then why stay in Treepoint?"

"You've met Ben. What do you think?"

"I think you and your father don't like each other."

"It's a love/hate relationship, one where there's never been any love between us. We're both alpha dogs who have always fought over the way we want to run the ranch."

"You live with a clubhouse of alpha males, and you're all close."

"Viper, me, and the brothers like the life we lead at the club. We've seen firsthand that if you're content doing just one thing, then at the first catastrophe, it can wipe you out. We're not content putting our faith in one business. But as a team, we can divide and conquer."

"I'm glad you made friends like them. They've become your family."

"That's why I stay in Treepoint." Rider turned his horse so he could gaze back at the beauty of his birthright.

She raised her head so she could see him better, a tight ball forming in her throat at the stunning profile of a man who constantly changed, assuming the qualities of each environment he was in. It was like if he stepped into a room of mirrors, a different reflection would show when he stopped in front of them.

"I'm sorry."

Rider looked down at her, his laugh lines crinkling. "What for?"

"I can see how it would be hard to live in the same house with Ben and your stepmother. I wish you shared a closer relationship with them. Were you close to your mother?"

"Very." His voice cracked, showing a reflection of the pain he felt at losing her. "She died when I was sixteen." Raising his eyes, he turned the horse forward again.

During the rest of the ride back to the main house, he described his mother. The lump in her throat grew at how much Rider had loved her and the close relationship they had shared.

In the barn, he got down before lifting her off.

She wrinkled her nose at him. "We need a shower."

"Go ahead. I'll see you at dinner."

Jo left him unsaddling his horse, going to the bedroom

that his stepmother had shown her to the first day they had gotten there. It had been decorated with luxury in mind and would make up four of hers in Treepoint. His stepmother had expected Rider and her to share, but after showing her the room, Rider had carried his suitcase to the bedroom across the hall.

Over the last two weeks, Rider had been nothing but a gentleman. Other than small touches when she rode with him, he had kept his distance, a distance that was beginning to grate on her nerves.

When they had been in Treepoint, she had never seen the man he was showing her in Texas. He didn't walk with a confident swagger. In Texas, when he came into a room, he took it over, dynamically dwarfing his father and making him seem smaller, a shadow of Rider, unable to compete with the real thing. Even the cowboys who worked the cattle and the land showed him deferential treatment when they were together, looking to him when they wanted their orders confirmed instead of asking his father.

Still, nothing he had shown her had changed her opinion of him until she had seen him with his half brothers. Their father would show his impatience with them when they would beg to help the cowboys work the cattle. However, Rider would agree without hesitation. Then he would patiently correct them by showing them how to do something right. When his youngest brother had managed to rope a calf, Rider had ridden over to him to congratulate him as their father had returned to the house.

An ache settled in her chest at imagining Rider teaching his child the skills he was showing his brothers. He was going to make a caring father, that his children would never doubt his love for them. The type of father that other children would wish was theirs.

Showering, she decided she wanted to look pretty for him

tonight, with it being their last night together at the ranch. Unfortunately, the clothes she had brought weren't cooperating.

Taking a dark navy blue dress out of the closet, she wished it were fancier, yet was satisfied that it showed off her feminine curves. Brushing her hair out, she slipped her feet into the low-heeled shoes she had found in her closet at home. She had packed the dress and shoes as an afterthought and was glad she had. It didn't compare to Rider's stepmother's tailored clothes, but she didn't have the desire to have them either.

Jo went down the staircase and to the dining room. She knew she was too early, but she had wanted to spend more time with his half brothers. The gregarious boys always made her laugh and lessened the strained atmosphere between the adults. They were already showing signs of Rider's personality. The three together made the nights fun as they ended up watching movies together before going to bed.

The stairway ended with a foyer and two huge rooms on each side. One side was the living room, and the other was the dining room. Smelling dinner cooking, she went back to the foyer, making her way down the hallway and passing Rider's father's study.

As she walked by, she heard a raised voice coming from the other side of the door.

"What time are you leaving in the morning?"

Jo wanted to snatch the door open at the hostile way his father was talking to Rider.

"Long before you'll be up."

"Good."

"Ben, don't be that way. Ty, you're welcome anytime—"

"Shut up, Quinn. We need to talk about the orchard

before you leave. You've put me off for two weeks. I told you it's a waste of our men. I want—"

"Do what you want. After tomorrow"—Jo pressed her ear to the door, listening to the sound of crackling papers coming through the door—"it will all be yours."

The silence coming from the room had her frowning, wishing she could see the papers Rider must have given to his father.

"About damn time. Your mother should have never left it to you anyway."

"She left it to me because it was hers to give. She knew you would destroy the ranch, even before you married her for it. That's why she had you sign the prenuptial agreement before she married you. She fooled you, didn't she, old man? You weren't able to tear it up, were you?"

"The stu—"

"Be careful ... I'll kill you, and you won't benefit from one dime of that piece of paper you're holding in your hand."

"You always were too soft where your mother was concerned."

"I agree with that. If I didn't love her so much, I would have kicked your ass out the day I turned eighteen. Instead, I let you stay; even trusted you to take care of the ranch while I went to basic. Of course, I didn't expect you to have an affair with my wife while I was gone."

"Ty, I told you it didn't mean anything. I was lonely. You left me all alone."

"You were the one who told me to follow my dreams of joining the service. But your dreams were bigger than being married to me. I bet you shit your pants when I came home on leave for you to tell me you wanted a divorce to marry my father and then found out I was the one who owned the ranch."

"It was a mistake I will always regret, Ty. I handled it badly."

"You can say that again. You both have what you want now, and you can let the ranch go down the toilet together. With the interest you managed to wrestle from me when we divorced, if you divorce Ben, you should be set for a couple years. I would say for life, but with the way you like to spend money, he won't be able to keep you afloat for that long."

"She won't be divorcing me." Ben's usually harsh voice had a hint of doubt that Jo picked up on.

"I'd get a bodyguard if you do. I haven't seen Reno since I've been here."

"He's on vacation."

"I bet. He's lucky no one was hurt from that stunt he pulled in Kentucky."

"I don't know what you're talking about."

"You're lucky Shade hates Texas, or you'd be searching for another foreman. At least with that paper in your hand, it's one less target on my back. And you can quit breaking into the church. What you want isn't there. Here"—Jo heard a paper crinkling—"I made an extra copy of my will to save you the trouble. If I die, neither of you nor my brothers will see a dime. I'm leaving everything to The Last Riders, who will administer a trust I have set up. A piece of advice, Quinn; make a will in case an unfortunate accident happens to you. Leave the ranch completely to Ben. Don't let my father put a target on the boys' backs."

"Ben wouldn't harm a hair on their heads." Quinn's uncertainty was plain to hear.

"Regardless, I've warned you. What you do with it is on your own conscience." Rider's warning had Jo shivering outside the door. "If I have to come back to Texas because of anything you've done to those boys, the whole state of Texas won't be large enough to hide in, and The Last Riders will be coming with me."

"Don't threaten me with those thugs!"

"They aren't thugs. Every damn one of them has a medal showing their bravery. They have more courage and honor in one cell of their bodies than you have in all of yours. The only good thing about me signing ownership over to you is that I'll never have to see you again after tonight."

"Then I'll make it better for you. I'll stay in the bunkhouse tonight."

Jo hurried down the hall when she heard Ben slide his chair back.

The housekeeper stared at her curiously when she hurried into the kitchen.

Jo tucked her hair behind an ear. "You mind if I watch? I promise I won't get in your way this time." She moved toward the large stove, hearing someone coming in just as she was sniffing the large pot of chili.

"Are you still trying to steal Mary's recipes?" Rider teased.

"I promised to behave." She stealthily picked at the corn-bread sitting on the stove.

"How's that working for you? It's been hell for me behaving around you." He grinned, reaching over her shoulder and confidently stealing a whole slice.

She raised imploring eyes to his teasing ones, seeing the lurking pain in their depths.

She turned around, pressing her hand to his chest. "Don't. We can leave tonight if you want."

His feigned grin faded, and he stared down at her before pressing his cheek to the top of her head. "You were listening, weren't you?"

Jo nodded against him. "I hate him."

"I feel sorry for him. He's going to destroy the ranch, and Quinn will cut and run when he does."

"Your mother wanted you to have it."

"I found something I care about more."

"The Last Riders or Treepoint?" She lifted Rider's hand to take a piece of his cornbread.

"You."

"Why are we stopping here?" Jo asked as Rider turned the blinker on and pulled to the side of the road.

"I want to take a picture of you," he stated after stopping the car. "Do you mind?" Picking up his cell phone, Rider waited for her answer.

"Why here? There's nothing here." She rolled her window down, seeing nothing but a landscape of overgrown flowers growing on the side of the road.

Rider raised his hand, pointing out the window. "Those are bluebonnets."

Jo got out of the car, her knees trembling as she followed him.

As she walked deeper through the flowers, she trailed her fingers over the blue blossoms.

"It's beautiful." She looked over to see he was videotaping her walking through the flowers.

"Yes, it is."

Blushing, she made a comic face at him, then stopped when he put the phone to his side and just stood there, staring at her.

Jo tilted her head. "What are you doing?"

"Remembering how you look."

"You're really not coming back to Texas anymore, are you?"

"No. It's not like I come that often anyway. After my divorce from Quinn, I only came back when I needed to take care of something concerning the ranch and it was too big to take care of from Treepoint."

"You loved Quinn, didn't you?"

"I did. I was young and missing Mom, and my father and I living alone in the house was not a good thing."

Jealousy tore at her composure. She would never again be able to brag that she wasn't jealous-natured.

"Not even to see your brothers?" she prodded, trying to make him change his mind.

"In a few years, they'll be men, and then they can come see me. They have my number if they need me before then." He took her hand, leading her back to the car. "We need to leave, or we'll miss our flight."

"Are we going to drive from Lexington back to Treepoint tonight, or are we going to stay the night in Lexington?" she asked once they were back inside the car.

"We're going to stay the night in Lexington. There's someone I want to introduce you to."

———

JO CAUGHT Rider's arm when he got in line to check them into the hotel for the night.

Her cheeks felt like they were on fire as he waited to see what she wanted.

"We only need one room."

He placed his hand on the side of her neck. "As much as I want to take you up on that invitation, I have to wait."

Disappointment filled her. She had thought they had drawn closer over the last two weeks. She knew she had fallen deeper in love with him. Had Rider already decided there wasn't a chance he was going to fall in love her? Had she just been giving herself false hope that he would?

"Jo, bear with me one more day."

So, it was true. He wasn't going to love her.

Giving him a shaky smile, she released his arm. "I guess that's what friends are for."

Rider frowned, searching her face. Then his eyes darkened at what he must have seen. "Just wait. Tomorrow—"

"It's okay, Rider. I understand. I can wait one more day." She had one more day to pretend that there was a chance for them. It was more than some other couples had before deciding to break up.

She hated herself for wanting more than he was able to give her, for the years ahead of her without Rider.

How was a woman supposed to get over the Winston Hero?

45

"This is where the person you want to introduce me to lives?"

"Yes," Rider answered as he opened the car door for her.

At the front door, Rider knocked.

As they waited, he felt Jo's curious eyes on him. It was always hard for him to come here for a visit. That was why he had never taken anyone before. It wasn't a place where he could hide his emotions, but if he wanted Jo, he had to show her all the parts of his life.

What he had shown her in Texas had been hard for him. Usually, when he returned from Texas, he would fuck his way through The Last Rider women until the bitterness could be hidden away until his next visit.

"Gabby, you're prettier every time I come for a visit." Rider swooped down on the middle-aged woman who answered the door.

The woman reached up, hugging him, then pushed him away. "You're lying, but go ahead. I don't mind."

"Jo, this my aunt, Gabby. Gabby, this is Jo Turner."

His aunt gave her a sweet hug, then kissed Jo on the cheek. Jo turned crimson at the attention she was receiving.

"She can't be your father's sister."

Rider laughed when her hand went to her mouth, giving him a mortified look.

"I am." Gabby laughed with him at Jo's consternation. "It's okay, sweetie. He isn't worth the bullet to put him out of his own misery. I take it Ben was his old, reliable self during your visit with him?",

"You can say that again," Rider commented, taking Jo's hand to follow his aunt into the living room.

"It's not worth repeating to talk about that son of a bitch." Gabby motioned them to take a seat on her couch as she sat down on the arm of a pretty, green chair.

"How have you been doing?"

"I can't complain, and Carsen is good, too. He's with Delara. Are you going to introduce her to Jo?"

"Just for a moment. Then I thought you could keep Jo company while I spend some time with Delara."

"Go ahead. I'll make Jo and me some coffee. I made your favorite cake for you. I'll try to save you a piece." His aunt nudged him toward the hallway when he would have gone into the kitchen. "I made one for you to take home. Go ahead. Introduce her to Delara," she said gently.

Rider went down the hallway, making a left turn that opened into a large bedroom filled with windows. When he and Jo entered, the man who was reading to the woman on the bed closed the book and stood, meeting them halfway.

"Good to see you, brother."

"It's good to see you, Carsen." Rider shook his aunt's husband's hand as Jo moved around them to look at the woman on the bed. "Jo, this is Carsen, Gabby's husband."

Jo tore her eyes off the bed, taking the hand he held out to her.

After a brief shake, Carsen gave him the book he had been reading to Delara. "I'll leave you to make the introductions."

At the soft click of the door shutting, Rider put his hands in his pockets as he walked to the bottom of the bed.

"Delara, this is Jo." Taking a deep breath, he finished the rest of the introduction. "Jo, this is Delara ... my wife."

The hurt on her face cut him off at his knees.

"Does she understand ...?" Jo tried to get her question out. "Can she ...?"

"The doctors say no." Rider didn't want to think the woman he had loved so deeply was in any pain or knew what was going on around her, trapped in the shell that remained.

"Her eyes are open." Jo moved closer to the bed.

"They say it's a reflex." Rider clenched his hands in his pockets.

"What happened?"

Rider moved to the side of Delara's bed, making sure he didn't interfere with any of the machines that were on both sides. The largest on the other side of the bed breathed for her.

He lifted a trembling hand to the rail of her bed. It was still hard for him to be in the same room with her. The lovely, vivacious woman he had fallen in love with was gone, and all that was left was the shell of her body that had once held her soul for the brief time she had been on earth.

"Rider ...?" Jo's voice drew him out of the past.

"The brothers know what I'm about to tell you, but it can't go any further."

"I won't tell anyone," she assured.

"I know you won't, Jo. That's one of the things I've grown to love about you." Rider lifted his eyes from Delara's blank face to Jo's pain-filled one. He wanted to snatch her into his arms. Resisting the impulse, he turned back to Delara.

"I met Delara when I was in the service. It was five years after my divorce, and she was everything Quinn wasn't. I had been given the job of infiltrating a camp that was blocking a convoy of trucks that was trying to render medical aide to a town that was under constant attack. I had been ordered to find a way for our men to get inside and take it over so the trucks could get through.

"I had already been involved with Delara. We had already been married when the order came from my commander. We were just waiting for her passport to come through before she joined me. That's why she was in the town where I had met her. Her father was the leader of the camp that needed to be neutralized. She didn't want to live in her father's world.

"I was to go in and find a way to get our squadron inside without getting them all killed. I had sneaked in once to memorize the buildings and where most of their guns and ammunitions were being placed.

"Gavin's order was to get the job done, but he was uneasy about it. He had tried to get the commander to wait a few more days. They didn't want to wait."

"Why did he want to wait?"

"Gavin didn't trust Delara. He said she was a spy; that I couldn't trust her. He even tried to get Viper and Knox to convince me so that I would second his opinion to wait. I wouldn't. I wanted her away from that world. I was terrified her father would have her killed."

"You loved her."

"I loved her," he acknowledged. "She was carrying my child, Jo. How could I not trust her?"

How naïve he had been still haunted him. So many could have died—his child had—because he had given that trust to Delara.

"The day before executing the attack I had planned, I

spent with our commanders, coordinating the attack. Delara was supposed to stay put until I came back the next day."

"She didn't."

"Gavin and I were coming out of where the meeting had taken place. There were barriers, so no one could get through unless they were military personnel. We had left the restricted area and were making our way back down the street when Gavin spotted her. We took off after her. I couldn't understand why she was there. That was when I noticed she was carrying a basket. I swear to God I didn't know what it was."

Jo went to his side, easily wrapping her arms around him to steady him. "I don't need to hear any more, Rider."

Rider broke. The ice encasing his heart that Jo had steadily chipped away since the day of the auction didn't have enough strength to withstand the power of Jo's love. And so, he stood there, crying over the woman who had betrayed him.

"There's not much left to tell. We ran after her to stop her before she could reach the barricade. I yelled at Gavin that I would take the basket and he was to get Delara the hell out of there.

"Delara saw us running toward her and reached inside the basket. I would have gotten it away from her before it exploded if Gavin hadn't held me back. Whoever had wired the bomb had done it wrong. It misfired."

"It could have been you."

"I wanted it to be me. My child would have lived." The torturous thought had kept him up sleepless nights since … until those sleepless nights had been filled with Jo.

"You had her brought to the States."

"Gavin had warned me that her father had too much control over her. I didn't listen."

"Rider, you loved her. That's what you do when you love

481

someone. She was carrying your child; her obligation should have been to you and that baby. She failed you both."

"I can't bring myself to divorce her. I gave her my oath to protect and care for her when I married her. I can't break that oath when she can't understand me."

"I understand, Rider. I loved my father despite him preferring a bottle of liquor to the promises he made to me." Jo took a deep breath, shaking off the despair the room held. "I'll leave you to have some time alone. I'm anxious to taste Gabby's cake."

"Jo, I brought you here to prove to you that I can be the man you want me to be. He was there all along. I was just too stupid to show him to you."

"I don't think you were stupid, Rider. Two women betrayed you. A heart is a precious thing to trust to someone. It hurts when that trust is broken."

"I'm sorry. I never cheated on you with my body, but I did with my actions. If you take me back, I swear I'll never let another woman buy me presents, or buy my favorite cereal, or give me extra french fries." Rider tried to rack his mind on how to convince her to give him another chance.

Jo gave him a tight hug before letting him go. "Can I say something to her?"

"Go ahead. Like I said, I don't know if she'll hear you." Rider moved aside, letting Jo take his place at Delara's side.

"Girl, you screwed up so bad. You could have had it all with Rider. I don't care why you did what you did, but I'm telling you here and now, I will make damn sure he won't be thinking of you when he's in my bed, or when I have his child, or when I make him show me that beautiful smile of his." Jo leaned farther over the bed, filling the blank eyes with the vision of what she looked like. "After I leave this room, I'm never going to give you another thought, but I hope there's enough of a spark of life in you to see the woman who's going to fulfill the promises you gave him."

Seconds later, Rider watched as Jo casually walked out of the room as if she were strolling through a park, taking the last piece of his heart with her.

46

G abby poured her a cup of coffee as soon as she came in. "I put a little brandy in there for you."

Jo took a seat at the small table as Gabby cut her a slice of the dark cake. "I use a devil's food cake mix to make it. That's why Rider likes it so much. That boy has a little bit of the devil in him," she said with a wink.

"A little? Gabby, I feel as Rider's aunt, you deserve to be told the truth." Jo took a bite of the chocolate cake, her eyes nearly rolling back in her head. It was pure sin on a spoon.

"I'm waiting." Gabby grinned proudly at her expression.

"Sorry. This is delicious." She took another bite. When her eyes came back from heaven, it took a second to remember what she had been about to say. "Oh, I remember." She leaned forward conspiratorially, lowering her voice. "He may have been a little devil when he was younger, but now he's an angel in disguise."

"Rider's no angel." Gabby slapped the table, laughing.

Jo took another bite. "I can prove it. I'm not saying that his halo isn't tarnished, but it's still there."

"I'll believe it when I see it."

"You'll see."

They were still sitting there when Rider came out of the bedroom. Jo was on her third cup of coffee and her second slice of cake.

Taking a seat at the table, Jo gave him a bite of her cake as Gabby fixed him a plate and a glass of milk.

Jo screwed her face up at the milk. "You're giving him milk instead of coffee? Here, you can have a sip of mine. It's the best I've ever had. What brand is it?" Jo asked, giving Rider the evil eye when he took another sip.

"I don't know what brand of coffee it is, but I'd say the brandy is about 90 percent. How many cups have you had?"

"A couple."

"It's her third cup."

"Tattletale." Jo glared at Gabby from over her coffee cup.

"I like her, Rider." Gabby cut him another slice of cake after he wolfed down the first one.

"I'm in love with her."

"No, he's not." Jo leaned back in her chair, pouting.

Rider frowned. "Yes, I am. I wouldn't lie to you about something as serious as that."

"Prove it."

"How do you want me to do that? Tell me, and I'll do it. Do you want me to get Diamond to help me get a divorce? I will."

"No, you made an oath. I never expected you to marry me anyway."

Rider's frown drew so deep Jo ran a finger over the lines that marred his forehead.

"How do you want me to prove it, then?"

"I want the cake." Jo lightly touched the extra cake that Gabby had made for Rider to take home.

"You want my cake?"

"Yep." Jo took the last bite of her cake before airily waving her spoon around. "I want the cake."

"And that'll prove my love to you?"

"Yes, that'll prove it."

When he didn't answer immediately, it was her turn to grow worried.

"Well?" she prompted him.

"I'm thinking. It's a damn fine cake."

When he started laughing at her expression, she playfully whacked him with her spoon.

"Yours, Bluebonnet."

"Then I love you back."

Jo was enjoying herself so much she didn't want to leave, but when he kept rushing her, promising to bring her back for a visit, she unsteadily placed her hand on the table to brace herself.

Getting her legs back under control, she reached for the cake.

"I can carry it for you," Rider offered as they walked to the door.

Jo refused, and then waited patiently as Rider hugged his aunt goodbye. Carsen came out of Delara's room to give his own goodbye.

"Go ahead and start the car. I'm coming," Jo told Rider, waiting for him to go to the car. Once he was gone, she gave Gabby a wink. "I told you I could prove he was an angel. Anyone who's willing to give this cake away deserves his wings."

Laughing, Jo walked to the car, making sure the cake was settled securely in the back seat before getting in the front and buckling herself in. Her head hit the headrest as he spun out of the driveway.

"Jesus, what's the hurry?"

"I have a surprise for you." He gave her a grin that never failed to melt her panties.

"What is it?" She shifted in her seat to face him, eager to hear about her surprise. "Is it a good surprise or a bad one?"

"A good one." He laughed, getting into the game she loved to play.

"Is it bigger than a bread box?"

"A lot bigger."

"Wow. Okay …" Jo tapped a finger on her chin as she thought. "Is it twice the size of a bread box or smaller than a car."

"Bigger." Rider sped up, getting on the interstate.

The rest of the way home, he fielded her guesses, not giving anything away. When they finally reached Treepoint, Jo was practically bouncing in her seat, anxious to get home to find out what her surprise was. The slowing of the car as they neared The Last Riders' clubhouse had her looking at him.

"You need to go inside to get my present?"

"You have to come inside. It's too big to carry."

She hesitated. "This isn't going to be like the last present you gave me, is it?" Jo asked as she got out.

"No, Bluebonnet. Nothing is going to spoil our night."

She warily went up the steps. She really didn't want the night to be spoiled.

She was slightly less nervous when Moon gave a sharp knock on the door as they approached, thinking he was being considerate to her by giving everyone time to stop what they were doing and get their clothes back on. Watching a Friday night party on one of the monitors in the security room was one thing. Full throttle was for the …

As Rider let her go first, Jo stepped inside, practically shielding her eyes. It was the cheers of "Happy birthday!" that had her emotions in a tailspin.

Balloons had been tied to the staircase, and when she walked through the crowd and saw Mag, she broke down in tears, running to the old woman. She dropped to her knees in front of her.

"You're going to make me cry with the way you're carrying on!" Mag's rough pats on her head had Jo raising her shining eyes to hers.

"I missed you," she said, wiping at her tears, self-conscious of everyone staring at her.

"I missed you, youngin. Go enjoy your party, and if you get a chance, sneak me one of those beers."

"I'll try," she promised.

Jo took the hand Mick held out to her, lifting her off the floor.

"I'm glad you're back." The bear hug he gave her almost had her crying again. "There're a bunch of Big Reds behind the bar. Don't let Moon drink them all. He's been drinking them since I brought them in."

"I won't." She loved the big man. He had let her cry all the way to the hospital to see Mag after she had left The Last Riders'.

He looked over her shoulder at Rider. "I hope you treat her better this time," he warned.

Jo leaned back against Rider. "Don't worry; he learned his lesson."

"I hope so. If not, I'll remind him," Mick was saying as Mercury walked by to watch a game at the pool table. Jo gave him a reprimanding glare. "You go open your presents, Jo. I'm in the mood for a good game of pool."

"Trip is a pool shark," Jo whispered as he started around her.

"Well, that'll be an interesting game. I am, too."

Jo spent the next hour talking to the others in the room until Rider dragged her to the couch where Lily and Shade were sitting, tired of following her around the room. Scooting over, he made room for her to sit next to him.

"Enjoy your trip?" Lily asked after she settled comfortably next to Rider.

Rider's arm around her shoulders tightened. Jo turned her head to give him a curious look, seeing the warning in his eyes. Not understanding what he was warning her about, she became noncommittal as Lily questioned her.

"Shade said you went on a small trip, but he didn't say where."

Rider's hand tightened across her shoulders again. She didn't want to get Rider in trouble, but she didn't want to lie to Lily either.

"We went to several states." *Technically, we* had *flown over several states*, she soothed her conscience.

"Did you go anywhere out West? I've been begging Shade to take me, but he won't."

"Why not?" Jo looked at Rider out of the corner of her eye.

"I had a thing for cowboys when I was younger. I keep telling him he's being ridiculous, but he keeps planning vacations anywhere but the western states."

"You find cowboys attractive?" Jo couldn't help prodding the devil whose wife was sitting between them.

Shade's eyes narrowed on her innocent expression.

"I used to, but I don't anymore." Lily shot her husband a quick glance.

"I don't blame you. I find cowboys attractive, too. There's an old saying that a cowboy's horse mirrors their soul."

Jo had to bite her lip when Lily looked like she was about to swoon.

Jo nestled closer to Rider. He bent to nuzzle her neck, whispering, "You're playing with fire," before he nipped her ear.

Her hand went to his thigh. "It won't be the first time."

"Did you say something, Jo?" Lily asked.

Jo cleared her throat. "I was just asking Rider if he will take me out West the next time he takes me on a trip. I can just imagine him on a quarter horse with a Stetson. Can't you, Lily?"

Her friend shook her head, laughing. "He'd fall off."

Rider stiffened next to her. "I wouldn't fall off."

"You would. Besides, a cowboy needs to be able to throw a rope to catch the strays. If you tried, you'd tie yourself up."

"I'll have you know—"

"Rider, do you mind getting me a piece of a cake and one of my drinks?" Jo hastened to distract the man from the burgeoning brawl she had instigated.

Shade's expression had turned deadly. Rider's injured pride was going to land him in a world of pain if he wasn't careful.

"Will you get me one? Just the drink." Lily shifted to the side to let her husband up.

Shade hesitated, not wanting to leave his wife alone with her.

"How are John and Clint?"

"They're getting bigger every day." Lily took out her cell phone and started showing her pictures of her two sons.

When the men left, Lily gave a quick glance at Shade and Rider's backs before turning back to her. "Hurry, tell me before they come back. How did he look on a horse?"

Jo gaped at her. "You know?"

"Killyama told me. She hates it when the men try to pull one over on us. So, did he look good?"

"Lily, he was magnificent."

"For our next anniversary, I'm going to make Shade take riding lessons." Lily turned to take another quick look at the men. "I want to tell you something, but I don't want you to get mad at Rider. You promise?"

"I won't get mad at him tonight. Plus, I'll be too full to care. I've lost count of how many slices of cake I've eaten."

Lily leaned over and started whispering to Jo, who had to control her reaction to what Lily was telling her. She wanted to take what was left of the cake and throw it at Rider.

"You're sure?"

"Positive."

"We girls have to stick together, don't we?" She kept tabs on Rider as he went from the table to the bar, where Shade was still waiting for Lily's drink.

"Yes, that's why I told you about the camera." Lily nodded.

"Who's working security tonight? Do you know?"

"Train and Diablo. What are you planning to do? If Shade finds out, I'll be in trouble."

"I have to tell Shade, or my plan won't work. But I'll make it a condition that if he does what I want, I won't tell you Rider is a cowboy."

Lily started wringing her hands.

Not wanting to get the woman upset, she scrapped the plan. "Never mind. I'll find another way to pay him back."

"No. I was just thinking. I changed my mind. You can tell Shade I told you."

"You're sure? You won't get in trouble?" She wanted to know why, but she didn't have time to ask since the men were almost back.

"I'm looking forward to it."

Jo excused herself after she forced down the cake, telling Rider she wanted to spend some time with Mag. Rider didn't object, preferring to stay and talk to Shade and Lily rather than deal with the old woman.

Jo found a seat on the couch where Cash and Rachel were sitting with Mag. She tried to concentrate on the conversation, waiting for the moment she needed. The opportunity struck when Shade went to the bar for a beer.

"I'll go get you that drink, Mag. I'll be right back."

Jo went to the bar, sliding through the crowd to stand next to Shade.

"I want a favor," she demanded.

"Usually, when you want a favor, you ask." He stared down at her with his harsh, impassive features.

Jo reached for every ounce of courage she possessed. "If you don't do what I want, I'm going to show Lily the pictures of Rider I took of him in Texas."

"What do you want?"

4 7

"Are you sure you don't mind that I have to work?" Rider motioned Moon to go inside as he said good night to Jo.

"Not at all. I was there when Shade told you that Diablo wasn't feeling well. It's probably the flu. You shouldn't keep him waiting."

"It's not the flu. He's the one who cut the cake before we got here." He was planning on kicking Diablo's ass as soon as he got to the security room.

"I have a whole German upside-down cake in the rental car. I'm good. I better be going; Cash is getting out of the car."

He tightened his hands on her arms, pulling her closer. "You sure you don't want to keep me company?"

She gave him a pained look. "I would if I could, but I'm exhausted."

Kissing her forehead, he then placed another on her cheek. He hated to let her go. "I haven't even been able to give you your present yet."

"Bring it by in the morning. I'll open it when I wake up."

"I'm going to hold you to that." Giving her a final kiss on the lips, he released her. "Good night, Bluebonnet. I love you."

Jo rushed back into his arms, flinging hers around his neck. "I love you, too."

The horn from the parking lot had her pulling away. "Good night, Rider."

He watched her until she was safely in Cash's truck before he went inside to make himself a plate of snacks and take a few drinks from the cooler. Then, going out the back door, he made his way to the security room.

Taking inventory of Diablo, he sat down on the chair that Diablo quickly vacated at his stare.

"You don't look sick to me." Rider pulled the computer chair under the desk as he set his snacks down.

"I have to keep running to the restroom. Train's not feeling any better. He'll be back in a few. He's already—"

"Call Train and tell him not to come back." Rider reached for the Clorox wipes, wiping everything down as he started scanning the monitors. "I don't need him, and I don't need you fuckers getting me sick. Get Gavin to go to the store and get you both a bottle Pepto. And if I get sick, you sons of bitches are ..." Rider took his eyes off the screens to see that Diablo had already left.

Snorting, he turned back to the monitors, pressing a key on the keyboard to light up the one in Jo's living room. The lights were on in the room, showing she was already home.

Taking a bite of his cake, he leaned back in his chair, using his boot to pivot it so he could easily see the rows of monitors. He was taking another bite of his cake when Jo came out of the bathroom.

His teeth raked the spoon when he saw her wearing a little black teddy that was high-waisted.

"She doesn't wear shit like that when I'm there," he spoke

out into the empty room.

Setting the plate down, he twisted the top of the bottle of his Big Red, wetting his dry throat. He stopped pivoting his chair when he looked at the screen and saw she had sat down on the couch and raised her feet to the coffee table. He barely managed to force himself to focus on the other screens, relieved when she turned her television on.

He was grasping for any distraction to keep himself from focusing on her brushing her hair. Each stroke made his dick strain in his jeans. He was castigating himself for not fucking her the night before.

"That's the last time I'm a gentleman." He forced himself not to look at her screen for a full two minutes before his eyes returned, and what he saw had him reaching for his phone.

"Hello?"

Jo's seductive voice had him trying to find his.

"Hello?" she asked again.

"I just wanted to make sure you made it home."

"Sure did. Cash is a safe driver."

The way Jo said Cash's name came out as a caress. Had the brother flirted with his old lady on the way home? With Mag and Rachel in the car? Deep down, really deep down low, Rider knew Cash hadn't, but it was that hesitation that had him darting quick glances at the other monitors before turning back to Jo's.

"What are you up to?" He gruffly managed to get the words out.

She was stroking one of her thighs. Reaching the top, she glided her hand to her waist as her other hand held the phone to her ear. Reaching behind her, Jo picked up a throw pillow, laying it on the arm of the couch before lying down so she could watch the television. "It's a shame you can't be here. I'm watching *Smokey*."

Rider squinted at the computer screen. His old lady wasn't watching Burt Reynolds.

Where in the fuck had she found that movie?

In the morning, before he woke her, he would for damn sure be finding out ... if he didn't rip the cable cord out of the wall first. His old lady didn't need to be watching a wanna-be fuck a woman without him being there. How couldn't she see he would be better?

"Believe me, I want to be there. You have no idea."

Frustrated, he went to the trash, memorizing the monitors before dumping the cake in the bin. Coming back, he gaped at Jo's screen. Her hand was slipping under the black lace at her breast.

"Give it to me," she purred, watching the actor spank the woman on the television.

"What did you say?" he croaked out.

"I said, give me an idea. Are you feeling okay tonight?"

"I'm fine. It's been a long day." More like a fucking long three weeks. If any of the brothers knew he had abstained from sex for that long, they would throw him out of the club.

"Yes."

Squinting at the screen, he watched what was taking place on the television, when a movement from the couch drew his eyes to her. She was draping a shapely leg over the back of the cushions.

"Rider, are you there? Are you okay?"

With a raspy voice, he reminded her, "You already asked that question."

"I forgot. I should go to bed." Jo moved her hand away from her breast to slide it under her black lace panties.

"Don't you dare." Standing up, he tried to concentrate on the screens and failed ... badly.

"Why not? I'm tired."

She wasn't tired! She was fucking getting off watching

another man give it to another woman the way he was supposed to do her but had been too leery of frightening her off.

"I need you to keep me awake. I've got to take a call. I'm going to put you on hold." As he moved his cell phone, he saw she had disconnected the call.

His thumb went to the number he wanted.

Shade's amused voice answered immediately.

"You have five minutes to get here, or security will be left unattended."

"You can't leave."

"Watch me." Rider shoved his phone into his pocket.

He wanted to call Jo and tell her he was going to spank her when he got there if she didn't stop, but the longer he had to watch, the angrier he became.

"Oh ... Bluebonnet, you're going to get it when I get there." Rider pushed the button, letting Shade and Lily inside at the same time he turned the screen that showed Jo playing with herself off.

"You can't just run off," Shade said, letting Lily go in the room first as he held the door open for her.

Rider waited impatiently until she was in the room, then took off at a run before Shade could get inside, saying, "I'm sick. Gotta go."

Shade walked to the desk, pressing the button to let Rider out of the garage.

"HE'S IN A BIG HURRY," he commented, not expecting an answer. He stood at the desk, familiarizing himself with where everyone was, seeing nothing was moving outside, other than Rider hell-bent to get to Jo.

Shade glanced at the mess that had been left for him to

deal with. "I hate when he doesn't clean up after himself." Shade tossed the remains of Rider's food orgy away. Then he turned the heat up before sitting down on the chair facing the computers.

"Take your coat off," he ordered, not looking back to make sure his wife was obeying him.

"Shade …"

"Lily …" he mocked, hearing her take off her coat.

Pivoting in his chair, he watched her ass as she hung her coat up, then returned to his side.

"Sit." Shade kept his hands on the arm of the chair as Lily climbed onto his lap. Then he began his interrogation.

"How long have you known Rider is from Texas?"

"Two weeks."

"Who told you?"

Lily folded her arms over her bare breasts mutinously.

"Who told you?" He lifted his hand to his wife's breast, taking a nipple between his fingertips. He didn't have to exert any pressure before his gentle bride caved with a whimper.

"Killyama."

Shade texted Train how disappointed he was that Killyama had revealed a fact he didn't want his wife to know. Satisfied that the brother knew exactly how disappointed he was, he turned back to the monitors, ignoring his wife as she sat trembling on his lap, drawing out the suspense of what he was going to do next while keeping track of time passing on the clock.

"Did Jo show you her pictures?"

"No."

"Do you know when you're going to see those pictures?"

"No. I was going to stop by her hou—"

"You're never going to see Jo's pictures, my darling little wife … never. Do you understand my meaning?"

"Yes, sir." Lily trembled harder against him.

"Good." His eyes flicked to the clock again.

"I'm in the mood to watch a little television. And you're going to watch it with me." Shade pressed a button, lighting the screen that Rider had turned off before he had left.

Grinning, he squeezed her nipple. He loved it when art mimicked life. Before he was done with his wife, she would appreciate it, too.

JO JERKED her hand out from under her panties at the sound of the motorcycle outside. Using her elbows, she half-raised herself from the couch, listening, becoming afraid at the late-night visitor she hadn't been expecting.

At the sound of the key turning in the lock, she jackknifed into a sitting position, almost tumbling over at the quick movement.

Staring at the door as it opened had a myriad of horror movies she had previously watched playing out in her mind. Her lips parted, preparing to give a blood-curdling scream.

Jumping up, she was going to run to her bedroom, but Jo only made it to the arm of the couch before Rider came in, then closed the door behind him.

"What are you doing here? You scared me to death!" Picking up a throw pillow, she threw it at him. "You jackass! Why didn't you call?"

Rider caught the pillow, coming farther into the room and letting it drop to the couch as he took off his jacket. "I didn't want to wake you if you were sleeping."

Jo cautiously watched as he sat down on the chair to remove his boots. "You're not supposed to leave …"

"I called Shade." Rider took off his T-shirt, throwing it to the back of the chair. "That doesn't look like *Smokey*."

499

Jo's eyes traced over the tattoo on his broad back. Shivering in the black lace teddy, she began to regret her plan. She had overestimated her courage and her anger when confronted with the sexy male standing a few feet away.

Mentally shaking herself to get her libido back under control, she managed a serene smile. "I was bored. I wanted something a little more stimulating."

"Are you bored now?" Rider started to walk toward her.

Jo moved behind the couch, keeping it between them. "I can't say I am."

He was staring at her in the same way she had only seen him look at Willa's candy.

"Have a seat. We can watch your movie together."

"I'm not in the mood anymore." She sidled to the side of the couch as Rider moved toward the opposite arm.

"Why not? You can't play with yourself watching *Smokey*?" he taunted with a lust-filled glance.

"How do you know what I was doing?" she taunted back. Feeling emboldened by the distance separating them, she jutted her breasts out, jiggling them. "Did you see anything you liked, you Peeping Tom?"

As Rider started to move around the couch, she matched him step for step.

"I saw plenty I liked," he goaded, stopping when they were once again on opposite sides of the couch arms.

"I want the camera out!" She pointed in the direction where Lily had told her it hidden.

"How'd you find out?"

She was debating if she had enough time to make it to her bedroom before he caught her when his question had her turning to look back at him.

"It doesn't matter. It's there. I want it out."

"No."

She frowned at his firm refusal. "Why not?"

"That fucking camera saved your life and the other women's. And because you're a lousy cook. Do you know how many times I've almost had to call the fire department when you were cooking?"

"No."

"A lot. That's why I bought the fire extinguisher to keep under the counter."

"Okay." She waved her hand airily, giving him that excuse. "But the camera didn't save our lives that night, you did. Lily told me that you told Gavin, Shade, and Jewell how to get into my father's room from the back of his closet that once led to the root cellar. How did you know it was there anyway?"

"I found it when I had a new furnace installed when you were knocked out with the flu. If you hadn't been such a chicken about going down there, you would have known it was there."

"You bought me a new furnace without telling me?"

He snorted. "I wasn't going to freeze my ass off."

"I'm going to pay you back."

"Go ahead. You're going to have plenty of money when your father's insurance pays off because he wasn't driving drunk. I already made sure the money Aly stole from you was applied to the loan you owe The Last Riders."

She looked down at the arm of the couch. "I didn't hear a gunshot that night when I was running toward the garage ..."

Rider's expression went lethal. "Don't ask questions you don't want answered."

Jo's eyes went to the spot where F.A.M.E had lost his life and where Mag had lain helplessly as Aly had stepped over them without a care.

"I don't want it answered."

"Cool. Then I won't."

"That doesn't mean that camera was responsible—"

"Jo, do you really think her phone just happened to ring as Gavin and Shade were coming down the hall?"

She would never forget the terror she had felt that night. She had thought it was a miracle that it had rung at that precise moment. God had been responsible for that miracle … with a little help from Rider.

"Lily's the one who told you, isn't she?"

"Shade told her because she was worried about that computer screen being out. She must have kept bugging him to get it fixed, so he just told her to get her off his back."

"That fucker doesn't get bugged."

"Then why did he tell her? I'll make damn sure to ask him."

Jo accidentally took her eyes off Rider when she saw what was happening on the television. Rider turned to see what she was looking at.

Turning back to her, Rider gave her lascivious grin. "That making you horny?"

"No," she lied, sliding behind the couch when he started to move.

"I am. I haven't had sex since you broke up with me." He pouted.

"That's your fault. I offered last night, but you wanted your own room."

"That was a mistake I'm going to rectify right—"

At his sudden movement, Jo screeched, making a run for the front of the couch, expecting him to keep going around the back. The jerk unexpectedly jumped over the back, grabbing her. They tumbled down onto the couch cushions.

Staring up at his satisfied smile reminded her of when he'd chased after strays.

Circling his shoulders, she lifted her mouth to his. "I love you," she breathed into his mouth.

"I love you, too."

Playfully teasing his bottom lip, she ran her hand over the tattoo that always made her feel protected.

"You like the teddy I got you for Valentine's Day?"

"That day just keeps on giving."

"How?"

"That's the day I realized I was fighting a losing battle of not falling in love with you. The next time Colton comes for a visit, I'm going to have it tatted under the one on my chest."

Jo frowned. "The one that means *light it up*? I don't know if I like that one higher than the day you fell in love with me."

"4:20 is the day my son died."

Tears filled her eyes. The beautiful soul staring down at her with his heart in his eyes was one she would thank God for every day. The mirrors he had hidden behind were gone, exposing the clear reflection of a soul that had endured his fair share of pain yet still held the capacity to love. He hadn't let it drag him down to a depth he couldn't recover from. He was merely waiting to find someone who could thaw his heart out so it could beat again.

Her Winston Hero deserved his chance. However, it was really she who had to deserve the chance he was giving her.

"Rider …" Jo nuzzled his neck. "I want a baby. Can you make it happen?" she whispered.

"Yes," he groaned.

She ran her hands down his trembling back. "I already picked out his name."

"You have?"

"I want to name him after his father."

Rider frowned. "I'm not crazy about my given name."

"I'm not talking about Ty. I'm not crazy about it either. Now Crux"—Jo gave a heartfelt sigh—"that's the name legends have been borne from."

EPILOGUE 1

Her hands on her hips, Jo stared in dismay at the mess in her living room. "Rider, have you seen my cell phone?" she yelled out, lowering her voice when he came out of the bathroom, running a towel through his hair. "I can't find it anywhere."

"I'll get my phone and call it."

She started picking up the tumbled cushions, then picked up the scraps of black lace. Going to the camera, she removed the pillow that blocked the view of the couch and kitchen, tossing it onto the couch as she went to the trash can.

"Are you calling it?" Jo asked, going down the hallway to her bedroom, seeing him lowering the phone as she neared her room.

"I did. If you didn't hear it, the battery must be dead."

"I charged it all the way from Lexington. It should have plenty of charge left."

"We can find it later. I want to give you your birthday present."

Jo jumped on the bed, bouncing, holding her hands out.

"I don't have it here. Let me get dressed." He laughed,

taking out a clean pair of jeans from her dresser. "I'm glad you didn't throw my clothes out after you broke up with me."

"I was getting around to it." She watched as he dressed.

"You ready?" He held his hand out for hers to help her from the bed.

"Yep."

Laughing, they left her room, going out the front door.

"Are we going to the club?"

"No, it's in the garage."

She tried to skip ahead of him, anxious to see her present, but he wouldn't let her hand go.

"You're no fun."

"I had a lot of fun last night."

She stuck her tongue out at him. "You're not the one with a sore ass."

"Your ass isn't sore."

"How do you know? It isn't your ass that's sore." She bristled at his surety.

"I was very careful with you being a first-timer."

"Rider ... I can feel another dry spell coming for you."

"I don't have to worry about that. You kept screaming out *more ... more ... Rider, more ...*"

She was still pummeling his shoulder when he opened the garage door. Her eyes widened at what she saw inside.

"For real?"

"For real." He threw her the keys. "Let's go for a ride."

Jo caught the keys before removing the gigantic bow off the car he'd had her restore. She carefully carried the bow to the worktable.

"You're not saving that bow," he said as they got in the car.

"Yes, I am. It isn't often I get a present like this. I want to remember it forever."

"The car is the reminder, Bluebonnet," he said, buckling the seat belt.

"I know I'm being ridiculous"—she grinned as she started the engine—"but I'm going to do it anyway. Where we going? I'm hungry."

"Me, too. Let's go by the club. It's lunchtime, and I need to check and make sure an order went out. We can go anywhere you want after that."

"I can live with that deal." She had to hold herself back from gunning out of the garage. The car ran like a dream, and she wished they could keep going. Unfortunately, her stomach was protesting.

"After we eat, I'm going to show them my car," Jo said excitedly as they went up the steps.

"They've seen it."

"They saw it when it was yours. Now it's mine." As she went up the last step to the porch, it wasn't Moon who attracted her shocked amazement.

Gripping his arm to keep him from going through the door he was holding open, she couldn't take her eyes off the holes in the walls she hadn't noticed before.

"When did that happen?" she asked, concerned that something had happened after they'd left last night.

Rider pulled his arm out of her grip, then put it around her shoulders, urging her inside. "Jo—"

"I'm asking," she cut him off.

When he moved her forward into the alcove, out of view of the camera, she knew he was giving them privacy.

"The night Aly took you hostage." His expression was filled with rage, grief, and a pitiless resolve that had her clutching his shirt.

"Who was hurt?"

"Driver."

Hearing the name of the man she had eavesdropped on at the diner had sorrow filling her. Her lips started quivering.

"He was nervous about meeting Viper. If I hadn't talked

507

you into letting Jewell stay, he would still be alive."

"Look at me, Jo." Rider gently gripped her jaw, forcing her to look at him. "You're not the reason Driver is dead. Curt is, and so are his family members who took part in the attack. If it was anyone's else fault, it was mine. I knew the repercussions of firing Curt, but I've never run from a bully, and I wasn't going to start that night."

"Did he really die using a broom to take a transformer out?"

"He really did." He caressed her cheek with his thumb as she tried to wrap her mind around the cruelty Curt had inflicted since he'd been a young man. If his family had stopped protecting him when he was younger, two men might still be alive.

"I'm glad he's not going to hurt anyone else."

"He'll never hurt anyone else again, nor will the men who helped him carry out the attack."

"How many?"

"Eight. They tried to get into Shade's, Viper's, and Razer's houses, and the club. It was an all-out assault."

"There were babies in those houses!"

"They didn't care."

"Are they in jail?"

"No, they aren't."

"How …?" She clutched his hands tighter. "Never mind. I don't want to know. It can't be traced to The Last Riders?"

He lifted a mocking brow. "What do you think?"

Jo unclenched her fingers, smoothing his T-shirt out. "I'm not hungry anymore."

"Then you can sit with me. It won't take me long to check the order. Then we can go."

Nodding, she followed him into the kitchen, going through the dining room. Finding a seat next to Killyama, she waited for Rider to fix his plate.

"You look like someone took a piss on your leg. What's wrong?"

"Nothing."

"I hope you're better at lying to Rider than to me. Come on; tell me. Another bitch buy your man another box of cereal for him? Tell me who it is, and I'll whip her ass for you."

"No, that's not it."

Killyama gave her a critical look. "One of them buy him another present? If they did, I can take it off your hands for you."

"No, they didn't."

"Someone watched you and Rider boinking last night?"

Flabbergasted, Jo didn't know how to respond to the question.

"Don't look so uppity. It's just sex. Jesus."

"Then why did you break all the computers in the security room when I let you talk me into keeping me company when I was working?" Train asked.

"Because of the camera in the living room and the kitchen." Killyama's killing glare would have had any sane man backing off. Train was obviously unstable.

"It was just sex," Train mocked.

Killyama grabbed his T-shirt as Rider took a seat next to him. "Brother, haven't you learned not to antagonize her?"

"You fuckers both ..." Killyama broke off what she was about to say, going back to eating her food. "Yo, Mercury, that's some killer meatloaf."

"What were you about to say?" Jo didn't let her escape so easily.

"Nothin'," she muttered.

"Did you, Train, and Rider have sex in the living room?" Jo's teeth snapped together when they denied it.

"Jo ..." Having been in the military, Rider knew when a

shitstorm was brewing. "I'm done eating. We can go—"

"Shut up." Jo glared at him. Out of the corner of her eye, she saw Winter sliding out of her chair, taking her full plate. "Winter, have you been with Rider?"

"I have to ..." She sat back down at the table when Jo gave her a warning glare. "Hell no. I'm too much woman for him."

She saw Mercury and Sasha slipping out of the kitchen and into the dining room. It didn't take a genius to figure out why.

Jo was so furious she wanted to ... wanted to ... Giving Rider an evil grin, she relaxed back in her chair.

"How about Rachel? Was Cash there too?"

Rider shifted uncomfortably in his chair. "Bluebonnet ... this is a private conversation that we can talk about in the car. Remember, we're going where you want to go."

Lucky, who was sitting at the table and listening to Rider get put on the spot, was clearly enjoying it too much by the big smirk on his face.

"Lucky, has Rider—"

"God, no." He shuddered.

Jo had learned one thing since she had been with Rider—things were never as they seemed. "Then how did you know Rider's leather pants would fit you?"

Consternation filled his face. "We may have used him with a little bit of role-playing," he admitted.

"Bluebonnet—"

"Okay ... I see how it is." Jo nodded, getting out of her chair.

Confused, Rider watched as, instead of running out in tears, she went behind the counter to make herself a plate of food.

She had just pulled a plate out of the cabinet when Razer and Beth came in from the back door. Seeing everyone looking at them, they stopped.

"Is anything wrong?" Beth asked, looking at Razer, who looked just as confused as her.

"Nothing much, except I found out Rider has been with most of the wives here."

When Beth paled, Jo waved her fork airily. "Don't. I'm not upset. After all, it was before Rider and I were a couple. Isn't that right, Rider?"

"Yes."

Seeing the truth in his eyes, she stabbed a large chunk of meatloaf. "You know, Rider, I've changed my mind. I think I could get into the lifestyle." She put the last of the potatoes on her plate.

"Which lifestyle?" Rider tensed.

"Sharing. My only hesitation is … Do I get to pick, or do you?"

Rider's jaw jutted out. His eyes went dark. "Who would you pick?"

Jo took a heaping spoonful of macaroni, pretending to give it some thought. She almost laughed when she saw Killyama evilly smiling back at her.

"Train's good. You could give him a try."

Beth moved forward, reaching for a plate. "Razer's very nimble, if that helps. Are you going to take that roll?"

"No, you can have it."

"Viper is a control freak, but if you can deal with that, go for it." Winter turned back to the table and started eating, ignoring her husband's infuriated face.

"How about Lucky? I've never tried role-playing. I'm open to new experiences." Jo set her plate down on the table, then went to the fridge for a bottled water.

"That's one experience that won't be in your future," Rider snarled.

Jo was closing the fridge when Shade came through the swinging door.

"What's taking so long?" he asked Rider. "Lily is waiting for me to take her and Clint to the pediatrician's office."

"How about Shade?" Jo asked, going back to her chair. "Any of you girls have any experience with Shade?"

Shade's brows lifted in unison.

"No, but if you find out, let me know how it goes. Lily won't tell us a damn thing," Killyama complained.

"We won't be having a threesome with Shade!" Rider scowled at her as she calmly began to eat.

"I was thinking more of a foursome or a fifth-some."

"I don't think it's called a fifth-some." The teacher in Winter wasn't going to let that get by her.

Jo's interest piqued. "What's it called?"

"An orgy," Winter supplied helpfully.

"You're not having sex with four or five men!" Rider fumed.

"Have you ever had sex with four or five women?"

Rider met her gaze head-on. "No."

"You're lying. What's good for the goose is good for the gander." Jo airily waved her napkin around, then placed it neatly on her lap. "I think I should start small," she mused out loud. "A foursome is more feasible. Of course, I already have Killyama's permission. I can text Rachel and ask her if Cash is available. We're friends; I'm sure it will be fine."

Beth nodded agreeably, tearing her roll in half. "I'm sure it will be, too."

Moon came through the swinging door, nearly running into Shade. "I'm starved. Is there any food left?"

"There's plenty of meatloaf left, Moon. I'm trying to decide who I want to have an orgy with. Are you in?"

Moon, who had been going around Shade, stopped in his tracks, giving her a lecherous grin. "Hell yeah! Brother, I knew you'd come around. Do I have time to eat? I'm going to need my strength—"

Jo managed to catch her water before it spilt as Rider stood, sending the table legs wobbling.

Moon dodged behind Shade when Rider went for him. Shade, to his credit, got Rider, shoving him back toward the table. Killyama was quick enough to move out of the way. Train wasn't. He was knocked backward, both men falling to the floor.

Rider started to get up when Train punched him in the face.

"Get off! Your fat ass is crushing my dick!"

Rider stopped trying to get off Train, striking him back.

Moon looked like he felt bad that Train was taking his beating. He tried to break up the fight, only to have Rider sweep his feet out from under him.

Seeing the fight getting out of control, Viper and Lucky tried to break them apart, only to find themselves down, too.

Jo took another drink of her water, watching them.

"Aren't you going to stop him?" Winter asked, carrying her plate to the counter.

"No, I don't see any blood yet. Hey!" Jo brightened. "I got a new car for my birthday. Do you girls want to go for a ride?"

Beth got up. "It's better than watching them kill each other."

"Let's stop by and pick up Willa. You can ask her about Lucky." Winter followed Beth out the door, giving Rider a swift kick in the rear before patting her hair down and going out after them.

Shade stood back, watching the fight, making no move to interfere. "Happy now?"

"Not yet," Jo snapped, holding her hand out and wiggling her fingers. "My phone?"

Shade reached into his pocket, taking it out and giving it to her.

"I blame myself for telling you about those pictures. Next time, I won't be so generous when you break into my house."

"Rider tell you I had it?"

"No, Rider was too anxious to stop by to get an order out. When has he ever been worried about work?" Jo swung her foot out, kicking Lucky in the ass for hitting Rider so hard. "Can I ask you a question?"

"Go ahead. I don't have anything better to do, other than keep Lily waiting."

Jo ignored the jibe. She would call Lily when she left and offer her a ride.

"So, if by any chance I did manage to save those pictures you deleted to the cloud, would I have enough votes to become a Last Rider?"

Shade's lips settled into a firm line. "More than enough."

"Thanks, Shade. It's always a pleasure doing business with you."

Sidestepping Moon and Lucky's feet, she went to the door. "Rider!" Jo yelled over the cursing men. "Rider! Shade said he's in, too!"

She was satisfied when she saw Rider manage to wiggle out from under Viper.

Razer, seeing the savage visage on Rider's face as he fought his way toward Shade, rolled his sleeves up, preparing for the coming battle between the two men.

"Shade, now I'm happy."

"What made you come back and pick me up?"

Jo lay languorously on top of Rider. Tilting her head, she stared at his battered face.

"We never left. As soon we were in the car, Winter changed her mind about going. She said that fighting makes

Viper horny and she wasn't going to miss out on that to teach you a lesson. The rest of them... me included, followed her lead. I'm willing to admit, I may have hoped you got a big adrenaline rush as Viper does."

She grinned when his hands went to her upper arms, dragging her breasts up his chest so his mouth could torment hers the way she had his.

"I always get a big adrenaline rush around you. I don't need to get in a fight to make you see stars."

"Rider your good, but not good enough to make me see stars. If you want me to see stars, let me drive your Ferrari."

"No."

"You're seriously not going to let me drive it?"

"Bluebonnet, you want to drive my car, you're going to have to make *me* see stars."

Laughing at his lecherous smirk, she started tickling him until he had enough and rolled her over so she was pinned underneath his body.

Becoming serious, she stared up at him, a lump coming to her throat at the way he was looking down at her. It was a Rider, with his heart in his eyes, as if all his past heartbreaks were nonexistent.

"Do you believe in everlasting love?" Jo held her breath after asking her question.

Rider stopped trying to tickle her back when he saw she had turned serious.

"I would have to believe I'm going to heaven to believe in that. I plan to take my sins to hell with me."

She whacked him on his shoulder. "You promised me forever and ever, and I'm going to hold you to it." Her arms wound around his neck, clinging to him, her eyes staring up at him with all the love she felt for him shining through. "Don't you want to go to heaven with me?"

"Jo, anytime you're with me, I'm already there."

EPILOGUE 2

"Shh ... they'll hear us," Crux warned as they sneaked to the hidden spot where Noah and Chance had trailed their fathers earlier that day. Noah had bragged that it was the spot The Last Riders' initiations took place.

"No one is going to hear. Everyone is sleeping. We shouldn't have brought you anyway. You're always trying to tag alone when you're not wanted," Noah griped.

"Shut up, Noah. Crux is right. You're making enough noise for Viper to hear us, and he's farther away."

"I told him he could come. I had to," John said, stepping over a dead tree. "He was spending the night with Clint, and he saw me slipping out of the house."

"I don't know why I even told you we're coming tonight. Me and Noah should have come ourselves and told you tomorrow what it was like," Noah complained.

Crux felt the chill on the back of his neck grow colder the deeper they went into the woods. He nearly fell trying to climb over the tree that John had easily stepped over.

"If you didn't want me to come along, then why did you

bug me all day? If our parents find out he snuck out, we're going to be grounded for life."

Crux quit listening to the older boys arguing. "I think I hear something." He lowered his voice, trying to keep up with John. He didn't want to get lost in the dark. He was the only one without a flashlight.

"Chickenshit. Keep up, or we're going to leave you … Here it is." Noah's voice had gone from irritated to excited.

Crux hurried forward, slipping through the huge rocks to come out at a clearing on the other side.

"How do they get through there? I barely made it through." John flashed his light, showing the clearing that was just dirt and mostly rock. "I wonder where that goes?" he asked, stopping the light on the dark woods that led from the other side of the clearing.

"How the hell would I know? Let's go see—"

"Wait, Noah …" Chance stopped his twin brother. "Let's go. It's creepy here."

"Not you, too! I just want … What's that?" The flashlight wavered as a shadowy figure came out of the dark where Noah had been about to explore.

Noah and Chance dropped their lights to the ground as boyish screams filled the air. They took off at a run, slipping through the rocks to the other side.

Crux nearly wet himself when the shadow grew closer.

"Run, John!" Crux stood still as John's light wavered within his frightened grasp.

Noah and Chance's screams had him just as scared, but he couldn't leave his best friend behind.

Crux didn't know whether to run or cry in relief when he saw who bent down to pick up Noah and Chance's flashlights.

"John, your father is waiting for you on the other side,"

his father said, walking toward him to hand him one of the flashlights.

"Do I have to?"

Crux raised the flashlight to see John.

His father laughed. "It'll be all right. He's not mad."

"He never gets mad. He's going to be disappointed," John said glumly, walking toward the rocks.

"It could be worse. You could be Noah and Chance. Razer and Knox will be lucky to catch them before they get home they were running so fast."

Now Crux understood Noah and Chance's heightened screams when they had come out the other side. If Knox had come out from the dark, he would be returning home with more than wet jeans.

Crux remained where he was as John slipped through the rocks.

"I'm sorry," he said as he watched his father sit on a large rock.

Crux kept the flashlight pointed on him as his father took something from his pocket. When he saw a flame, Crux curiously stepped closer.

"What are you doing?"

"Nothing."

Crux sniffed the air. "That smells like a cigarette. You don't smoke."

"There're a lot of things I do that you, your sister, and your mother don't know about."

"Like what?"

"Those secrets are for when you're older and not in trouble for doing something you shouldn't have been doing."

Crux lowered the flashlight, not wanting to see the disappointment on his father's face. "I didn't want to be a tattletale."

Crux saw the glow of the cigarette grow brighter before becoming a light red.

"I can understand not wanting to betray a friend."

"They aren't my friends. They don't like me. John might a little, but he doesn't tell me so," he said dejectedly.

His father laughed. "I bet he doesn't."

"Aren't you mad at me?"

"No, I'm not mad. I don't get mad."

"I've seen you mad."

Crux saw the cigarette glow again.

"What you've seen is me letting people see what they want to see. If they want to see me angry, I show them anger. If they want to see me happy, I show them that, too."

"I don't understand ..."

"You do. You pretend just as well as I do when you're hurt because your mom shows your sister more attention than you, or when you're angry when Noah doesn't want you to hang out with them, or when you're scared enough to wet yourself but you don't run."

"It was an accident," he mumbled.

"Son, it won't be the last time you wet yourself because you've been scared shitless. I've wet myself a couple times, and so have all The Last Riders. I'm not mad. I'm too proud that when Noah and Chance ran, you stayed."

"I didn't want to leave John."

"I know that. That's why I'm proud of you. You're much younger than them, but where courage is concerned, you're ahead of the curve."

Crux frowned. "What does that mean?"

"That one day, Noah and Chance will be as brave as you are now, but it won't come until they get older and their experiences shape them. Your courage is a part of you. It will just grow stronger as you get older."

"How about John? He was brave, too. He didn't run."

"No, he didn't. He's like you, which I'm sure Shade is going to take into consideration for his punishment, just like I will."

Crux nodded. He didn't understand a lot of what his father had said, but he understood he was still going to be punished.

"Are you going to tell Mom?"

"No." His dad gave a soft laugh. "Then I would have to pretend to be mad at you. I try not to pretend too much around her."

"Do you pretend around me and Val?"

"No, that's why I'm having this talk with you now, so when I act differently when others are around, you will know the difference."

"I wish I had as many friends as you do."

"You'll be friends with Noah and Chance when you get older."

"They make fun of my name."

"They're just jealous, which is a good thing. All their fathers are jealous of me," his father bragged, standing as he threw his cigarette away. "Let's go. I have to get back to work."

Crux started toward where the others had gone through.

"This way, Crux. I'm too big to go that way."

Crux held the flashlight as he walked next to his father, trying hard not to be afraid.

"Don't let it bother you when they make fun of your name. By the way, blame your mother. I was going to name you Brandon."

"Ewie. That's even worse than Crux."

"A name doesn't wear the man. A man wears the name. I learned that in the service."

"I want to go in the Navy like you when I grow up."

521

"You can do anything you want to, just do it better than everyone else."

"I will. Do you think Uncle Knox and Uncle Razer found Noah and Chance?"

"I'm sure they did. I don't hear them screaming anymore." He laughed. "By the way, the next time Chance calls you chickenshit, remind him he was the one who shit his pants and ran."

"They'll beat me up if I do that!"

"No, they won't."

"Yes, they will."

"No, son, they won't, because their father would have warned them."

"What would their father warn them about?"

His father laid a strong hand on his shoulder, guiding him over the dead tree that he had almost fallen over on the way to the initiation spot. "That I will always have your back."

EPILOGUE 3

Jo sat on the blanket that her grandson had laid down for her on the beach. Laughing, she hit the beach ball back to the children, who were playing nearby.

"You having a good time, Mom?"

Jo smiled up at her son as he threw himself down next to her on the blanket.

"The best time I've had in a long time."

Crux picked up a towel he had laid down before going swimming, rubbing it over his legs and arms. "You still miss him, don't you?"

Jo looked at her son, who looked so much like Rider it made her ache every time he smiled at her. "God, yes. Don't you?"

Her son stared out over the ocean, his own sadness apparent as he twisted the towel to place it over his shoulders. "At first, I thought you were crazy for wanting to come back here, but I'm glad you talked me into it. I feel closer to him. I don't know why."

"Because of the vacations we shared here when you were younger, and ... it was where we lost him."

She unconsciously rubbed her thumb against the tattoo on her fourth forefinger. She and Rider had both gotten the tattoos the day Lucky had performed their wedding ceremony. She had felt like a princess that day, and Rider her prince.

Some years had been great; others had been hard. Through it all, their love had continued to grow and blossom, just like the bluebonnets he had nicknamed her after.

She had given Crux her and Rider's wedding rings last year when she had become ill. He had wanted her to take them back when she had been released from the hospital, but she wanted him to keep them. Like Mag, she knew her time was nearing its end, and she wasn't afraid. Her Winston Hero would be waiting for her. They had been separated for twenty-two years now.

Jo didn't remember much about that first year. She had slept it away. Or when she had been awake, she had drifted through waves of despair and anguish. Crux had taken leave from the Navy. It was only when he'd been about to give up his commission that she had dragged herself out of the fog that had been blanketing her and began to live again. By the second year after she had lost him, Jo had moved to the state he had been born in and the one they had lost him in, too.

After his death, Rider had received the medals he had been denied in life, each placed in his casket by the remaining Last Riders, or by their descendants who had promised to fulfill their parents' requests.

Even at the very end, he had sacrificed his life to try to save two boys who had swum out too far and couldn't get back.

She remembered she had gone into the house for drinks, and when she had come out, he had disappeared. Frantic, she had finally spotted him helping one of the boys. Jo had managed to run out into the surf to help. Then he had taken off again before she could stop him.

Jo had made sure the boy was safe, then ran to her phone to dial for help. Racing back to the water, her prayers were answered when she saw him nearing the shore with the other boy. Crying, she saw another man running into the water to help, taking the boy from him.

Jo had taken her eyes off Rider for a second at the sound of the EMTs, and when she had turned back, he was gone.

She had run out into the water to search for him, but each time, the water had pushed her back. Sobbing, she had tried again when the stranger who had helped with the boy dragged her out of the water, then returned to search for Rider.

She was in the same spot then as she was now, sitting on the sand with a blanket the EMT had put around her, when they had found Rider.

"Mom?"

"Yes, baby." Jo blinked back the tears she was determined not to shed.

Crux gave a small laugh. "It's been a long time since you called me that."

"You'll always be my baby, no matter how old you get." She gave a trembling smile, turning to look at the son she was proud of.

Crux had earned Rider's respect, assuming the same position he had held in the club.

"It's getting late. Come on; I'll help you inside."

"I don't need any help. I can do it on my own."

"Then you can help me." Crux rose, waiting patiently for her to do the same.

Using her cane, she managed to get to her feet. She didn't want to show any weakness in front of Crux, or she would find herself leaving in the morning to go to Treepoint. She had to stay here. She was waiting for him.

As much as Rider loved The Last Riders and Treepoint, his heart had never strayed from Texas. Just like his heart had never strayed from her. It had been hers since the day he had promised her forever and ever, and he had stayed until his death had separated them.

"I wish you would come home with us, Mom. Val and Tom and their kids miss you. So do Keira and Ridge."

Jo lightly took her son's arm as they walked toward the beach house. "I miss all of you, too, but your sister and her husband don't need me sitting around the house. She's too busy taking care of the kids to be worrying about me. You and Keira have your own lives to lead, too. With Ridge going into the service, you can finally have time alone again. I'm content, Crux. I get plenty of company to keep from being lonely. Rachel was supposed to come with you all, but Greer wasn't feeling well. Hopefully, they'll be coming soon. I miss Rach."

"They wanted to be here for your ninety-second birthday, but Greer was having trouble getting over the flu, and the doctor didn't want him to travel. Rachel looks as young as you do. Probably because you keep each other young when she comes to stay the winters with you."

"They miss the deep snow, but not enough to live in Treepoint during the winter. Our old bones can't take it anymore."

Jo smiled at her grandchildren as they gathered around the table, while their mother scolded them for not wiping the sand off their feet before coming inside to eat.

"Leave them alone, Valentine. I don't blame them. They were probably worried all the cake would be gone with Tom sneaking inside all day to get a slice." Jo went to her two grandsons, kissing them on the cheeks. The sixteen- and seventeen-year-old boys gave her mischievous smiles that reminded her of Rider.

Moving to the end of the table, she kissed her twenty-year-old grandson, who was constantly watching the environment around him with a solemn expression. Jo knew he had been gifted with the same abilities as Rider and Crux. Ridge was the one she worried about the most.

It would take a special woman to see beneath the reflections that were such an intrinsic part of him. She'd had the same worry about Crux before Kiera had fallen in love with him. It would take a discerning woman to see through Ridge and accept his strengths without being overwhelmed by them.

It took courage to love a hero. Maybe more than the man they loved. That was why she had already decided to go back to Rider before he had shown up at her garage, wanting another chance.

"You want my chair, Granny? I'll go sit on the couch," he offered.

"No, you stay there. I'm going to bed." Patting him on his back, she went to Crux, kissing him on the cheek. Then she took a second to catch her breath by resting an arm across Tom's broad shoulders. "You keep eating that cake, when you get back, the club won't be calling you Tomcat, they'll be calling you Garfield."

"I'm a growing a boy." Giving his wife a worried glance, he pushed his plate away, rising to stand. "Mind if I get the photo albums out of your room? I want to show the boys pictures of when me and Crux were in high school."

"You and Crux have shown them those pictures a million times, but if you want to walk me to my room, I won't mind." She gave her son-in-law a loving pat as she kissed her daughter and daughter-in-law good night. "We can clean the sand in the morning. They'll want to go again in the morning before you leave. No need to do it twice."

"You spoil them too much." Valentine returned her kiss, giving her a gentle hug, too. "I love you, Mom."

"I love you, too, baby girl. I love all of you. Good night. I'll see you in the morning. Kiera, don't keep Crux out too late when you go for your midnight swim." Winking at Kiera, Jo went to her bedroom that was next to the front door with its own bathroom. She sat down on her bed as Tom got the album she always kept on her dresser.

"Can I get you anything?" he asked.

"No, I'm fine. I'm just going to read a bit before I fall asleep."

"Good night, then."

"Tom," she stopped him. "I couldn't have asked God for a better husband for my daughter. You've been a good man to her and a good father. Don't screw it up."

"I promised you and Rider when I asked your permission to marry her. I don't ever plan to break that promise to you and Rider, or the vows I made to Val."

Jo nodded tiredly. "Night, Tom."

Her son-in-law gave her a concerned look before going to the door. "The boys have a few more days before they have to be back at school from Christmas break and want to stay a little longer; is that okay with you?"

Jo rolled her eyes heavenward. The man had never been good at lying. "I'll enjoy having you here longer." She knew it would be useless to argue.

Left alone, she slowly got up off her bed, making her way to her bathroom, where she got ready for bed. The mirror over her sink showed her snow-white hair. Her blue eyes looked duller. Her lips twisted into a smile at the nightdress she was wearing. Rider had hated flannel.

Her arthritic bones ached as she lowered herself to her bed. Then she lifted the necklace out from under her gown, staring down at Rider's grinning face. Kissing the picture, she placed it back underneath her gown so it could rest against her heart.

Turning off the light, Jo covered herself, too tired to read tonight. Closing her eyes, she drifted off dreamlessly.

The faint rays coming through her window woke her. She hadn't been awake to see a sunrise in a long time.

Suddenly wanting to see it from the beach, she jumped out of bed and raced out of her home, running to the beach, feeling as lithe and limber as she did as a young girl.

Sinking to the sand, she curled her hands around her knees, gasping at the beauty before her as the morning sun glistened off the water.

As the sun drew higher, she had to look down to keep her eyes from burning. When she did, she saw a lone figure running along the beach toward her. At first, she thought it was Tom out for his morning run, but the man running toward her was too tall. As he grew closer, she thought it was Crux and was about to tease him for being up so early, until the sun rose higher and the shadows on the beach disappeared. Then she realized it was Rider.

"Rider!" Jumping up, she started running toward him, hurdling herself into his arms when he came close enough. "Rider!" Sobbing, she wrapped her arms around his neck as he swung her around in a circle. "I've missed you so much." Nuzzling his neck, she cried out all the anguish she had experienced since he had been taken from her and all the joy of being reunited with him.

He set her firmly back down on the sand. "Stop crying, Bluebonnet. I'm never going to leave you again."

"I won't let you." She grinned, tears still streaming down her face.

They walked along the beach in the direction she had seen him coming from, holding hands.

"I won't *ever* let you get away from me again," she swore.

"It wasn't time, Bluebonnet. I have a present for you. A beautiful, glorious present I've been waiting to show you."

"Can I see it now? I don't have to wait anymore?" she asked excitedly.

"You can see it now. That's where we're going." He indulgently held her back when she would have dropped his hand to run ahead.

"Is it bigger than a ring box?"

"Bigger." His eyes crinkled in amusement. "So much bigger."

She quit trying to run ahead, lifting shining blue eyes to his. "Bigger than a bread box?" she insisted, gripping his hand tighter.

"A little bigger." Rider tenderly caught her lips in a passionate kiss before twirling her around again.

Jo couldn't resist one final look back along the beach from where they had started their journey.

His smile slipped when he saw what she was doing. "It's not too late to turn back."

"No, I've been ready to leave since the day I lost you. I have so much to tell you." Jo's gaze went to the sand behind them, seeing their footsteps hadn't disturbed the pristine sand.

"We have plenty of time," he told her, pulling her even tighter against him as the sun rose higher, exposing the ethereal beauty of the Kingdom that had been waiting for her.

Her lips parted in awe. "Rider, this is definitely bigger than a bread box."

Rider stopped, cupping her cheek while holding her hand. As he traced her cheek with his knuckles, Jo lifted her other hand, laying it atop his tattoo ring, the exact duplicate of hers.

"It has to be to hold forever and ever."